Secrets and Second Chances at Saffron Bay

LK Wilde

ISBN 978-1-0685491-7-5

Chapter 1

Then

With his bag at his feet, Daniel stared down at Saffron Bay and the village that had once been home. Beyond the houses and winding lanes, the sea stretched out towards the horizon, sparkling beneath a bright summer sun. Tears rushed to Daniel's eyes, and he brushed them away. He had burned his bridges, and there was no going back now.

Of everything he had lost, the thought of leaving his daughter behind broke his heart. Would she hear the rumours? Would she ever be welcomed into the place that had seen him grow from boy to man? Perhaps, but not for as long as Daniel was around, of that he was sure. There was so much he wanted to give his little girl, but all he ever brought people was pain. The kindest thing he could do was turn and walk away.

Daniel shielded his eyes from the sun and squinted at the white clapboard cottage, just visible behind the blooming lilac bushes lining its plot. One day, his daughter would receive her inheritance. One day, memories would fade. New residents would move into the village, and those who knew what he had done would leave or pass away.

Whether the cottage would still be standing by then was another matter, but the plot alone would be worth a small fortune in twenty-five years' time.

Daniel dried his eyes, said a silent farewell to the place he'd loved for his entire life, turned, and walked away.

Chapter 2

Alice pulled into a layby and jabbed at her phone in frustration. Of all the times to lose signal, this was the worst. She had followed the sat nav as it led her along narrow tree-lined lanes, feeling like a rabbit trapped in a warren of tunnels with no obvious way out.

She hadn't realised how hot and bothered she'd become until she climbed out of the compact car and a blast of cold air hit her skin. Above her head, a canopy of skeletal branches clawed at each other in the breeze, blocking out the weak winter sun. The only sounds were the rustle of fallen leaves and the strange cries of wild animals. How could a place like this exist so close to the city?

In the fifteen minutes since leaving the last major road, Alice felt she'd entered another world. It was impossible to believe the coastline lay a mere few miles away, let alone any sign of civilization. With the paper map she kept for emergencies spread across the car bonnet, Alice traced the distance between her rough position and the city. It couldn't be over ten miles as the crow flies, but on the snaking narrow lanes, she must have driven closer to thirty. The petrol gauge had been hovering just above red for a while now, but Alice couldn't imagine there'd be anywhere to fill up in the back of beyond.

Alice's finger skimmed the soft paper as she tried to pinpoint her location. Perhaps if she weren't so reliant on her phone, she could have done, but her map-reading skills had grown rusty; she hadn't used them since a Duke of Edinburgh expedition at school ten years earlier.

'Are you alright there? You look lost.'

Alice jumped out of her skin as a face appeared from behind a tree. The figure stepped forward, and Alice breathed a sigh of relief. This was no axe murderer, just a lady out for a hike.

'Actually, I am. I'm trying to get to Saffron Bay, but my phone has no signal and I'm completely lost.'

The woman smiled, her silver bobbed hair catching the light as she shook her head. 'You're closer than you think. I've walked from the village, so it's really not far. I'm president of the local ramblers' association, so I'm scouting out the route for our next walk.'

Alice swallowed a sigh, wishing the woman would give her directions rather than her life story. 'I reached a T-junction about a mile back, but there was no signpost.'

The woman shook her head, leaning heavily on one of her walking poles. 'You poor love, no wonder you're lost. Storm Bert took out the signpost last month, and the council is yet to replace it. I've sent several emails about it, all of which have been ignored. It's only when the tourists come the council remembers we exist.'

'I see.'

'You should have turned left at the T-junction, not right,' said the woman, walking over to Alice and leaning over the map. She smelled of lavender and coconut, and Alice suspected there was a glamorous woman beneath all the hiking khaki.

'Here,' said the woman, resting a delicate finger on the map. 'See? This is where we are. You need to go back this way. There's where you went awry. Keep following the road down the hill and you can't go wrong.'

'Thank you.'

'No problem. Are you just visiting the village for the day?'

'Something like that.' The woman seemed keen to talk, but Alice's mind was too scrambled for conversation. Perhaps she was being paranoid, but Alice was sure the woman was looking at her strangely, almost like she recognised her, which was impossible as Alice had never heard of Saffron Bay until two weeks ago, let alone visited the place.

Alice gave the woman a polite smile, folded up the map and shoved it in her back pocket. The past fourteen days had had a dream-like quality to them, filled with shocking revelations and solicitors' visits. Now that all the paperwork was sorted, Alice needed to get to Saffron Bay to find out what she was dealing with and regain a little control.

'I'd best be on my way. Thank you for your help.'

'You're welcome. Enjoy your visit.'

Alice climbed back into the car, turned it around, and waved at the woman who stood watching her. Only as she turned a corner did Alice relax. She checked her rearview mirror, relieved she was alone once more. The last thing she needed today was an audience.

Before long, the road began a sharp descent, the forest giving way to driveways and gates hinting at the million-pound properties hidden behind them. Alice turned another corner and was rewarded with her first glimpse of the sea.

She pulled the car to a stop at the crest of the hill, her fingers tightening on the steering wheel as she took in the view below. Saffron Bay sprawled out beneath her, a tapestry of rooftops, winding lanes, and chimneys trailing wisps of smoke into the crisp coastal air. The village nestled in the valley, spilling down to the ribbon of sand where sea met land.

The forest surrounded the valley like a dark green piece of cloth, its edge fraying into neatly arranged gardens and the sprawling estates that formed the outskirts of the village. Grand houses stood proudly, their windows reflecting the wintry light of the morning sun. Beyond them, more modern housing estates jostled for space, their slate roofs forming a patchwork of the village's expansion.

At the very bottom of the valley, butting up against the beach, were rows of higgledy-piggledy rooftops, which Alice assumed must form the heart of the village. The bay sparkled like silver beneath the sun, its horseshoe shape enveloped as though hugged by arms of forest on either side.

Alice knew that just beyond the peninsular lay Plymouth, with its hustle and bustle, traffic, noise and muddle of lives, but looking out of her car windscreen, the city felt a world away. Alice sighed and let her eyes drift back to the village. Through no choice of her own, Plymouth was her past; Saffron Bay, her future. She switched on the engine, put the car into gear, and, with a deep breath, set off to find out what was waiting for her.

Chapter 3

A light on the dashboard flickered red, hinting at yet another thing wrong with her awful car. Ignorant of anything to do with engines, the only warning the light gave Alice was that she was likely about to throw more good money after bad. Not for the first time, she considered how unfair it was that those with the least money always ended up spending the most. The car had seemed such a bargain when she bought it; it was rare to find a vehicle for five hundred pounds with a year's MOT. She should have known her dodgy neighbour Kevin wouldn't be selling off the car cheap out of the goodness of his heart.

It came as a relief to arrive in the quaint heart of the village, pull the car to a halt, and turn off the engine. Through a gap in the buildings, she could make out a pale, grey-blue band of sea. Other than a few hungry-looking seagulls, the street was deserted. Did anyone actually live in Saffron Bay at this time of year?

Buttoning up her jacket, Alice climbed out of the rusty car and pulled a piece of paper from her pocket. It was crumpled, with an aging coffee stain visible in one corner, and the writing on it was scrawled, as though the author were in a hurry.

In case she ever sees this, on turning twenty-five, the ownership of Seashell Cottage transfers to Alice. The cottage belongs to her, and I lay no more claim to it.

Taped to the bottom of the note was a key. The tape had turned yellow and cracked, and Alice was surprised it could still cling to the paper. Just above the key was a roughly drawn map. Alice turned her back to the sea and glanced from the map to the street and back again. According to these instructions, the cottage was only two streets back from the beach, so it should be easy enough to find.

As she trudged through the village, Alice pulled her jacket tighter around her. She was unprepared for the changeable coastal weather and feared the umbrella she used in the city would be useless against the elements here. She passed by stone cottages, their windows dark and no signs of life evident from behind their closed curtains. One cottage was now a gift shop, with a handwritten sign on the door announcing it would reopen at Easter.

A light was on in the General Store, a sign outside flapping in the breeze, informing potential customers that they could purchase local clotted cream here. Opposite the General Store, Alice paused for a moment outside the cosy-looking Bayside Café. The smell of fresh coffee overtook the faint tang of seaweed in the air, and Alice was tempted to treat herself. But she was on a mission and didn't want to be derailed before she'd even got started.

Alice studied the hand-drawn map once more and pressed on through the village. The distant sound of children playing reached her on the breeze, and the unadulterated joy in the children's squeals lifted her mood a little. Perhaps she should be more excited by her unexpected inheritance, but as with everything concerning her father, Alice's feelings were mixed.

'You lost, maid?'

Alice jumped and looked around her. The voice had come from an elderly man who was camouflaged against a wooden bench in his brown corduroy jacket and flat cap.

'Oh, hello. I'm sorry I didn't see you there.'

The old man tapped the walking stick he was holding against the pavement. 'It's always the way when you get older. You become invisible.'

'Oh, no, I didn't mean it like that.'

'Don't worry about it, maid. We rarely get tourists at this time of year. Are you looking for anywhere in particular?'

'Cliff Lane.'

'You need to head in that direction,' said the man, pointing down the road with his walking stick.

'Thank you, that's really helpful.'

'You got friends living along there?'

'Something like that.'

The man nodded, and Alice walked in the direction he'd shown her. She'd expected Saffron Bay to be packed with quaint fishermen's cottages, but as she left the centre of the village behind, quaint cottages gave way to retirement-style bungalows, a Victorian terrace, and a couple of new-builds that wouldn't look out of place on *Grand Designs*. It was the kind of mishmash that made Alice even less sure of what to expect from the unimaginatively named Seashell Cottage.

After consulting the map once more, Alice turned right up a steep hill. The incline strained her calf muscles, and she wished she hadn't let her gym membership expire. Halfway up the hill, Alice paused to catch her breath. She must be almost there. According to the map, the cottage was somewhere on her left.

Alice walked higher, then retraced her steps. Most of the houses along this street seemed to have been built in the 1960s, with driveways and front gardens. Just as she was wondering if the map was wrong, Alice noticed a rotten wooden sign poking out from between the branches of an overgrown bush. She brushed a layer of dirt away and squinted at the peeling paint. *Seashell Cottage*.

With a bit more exploration, Alice found a rickety wooden gate hidden within the bush. When she pushed it, the gate fell from its hinges, clattering against the pavement below. Alice picked up the gate and rested it against its frame. Then, bending to avoid the thick branches, she pushed her way into an overgrown garden.

Alice didn't know whether to laugh or cry as she got her first view of the cottage. In the end, she opted for a surprised yelp, followed by a shudder and a strong sense of doom. *Look for the positives*, Alice told herself, repeating the words like a mantra as she fought back tears. She took a deep breath and made a mental checklist.

1. It's on a big plot.

2. If some of the foliage were cut back, there would probably be spectacular views.

3....

3....

No, it was no use. There was little to redeem the building in front of her, the building that was supposed to be her home. The clapboard cladding looked rotten, green where once it should have been white. Was it even cladding? Was the entire building made of soggy planks of wood?

Several tiles were missing from the roof, and one of the two windows framing the front door was missing its glass. Weeds had grown halfway up the outer walls, as if nature were reclaiming land that had once been stolen.

When she first heard about Seashell Cottage, Alice's immediate thought was to sell it and bank the large sum it would inevitably fetch because of its location. But as with most things in her life, nothing was ever straightforward. This was no ordinary inheritance. Yes, her father had given up all legal claim to the place, but what if he came looking for her one day? What if he'd been waiting for this moment, when he would know where to find her? To sell up now was too great a risk, despite the little voice in her head telling her fairytale endings didn't exist for women like her.

With some trepidation, Alice walked towards the faded front door. She ran a finger along the door's wood, flecks of red paint clustering against her skin. With a deep breath, she lifted the key to the lock. Part of her was hoping she'd got the wrong house, but when the key slid neatly into its lock, she knew this was no mistake.

Alice turned the key and, after several shoves with her shoulder, the door gave way and opened with a loud creak. After allowing her eyes to adjust to the gloom, she took a deep breath and stepped inside.

Chapter 4

Alice had glanced inside each room before the reality of Seashell Cottage overwhelmed her and she sank to the living room floor in despair. When tears came, they rushed down her cheeks in a torrent. She couldn't tell how long she'd sat there, head in her hands, but it was long enough for the cold to seep into her bones and for her backside to go numb.

'Hello?'

The voice made Alice jump out of her skin. She scrubbed her eyes with a piece of tissue and staggered to her feet.

'Hello?'

'Yes?' The word came out as a croak, the hurt and confusion she felt stealing her voice.

A man appeared in the doorway, his broad shoulders filling the space, his sandy-coloured hair tickling the top of the doorframe. If he were a serial killer, she was screwed, for there was no way she was getting past him.

'Who are you?'

'I was about to ask you the same question,' said Alice, standing up and folding her arms. If she were about to be attacked by this stranger, she'd go down fighting. She should have told someone she was coming here. Mind you, who was there to tell? Yes, she probably should have let May know, but May was so wrapped up in her own dramas that Alice could have told her she was moving to the moon and she wouldn't have listened.

The man stepped forward and squinted at Alice. 'You go first. Are you a squatter? If you are, I can tell you right now you've picked the wrong place. This cottage's more likely to fall down around your ears than provide any shelter.'

'I'm not a squatter.' Alice spread her feet wider and stuck out her chin. Did she look like a squatter? She'd not had money for new clothes for a long time, but a squatter? How rude!

'Then what are you doing here? No one's been inside this place for as long as I can remember.'

'Well, that clearly isn't true,' said Alice, scowling at the man and pointing to the graffiti-covered wall in front of her.

'Fine,' said the man with a sigh. He stepped further into the room and began examining the defaced wall. 'No one's been inside here for years, except local teenagers wanting to party.'

'Well, I wish they hadn't used my house as their destination of choice.' Alice pouted, aware her tone was accusatory.

As the man turned to face her, his eyes widened. '*Your* house?'

'That's right.'

'You mean you bought this dump? Wow! I didn't even know it was for sale.'

'It wasn't.'

'It wasn't? Then how...?'

'It belonged to my family and has now been passed down to me.'

'To your family...'

'Will you please stop repeating everything I say?'

'Sorry.' The man scratched at the stubble on his chin and let out a low whistle.

Alice tried to ignore his good looks, annoyed that he'd barged into her home. Her home? Could this shack of a place really be described as that? It would have to, given the lack of alternatives.

'You still haven't told me who you are,' said Alice, placing her hands firmly on her hips.

'Sorry, I'm Luke. My gran lives next door. I was visiting her and saw you letting yourself in. I'm sorry, I thought you were trespassing. I didn't realise this place belonged to you. It's been empty for years.'

'Has it?' asked Alice, her voice dripping with sarcasm as she rolled her eyes.

The corners of Luke's lips twitched in a move that annoyed Alice even further. She usually prided herself on her politeness and adherence to social convention, but the past couple of weeks had stolen her energy and reason. Her tears and plan to wallow in them had been interrupted by this stranger, and as a result, her patience was hanging by a thread.

'This place is going to take a hell of a lot of work to get into any sort of livable condition.'

Alice bit back a stinging reply. 'I'll have to do the work a section at a time.'

'That will take a while.'

'Yes, but as I'll be living here, I'll have plenty of time.'

'You're planning to live here?' asked Luke, his mouth hanging open.

'Yes,' said Alice, who knew the idea was ridiculous, but also had nowhere else to go.

'Is there even running water?'

'I don't know, I haven't checked.'

Luke left the room, and Alice heard him scrabbling around in what passed for a kitchen.

'What are you doing?' she asked, walking into a kitchen that seemed stuck in a 1970s time warp.

'Looking for the stopcock.'

'Why?'

'To see if you have water. I checked the taps, but unsurprisingly, nothing came out.. It could be the water's been turned off, or you might have been disconnected.'

Alice prayed it was the first option. She had no idea how to go about reconnecting utilities on a property. Would a utility company ask for proof of ownership? The folder she'd been given containing deeds and other documents looked official, but what if it was a scam? What if the solicitor Maz had taken her to was a fraud? The only other evidence Alice had was her father's scribbled note, which, for all she knew, had been written while he was drunk.

'You said this place had been in your family?'

'Yes,' said Alice, 'it belonged to my dad.'

'Oh, right. What was his name? I don't remember anyone ever living here, but Gran might remember him.'

'His name is Daniel Loveday.' His name *is*? Or *was*? Alice supposed most people knew if their father was dead or alive. Maz talked as if he were dead but didn't have any evidence to back up her claim.

'OK, I'll ask Gran if she knew him. Sorry, I haven't even asked your name.'

'Alice.'

'Alice Loveday?'

She nodded. The only things her father had given her were his name, his white-blond hair, and now this cottage, which felt more like a curse than a blessing. *Look for the positives*, she told herself. At least the cottage was in a fairly built-up area, so connecting things like water and electricity shouldn't be too difficult, and the cottage had an undeniable charm. *Charm?* Said the little voice in Alice's head. *Charm? More like drug den meets city underpass.*

'Sorry, what did you say?' Alice realised Luke had been speaking.

'I said the water seems to still be connected, but you're going to want to run it for a while so you're not at risk of catching Legionnaires.'

'Right, thanks for the advice.' Alice wanted this man gone, but couldn't deny his knowledge of stopcocks and utilities was greater than hers.

‘Let me check in here.’ Luke ducked his head into a small cupboard and began fumbling around. When he pulled his head from the cupboard, his hair was full of cobwebs, and Alice had to fight the urge to brush them off for him. ‘When are you planning on moving in?’ asked Luke.

‘Next weekend.’

‘Next weekend?’ Luke’s eyes were wide, his mouth hanging open.

‘Is that a problem for you?’ Alice placed her hands on her hips.

‘It’s not a problem for me, but by the looks of things, it might be for you. You’ve got running water, but no electricity.’

‘I can sort that.’ Could she? Luke must think her a nutter for moving into a tumble-down cottage with no electricity. Perhaps Alice should tell him that by the weekend she’d be homeless, and whilst she could probably manage a couple of months of sofa surfing, it wasn’t only herself she had to think about. But he seemed so sure of himself, Alice felt that admitting the truth would be to lose face. ‘It will be fine. I’ll come here every day this week and get the place cleaned up.’

‘OK. Well, I’m a builder, so if you need any help, you can call me.’

‘Thank you.’ Luke handed her a business card, and Alice slipped it inside her pocket, knowing she wouldn’t call. How could she on such a tight budget? Builders charged extortionate rates these days. The money she’d saved for uni wouldn't last long, and Alice would need to spend it wisely.

'Do you mind if I have a quick look around before I head off?'

Yes! Alice wanted to yell, but once again, politeness won out. 'Sure, help yourself.'

As her new neighbour began knocking on walls and poking about in nooks and crannies, Alice fought to keep her emotions in check. May would hate this place. How was she going to break the news to her city-loving sister that they were going to be camping out in a tumble-down shack in the middle of nowhere for the next goodness-knows-how-long? If her new neighbour weren't on the other side of the thin wall, Alice would have given in to tears once more.

Chapter 5

As he moved from room to room, Luke told himself it was professional curiosity keeping him in the building, and not the woman in the other room whose tear-stained, scowling face was the most beautiful he'd ever seen. He shook his head and laughed at his straying mind. *You need to get out more, mate*, he told himself.

Luke left Alice staring at the water pouring from the tap and started his exploration in the long hallway. Before looking behind any doors, he peeled away the edge of a carpet so threadbare it was hard to tell what colour it had once been. Beneath the carpet lay floorboards in pretty good shape, and Luke made a mental note, as he suspected it would be one of very few positives.

Luke tried another door, which creaked open to reveal what must have been a bedroom, for it was too small to be anything else. One patch of carpet still held a faint blue colour, and from its shape, Luke guessed this must have been where a bed once stood. He walked to the window and poked a finger into the spongy wood. He could feel a draft seeping through the thin pane and the tiny holes created as the frame rotted.

Luke took a step back, puzzled. Something was missing. He paced around the room, trying to identify the nagging in his brain, and then it came to him. The room was free of dust. In fact, despite its shabby state, it was relatively clean.

'Alice? Can you come here for a minute?'

'What is it?' she asked as she joined him in the small room, sounding unimpressed at being summoned.

Alice looked directly at Luke, and he found he couldn't meet her gaze. How could a total stranger have this effect on him? It was ridiculous. 'Have you been here before to clean?'

'What? No, of course not. You saw me arrive.'

'Someone has been in here, and not the kids who painted that graffiti.'

'What are you talking about?'

'Run your finger along the windowsill.'

Alice walked to the window and shivered as the draft met her. She rolled her eyes at Luke, but then did as requested. When she held her finger up to show him, other than a few flecks of paint, her skin was clean.

'That's not normal for a house that's been sitting empty as long as this one.'

'Maybe the draft has blown the dust away?' asked Alice, wrapping her arms around herself.

Luke fought the desire to offer her his jacket. He had a feeling she wouldn't appreciate any attempts at chivalry. 'Let's check out the other rooms.'

'This is grim,' said Alice, following Luke into the small bathroom.

'It's old-fashioned,' said Luke, running his hand across the peach floral tiles, their grout black with age and mould, 'but it's not dirty.'

'What about all the mould?'

'Even that's not as bad as it could have been. Look, there are scrape marks in the grout where someone has tried to remove it.'

Alice lifted the toilet seat and stepped back, frowning. 'There's bleach in the toilet bowl.'

Luke peered over the toilet. 'This is so weird.' He returned to the bath and ran a finger along the bottom before lifting it to his nose and sniffing. He held his finger up to Alice to show her a cream residue. 'That's not dust, that's cleaning product. Can we go back into the living room and have another look at the graffiti?'

'Be my guest.'

They walked along the narrow corridor, and Luke blinked as they stepped into the living room. Light poured through the tall windows, and even on a bleak winter's day, the view being teased from behind overgrown shrubs was beautiful. He dragged his eyes away from the window and stood close to the wall.

'What is it?' asked Alice.

'I think someone's tried to clean this off.'

'They haven't done a very good job of it.'

'Soap and water won't work on this stuff.'

Alice walked to the window and placed her hand on the cold glass. 'What are you thinking?' she asked.

'I'm thinking someone has been in here trying to get the place ready for you.'

'What? And they thought they'd cover the walls with their artwork while they were at it?'

'No, of course not. I highly doubt your graffiti artists were also your cleaners. Do you know anyone in the village who might have done this?'

'I'd never even heard of Saffron Bay until two weeks ago!'

'Right, but someone knew you were coming here?'

'No! I haven't even told my sister yet.'

'Then it looks like you have a fairy godmother.' Luke laughed as Alice rolled her eyes at him. When he noticed the corner of her lip twitching, he felt an irrational burst of happiness. To distract himself, he pushed open a door that led off the living room. 'Wow, this room also has amazing views. I'm guessing this must have been a bedroom.'

Alice placed her hands on her hips and took a deep breath. 'So,' she said, 'in your expert opinion, is this place going to fall down around me?'

'You'd need a surveyor out to give you a definite answer, but let me have a quick look outside and I'll have a better idea.'

As he stepped outside, Luke breathed a sigh of relief. Being in the cottage with Alice felt claustrophobic. Something about her got under his skin, and part of him wished he'd never darkened her door. Now he felt responsible for making sure the cottage was safe, and he already had more work than hours in the day. And he was in danger of breaking his golden rule–*never trust a beautiful woman.* He'd had his fingers burned on that count one too many times before.

At least the fabric of the building seemed sound. On closer inspection, it transpired that the clapboard cladding was a later addition to protect a brick-built structure that had survived the decades remarkably well. As he checked the wood around the back door leading off the living room, Luke noticed that the grass was flattened, and a makeshift path had been created through the undergrowth. So this was how the mystery cleaner had got in and out of the building without being seen. Even so, how could anyone have known Alice would arrive to claim the cottage as her own? Someone in the village knew more than they were letting on about Seashell Cottage, but Luke was blowed if he knew who.

Chapter 6

'Penny for them.'

'Hello, Tricia.' Luke tried not to smile as Patricia winced at the name. She was no longer the carefree girl he remembered. Her once-perfect skin now showed the passage of time all too well, but rather than laughter lines, her creased forehead suggested that the past few years had not been happy ones. She'd tried to cover up the signs of a difficult few years with makeup, but he knew her well enough to spot the red tinge around her eyes, and how their sparkle had dimmed. Luke reminded himself that Tricia's happiness was no longer his problem, but he couldn't help hating her ex for hurting her, despite the hurt she'd caused him. Some might have seen it as karma, but Luke wouldn't bring himself to sink that low.

'What are you doing in here all alone?'

'I'm not alone. Nick's just gone to the toilet.'

Right on cue, Luke's best friend Nick strolled towards them, doing up his fly.

'Hello, Nick,' said Patricia, batting her eyelashes. Luke hid a smile. Patricia clearly wasn't fussy about who she hooked up with, so long as she could make her ex-husband jealous.

'Alright, Tricia. How's things?'

'Fine, but you know I like to go by Patricia these days.'

'Course you do,' said Nick, winking at Luke.

'Right, well, I'll leave you lads to it, but don't forget, it's my divorce party on Friday. I'm a free agent again! If that's not something to celebrate, I don't know what is. I expect both of you to be here. We're having a buffet and karaoke, so it should be a right laugh.' Her tone was brittle, and her forced cheeriness wasn't fooling anyone.

'Sounds great,' said Luke, taking a swig of his pint.

After Patricia had wandered off, Nick leaned over to his friend and said under his breath, 'She's still got it, right?'

'Really? That woman needs therapy, not a new boyfriend.'

'You're feeling sorry for her?' asked Nick, his eyes wide. 'Luke the saint strikes again.'

'Hey, just because I don't like seeing her suffer doesn't mean I'd trust her as far as I could throw her. I'm not the kind of bloke to make the same mistake twice.'

'Really? She's single, you're single...'

'Are you forgetting what she did to me?'

Nick had the good grace to look sheepish. 'Sorry, mate. But you're over that now, surely?'

Luke sipped his pint. He wasn't sure he'd ever be over the way Tricia had humiliated him in front of the entire village. It wasn't Tricia's betrayal that still hurt, but losing what might have been. He felt a pang as he pictured the little girl he'd been all set to adopt as his own. What a fool.

Luke's thoughts turned to the spiky young woman he'd met in the run-down cottage. She wasn't his type at all and was the polar opposite of Tricia from the little he'd seen. He was pretty sure she disliked him and seemed to resent his offer of help. But something about her determination not to let the cottage beat her resonated with Luke, and, against his better judgment, his thoughts kept returning to ways he could help.

'I know that look,' said Nick. 'You've met someone, haven't you?'

'No, nothing like that.'

'Shame, I thought something exciting might happen around here at last.'

'What about Tricia's divorce party? Isn't that excitement enough?'

'You know what I mean. Sometimes I wonder why we didn't get out of here at the first opportunity.'

'Things get livelier in the summer.'

'What, for those four days in a year it doesn't rain?'

Luke laughed. 'Same again?' he asked, holding out his hand for Nick's empty glass.

When Luke returned with their second pints, he found Nick looking through the village magazine.

'See what I mean,' said Nick, throwing the magazine down on the table. 'We're too young to be stuck in a place like this.'

Luke pulled the magazine across the table. 'There's a cinema night in the community centre next week, and the amateur dramatic society is recruiting for their next performance. I seem to remember you having a fine voice.'

'When I had dreams of being a rock star or actor, maybe. These days I only sing in the shower.'

'You're missing a trick,' said Luke. 'You should audition. Where's all this discontent coming from, anyway? You know loads of people would kill to live a stone's throw from the beach.'

'Even if it meant living with their parents at twenty-six?'

'My God, you are in a foul mood. Last I checked, your parents go swanning off around the world for most of the year, leaving you all alone in their plush property with sea views.'

Nick smiled. 'Yeah, I suppose I don't have it too bad. Don't you ever think of moving away?'

'Nah, at least not while Gran's still around. It's not like there's anyone else to look out for her.' Luke found he couldn't meet Nick's eye and stared into his pint. He'd have to tell his best friend about the letter soon, but now wasn't the right time.

'No, sorry, mate.'

Luke waved his friend's concern away. 'It's not a chore. I love living near Gran.'

'Yeah, but you must feel the pressure sometimes.'

Luke shrugged. 'Maybe if I hadn't lost Mum and Dad so young, or if things had worked out with Tricia, my life would have turned out differently, but there's no point thinking like that. I'm happy with my lot.'

'Good for you.'

'Anyway, I'd best head home,' said Luke, downing the last of his pint. 'I've got so much work on at the moment. I need all the sleep I can get.'

'Alright, catch you on Friday if not before.'

'Sure.'

Luke stepped out into the freezing air. Rather than heading straight home, he walked into the beer garden, leaning against a glass balustrade that stopped drunks from falling to the beach below. The sea, whipped up by a fierce wind, roared as waves pummelled the shoreline. Luke squinted into the darkness, just making out the white crests of waves against the inky night.

Nick could moan all he liked about winter in Saffron Bay, but it was Luke's favourite time of year. The elements were at their most dramatic, the sunsets blistering and the beach empty. He could explore the coastline from the water without dodging kids in inflatable boats or louts on jet-skis.

Luke pulled his hat from his pocket, tugged it down over his hair and set off on the five-minute walk to the holiday let he was renting over the winter. He'd thought his two-bedroom temporary home shabby until he'd seen the inside of Seashell Cottage. It made his own place seem like a five-star hotel, and his gran's house like a palace. *Poor Alice*, thought Luke, then promptly shook the thought from his head. He had to stop thinking about the strange young woman. No good could come of it. Turning up his collar, Luke put his head down and strode toward home.

Chapter 7

'It's only me, Gran.' Luke walked through to the kitchen and placed a bag of shopping down on the kitchen worktop.

'I'm through here.'

Luke followed the sound of Sylvie's voice and found her in an armchair, a blanket spread across her lap and her feet up on a footstool.

'Are you cold?'

'No, I just fancied getting cosy. It's blowing a hoolie out there. Did you manage to get any work done? I was worried about you out in the storm.'

'I was fine. It wasn't a storm really, just a bit blustery, and I was working inside today.'

'On what?'

'A bespoke kitchen that costs more than I'll earn in ten years.' Luke laughed at the scowl appearing on Sylvie's face. 'I know,' said Luke in answer to her unspoken comment, 'but at least the rich folk moving in provide plenty of work for me.'

'But they're not moving in, are they? Not properly. I don't understand why they need such big houses. In my day, a holiday home was a little shack on the cliff, not some concrete and glass monstrosity. And whilst they might throw a bit of work your way, what about how they're pricing youngsters like you out of the area? Huh?'

'Railing against it won't help any of us. Anyway, speaking of shacks, have you met your new neighbour yet?'

'New neighbour?' When Sylvie looked at Luke, she had a glint in her eye. 'Please tell me the foul Merryweathers have sold up at last.'

Luke grinned. 'No, unfortunately not. I'm talking about your neighbour on the other side.'

'Not that tumble-down cottage?'

'That's the one.'

'So someone has bought it at last. To be honest, I'm surprised it's taken so long. I'll be looking forward to months if not years of bulldozers, diggers and foul-mouthed workmen just the other side of the fence. Wonderful.' Sylvie let out a long sigh.

'No, Gran, the place isn't being demolished, and no one's bought it. A young girl, a woman really, is moving in. She says the cottage used to belong to her family.'

'That can't be right,' said Sylvie with a frown. 'The last people to live there were... never mind.'

'The Lovedays?'

Sylvie's eyes opened wide, and her hands began to shake. 'The Lovedays?' she asked, her voice little more than a croak.

'Are you alright, Gran? You've gone pale.'

'I'm fine, I'm fine,' said Sylvie, waving a hand to bat away Luke's concern.

'The woman's name is Alice Loveday. Apparently, she's been given the cottage by her father.'

'D... Daniel Loveday is back in the village?'

Luke studied his grandmother, who had gone a deathly shade of grey. He kicked himself for upsetting her, although, to be fair, he thought the idea of new neighbours would have been a pleasant surprise. 'No, Alice, that's his daughter, seemed very vague about him. I got the impression they're not close. In fact, I think she hinted he might be dead.'

'Well, I suppose that's something.'

'That he's dead?' asked Luke, incredulous that his mild-mannered grandmother would say such a thing.

'No, of course not. I meant it's good the girl's not close to her father.' Sylvie frowned, her hands gripping the blanket tight.

'Gran, what is it about this man that's got you so upset?'

Sylvie shook her head. 'I'm not one for spreading gossip, Luke. All I'll say is that girl will need to be careful around here with a surname like Loveday. Things happened in the past with her father that folk won't want to be reminded of.'

'What things?'

Sylvie shook her head again, and Luke knew there was no point in pressing her. His gran was right; she was the most ungossipy old lady he'd ever come across, a quality he'd always admired, although just this once he wished she'd open up. Luke stood up to make them a pot of tea, but before he could walk away, Sylvie grabbed hold of his arm.

'You need to keep her away from Jack Tyler.'

'The old guy who lives up on the hill? Solly's brother?'

'That's the one.'

'And I don't suppose you'll tell me why?'

'You suppose correctly. Now, am I going to get a cup of tea anytime soon?'

Sylvie let go of his arm, and Luke smiled at the grandmother he loved more than anyone in the world. 'Your wish is my command.'

As Luke filled the kettle in the kitchen, he couldn't shake a sense of unease. Why had Alice's name upset his grandmother so much? When he'd mentioned Daniel Loveday, it was as though Gran had seen a ghost. Should he warn Alice? No, he hadn't gotten the warmest reception from the woman last time. If there was something dodgy in her family history, surely she'd be aware of it? It wasn't his place to go meddling.

Chapter 8

Alice sat cross-legged in the middle of her new living room, trying to get her body to move. She felt pinned down by the change thrust upon her against her will. Yes, most people would give their right arm to own a cottage in Cornwall with sea views, but Alice was not most people. Her escape into the life she'd dreamt of had been tantalizingly close, and now, in one fell swoop, her dreams of finally putting herself first and making it to university were in tatters.

From her pocket, she pulled out the deeds Maz had thrust at her two weeks earlier. *It could be worse*, said the voice inside her head. *You could be homeless*. But the last thing Alice felt was gratitude. After all she'd done for her family, how dare Maz steal her one shot at freedom?

Alice had hoped that her second visit to Seashell Cottage would prove more positive than the first, but with the wind howling outside and rain battering the leaky windows, if anything the cottage seemed worse. When she closed her eyes, Alice pictured Maz living it up on a beach somewhere in Thailand, sipping cocktails, free from all parental responsibilities. In that moment, it was hard to feel anything but hate toward her mother.

'This was supposed to be *my* time,' said Alice through gritted teeth. She banged her fists against the floor. It felt good to indulge her anger, and Alice would have given herself more time to wallow were she not rudely interrupted. A chirpy ringtone echoed around the empty room, and Alice reached across and picked up her phone.

'Hello?'

'Oh hello, is that Alice Loveday?'

'Speaking.'

'I've been trying to get hold of Mathilda Green. We need to speak to her about her daughter, May Green.'

'Sorry, who is this?'

'My name's Kim Mason and I'm calling from St Felix Community College. You are listed as the second emergency contact, but ideally, we'd like to speak to May's mother.'

'She's out of the country,' said Alice, picking at a loose piece of carpet. 'What's the emergency?'

'May has been suspended for fighting.'

'Fighting?'

'Yes. The principal would like you to come in for a meeting this afternoon.'

'I see. How long has May been suspended for?'

'That's what the principal would like to discuss with you. As I'm sure you're aware, this is an important year for May, so time out of school is less than ideal. Could you get here by two o'clock?'

Alice checked her watch. 'I suppose if I leave now...'

'Wonderful, I'll let the principal know.'

The screen went blank, and Alice threw the phone down onto the floor. She needed to be here at the cottage, trying to make it habitable, not rushing back to Plymouth to clear up yet another crisis involving her little sister. A rush of rage was swiftly followed by resignation. May had always been her responsibility, now more than ever, and fighting against her sisterly duty would solve nothing.

Alice locked up the cottage, noticing how the air felt warmer outside than in, then trudged back to her car, her mental to-do list growing longer with each step. Hers was the only car parked on the street. Only a handful of cottages had their lights on or curtains open, and Alice wondered how many were second homes. Warm light spilled out from the café, and although a coffee was tempting, there wasn't time.

When Alice turned the key in the ignition, nothing happened. She tried again, but the only sound was a clunk of metal, then silence. Once more, tears threatened, and Alice scrubbed her arm across her eyes, determined not to give in to the feeling of despair. She was the capable one, the sensible one, the only female member of the family not prone to flights of fancy or victim to tumultuous emotions. Now was not the time to lose her cool.

Alice tried again and again to start the engine, but to no avail. A sudden rage overtook her, and she hammered the heels of her palms against the steering wheel, letting out a cry of frustration. A knock on the window made her jump, and heat flooded her face as she saw Luke peering in. Of all the people to catch her in this state, it had to be him.

With a deep breath, Alice unwound the window but couldn't bear to turn her head.

'Is everything alright?' asked Luke.

'Does it look alright?' asked Alice through clenched teeth.

'No, I suppose not.'

From the corner of her eye, Alice saw Luke run his hand through his hair and give her a nervous smile, and she instantly regretted the sharpness of her tone. 'I'm sorry, I'm having a terrible day.'

'Car troubles?'

'Car troubles, sister troubles, house troubles, money troubles, you name a trouble and I bet I have it.'

Luke laughed. 'Want me to look at your car?'

'You know how to fix cars?'

'No,' said Luke, laughing. His cheeks turned rosy as he added, 'I was trying to sound manly.'

Alice let out a surprised laugh. 'You've proved your manliness by giving your professional opinion on the cottage. This car is an old banger I picked up for a few hundred quid. It's been on its last legs for ages.'

'Do you have somewhere you need to be?'

Alice looked at her watch and groaned. 'Yes, I'm meant to be at my sister's school by two. She's been suspended.'

'What for?'

'Fighting, apparently.' Alice rolled up the window, grabbed her bag, and climbed out of the car. 'I'd better check when the next bus gets in.' She began striding towards the bus stop outside the community centre, but Luke jogged up to her and grabbed her arm.

'There's no point,' he said. 'There's a bus at eight, then another at three.'

'That's it?'

'I'm afraid so.'

Alice walked to a nearby bench, sat down, and threw her head in her hands. Somewhere nearby, a gull squawked angrily, and Alice wished she could do the same. She felt the air change as Luke sat down beside her, and she lifted her head. She pointed to the sliver of sea visible between two houses and said, 'This place is beautiful, but I don't think I've ever been anywhere so impractical.'

Luke laughed. 'That's true enough, although it could be worse. For a couple of years, we didn't even have a shop in the village. It's positively cosmopolitan compared with what it used to be. Listen, why don't I drive you to Plymouth?'

'That's very kind, but I'm sure you have better things to be doing with your time.'

'It's OK, I need to go to the builder's merchant either today or tomorrow, so it might as well be today.'

Alice looked at Luke through narrowed eyes. She wasn't used to accepting help, and hated the fact she needed it now. But what choice did she have? 'If it's not too much trouble, that would be really helpful. I was going to stay at our flat tonight anyway to do some packing, so I can get a bus back to Saffron Bay tomorrow morning, and I'll sort the car out then.'

'Great. I'll get the van. Oh, and I have a mate in the next village who's a mechanic. I'll call him and ask him to look at your car.'

Before Alice could either protest or thank him, Luke was marching off down the road to get his van. She pulled her coat tighter around herself and studied her surroundings. The centre of the village was compact, with the café, community centre, doctor's surgery and General Store all within a few metres of each other.

Despite the quietness of the street, the windows of the café were steamed up, and Alice could see the outlines of customers filling every table. Several cars were parked in the community centre car park, and Alice wondered what could draw locals out on a chilly midweek lunchtime. She left her position on the bench and crossed the road to read the notice board. For a relatively small village, the amount of clubs and events was staggering; chess club, ballroom dancing, line dancing, cinema club, men's breakfast, WI, mothers and toddlers, over-sixties supper, not to mention the one-off bingo, quiz, and music nights booked in over the next few months. *Perhaps there's more to this village than first meets the eye*, thought Alice, as Luke pulled up in his van.

Chapter 9

As Luke pulled the van to a stop beside Alice, he wondered if he was making a huge mistake. After Sylvie's reaction to the Loveday name, surely he should be keeping his distance, not offering to spend the best part of an hour with Alice in close quarters. She unsettled him and drew him to her in equal measure. It was as if the harder she tried to assert her independence, the more he wanted to break down her defenses.

You're playing a dangerous game, he told himself as she climbed into the van. *Don't you have enough problems of your own without taking on someone else's?*

'This is really kind of you,' said Alice, and warmth flooded Luke's body.

'Does your sister often get into trouble?'

'No!' snapped Alice, and Luke cursed his insensitivity.

'I'm sorry, it's none of my business.' He turned on the radio, and they drove out of the village in silence. As the van struggled up the steep, tree-lined hill, Alice turned the radio down and shifted in her seat.

'It's me who should apologise. I shouldn't have snapped at you, not when you're doing me such a big favour. It's been a tough couple of weeks for my sister, on top of the usual stress of being a teenage girl and looming exams.'

'It sounds like it's been a tough couple of weeks for you, too, what with the move and everything.'

'Hmm.'

Luke tapped his fingers against the steering wheel as silence stretched between them. Should he turn the radio back up? Would that seem rude? What if Alice wanted to talk? But Alice seemed lost in her own world, staring out of the window, chewing on her bottom lip. Luke forced his eyes on the road, ignoring the quick beating of his heart and the way his clammy hands kept slipping from the steering wheel.

'Do you work for a company or are you self-employed?'

The sudden break in the silence made Luke jump, and he cleared his throat. 'I'm self-employed.' *What's wrong with you?* He thought. *Is that the best you can do?* He cleared his throat again. 'I've worked for myself for the past ten years. The business is almost at the point I can take someone else on, but I don't want to run before I can walk.' *Wow, you must be thrilling her with your scintillating conversation.* 'How about you?'

'I'm not self-employed.'

'Right.'

Luke breathed a sigh of relief as the city finally came into view. He met so many people through work, making small talk with people from all walks of life was a skill Luke prided himself on, but Alice was a different story. Either she didn't enjoy talking, or she didn't enjoy talking to him.

Neither option was great, especially as they hit another patch of traffic, extending the time they'd have to spend together stuck in the van.

'Did you mention my dad's name to your gran?'

Alice spoke so quietly Luke had to strain to hear her, and as he noticed the shake in her voice, he wondered if this explained her silence. Had she been building up to this question the whole journey?

'Um, yes, she said she recognised the name.'

Alice sat up straighter in her seat, and Luke felt like an animal caught in a trap. Tell her Sylvie's genuine reaction and it would crush her, palm her off with platitudes and she'd be disappointed.

'And?'

He opted for what he hoped was the gentler approach. 'She couldn't remember much about him.'

'Oh.'

Luke ground his teeth. His irrational desire to make the woman beside him smile was being thwarted at every turn. 'The college is around here somewhere, isn't it?'

As Alice rattled off directions, Luke leaned back in his seat, his shoulders aching from the tension of the drive. It was only another five minutes before the school came into view. Alice had her seatbelt off before he'd even pulled into the car park. It seemed she'd enjoyed the journey as much as he had.

'If you have any problems with buses tomorrow, let me know.'

'We'll be fine,' said Alice, climbing down from the van and giving him a smile that seemed to take all her effort.

'OK, but I mean it. It's no trouble to come and get you if you need a lift.'

'Bye, Luke,' said Alice. She threw him another fleeting smile before slamming the door and hurrying off to find her sister.

Luke turned the van around. There was nothing he needed from the builder's merchant, but he may as well call in for a visit while he was in the area. He opened the window to let out the delicate scent of Alice's perfume. The less he thought about Alice, the better. He had enough on his mind already. The last thing he needed was the complication of a ridiculous crush on a woman who couldn't be bothered to string more than two words together.

Chapter 10

Alice kept looking forward despite wanting to check Luke had actually driven away. Was he watching her? She was suddenly acutely aware of her gait. Did she lean to one side as she walked? Did she stomp? Shuffle? A memory flooded back of Maz trying to teach her how to walk like a model. *Swing your hips! One foot in front of the other!* Alice tried it now, but decided she looked more like a newborn foal than a catwalk model.

Only when she arrived at the school reception did she turn and breathe a sigh of relief when she saw the empty parking space where the van had been. Accepting kindness from strangers made her skin crawl, however well-intentioned. She needed to manage on her own, just as she always had.

Alice side-stepped a group of teenagers dragging their feet on the way to their next lesson, grateful she no longer had to navigate the complex social structures of high school. She'd enjoyed the actual learning; it was everything that went with it that was hard.

After introducing herself to the receptionist, Alice was shown along a corridor to a waiting area, tucked in a corner of the building away from the disobedient cries of ill-managed students and harassed teachers. On one of the plump armchairs sat May, head down, her arms folded across her chest.

'The headteacher will be with you shortly,' said the receptionist. 'Please wait here until you're called through.'

Alice nodded her thanks and flopped down in a chair beside May. When May looked up and saw Alice, she groaned. 'What are you doing here?'

'The school called me. They said you've been suspended. What happened?'

'Becky Gill started it.'

'Started what?'

'The fight.'

'Oh, May, what have you done?'

May scuffed the toes of her shoes against the carpet. 'That's just like you, assuming it was my fault.'

'Then tell me what happened.'

'Becky called Maz names. She said she's a home-wrecker.'

'A home-wrecker?'

'Becky said her mum caught our mum in bed with her dad. Now Becky's mum and dad are getting a divorce.'

'Maz slept with Becky Gill's dad?'

May nodded.

'And you think she's telling the truth?'

'Don't you? There can't be many men in Plymouth Maz hasn't slept with.'

'But if you think it's true, why did you get into a fight?'

May tilted her head back and let out a long sigh. 'She said I was a slapper like my mum.'

'I can see why that would annoy you.' Alice took May's hand. 'You know that's not true, don't you?'

'Of course I do. I've never even kissed a boy!'

'Oh,' said Alice, surprised at the revelation. May often stayed out late with friends, occasionally arrived home drunk, and Alice had imagined many disastrous situations her little sister might have been getting herself into.

'Miss Loveday?' A middle-aged man in a cheap suit, with a paunch hanging over his trousers, was holding open the office door. 'I'm Mr Murry, the head of school here at St Felix's. Perhaps I could have a chat with you, and then we'll invite May to join us?'

'Alright,' said Alice, feeling like a student again. She hated how male authority figures cowed her, even now she was a grown woman. She wouldn't have dared even talk in class when she was at school, let alone get into a fight.

'Take a seat,' said Mr Murry, pointing to three comfortable chairs positioned around a low coffee table. 'As I'm sure you've heard, we've had to make the tough decision to suspend May for two days.'

Two days? Alice breathed a silent sigh of relief. It could have been a lot worse. 'I see.'

'She's usually one of our better-behaved pupils, but this past week her behaviour has taken a turn for the worse. I wanted to speak to you to find out if there is anything going on at home we should be aware of?'

'Yes, actually, there is. Our mother has moved to Thailand, leaving May in my care.'

'I can see how that would have disrupted things for May. Has this move been a long time in the planning?'

Alice couldn't help laughing. 'No, as with everything concerning our mother, it was last-minute and ill-thought-through. May and I are going to have to move, so my sister's world has been turned upside down.' Alice frowned, questioning herself. Was it really a coincidence Maz had found the letter about the Seashell cottage whilst packing? What if she'd known all along and had been biding her time? No, Maz could never be that cunning. She was too disorganised.

'Where will you be moving to?'

'To a small village in Cornwall called Saffron Bay. May will get the bus to school, but she'll have a long commute, and won't be able to spend as much time with her friends.'

'I see. Still, I'm afraid it doesn't excuse her use of violence. We caught her pulling another girl's hair and trying to scratch her face.'

'May told me the girl had been taunting her.'

'And you think that's an excuse for violence?'

'No, that's not what I'm saying. Will you also be punishing the other girl?'

'I can't discuss other pupils with you. I'm sure you understand. Now, let's bring May into this discussion, shall we?'

As Mr Murry stood to open the door, Alice understood his question wasn't a question at all. *Just keep your head down and say yes and no in all the right places*, she told herself. The last thing she and May needed was some busybody questioning the legality of their unusual guardianship arrangement. What if social services got involved? As May trudged into the room, a shiver of fear rippled through Alice. She pictured someone coming out to inspect the cottage. Would May be taken into care? There were four months to go until she turned sixteen. Four months of separation would be four too long.

May slumped down in a chair, and Alice squeezed her hand, probably a little too hard. She needed to convey the silent message that May needed to comply, just this once. *Don't draw attention to our situation*, she tried to say silently through a pleading look. To Alice's immense relief, May must have used all the fight she had on Becky Gill, for she responded to the headteacher's admonishments meekly, nodding her head in the right places and apologising when required.

'And I'd like you to write a letter of apology to Becky.'

Alice felt May stiffen and gripped her sister's hand again. 'I can help May with that,' she said.

'Good. Well, we'll see you on Thursday, May, and we'll need to see an improvement in your attitude.'

'Yes, sir.'

Alice and May walked back through the school in silence. As they stepped out of the gates, Alice doubled over, struggling for breath.

'What's wrong?' asked May, rushing over and putting an arm around her sister.

Alice pushed her away, trying to pull in deep breaths. When she straightened her body, her head swam, and May guided her to a low wall before her legs gave way.

'Alice, I'm so sorry for all the trouble I've caused.'

When Alice looked at May, her eyes were swimming with tears. 'Please, May, promise me you'll try to keep your head down and avoid getting into trouble. I don't know where Mum running off leaves us, and if social... if social services...' a lump in Alice's throat blocked all speech and May wrapped an arm around her shoulder.

'I get it. I'm so sorry. I've been so selfish thinking this is all about me, when it's you who's had a teenager dumped on you. You're the one having to sort out this mess.'

'We'll sort it out together,' said Alice, regaining some of her composure. 'We're a team, remember?'

May laughed as they reenacted the secret handshake of their youth. 'What do we do now?'

'Go back to the flat and pack up the last of our things. You may as well use your unexpected two days off to help us move. The flat is going to need a good clean. Maz was so far in arrears with the rent that we don't stand a chance of getting our deposit back, but cleaning the place still feels like the right thing to do. By the end of the week, we should be settled in Saffron Bay.'

'Great,' said May, though her tone told Alice it was anything but.

Chapter 11

Luke opened the curtains and sipped his coffee while staring at the view. His temporary home was shabby and unloved, but with a view that encompassed not only the village, but a long stretch of coastline, he could understand why holidaymakers paid through the nose to stay there in peak season.

To the untrained eye, the village would have seemed sleepy, if not half dead, but Luke knew where to look for signs of life. The lights flicked on in Bayside Café, then the door flung open and Margot staggered out onto the pavement, wrestling a blackboard advertising her latest cakes and daily specials. Across the road from the café at the General Store, Steve, still in his dressing gown, ducked outside to grab a pile of newspapers and a crate of milk waiting for him. Outside the community centre, one of the many retirees who lived in the village was hanging up a sign advertising a men's breakfast.

Luke shook his head as he spotted a young mum battling the wind to push a buggy along the pavement. Behind her, a sulky little boy in a school uniform dragged his feet, and she had to keep stopping to let him catch up. Luke couldn't tell if the pang he felt watching the young family came from memories of his own mother, what had happened with Tricia, or a deep-seated fear that the chance of creating a family of his own was passing him by.

Luke picked up a letter from the coffee table and held it by one corner, as if it might burn him. Time was running out to reply, the opportunity slipping through his fingers. Burying his head in the sand and ignoring the dilemma wouldn't work. He needed to talk to Sylvie about it, but it never seemed the right time. And now there was Alice in the mix, confusing his thoughts even more. Luke dropped the letter back on the table, rinsed his mug in the sink and pulled on his coat.

Just as he was climbing into his van, Luke's phone buzzed in his pocket. 'Hello? Oh, alright, mate?'

'Yeah, just calling to let you know I've fixed your friend's car. The starter motor had gone. It was a pain to get in and replace it, and a few of the bolts had rusted, but it's all sorted now and ready to pick up.'

'Great, I'll let her know. How much does she owe you?'

'A hundred will cover it.'

'Thanks, mate.'

'No worries, see you later.'

Luke's thumb hovered over the number he needed to dial. Would she think he was pestering her? Don't be ridiculous, he told himself, you're just helping a friend.

'Alice, hi.'

'Hello? Who is this?'

Luke swallowed down the disappointment that she hadn't bothered to save his name when they swapped numbers. 'It's Luke. I'm calling about your car.'

'Oh, right, sorry, hi.'

'My mate just called me. It needed a new starter motor, but it's all fixed and ready for you to collect. He said it will be a hundred.'

'That's not as bad as I was expecting. Can you give me the address of the garage?'

'Sure, I'll text it to you. It's on the bus route from Plymouth. Sorry, I'd offer to pick you up and take you there, but I've got a big job on today.'

'Don't be silly, you've already helped me more than enough.'

'Did you get everything sorted yesterday?' The pause on the line made Luke wish he'd just said goodbye.

'Yes and no,' said Alice eventually. 'May is suspended for two days. I don't want her seeing the cottage yet, not until I've spruced it up a bit, so I'm leaving her in Plymouth to finish packing and make a start on the cleaning, and I'm heading back to Saffron Bay this morning.'

'Sounds like a plan.'

'Yes, so could you text me the address of the garage?'

'Sure, I'll do that now. Bye.'

'Bye.'

Luke drove down into the village, but rather than heading straight to his next job, he parked up outside the café.

'Morning, Luke. The usual?'

'Yes, please, Margot,' he said, walking up to the counter. The café was so warm, he removed his jacket and draped it over one arm. 'Got a busy day ahead?'

'The knit and natter lot are in this morning,' said Margot over the noise of the coffee machine. 'They'll keep me busy for hours. I keep inviting Sylvie to join us, but I've had no luck so far.'

Luke laughed. 'Gran is a woman of many talents, but handicrafts are not one.'

Margot smiled and handed him his cup of coffee. 'Where are you working today?'

'Up on Villa View, one of those new builds. Guess what they've named it?'

'Seaview?'

'Got it in one.'

Margot laughed and handed him a coffee in a takeaway cup. 'Is it even legal to have so many Seaviews in one village? The poor postman is going to get so confused!'

'I know. Some people I work for have more money than sense.'

'And not a scrap of originality between them.'

'You said it. Right, as lovely as it is having a good old moan, I'd better get on and actually do some work.'

'Likewise,' said Margot, as a group poured in through the doors.

'Oh,' said Luke, turning back to Margot. 'Before I go, I don't suppose you know anything about the Tyler family who live up at Saffron Manor?'

Margot fiddled with the apron around her waist, and Luke couldn't tell if she was impatient to get on with her work, or uncomfortable with his line of questioning. 'No, sorry. But I know there's no family living up there now, just old Jack Tyler. Solly's brother.'

'Oh yes, of course.'

'The rest of the family left years back. Why do you ask?'

'No reason, just curious.'

'Right,' said Margot, her tone wary. 'Sometimes it's best to let sleeping dogs lie, Luke.'

The group of knitters arrived at the counter, and Margot turned her attention to them.

'Best let sleeping dogs lie?' muttered Luke, frowning as he headed off to work.

Chapter 12

Alice took her hands off the steering wheel and rubbed her eyes with the heels of her palms. The bus ride back to the garage had felt never-ending, handing over a hundred pounds had been painful, and the thought of a day of cleaning and painting the wreck of a cottage made Alice want to scream. Perhaps among the many items of furniture she needed for the cottage, she should include a punching bag to release some of her frustration? The thought made her smile, and she felt strong enough to face the day.

Alice lifted her arms in a stretch and let out a wide yawn. She'd been up half the night worrying about May's suspension and the effect the move was having on her. May had been remarkably calm when she first found out their mum had done a runner, and Alice should have recognised it as the calm before the storm. It was bad enough to be abandoned by your mother at fifteen without having to lose the only home you'd ever known.

After Alice had shown her the photos of Seashell Cottage, May had hit the roof. Alice's pleas that living by the beach would be fun had been met with an increasingly hysterical list of reasons city life was preferable.

Her sister's reaction didn't surprise Alice. May had a wide group of friends, an active social life, and, thanks to a part-time job at a local bakery, money for shopping, all things Alice craved but never had at that age. Another major difference between them, other than looks, was that May still had something of a relationship with her father. Phil was as useless as a chocolate teapot with parenting, but he took May out for dinner occasionally, where he'd hand over a few banknotes to salve his guilt. No wonder May didn't want to move out to the sticks.

May saved the money from Phil in a metal tin under her bed, but Alice would never ask her to part with the money to help get the cottage into good shape. Perhaps if they had shared a father, things would have been different. But the cottage was Alice's problem, and she'd need to resolve it alone.

Alice knew what May thought of her: dowdy, middle-aged, a spinster at twenty-five. But what was Alice supposed to do? Their mother had worn the mantle of irresponsibility, forcing Alice to become old before her time.

A gentle rap on the car window startled Alice from her thoughts, and she looked up to see the old man she'd met previously, leaning on his walking stick. Given the twinkle in his eye, Alice couldn't help but wonder how much he really needed the stick. She wound down her window, letting in a blast of freezing air.

'Back again so soon,' said the man.

'I can't keep away. Nice to see you again,' said Alice, returning his warm smile.

'Did you find what you were looking for the last time?'

'I did, thank you.'

'Good. My name's Solomon, in case you were wondering, but please call me Solly. Everyone around here does.'

'Alice,' said Alice, stretching her hand out of the window for Solly to shake. 'Sorry, it's rude talking through a window.' Alice wound up the window and climbed out of the car, leaning on the door as the wind buffeted her and smiling at the man she'd instantly warmed to. 'Have you always lived in the village?'

'No, but I was born in one of those cottages,' said Solly, pointing his walking stick to a nearby row of small stone cottages. 'My brother Jack lives up on the hill. He never left Saffron Bay, but I was in the Navy for years, then moved back here when I retired. Anyway, I can see you're busy, so I'd best not keep you.' Solly lifted his walking stick and pointed to the many bags Alice had on the back seat.

'Yes, I've got lots of work to do, so I'd best be getting on.'

'It was good to see you again, and to meet you properly, Alice. Do you think we'll be seeing you again?'

'I think you'll have a hard time getting rid of me.' Alice smiled, and Solly turned with a laugh and headed back to his usual bench. Alice appreciated that he'd not quizzed her too much on her plans. The entire village would know soon enough about their new residents, but as far as Alice was concerned, the longer she had to fix up the cottage in peace, the better.

Alice was about to collect her bags from the car when the smell of the sea reached her on the breeze. In all the surprise of discovering the cottage, she hadn't yet ventured down onto the beach. Keen to delay the start of her endless to-do list, Alice abandoned her bags of cleaning products and turned down a narrow path that sloped steeply downwards. Trees with bare winter branches hung across the path like clawed hands, creaking back and forth in the wind.

Alice pulled her hat down and zipped up her coat. Clouds scudded quickly in the sky above, clustering together to form an ominous mass. She picked up her pace, jogging the last few meters until her feet left the tarmac for sand. There was no one else on the beach, the sea stretching out as far as she could see. The tide was on its way out, receding to reveal a dark shelf of rock, which rose in ragged formations from the water like ink stains on a page.

Bracing herself against the wind, Alice staggered a few meters along the beach. Sand whipped up into her eyes, and she felt tears dampen her cheeks. Despite the unpleasant conditions, she could appreciate how lovely the beach would be on a warm summer's day. Perhaps she could buy a stand-up paddleboard and explore the coastline with May. Alice smiled as she imagined May's response to the invitation, likely to be something along the lines of, *so lame*.

As the wind grew fiercer, tearing at her coat, Alice decided the beach was best saved for another day and turned back the way she came. She squinted against the whipped-up sand, surprised to see another figure on the beach. The man was hunched, his head bent as he held on tight to a hat. At his feet, a Scotty dog yapped and chased pieces of seaweed caught by the wind.

'Morning,' called Alice, as their paths crossed. The man looked up, but rather than return her greeting, he scowled. Alice hurried on her way, keen to get out of the weather and on with her day.

Alice didn't trust the handbrake on her rust-bucket car, so left it at the bottom of the hill and carried the bags up the street. Once she'd got the last supplies into the cottage, she slammed the door behind her and leaned against it to catch her breath. Rather than providing the shelter she'd hoped for, the cottage rattled and howled amid what had escalated to a full-blown storm outside.

'It's only the wind; there's nothing to be frightened of,' Alice told herself, as a ghostly scream tore through the chimney. The windows rattled in their frames. A loud bang came from the kitchen, and Alice wrapped her arms around herself for comfort. May was going to hate this place. Alice prayed the weather would have at least calmed down a little by the time they officially moved in.

Chapter 13

'Morning,' said Alice, waving at the old lady who, despite the cold weather, was kneeling on a mat weeding a flowerbed. The woman nodded in response, then turned her head. 'And what a fine morning it is,' muttered Alice, wondering if all the locals were going to be this unfriendly.

Alice squatted down and squeezed through the foliage, blocking the garden path. She reached behind her and yanked the box of belongings she'd brought with her into the overgrown front garden. She should probably tackle the foliage before anything else, but Alice liked the privacy it provided while she tried to make the cottage livable.

The key turned in the lock, and Alice stepped inside, rubbing her feet on a newly purchased mat. After spending two days ripping up old carpet and washing down the walls with sugar soap ready for painting, she had no intention of adding any dirt to the relatively clean floors.

With her fingers crossed, she walked through to the kitchen and turned on the taps. As cloudy water stuttered from them, she breathed a sigh of relief and decided she'd need to thank Luke again for finding the stopcock for her.

Thoughts of Luke provoked a shudder of guilt. She'd been rude to him, she knew that, but she still didn't trust his motives for wanting to help. No one gave something for nothing in this world.

Hands on hips, Alice wondered where to start. The windows needed a good polish, but it was the graffiti that would probably freak May out the most. She filled a bucket with water, added half a bottle of washing-up liquid and carried it through to what she had already earmarked as the sitting room. Being able to visualise the rooms' uses had given Alice the first flutters of excitement rather than the feeling of drowning which had plagued her recently.

'Knock knock.'

Alice frowned as Luke walked into the sitting room. 'You again?'

'Me again.' Luke grinned, and Alice's frown deepened.

'Look, if you're here about work, I'm really sorry, but I have zero money to pay for any hired help.'

Luke laughed, a deep, throaty laugh that creased dimples into his cheeks and made his eyes sparkle. 'I'm not here for paid work, and trust me, with what those holidaymakers are prepared to pay, you couldn't afford the going rate.'

'OK. So why are you here?'

'I called in on Gran and thought I'd see if you need a hand. My next job doesn't start until after lunch, so I'm at a bit of a loose end.'

'How do those holidaymakers feel about you working half-days?'

'They don't want me getting under their feet this morning as they've got a fancy interior designer from London visiting.'

'Shouldn't you be spending time with your gran?'

'Nah, she's off to a coffee morning. She doesn't want me there when she's chatting to her mates.'

Mates? Alice tried very hard not to smile. 'Don't you have anything else you could be doing?'

'Nothing productive.'

'I don't get it,' said Alice, bending down to rinse a cloth in hot water, then making a start scrubbing the wall. 'You have the morning off and you want to work here for free?'

'Yes.'

'Why?'

'Because I don't like being bored.'

'Oh, come on, no one gives something for nothing. What is it you want? You know I don't have money, so is it gossip? A few stories to tell your mates down the pub, is that it?'

'You realise how rude you can be, don't you?'

Alice felt her cheeks redden and scrubbed harder at the wall. Flushed cheeks were the bane of her life. Thanks to the pasty pallor inherited from her father, she could never hide her feelings, as they blazed like a beacon across her face. 'Sorry,' she muttered, 'I guess I don't buy this good-guy act, that's all.'

'You've never lived in a village before, have you?'

'What's that got to do with anything?'

'If you had, you'd know that unlike in towns or cities, in villages like this one, people help each other out. That's all I'm doing here, trying to be a good neighbour.'

'Humph.' As annoying as Luke was, Alice wasn't in a position to turn down an offer of free labour. 'Alright then, if you insist. I'm trying to get this graffiti off the walls. I know it will freak my sister out otherwise.'

Luke crouched down and picked up a cloth. 'How is your sister feeling about the move?'

Alice shrugged. 'She's only fifteen, and would much rather be staying in the city, so I need this place to be as nice as it can be for her.'

'Isn't there somewhere else you can stay while you're doing the cottage up?'

'Nope.'

'Have you considered selling it?'

'Can't do that.' *At least not until I know whether my dad is dead or alive.*

'Right,' said Luke, looking puzzled.

As much as Alice hated that look, she would probably feel the same if the roles were reversed. How could she explain that by living in the cottage, her dad could find her if he wanted to? If he isn't dead. It was a stupid fantasy, and there was no way she would admit it out loud.

'I know your dad's not on the scene,' said Luke, 'but what about your mum?'

Alice grimaced. She hated discussing personal matters, but Luke was here helping for free, and at a bare minimum deserved her politeness. 'You really want to know?'

Luke nodded.

'She's run off to Thailand to open a yoga retreat with her friend.'

'Wow.'

'Exactly. I mean, she's always been restless, a free spirit tied down ever since she became a teenage mum. She always resented being a mother and made us call her Maz rather than Mum. But I thought she'd at least wait until May sat her exams before taking off again.'

'May?'

'My sister.'

'Oh yes, that's right. You sound remarkably calm about it, considering.'

Alice smiled and shrugged her shoulders. 'This isn't the first time she's run off. When I turned eighteen, she saw it as an opportunity to run off and join the circus. Hey, it's a true story,' said Alice, after seeing the look on Luke's face. 'Anyway, it didn't last long. She injured her throat trying to breathe fire and had to come home.'

'Sorry,' said Luke, trying not to laugh.

'It's OK. With the benefit of hindsight, I can see the funny side.'

'And she left you to look after your little sister that time, too?'

'Yep.'

'What do you do when you're not looking after your little sister?'

Alice sighed. 'I've been doing any old job for the past few years, trying to save enough to go to uni. I've done everything from dog walking to waitressing to office temping. I was supposed to be starting uni in September, but now it looks like I'll have to defer my place.'

'Can't you still go? I mean, your sister will have finished her exams by then, right?'

'She will, but she wants to go to sixth-form college, so I'll still need to support us financially. It's just not the right time to be taking on a load of student debt.' What Alice didn't say was that none of this was about getting a degree, or the worry of student debt. What she'd really craved was freedom, the chance to indulge her passion and think about herself for a change. A rush of anger flowed through her as she pictured Maz on a beach halfway across the world, having taken her eldest daughter's chance of freedom with her.

'What are you supposed to be studying?'

Alice felt her cheeks redden again but couldn't tell if it was from embarrassment or residual anger towards Maz. 'Music,' she muttered. 'It's always been a dream of mine. But life happens, and we can't always get what we want, can we?'

'What do you play?'

'Piano. I got free lessons at school as we were a low-income family, and from the first moment my fingers touched the keys, becoming a musician is all I've ever wanted to do. I realise now it's a childish idea, no different from the boys at school who said they wanted to be footballers. It's time I grew up.'

The intense look Luke gave her caused Alice to look away, and she hid her embarrassment by ringing out her cloth in the bucket of water she'd filled. 'Are you actually going to help?' she asked. 'Or are you going to stand there holding a damp cloth doing no work, just asking a load of questions?'

'I don't believe in wasting effort,' said Luke. He bent over the bucket and was so close Alice could smell the soap he'd washed with that morning. 'What have you got in there?'

'Washing up liquid.'

'You could stand here all day scrubbing, and I doubt a bit of washing up liquid will be much of a match for those walls. What you want is paint thinner. I've got some in the van. I'll grab it.'

'There's really no need,' said Alice, but Luke was already jogging towards his van. She sighed and wiped her arm across her forehead. It was kind of Luke to help, but a small, ungrateful part of Alice wished he'd leave her alone to get on with the job. It was distracting having him around, not to mention embarrassing. How many other twenty-five-year-olds would dream of living in such a manky house?

'Here you go,' said Luke when he returned. 'Got any gloves?'

Alice held up a pair of pink rubber gloves, and Luke pulled them on.

'How do I look?'

'Do you really want me to answer that?' asked Alice, unable to keep a straight face.

'Tell you what, why don't I make a start in here, and you can grab us a couple of coffees from the café? Tell Margot I sent you and she'll give you a discount.'

'Sure,' said Alice. She grabbed her bag and left the cottage, wondering who Margot was, and why she'd be so keen to give Luke a discount.

Chapter 14

The café door clinked, and Alice tried not to feel daunted as she stepped over the threshold. She'd spent so many years being the sensible one who took care of everyone, it hadn't allowed much time for making friends. She'd taken to hiding in her bedroom whenever Maz threw one of her famous soirées, and anyway, for the past few years she'd been juggling so many jobs she'd not had time for socialising. Being so out of practice made meeting new people scarier than it should have been.

'Morning,' said a bright-eyed woman from beneath a mop of shiny silver hair. Colourful feathered earrings hung down to her chin, matching the multi-coloured jumper she wore over her jeans. 'Oh, hello again, love.'

Alice frowned, then realised why the woman looked familiar. She hadn't recognised her without her kagoul and waterproof trousers. In the forest, the woman had been camouflaged in brown and khaki. Today, she was more like a rainbow. 'Hello again.'

'My directions must have worked then. I'm Margot, by the way. Sorry, I realised after I sent you on your way I hadn't even introduced myself properly.'

'I'm Alice. Pleased to meet you again.'

'What can I get for you, Alice?'

'A flat white and... I don't suppose you know what Luke usually drinks?'

'Luke?' asked Margot, her eyes growing wide. 'Luke as in builder Luke?'

'Yes, assuming there's only one of those in the village.'

'What a sly old dog. Where's he been hiding you then?'

Alice felt her cheeks heat to the point they had probably turned purple. 'Oh, no, it's nothing like that.'

'It's about time he found happiness again and made some friends his own age, rather than hanging around with old codgers like me and his gran,' said Margot with a wink.

'No, really...'

'Sorry, I didn't mean to embarrass you. But you are a friend of Luke's?'

'No, he's just helping me with some building work.'

'And he told you I'd give him a discount?'

'Um, well, yes, actually.'

Margot rolled her eyes. 'He did one job for me years ago for mates' rates, but I should have paid full price considering the amount of cheap coffees he's got out of me ever since.' She turned her back on Alice and began fiddling with the coffee machine. The way she hummed as she worked made Alice suspect she was no stranger to giving discounts to locals. For a small woman, Margot seemed to take up a lot of space, and Alice imagined the energy bursting from her in colourful sparks. Just watching her made Alice feel old and tired.

'You've got a lovely café,' Alice said, trying to move the subject on from Luke.

'Thanks, love, I do my best. I've lived in the village for donkey's years, but only bought the café five years ago. Before that, I ran a café at the community centre, but the place cost so much to run. I thought, why not buy this place and run the smaller groups from here, then use the community centre for larger events? It's worked out well. Of course, the café was a wreck when I first bought it. That's where Luke and his mates' rates come in. He did an amazing job helping me turn this place into what you see today.'

Alice looked around at the upcycled, mismatched furniture and sea-themed colour scheme of blues and greens. It was tasteful, homely, and just the place she could imagine relaxing with a good book.

'So come on then,' said Margot. 'How did you and Luke meet? I didn't think that boy ever leaves Saffron Bay, and I'm sure I haven't seen you around here before. Did you meet online? I know those online dating sites are all the rage with you youngsters.'

'We're not dating,' said Alice, trying not to sigh or roll her eyes. 'We're not even friends. Like I said, he's helping me with some building work. I've moved in next door to his gran.'

'Next door? Are you related to the Merryweathers?'

'The who? Oh, no, I'm on the other side, in Seashell Cottage.'

'Seashell Cottage,' said Margot, drumming her fingers against her chin. Alice felt Margot was hamming it up a bit, but couldn't think of any reason she'd be pretending not to know the name.

'Mouldy, falling down, being overtaken by plants. Ring any bells now?' asked Alice with a grimace.

'Oh my goodness, you've moved in *there*? But why?'

'The place used to belong to my dad. My sister and I have to leave the city, so it made sense to come here.'

Before Margot could respond, the door chimed and a hunched old man walked in, shooing his small Scotty dog back out onto the pavement.

'Morning, Jack,' called Margot. 'The usual?'

'Yes, please, Margot, if you'd be so kind.'

The man Alice now knew to be called Jack shuffled through the café towards them. He didn't look as old as his gait suggested, and it was like he had the weight of the world rather than old age weighing him down. She noticed he had sand clinging to his shoes and, as he walked, he left a golden trail in his wake. Alice smiled at Jack, who studiously avoided her eye. *Perhaps he's shy*, she thought. Margot returned with two coffees in takeaway cups and one in a cup and saucer.

'There you go, Jack,' said Margot, handing the cup and saucer to him.

Jack took a sip of coffee and smiled for the first time. 'You know just how I like it. Perfect.'

'Thanks,' said Margot. 'Jack, this is Alice. She's just moved to the village.'

Jack gave Alice a small nod of the head, then turned back to his coffee.

'Yeah,' said Margot, 'Alice has moved into Seashell Cottage, if you can believe it. It belonged to your dad, didn't you say?' Margot turned towards Alice, but at the same moment the cup he was holding slipped out of Jack's hand and smashed against the tiled floor below. Alice screamed as hot coffee met her legs, and Margot rushed around the counter. 'Here,' she said, handing Alice a clump of tissue to wipe herself down. 'Are you OK, Jack? Jack?'

Margot and Alice looked up from their wiping to see Jack rushing with surprising speed towards the door.

'Jack?' called Margot. 'Jack, please don't worry, it's only a cup of coffee. I'll get you another.'

But the old man was out of the door, slamming it behind him. The two women looked on as he grabbed hold of his dog's lead and began hurrying along the street.

'Poor old Jack,' said Margot. 'I hope he's OK. It's not like him to be so clumsy.'

Alice nodded, but she'd seen exactly what had happened, and Jack hadn't dropped the cup out of clumsiness. It had been from shock. Shock at hearing the name Seashell Cottage. Shock at the mention of her dad. What on earth had gone on here, to let a prime seaside cottage go to rack and ruin, and to sully her dad's good name? Alice closed her eyes, longing for the chance to go back to her boring city life.

'Are you sure you're OK?' asked Margot, breaking into Alice's thoughts. 'You're not burned from the coffee, are you?'

'No, it's not that,' said Alice. 'Thanks for the coffees. How much do I owe you?'

'After what just happened, you can have them on the house,' said Margot, 'but don't go telling Luke or he'll be round here sniffing out more freebies.'

Margot's wide smile helped lift Alice's spirits, and as she left the café, she decided that with so much work to do on the cottage, any concerns about Jack's strange reaction to her arrival in Saffron Bay could wait.

Chapter 15

As Alice walked into the cottage, the sound of a man humming made her smile. Despite her reservations, she couldn't deny it was nice having someone else around. From the little she'd seen of him, Luke seemed genuine enough, and so long as she stayed on guard, Alice couldn't see the harm in softening her attitude a little.

'Everything OK?' asked Luke, taking the cup of coffee from Alice.

'What? Oh, yeah, sorry. Something strange happened while I was getting the coffees.'

'Strange? Like what?'

'There was this old guy in there, Jack. When Margot told him I was moving in here, he dropped the cup he was holding and ran off.'

Luke groaned and ran his hands through his hair. 'I should have warned you about Jack. Sorry, I didn't expect you to bump into him so soon. He's a bit of a hermit these days.'

'Why would I need a warning about him?'

'Truth be told, I don't know.' Luke held his hands out and shook his head in confusion. 'Gran told me to keep you away from him. All she'd say was that he and your dad had history.'

'But she didn't say what?'

'Gran prides herself on not repeating village gossip, unfortunately for you.'

'This is all I need,' said Alice, taking a sip from her coffee. 'Oh well, I don't have time to worry about some ancient feud right now. Thanks for what you've done while I've been gone. The walls are looking way better.'

'Yeah, it'll need covering up with paint, but hopefully I've got the worst off for you. Have you had any luck getting the electricity back on?'

'Yes, I rang them yesterday. They're sending an engineer over to check the place over before they reconnect me, but hopefully I'll have electricity by the end of the week. I'm not sure the boiler's up to much though.'

'I can probably find you a deal if it needs replacing.'

'Thanks,' said Alice, frowning as she thought of the dent a new boiler would make in her savings. Oh well, needs must.

'Oh, by the way, are you around on Friday evening?'

'I'm not sure. Why?'

'Nothing, really. It's just an old friend of mine is having a divorce party down at the pub. I thought it might be a good chance for you to meet some locals, some of the friendlier locals, at least.'

'Oh, right, I see. I'll have to check. May's usually out with her friends on a Friday night, so I probably will be free. I won't be able to come for long, though. May sometimes gets home in a bit of a state, so it's best I'm around when she does. Also, Saturday is moving day, so it will be an early start.'

Alice was babbling and knew it, but it had been so long since the hand of friendship had been extended in her direction, her responses had grown rusty. And she didn't know how to react to Luke himself. Finding him attractive was no big deal, but being drawn to his kindness and generosity was another thing entirely. He made her feel safe, but in her experience, there was no one she could rely on but herself, and she would do well to remember that.

'How much have you told May about this place?'

Alice grimaced. 'Probably not enough. I think I've been worried that if she knows the truth, she might refuse to move. I showed her a few photos of some of the better areas, and that was enough to freak her out. If she saw all this graffiti, she'd go nuts.'

'I get that. Listen, I have a bit more time on my hands than I thought I would this week. The owners of the house I'm working on called me while you were out. They have had a last-minute change of plans with flooring, so there's nothing much I can do until that's finished. Why don't I help you get this place as good as we can?'

'That's really kind of you, but like I said, I haven't got the money to pay you.'

'Maybe you could pay me in other ways. Oh, God, not like that...' said Luke after seeing the horrified look on

Alice's face. 'I meant maybe you could help a bit with my gran.'

'How do you mean?'

'Nothing too strenuous. She's really independent, but she's had a couple of falls lately, and I'm not always close enough to help her.'

'Don't her other neighbours help?'

'They used to, but most have sold up to holidaymakers. The only other permanent residents on this street are the Merryweathers, and let's just say Gran isn't their biggest fan.'

'What makes you think she'd like me?'

'She might not,' said Luke with a grin, 'but if she does, it would be a weight off my mind. And it wouldn't be forever. I live with Gran in the summer months.'

'Oh, right, and what do you do in winter?'

'I rent a holiday let, whichever one I can get for the best price. It suits the owners to have someone living in a property rather than it getting cold and damp. It also gives Gran a break from me. We rub along well, but she values her independence, and when I'm there, I cramp her style.'

Alice smiled, liking the sound of Luke's gran already. 'And does your gran have a name?'

'Yeah, sorry, you can't call her Gran, can you? Her name's Sylvie. Why don't we do a couple of hours' work here, then pop over there for coffee? I'm sure she'd like to meet you.'

'That sounds lovely.'

'Great. If you leave me to finish up these walls, you could start putting masking tape around the skirting boards ready for painting?'

'Good plan.'

As she attached long strands of tape to the walls of the kitchen, Alice smiled to herself. From the other side of the wall, she could hear Luke humming again. She regretted her earlier frostiness. It felt good to have someone on her side for once. She crept to the door and poked her head around. Luke had headphones in, his back to the door, and as he scrubbed at the graffiti, his feet shuffled from side to side. Only as Luke raised his arms and spun around did he notice Alice watching him. His cheeks turned pink, and he pulled his headphones down around his neck.

'How long have you been standing there?'

Alice covered her mouth with her hand. 'Long enough. You've got some good moves there.'

'I'm a trained dancer, actually,' said Luke, a grin spreading across his face.

'Really?'

'Yes, I went to Cornish dancing lessons when I was younger.'

'Cornish dancing? Is that even a thing?'

Luke's jaw dropped and his eyes widened. 'Is it a thing?' He slapped a hand against his chest. 'I have to say, Alice, I'm offended. I know you grew up across the border, but honestly, I expected more from you.'

'I really can't tell if you're joking.'

'Wait there.' Luke fiddled with his phone, then placed it in the middle of the floor. 'Stand here.'

Alice stayed where she was, but Luke's stare burned through her, and with a sigh, she relented and moved to the middle of the empty room.

'Ready?' asked Luke.

'Ready for what?'

Luke bent down and tapped his phone. The sound of traditional folk music poured out from it, and Luke's foot tapped. 'Here,' he said, holding out his hands. 'I'm going to give you a lesson.'

Alice felt a rush of nerves as she took hold of Luke's hands. Were her palms sweaty? What if she made a fool of herself? Being touched felt so foreign. The resulting sensation was a mixture of pleasure and pain.

'All you need to do is count,' said Luke, 'like this.' He began counting and leading Alice in a series of simple steps.

'Do you teach Cornish dancing to all your new acquaintances?'

'It's my USP.'

Alice smiled and tried to focus on the dance moves, and not on her constantly changing opinion of Luke. It wasn't like her to be so open with someone she barely knew, let alone dance with them. In fact, in the week she'd been working on Seashell Cottage, Alice had felt less like herself than ever. Or was it that this was the real her, and the sensible, boring woman had been left behind in Plymouth? She decided only time would tell.

Chapter 16

'What is she doing here?' hissed Sylvie, after pulling Luke into the kitchen.

'She's your neighbour, Gran. I thought you'd like to meet her?'

'Under normal circumstances, of course I would. But, Luke, she's a Loveday. I'm too old to be getting dragged into another Loveday mess.'

'Gran, I have no idea what you're talking about. Alice seems great from the little time I've spent with her. I thought you'd always prided yourself on not getting dragged into village gossip.'

'I have.'

'Well then, give Alice a chance. She's never met her dad and doesn't know if he's still alive, so it's not exactly fair to blame her for his misdeeds, is it?'

Sylvie sighed. 'I suppose you're right. And as we're to be neighbours... Why don't you make a pot of tea and I'll try to give Alice a warmer welcome than before.'

With Luke busy in the kitchen, Sylvie made her way toward the sitting room. Outside the door, she paused. It wasn't like her to be so rude, and if that poor girl really was a Loveday, she'd need all the friends she could get. With a deep breath, Sylvie opened the door. 'It's Alice, isn't it? I'm sorry for dragging Luke away before you'd even gotten through the door. It was very rude of me.'

'It's fine,' said Alice, who was perched uncomfortably on the edge of a hard-backed chair.

'Sit yourself somewhere more comfortable,' said Sylvie, flapping her hand toward the sofa. 'The chair you're on is the one I save for when the vicar visits. It's so uncomfortable I know he won't stay for long.' Sylvie chuckled, and Alice moved chairs.

'It's lovely to meet you, Mrs...'

'It's Mrs Trelawn, but please call me Sylvie. Everyone else does. Luke tells me you're moving into the cottage with your sister.'

'Yes, that's right. May's only fifteen, so it'll be a big upheaval for her, but hopefully she'll settle quickly.'

'Fifteen? That must be quite the age gap between the pair of you.'

'Ten years. Different dads.' Alice shrugged. 'Um... Luke... well, Luke said you may remember my dad?'

Sylvie shifted in her seat. Her initial instincts about having this young girl in her home were right; it would only lead to trouble. 'I knew of your father. I wouldn't say I knew him as such.'

'But you were neighbours?'

'Yes. Ah, here's Luke with the tea.'

'What were you two gossiping about?' asked Luke as he laid a pot of tea and three cups on the coffee table. Sylvie would have liked to kick his shins. Silly boy, she'd hoped his arrival would have changed the subject, not continued it.

'I was asking Sylvie what she remembered about my dad,' said Alice, her eyes wide in anticipation.

Luke turned to his gran and mouthed a silent 'sorry'.

After giving Luke a quick smile, Sylvie took a sip of her tea and turned back to Alice. 'As I said, dear, I don't remember much about your father. Just that he was an only child and lived in the cottage when he was in his early teens. The family moved in to care for Harry Loveday, who would have been your great-granddad. When he died, your father and his parents continued living in Seashell Cottage.'

'My grandparents,' said Alice, frowning. 'I always dreamed of having grandparents growing up. Mum was estranged from her own parents and never told me anything about Dad's. Do you know if they're still alive?'

'I'm afraid I don't,' said Sylvie, dunking a ginger nut biscuit into her tea. 'They moved away from the village such a long time ago...' Sylvie was expecting Alice to probe further, but to her relief, the young woman stared out of the window, lost in her thoughts.

'Alice is hoping to go to university,' said Luke.

Once again, Alice's cheeks flushed. 'I was, but I've had to put my plans on hold. In fact, only yesterday I contacted the university to defer my place.'

'And what were you hoping to study?'

Alice's cheeks burned a deeper red. 'Music,' she muttered. 'I realise now it's silly holding onto childish passions. It's probably best to have a rethink.'

'What tosh,' said Sylvie. 'I can't think of anything more important than pursuing your dreams. And why should moving here make you change your plans?'

'I don't have a piano for starters,' said Alice with a small smile. 'I used to go to a neighbour's house to practise.'

'I've got a piano in the dining room,' said Sylvie. 'You'd be more than welcome to use it. No one's touched it since... nevermind. That's one problem solved. And education is never wasted. You're young. You should follow your dreams.'

Alice smiled. 'I'm afraid I'm not that young. I'm in my mid-twenties and have responsibilities. When my mum was around, things were different, but now she's gone...'

'I'm so sorry to hear that, dear. Did you lose her recently?'

'Oh, no, I don't mean she's dead. She... she...'

'Alice's mother has taken up a once-in-a-lifetime business opportunity in Thailand,' Luke chipped in.

Sylvie frowned, not just because there was clearly more to the story of Alice's mother, but at the way Luke had rushed to her defence. She'd never seen her grandson behave so chivalrously before.

'Luke's being kind,' said Alice, smiling 'Truth be told, Mum's rather dropped me in it. She's left me to look after my sister and run off on some adventure. If it weren't for Dad giving me the cottage, I'm not sure what I'd have done.'

'So you've been in touch with your father, have you?' asked Sylvie, peering over the top of her teacup.

'No, unfortunately not. Mum passed on a note he'd left to be given to me when I turned twenty-five, and when I tracked down the solicitor's firm named in the letter, I found out the cottage is in my name. It's all been a bit of a shock. I mean, I've never even met the man, so why he'd be giving me this cottage is a mystery. It was left in a trust rather than a will, and even the solicitor couldn't tell me anything about him. The last contact they'd had with Daniel was twenty-five years ago, just after I was born. That's why I'm so curious about him, you see. He doesn't seem very popular in the village, but good or bad, it would be nice to know *something* about him.'

Sylvie fiddled with her long beaded necklace. It couldn't do any harm to throw a bit of information Alice's way, could it? 'As I said, I don't remember much about Daniel. But I know he had a shock of white-blond hair just like yours, and was extremely green-fingered. He'd just set up his own landscape gardening business before... well, before he and his parents left the village.'

'And I don't suppose you know why they left?'

Sylvie wound her necklace around her fingers. She hated lying. 'I'm afraid I'm getting rather old, dear, and my memory isn't what it once was.' Sylvie avoided Luke's eye, knowing the look he'd give her. She may be a little wobbly on her feet these days, but there was nothing wrong with her mind. *Oh well*, thought Sylvie, *if her grandson thinks badly of her, so be it. Some things from the past are best left there, and nothing would change her mind about that.*

Chapter 17

Then

Daniel tried to focus on the horizon, but it kept jumping and wobbling in front of his eyes. His bare toes clipped the edge of a beer bottle, and he winced. How many had he had tonight? The fact that he couldn't remember was undoubtedly a bad sign. Beside him, pop music blared out of a portable boombox Sam had brought along.

Unfamiliar faces appeared ghoul-like in the firelight. This was supposed to be the best time of year, when a bit of life finally came to Saffron Bay in the form of tourists, but so far, Daniel couldn't remember much about the summer. It was as though the local youths held all their desires in all winter, emerging like coiled springs into the warm summer sunshine, ready to embrace whatever opportunities came their way. For Daniel, this meant booze and girls, and too many nights blacking out after sampling too much of both.

'Hey.'

Daniel shifted his weight and tried to focus on the girl who sat beside him. 'Hi,' he slurred, his voice too loud even to his own ears.

'I'm Maz.'

'Dan.' Daniel held out his hand, and the girl laughed, taking and shaking it before raising her hand for a high five.

'I saw you were empty,' said Maz, handing Daniel another bottle of beer.

'Cheers, but I think I might call it a night.' *While I can still find my way home.*

'Aw, don't be an idiot. The party's only just starting.'

'There'll be plenty more.'

'Not for me. I'm only here for three weeks, then I'm off to my cousin's.'

Daniel frowned. There was something familiar about the girl, but he couldn't put his finger on it. 'Have we met before?'

'I think I'd remember if we had,' said Maz. She winked, then turned her attention to the group. 'Hey, does anyone want to go skinny dipping?' she called, already pulling off her T-shirt.

Shouts of agreement echoed into the night, as those too young to worry and those old enough to know better began staggering to their feet and shedding their clothes.

'What are you doing still sitting down?' asked Maz.

'I'll pass on the skinny dip,' said Daniel.

'Oh no you don't,' said Maz, grabbing Daniel's hand and hauling him to his feet. She reached across and pulled his T-shirt over his head. Daniel shivered, despite the warm summer evening. Then, without taking her eyes off him, Maz began removing her remaining clothes.

Daniel felt his cheeks burning and was grateful for the cover of darkness.

'Beat you there,' whispered Maz, reaching up and stroking his cheek.

Then, before Daniel knew what was happening, Maz was whooping and screeching her way toward the water's edge. 'Sod it,' he said, pulling off his clothes and chasing Maz into the water.

Beneath a star-filled sky, the silky black water turned to a churning froth as bodies hurled themselves in, scooping up handfuls of water and flinging them in the air. Daniel was the last one in, and as he dived beneath the water, the cold had a sobering effect. He emerged, treading water, unable to identify the dark shapes of his friends as they splashed around, making no attempts to protect their modesty.

This summer felt different from the previous ones. The air held a sense of danger, the usual pranks going up a notch, the dares more risky. Perhaps it was because of what had happened to Marty. Perhaps it was the tourists here this year, more wild, more unruly, with less to lose. Either way, it unnerved Daniel. He shivered, not from the cold water, but from a premonition he couldn't explain. All he knew was that under a starlit sky, surrounded by friends, a darkness descended. With it came a feeling that this was a summer of change, and not for the better.

'Oi, you're not getting out, are you?'

Daniel turned around to see Maz swimming towards him. 'Yeah, I'm getting cold, and I really need to be getting home.'

'Will Mummy be worried?' asked Maz, pouting and speaking in a baby's voice.

'It's not like that,' said Daniel, turning onto his front and cutting through the water with an experienced front crawl.

'Hey,' called Maz, as Daniel heaved himself back onto the beach. 'Catch you tomorrow, yeah?'

Daniel gave a thumbs-up in response, though whether Maz could see it in the dark was anyone's guess.

'Oh, and Daniel?' she shouted.

'Yeah?'

'Nice bum.'

Daniel gave another thumbs-up and ran up the beach to retrieve his clothes. He used his hoodie to dry himself off, then slipped on his T-shirt and shorts. As he walked back along the beach, the noise of his friends carried on the wind. They sounded so carefree, Daniel envied them. Of those who had summer jobs, he was the only one who had to get up at an ungodly hour, and the formidable Jack Tyler would only increase the workload if he got a whiff of a hangover.

The village lay in darkness, and Daniel strode along the empty streets wondering how many residents they'd annoyed with their beach party. Every window he passed was dark, so Daniel hoped everyone had slept through it. The week before, some busybody had called the police after a raucous session. Daniel thought that might have led to a calming down of their nightly rampages, but if anything, it seemed to have added fuel to the fire. Daniel let out a long sigh. He was getting too old for this. There must be better ways than booze to get all the rage and hurt out of his system, but if there were, he hadn't found them yet.

Daniel clicked open the gate, which led to his home, Seashell Cottage. The name was so cheesy, but it was his granddad's choice, so Daniel would never change it. He stuck to his old method of climbing in through the open bedroom window. He'd given his family enough to worry about already, the least he could do was not wake the entire household.

Chapter 18

Alice checked her watch and was surprised to find it was already seven. She brushed her fringe from her eyes and stepped back to admire her handiwork. There was still so much to do in the cottage, but at least May had a nice room to move into. Perhaps they could go shopping at the weekend for items to make it more homely? Alice had spotted a secondhand shop in the nearby town that, from the outside, looked like a treasure trove.

Using her phone camera, Alice checked her reflection. She had a streak of white paint across her cheek, and a few flecks in her hair, but the old shirt she'd worn had protected her clothes from the worst. White had been a good choice for the walls. May could change the colour later if she wanted to, but for now it made the room feel fresh, in stark contrast to the rest of the cottage.

Alice flopped down on the single bed Luke had helped her put together and unbuttoned her painting shirt. All day she'd been weighing up whether to accept Luke's invite to his friend's divorce party. On the one hand, turning up at the divorce party of someone you didn't know smacked of gatecrashing. On the other hand, she couldn't hide away in the cottage forever. If they were going to make a go of living in Saffron Bay, Alice would have to get to know the locals sooner rather than later.

In the bathroom, she filled the sink with cold water and washed her face the best she could. The skin beneath her eyes had a grey tinge, and she couldn't get all the paint out of her hair Her outfit of jeans, T-shirt and woollen jumper didn't scream party, but as she'd forgotten to bring a change of clothes with her, they'd have to do. Her final meager attempt at glamour was to run her fingers through her shoulder-length hair.

Alice shivered as she locked up the cottage. The night was still, but the star-filled sky, whilst beautiful, showed a spell of cold weather had arrived. Alice hoped the cottage wouldn't be too chilly by the time she arrived with May the following day.

As she walked down the hill towards the pub, the sound of music reached her. Warm orange light spilled through the pub windows onto the pavement. The windows themselves were steamed up, only the outlines of party-goers visible through the blurred glass.

The pub was heaving with bodies, and after walking through the door, Alice was tempted to turn on her heel and run back to the cottage. Before she had a chance, Luke spotted her and beckoned her into the melee. When she hesitated, he pushed his way through the main bar to greet her.

'You came!'

'Did you think I wouldn't?'

'You didn't sound all that keen when I asked you.'

'Well, it is a little daunting, especially knowing not everyone in the village is pleased I'm here.'

Luke laughed. 'Don't worry, I doubt you'll be bumping into Jack Tyler at a divorce party.'

'Let's hope not. Who is getting divorced anyway?'

Before Luke answered, a glamorous woman, who Alice guessed to be anywhere between thirty and fifty, sidled up to Luke and rested her head on his arm.

'Who's your friend, Luke?' she asked, draping an arm across his shoulder.

'This is Alice. She's moving to the village and will be Gran's new neighbour.'

The woman appraised Alice through narrowed eyes, then turned to Luke. 'I was rather intending this party to be invite-only.'

Although the woman had lowered her voice, Alice felt certain she was meant to have heard. 'I'd better be going,' she said to Luke.

'Alice, wait.'

Luke tried to grab Alice's arm, but she slipped out of his grasp and fled the pub. It had taken all her courage to step through the doors, and to find she wasn't welcome, well, that stole any shred of confidence she'd had left. Of course, she shouldn't have gone to the party. What had she been thinking?

Alice walked around the outside wall of the pub. Finding a dark corner, she leaned against the cold stone walls, then crouched down, her head in her hands. Through a nearby window came the sound of karaoke. Alice crept towards the window and peered inside. Luke was sharing a microphone with the woman who'd made Alice feel so unwelcome. They were grinning at each other as they took on the roles of Sonny and Cher, and Alice kicked herself for ending up in this position. She shouldn't have accepted Luke's invitation. He must have felt sorry for her, and the last thing Alice needed was anyone's pity. Her life may be veering off her carefully planned course, but she was a capable, intelligent woman and, most of all, she was self-sufficient. She didn't need new friends, she never had. From now on, Alice resolved to keep her head down and politely decline any offers of friendship. From what she'd experienced of the village so far, the less people encountered her, the better.

With the cold biting through her coat, Alice skirted the perimeter of the building and made her way back towards her car. It was just as well she'd be getting an early night, for the following day she'd need all the energy she could muster for the big move. Butterflies danced in Alice's stomach as she began driving away from Saffron Bay. The next time she was in the village, it would be for good. The keys to their Plymouth flat would have been handed back to the estate agent, and however rough things got in Saffron Bay, there would be no escape. Alice wound down her window, letting the freezing, salt-tinged air calm her thoughts. She was moving to a Cornish coastal village, something most people could only dream of. Alice wound the window back up and told herself to stop worrying. She would do everything in her power to make the move a success. After all, if a few unfriendly locals were the worst of her problems, she had nothing to worry about, didn't she?

Chapter 19

'What the actual f...'

'Language,' warned Alice.

May gave Alice a scathing look and picked a twig out of her hair. Alice wondered what the reaction would have been had she not cut down most of the excess foliage the day before.

'It's not in the best condition,' said Alice, 'but think of it as a work in progress.'

'Whatever. Let's just get in, shall we?'

Alice turned the key in the lock and took a deep breath. Of all the reactions Alice was expecting as they walked through the door, she hadn't expected May's silence.

'So, here's the kitchen,' said Alice, 'the other rooms all come off this main corridor. There's no hot water yet, but the new boiler should arrive early next week.'

'Right.'

'I know there's a lot to do, but I'm sure we can make it homely.'

'Which is my room?'

'I thought you could have the one at the back with the sea views.'

May threw Alice a small smile. 'Thanks, sis. Can you show me where it is and I'll unpack?'

'Of course. As you can see, the cottage is quite small.' Alice stood in the hallway and pointed to a series of doors leading off it. 'My bedroom is opposite the kitchen, then down here is the bathroom, the living room and this,' said Alice, walking to the far side of the living room and pushing open a door, 'is your room.'

May walked in and headed straight to the window. 'Wow,' she said, lifting her hand to the newly polished glass.

'I know,' said Alice, 'it's quite a view. Obviously at some point we'll have to get double-glazed windows fitted, but Luke's checked all the existing frames and they'll do for the time being, until I've been able to save up at least.'

'Maybe this place isn't that bad after all,' said May, spinning around to scrutinise her room.

Alice crossed her fingers behind her back, desperate for May to like it. She had found a used single bed and chest of drawers on Marketplace, and added a lamp, vase of flowers and a brightly coloured rug for extra homeliness.

'It's a work in progress,' said Alice. 'Obviously you can put your own stamp on it in time.'

'Thank you,' said May, walking over to Alice and hugging her. For a moment, Alice was reminded of the sweet little girl she'd had as a sister, before the hormones hit. 'Can I see your room?' asked May.

'Oh, no, mine's not as finished as yours. There's not really anything to see.'

May pushed past Alice and strode down the corridor. She pushed the door open, and her hands flew to her face. 'For f... flip's sake, Alice, you can't sleep in there!'

Alice stood beside May and saw the room through her sister's eyes. Although she'd scrubbed the walls, she'd not had time to paint them, and the remnants of decades-old wallpaper remained. There also hadn't been time to find a decent bed, so Alice had bought a cheap camp bed from a shop in town and hoped it would be sturdy enough to last a few weeks at least. Other than the camp bed, the room was empty. No curtains at the window, no carpet or rug on the floor. It looked a little like a prison cell.

'This will do me fine,' said Alice, forcing a smile onto her face. 'I can sleep anywhere.'

'Share with me.'

'You don't want me cramping your style, but thanks for the offer.'

'OK, suit yourself. I'd like to see the rest, please.'

Alice gave May the tour, sounding like a cheesy estate agent as she tried to find positives where there were none. The avocado bathroom suite was serviceable, but no amount of scrubbing could remove the black stains from between the tiles. The tiles in the kitchen were in a similar state, with several cupboards missing doors and the oven hob had rusted so badly Alice had bought a small camping stove after deciding it was a health hazard.

'This place has water, yeah?'

'Water, yes, but like I said, the new boiler isn't arriving until later in the week. In the meantime, we can boil kettles. And at least you have short hair.'

May rolled her eyes. 'Please don't start going on about my hair again.'

'Hey, I'm being positive about it. It must be so much easier to wash since you chopped it all off.'

'I didn't chop it *all* off,' said May, running her hand through her shiny black pixie crop.

'No, you're right, and as much as I hate to admit it, it does suit you.'

'Finally you see sense,' said May with a laugh. 'You know what, sis, I reckon we're going to get on fine without Mum around.'

'I hope so,' said Alice, amazed at how positive her usually sullen sister was being. 'How about we unpack, then I'll head over to the next village and pick us up some fish and chips?'

'Sure.'

It was a big job unpacking May's life into her new bedroom. Unlike Alice, who liked to keep possessions to a minimum, May had a normal amount of clutter for a teenage girl.

'I think we should make getting a wardrobe a priority,' said Alice, gazing at the enormous pile of clothes on the bed.

'Yeah, I could have a look in some shops tomorrow if you like?'

'Tomorrow? You mean you're going back to the city? I thought we could explore the village together and get to know our new home.'

'I've checked out buses and it's an hour and twenty minutes back to Plymouth, which is a massive pain in the bum, but could be worse. You've not forgotten I'm staying at Hayley's tomorrow, have you?'

'I don't remember you saying anything about it.'

The eye roll was back as May said, 'yeah I did. She's having a small get-together at her place.'

'Will her parents be there?'

'They're out for the evening, but they'll be back by midnight.'

'I suppose, as long as you don't raid their drinks' cabinet again...'

'Great, thanks.'

May turned back to her box of knickknacks, signalling the conversation was over, and Alice shook her head, feeling as though she'd been hoodwinked. She was certain May had mentioned nothing about staying at a friend's, and despite never having gone to one herself, Alice was sure in teenage speak *small get-together* was code for *party*. Alice suddenly felt as though she had the weight of the world on her shoulders.

Chapter 20

The floorboards creaked outside her room, and Alice's shivering reached new heights. She burrowed down into her sleeping bag, trying to block out the strange noises all around her whilst rubbing her frozen feet to bring back feeling.

When a weight landed on her camp-bed, Alice screamed, her head shooting from the sleeping bag, her hands grabbing a pillow as her only available weapon.

'Alice, stop, it's me, May.'

'May?' Alice pulled herself up and squinted in the dim light of a distant streetlight pouring through the window. 'Why are you in here?'

'I couldn't sleep. It's so cold. Listen.' May moved her head close to Alice's. 'Can you hear my teeth chattering?'

'Can you hear mine?' asked Alice. 'Why don't I make us a hot chocolate?'

'Good plan. Then, maybe we could top to tail?'

'Not on this camp-bed we can't,' said Alice. 'It can barely hold the weight of one body.'

'My bed's OK though,' said May. 'I'll go back and snuggle down so it's warm when you come through.'

'Alright.'

Alice climbed out of her sleeping bag and pulled on a second pair of socks. She rummaged in her bag and added a fleece jacket over the top of the jumper she was already wearing. She couldn't remember a time she'd been so cold. The cottage seemed to lack any form of insulation, the cold seeping through gaps in the window frames, the single glazing and even the walls. They may as well be sleeping outside for all the protection the building gave them.

With the kettle bubbling, Alice held her hands above it, enjoying the steam's warmth on her skin. She pulled two instant hot chocolate sachets from the cupboard and stirred water into the cups. A branch banged against the kitchen window. Alice jumped, spilling boiling liquid onto her sleeve. She fought back tears. What possessed her to think they could live here? She was supposed to be the responsible one, and yet look at her. The cottage she'd brought her sister to was a health hazard.

Alice carried the hot chocolates through to May's room and found her sister sitting up in bed, her knees pulled to her chin.

'It's...s... s... so.... C... c.... Cold,' said May, her body trembling.

'Here, drink this; it will warm you up. I'll see about getting some electric heaters tomorrow. I'm an idiot for not thinking of it before.'

'Hot water bottles might be useful too.'

'Thermal underwear?'

'Electric blanket?'

'Furs?'

'Goose fat?'

'A dog?'

'A dog?' asked Alice with a laugh.

'Yeah, I see loads of people on Instagram posting photos snuggled up with their pets. They're like a living, breathing hot water bottle.'

'We are not getting a dog. Not yet, anyway.'

'Not yet? So that's a maybe?'

'Don't push your luck. Come on, move up. I need to get in.'

Alice squeezed in beside May, enjoying the warmth of her sister. They chatted quietly while sipping their drinks, and once they'd finished, snuggled down together, still not warm, but a lot less cold. It felt like a sleepover from their childhood, and when they eventually gave in to sleep, it was the time together that had warmed them more than any blankets.

'What the hell?' Alice woke with a start, wondering where she was. Beside her, May was fast asleep, one foot sticking out from the blankets. 'Alright,' muttered Alice as a persistent knock sounded on the front door. She climbed out of bed, grabbing a blanket and wrapping it around her shoulders before running to open the door.

'Oh goodness me, I am sorry.'

'Morning, Sylvie.'

'If I had thought you'd still be asleep, I would have come round later.'

'What time is it?'

'Ten.'

'Ten? Oh, wow. I'm usually up by seven, but we had a very disturbed night.' Alice yawned. 'Sorry, Sylvie, come in.' Alice led her neighbour through to the kitchen, wincing as she saw it through fresh eyes. 'It's a work in progress, sorry.'

'You really must stop apologising, dear,' said Sylvie. 'You've lived here less than twenty-four hours.'

Alice smiled. 'Would you like a cup of tea?'

'I'd love one, thank you. What was the problem last night?'

'Hmm?' Alice flicked on the kettle and turned back to Sylvie.

'You said you had a disturbed night?'

'Oh, yes. It was the cold mainly. The new boiler isn't coming until the end of the week, and I'd forgotten to buy electric heaters.'

'You've got no heating in March? But you'll freeze!'

'I'll nip to the nearest town and buy some heaters today. We'll be fine.'

'Those things cost a fortune. I've got a better idea. Why don't you sleep at my house for a couple of nights?'

'Oh, no, it's very kind of you to offer, but we wouldn't want to put you to any trouble.'

'I don't see how it could be any trouble if I'm asleep. I have two spare rooms already made up, just sitting there doing nothing.'

'Even so, we'd be invading your home.'

'Hardly. I'm inviting you to come over at bedtime, not move in. Unless you fancy dinner this evening, of course. I must admit, it sometimes gets lonely in that house by myself. Don't tell Luke I said that though, or he'll be moving straight in.'

'He lives with you in the summer, doesn't he?'

'He does, but he's so busy with work he's out most of the time. He'd live with me full time if I let him, but I don't want to cramp his style.'

Alice smiled, thinking about how Luke had said much the same about Sylvie.

'Come on, dear, say yes. It's only a couple of nights and, by the looks of things, you could do with a good night's sleep.'

'Yes,' said Alice, 'but only for one or two nights.'

Sylvie reached across and patted Alice's hand. 'See,' she said. 'Accepting help isn't so hard, is it?'

'Alright then, if you're sure,' said Alice, handing Sylvie a cup of tea. She didn't feel comfortable at the thought of sleeping in a stranger's home, but anything was preferable to another night shivering in a single bed beside May.

Chapter 21
Then

Daniel trudged up the steep hill, his head pounding with every step. He'd gained a reputation this summer as the wild one in the group, but this latest batch of tourists put his own efforts to shame. He wasn't sure he could remember a hangover this bad. Two hours' sleep was nowhere near enough to prepare him for a day under Jack Tyler's scrutiny. But if he ever wanted to get his own business off the ground, sacrifices would have to be made.

'What time do you call this?'

Daniel jumped and pulled his headphones off. Behind him, Jack Tyler's Mercedes engine was idling while its owner leaned out of the window, tapping on his watch.

'You should have been here five minutes ago.'

'Sorry, Mr Tyler.'

'So you should be. You look like something the cat dragged in. More partying last night, was it?'

'No,' lied Daniel, 'just a touch of insomnia.'

'Huh,' said Jack. He wound up his window and steered the car through a set of wrought-iron gates.

As the car turned a corner, Daniel stuck his middle finger up and cursed his employer. Would it have killed

Jack to offer him a lift? His leaden legs dragged themselves along the tree-lined driveway, which seemed longer than ever. Gravel crunched beneath Daniel's shoes, his teeth grinding in time with his steps.

Although used to it by now, the sight of Jack Tyler's house still caused Daniel to pause in admiration when it came into view. By far the grandest building for miles around, the Georgian mansion was unashamedly out of place among its humble surroundings, and yet Daniel loved it. His grandfather had shown him photos of a time the house was derelict, but looking at it now, magnificent against a bright blue sky, it was hard to imagine.

Despite his dislike of the man, Daniel had a grudging admiration for Jack Tyler. None of his wealth had been inherited. Jack had raised himself up in the world, from the tiny fisherman's cottage he'd been born in, to the grand mansion overlooking Saffron Bay. He'd made his money in fish, sticking to his roots, but rather than catching the fish, he'd set up a business selling fresh Cornish catches to upmarket London restaurants. Although Daniel's own plans for his garden landscaping business were far more modest, he knew he could learn a thing or two from a business mastermind like Jack.

Not that Jack Tyler had any time for the hired help. The only time he engaged with Daniel was to lecture him about his mistakes. Although mildly annoying, Jack's monologues were mostly water off a duck's back. Daniel may not yet have Jack's business acumen, but with gardens, he was the expert.

'You took your time,' said Jack, standing on his front steps holding a cup of coffee. The aroma reached Daniel, and he had to force himself not to grab the cup from Jack's hand.

'I'll be working on the ornamental garden today if that suits you,' said Daniel, ignoring Jack's jibe about timekeeping.

'Yes, but the lawn could do with a mow.'

'Really? I did it only two days ago.'

Jack sighed and shook his head.

'But if you'd like it mowed again, I'll see to it,' said Daniel, too tired to argue.

'Good. Well, you'd best be getting on then, hadn't you?'

'Yes, sir,' muttered Daniel, heading round the back of the house to the shed where he kept his tools.

'Good morning, Daniel,' said Jack's wife Mary, who was sitting out on the lawn reading a book.

'Morning, Mrs Tyler.'

'It looks like it will be a hot one,' said Mary, glancing up at the sky. 'Mrs Jones has made fresh lemonade, and there's plenty to spare if you'd like a glass.'

'That's very kind of you, Mrs Tyler,' said Daniel, 'but I'd best be getting on.'

'My husband's been cracking the whip again, has he? Oh well, I'll bring you a glass in a little while once he's left for the office.'

'Thank you.' Daniel grinned at Mary, who was the polar opposite of her husband. Daniel wondered what she saw in Jack, other than his money, although perhaps money was enough. What he really wanted to do was get stuck into his redesign of the ornamental garden, but to please his boss, he tackled the lawn first.

As Daniel climbed onto the ride-on mower, the two youngest Tyler girls spilled out of the house, chasing each other with water pistols. Despite Jack and Mary having three daughters, he'd yet to meet the eldest child. Perhaps she found her younger siblings too irritating to spend time with? If that was the case, Daniel could relate. 'Careful you don't get in the way of the mower!' called Daniel.

The girls giggled and squirted him with water from their pistols.

'You'd better watch out,' said Daniel with a frown. 'I have a hose I could turn on you any time I like.'

The youngest girl stuck out her tongue, grabbed her sister's hand, and sprinted off towards the pool. Daniel smiled, thinking he wouldn't mind a family of his own one day. Although he had never been short of friends, being an only child had, at times, been lonely. There'd been no water fights for him, no hide and seek, no one to gang up against his parents with. Daniel loved his parents, but wanted a life very different from theirs; a busy house filled with noise, the chaos of a large family, he the provider and protector.

As he rode across the lawn, Daniel daydreamed of his future life. There would be no need ever to leave Saffron Bay. It would be the perfect place to raise a family, and with tourism picking up in recent years, not to mention all the new houses being built, he'd never be short of work.

In later years, Daniel would look back on that day as a painful memory. How innocent he was, how naïve about the world. If he'd known how those carefree days of summer would play out, he'd have abandoned the Tyler's lawn, packed his bags, and left Saffron Bay at the earliest opportunity.

Chapter 22

Alice rubbed her eyes, wondering where she was. She looked down at the floral bedspread and remembered she was at Sylvie's house. Her third bed in as many days. May's arrangement to stay with a friend in Plymouth had proved a blessing, as it was one less body invading Sylvie's home. Not that she'd been anything but welcoming towards Alice. The earlier frostiness had vanished, and Alice had quickly learned that as long as she kept the conversation firmly in the present, Sylvie was great fun to be around. The old lady had a wicked sense of humour and seemed far younger than her years.

A knock on the door made Alice jump, and she pulled on her dressing gown before calling, 'Come in.'

'I didn't wake you, did I, dear?' asked Sylvie, a cup of tea in her hand.

'No, not at all. I was just about to get up.'

'You stay there for a little longer and enjoy the warmth,' said Sylvie. 'I've brought you a cup of tea. Here you are.' She placed the cup and saucer on the bedside table and smiled at Alice. 'Come down for breakfast whenever you're ready, but there really is no rush.'

'Thank you so much,' said Alice. 'This is very kind of you.'

'It's a treat to have guests,' said Sylvie. 'Since my daughter...' she cleared her throat and took a deep breath. 'Let's just say the past few years have been rather quiet around here. Once upon a time, this was a bustling family home. My husband, George, was a loud, boisterous man whose laugh boomed around the house. I still expect to hear it some days, but time moves on. I sometimes wonder if I need all this space at my age, so it makes me very happy to see it being used.'

'I'm so grateful to you for letting me stay. This bed is ridiculously comfortable. But it should be me bringing you tea, not the other way round.'

'It's nice to feel useful,' said Sylvie. 'Now I'll leave you in peace. See you later, dear.'

'Thanks,' said Alice, as Sylvie let herself out of the room.

Alice finished her tea, then climbed out of bed and walked over to an old oak dresser. This must be the room Luke used in the summer, as the top of the dresser was crammed with family photos. Alice picked up a photograph of a young boy with sandy-coloured curls being swung in the air between a man and a woman who Alice assumed were his parents. The woman had to be Sylvie's daughter, sharing the same impish features and slight frame. The man was the spitting image of Luke, other than his shorter cropped hair and glasses. Alice wondered what had happened to Luke's parents and if one day he'd trust her enough to tell her.

After using the bathroom and pulling on some clothes, Alice found Sylvie sitting at a breakfast bar in a modern kitchen.

'You have a beautiful home,' said Alice.

'All thanks to my grandson,' said Sylvie. 'He's helped me modernise it over the years and, just like the house, he keeps me young. Speak of the devil.'

The sound of the front door closing and boots being rubbed against the doormat reached them, and Luke strode into the kitchen.

'Morning, Gran,' said Luke, kissing Sylvie on the cheek. 'Oh, Alice, I forgot you were staying here last night.'

'Yes, thanks to your gran I had a very warm and cosy night.'

'I'm pleased I caught you, actually. I was thinking I could start work on the kitchen for you? I'm sure at some point you'll want to get a new one fitted, but if I patch up the current doors and cabinets, the one in there should be good for a while.'

'That would be amazing,' said Alice, 'but I really don't want to put you to any trouble.' She felt she'd stepped into another universe and couldn't understand why Sylvie and Luke were being so kind. It was easier to accept from Sylvie, who was clearly enjoying the company, but Luke's motives were harder to pin down.

'Like I said, I'm at a bit of a loose end this week, so I'm happy to help. I'll go and get started if that's alright with you?'

'Don't you want a cup of tea first?' asked Sylvie. 'I've just made a pot.'

'Tea sounds great, but I'll take a mug next door with me if that's OK?'

'He's a man on a mission,' said Sylvie, throwing Alice a smile as she poured Luke's tea.

'Thanks, Gran. See you both later.'

'I'll be over to help you in a bit,' said Alice, 'once I've had breakfast.'

'Great. See you soon.'

When Luke had gone, Alice sat at the kitchen table and took a piece of toast from the rack Sylvie had provided. 'It's so kind of Luke to help me as much as he has. I wish I could pay him for his trouble.'

Sylvie batted away Alice's suggestion with a flap of her hand. 'Don't you worry about that. Luke enjoys being busy. He's never been very good at relaxing.'

'Even so, I'm sure he has better things to do with his time.'

Sylvie smiled, her eyes twinkling. 'He's a wonderful chap, although, given I raised him, I'm likely to be biased.'

'You raised him?'

'Yes, from the age of twelve. My daughter...' Sylvie's voice caught in her throat, and she pulled a handkerchief from her pocket and dabbed her eyes.

'You don't have to say any more if it's upsetting.'

'No, it's fine,' said Sylvie, sitting down opposite Alice. 'My daughter and her husband were involved in a car accident when Luke was twelve. Neither survived, so he moved in here with me and George.'

'Oh no, that's awful. I'm so sorry.'

Sylvie gave Alice a watery smile. 'It happened so long ago, some days I don't even think about it. But it's true when they say you never get over the loss of a child. Luke's been my sunshine in the dark times. It was a privilege seeing him through those difficult days, and I couldn't be prouder of the man he's become.'

'I'm not surprised.'

'Now all he needs is to find a nice young lady to settle down with. I intend to keep going long enough to meet my great-grandchildren, but he'd better get a wriggle on as I'm not getting any younger.'

Alice bit into her toast, aware her cheeks were warming and unsure what to say. With horror, she recognised the feeling bubbling deep inside her. If Sylvie wasn't sitting beside her, she would have groaned. Now was not the time to develop a crush, particularly on a man who seemed too good to be true. Besides, with everything else she had going on, the last thing she needed was to be swooning over a man. She'd hoped to test out Sylvie's piano that morning, but how would that look with Luke next door working on the cottage?

'Thanks for the toast, Sylvie, but I'd better get over to the cottage and give Luke a hand.'

'Yes, you do that. Between the pair of you, you'll have the place shipshape in no time.'

As Alice left the table, she thought she caught Sylvie winking at her, but she must have been mistaken.

Chapter 23

Rather than heading straight next door, Alice walked past Seashell Cottage and made her way to the café.

'Morning,' called Margot as Alice walked through the door. 'I'm glad you came back. I was worried your last visit might have scared you off for good.'

'With coffee as good as you serve? No chance.' Alice walked towards the counter, her heart sinking as she spotted the woman from the divorce party perched on a stool.

'You'll be wanting the same as last time?' asked Margot.

'Yes please, but I'll take a couple of pastries too today.'

Margot turned to the attractive woman sipping a cappuccino. 'This is Alice. She's moved into Seashell Cottage, and Luke's helping her do it up. Alice, this is Patricia.'

'We've met,' said Patricia, giving Alice a polite smile before dabbing her lips with a napkin.

'It's nice to meet you properly,' said Alice, 'and sorry about gatecrashing your party the other night. I didn't realise it was invite-only.'

Margot laughed. 'Patricia's divorce party? Who told you that? From what I heard, it was a free-for-all.'

Patricia shifted on her stool, and Alice thought there might be a blush forming beneath the makeup she was wearing. 'You weren't actually there, though, were you, Margot?'

'For which I've apologised many times,' said Margot, rolling her eyes at Alice, who tried not to smile. 'My cat Bella was poorly, so I was stuck at home playing nurse-maid.'

'So you've roped Luke into helping you, have you?' asked Patricia, her long fingernails tapping against her coffee cup.

'I wouldn't put it quite like that,' said Alice. 'He offered to help.'

'I bet he did.'

'Pardon?'

'Nothing.'

Alice frowned, sensing an underlying hostility from Patricia, but with no idea what she'd done to cause it.

'How is the cottage shaping up?' asked Margot, placing lids on the two takeaway cups.

'Not too bad. At some point, it will probably need a full refurbishment, but for the time being, I've painted the walls and Luke is fixing the broken kitchen cabinets this morning.'

'Good for him,' said Margot. 'It's about time that kitchen got a new lease of life.'

'You've seen the kitchen?'

'What? No, of course not,' said Margot, turning to place two pastries in a paper bag.

'Right, it's just it sounded like...'

'Didn't you say you've got a younger sister?' asked Margot. Alice couldn't tell if she was changing the subject or genuinely interested.

'Yes, May. She's fifteen.'

'Not much older than Paige, then? Paige is Patricia's daughter,' explained Margot.

'Right. It's good to know there are other girls May's age in the village. Maybe they could hang out sometime?' In truth, this latest interaction had only confirmed Alice's first impression of Patricia, and the last thing she wanted was for May to become chummy with this Paige girl, but it might help May to have a local friend.

'Hmm, we'll see,' said Patricia, raising an eyebrow at Margot. 'Just because they're of a similar age doesn't automatically mean they'd get on.'

'No, of course not. Right, I'd better get back to the cottage. There's a ton of work to do.'

'See you again soon, hopefully,' said Margot.

'I won't be able to stay away from this coffee for long,' said Alice. 'Bye.'

It was a relief to be out in the fresh air again. Alice hoped one day she'd be able to visit Margot's café without any awkward interactions with locals. After all, she wasn't developing the best track record.

'Only me,' called Alice, letting herself into the cottage. When she walked into the kitchen, Luke was lying inside a cupboard, with only his long legs visible. 'I've bought coffee and snacks.'

'You've been to Margot's?'

'Yes, and I met your friend again.'

'What friend?'

'Patricia.'

'She's not much of a friend these days. More like an old acquaintance.'

'Right,' said Alice, thinking back to when she'd seen Luke and Patricia singing karaoke together. They'd looked like more than old acquaintances then. 'What can I do to help?'

Luke slid out of the cupboard, his T-shirt riding up to reveal a toned stomach. Alice looked away.

'If you come here and hold this door for me, I'll attach the new hinges.'

'Sure. Do you want coffee now or after we've done that?'

'After, please. I hate leaving a job half-finished.'

'An impressive work ethic.'

'Yeah, well, I've always worked hard. After all they did for me, I wanted to make my grandparents proud, and I'm still trying, all these years later.'

'There's no question your gran's proud of you,' said Alice, lifting the cupboard door and trying to hold it still while Luke prepared the hinges.

'I hope so. Can you lift that side up a little? That's perfect. OK, hold it still.'

'Sorry,' said Alice as the door slipped in her hand.

'Don't worry, you're fine, just lift it up a little. There, all done. Great teamwork.'

'Coffee time?'

'Coffee time. Why don't we take it out onto the veranda? The weather's calmed down a bit, and I've checked the boards and they're all sound.'

'I've not been out there yet.'

'Then it's about time.'

Alice followed Luke through the cottage and into the living room, where two glass-panelled doors led out onto a veranda with spectacular sea views.

'It looks different out here,' said Alice, frowning. 'Hang on, I'm sure the view wasn't this good before?' She turned to Luke, who shrugged and looked a little sheepish.

'I knew we were in for a few sunny days, so I came over last night and cut down some of the overgrown shrubs.'

'Thank you, that's so kind. I'll need to get some chairs out here,' said Alice.

'A rocking chair would be perfect. You know, this place is going to be amazing when it's finished.'

'Hmm, I don't think it'll ever be able to compete with those fancy houses you usually work on.'

'I actually think it will be better. People with money have a tendency to rip out the old in favour of the new. Having a smaller budget can be a blessing. It allows for a more thoughtful approach to renovation.'

'In what way?'

'In not getting rid of things that can be salvaged. Like the floorboards, for example, or the fireplace in the living room. You know, I'm amazed at what good condition the wood is in after all those years standing empty. You'll need to replace the roof as you've lost a fair few tiles over the years, but I can patch it for now and the beams are fine.'

'When I first stepped inside this place, I thought nothing could be rescued. I thought it would need knocking down.'

'To be honest, so did I. You've got lucky with this place.'

'We were due some luck.'

'Have you thought any more about going to uni?'

'No, it would be too disruptive for May.'

'Are you sure? You wouldn't need to go away to study. I'm sure you could study music at Plymouth University.'

Alice couldn't find the words to explain the truth. The whole point had been to get away from her responsibilities, to live her own life for once. Even in her own mind, it sounded selfish, so she settled for an easier explanation. 'I'd still need to take out all the same loans. No, now's not the right time. My priority is finding a job to tide us over. My savings won't last forever. In fact, calling the amount in my bank account savings is a bit of a joke. It seemed a decent amount when I thought it would supplement a student loan, but now it's got to be used to fix up this place, it seems to have shrunk.'

'I don't think there are any jobs going in the general store, and Margot won't be needing anyone, but you could try the pub. They won't have many shifts at this time of year, but they may offer you something.'

'Thanks,' said Alice. She held up her cup and tapped it against Luke's. He caught her eye and smiled, leaving Alice in a quandary. She mustn't get too complacent around this man, but couldn't ignore the relief and warmth that came with making a friend. Alice tore her eyes away and focused on the sea, stretching out beyond the cottage. Things were looking up in Saffron Bay.

Chapter 24

Alice squinted at the figure walking towards her. 'What on earth have you got there?'

May held up a large plastic cup filled with something pink, the cream on top sticking to the sides. She clamped her lips around the straw and made a loud sucking noise. 'I got it from the café,' she said, wiping cream from her lips.

Alice bit back thoughts of how much it must have cost. She could hardly criticise May having bought coffees for her and Luke the day before, but that felt more like payment for his work rather than a treat. With the huge to-do list of jobs in the cottage, treats should be the last thing on their minds.

'How was it being back at school?'

May rolled her eyes. 'Fine, just like it was yesterday, and just like the day before that.'

'You've had no more hassle from that Becky girl?'

'Nope.'

'And you've been keeping out of trouble?'

May shook her head and let out a loud sigh. 'You're talking like I get in trouble all the time. That was my first ever suspension, and I've only had three detentions in my life!'

Three more than me, thought Alice, but was wise enough not to say it out loud.

'What are you doing wandering around the village?' asked May. 'I thought you'd be busy working on the cottage with your hunky builder friend.'

'He's not hunky, and he's not my friend,' said Alice, realising she sounded more like a stroppy teenager than the actual stroppy teenager.

'Whatever,' said May with a snort.

'I needed a break. I'm only going for a quick walk. Want to come?'

May shrugged. 'Why not?'

They walked along the main street that ran through the center of the village, and when they passed the café, Margot waved through the window. 'Margot seems nice,' said Alice. 'Did you meet her when you got your milkshake?'

'Yep. And yes, she seemed nice, but also kind of sad.'

'Sad? Are you sure we're talking about the same woman?'

'The one who just waved?' asked May, and Alice nodded. 'Then yeah. She was putting on a good show, but there was something about her eyes.' May fiddled with her straw, swirling it around the cup. 'She was really smiley, but her smiles never reached her eyes.'

'I hadn't noticed,' said Alice, wondering if May had been uncharacteristically perceptive or simply got it wrong.

They walked on past a row of grand Victorian terraced houses, one of which, according to a sign outside, housed the local doctor's surgery, and found themselves outside a small primary school.

'Look at that,' said May, pointing past the building to where a playground ended and the beach began. 'What a cool place to go to school.'

'Isn't it? I'm surprised there are enough families here to justify a primary school, but I've heard their screams and giggles at break times and it sounds like there are a fair few kids.'

'We probably haven't seen them because anyone in their right mind will be getting cosy beside a fire,' said May with an exaggerated shiver.

'You're the one drinking a cold milkshake,' pointed out Alice. 'And at least the sun is shining. Look, there's a path beside the school heading down to the beach. Let's go that way and loop back around.'

'OK.' May slurped the last of her milkshake and threw the cup into a conveniently placed bin.

'Do you want me to carry your bag? It looks heavy.'

'Textbooks,' said May, handing the backpack to Alice.

'Old school.'

They crossed the road and headed down the path. 'Yeah, well, it's not like I can use the internet, is it?'

'I'm sorry,' said Alice as they reached the beach. 'I contacted the company today, and they said they'll be over on Monday to connect us.' She didn't add that the quote she'd been charged had almost seen her fall off her chair and slam down the phone.

Away from the shelter of buildings on the beach, the wind hit them with full force. As a result, the temperature was a good few degrees cooler, gusts stealing any words they tried to speak. They bent their heads against the wind and marched across the beach.

'This was a great idea,' yelled May as her scarf was ripped from her neck. Alice caught it and handed it back.

'Let's head up there,' shouted Alice, pointing to a path that led from the beach past the pub.

When they reached the outer walls of the pub, they were sheltered enough to stop and catch their breath. 'Oh, I do like to be beside the seaside,' sang May, in a tone that suggested she really didn't.

'It will be lovely in summer,' said Alice, praying it would be true.

'Can we just get home? I've got a ton of revision to do, in case you hadn't noticed.'

Alice adjusted the heavy bag on her shoulders. With the cold nipping at her fingers, and her hair a tangled mess thanks to the wind, when Alice pictured returning to the cottage, for the first time she viewed it as a place of shelter and sanctuary. May had asked if they could go home. Home. It was a big word the cottage had yet to earn, but as they pushed on up the steep path, Alice knew they were heading in the right direction, metaphorically as well as literally.

Chapter 25

Luke saw Patricia's name flash up on his phone and inwardly groaned. He was having fun helping Alice whip the cottage into shape, and resented the intrusion, even if it was at the end of the phone.

'Hello?' he said.

'Oh, are you alright, Luke? You sound tired.'

'I'm fine, Tricia. What do you need?' She never called unless she needed something, but even so, Luke heard the humph she tried to hide.

'I wondered if you have time to meet for a coffee? Things have been so tough lately, I could do with a friend.'

'I'm busy at the moment.'

Patricia sniffed. 'O...K... I... I'm sorry,' sniff, 'to bother you.' Sniff. Sniff.

Luke sighed. 'Where are you now?'

'I'm at the café. Luke, I'm sorry, I know I can be a real pain. I shouldn't have bothered you.'

'It's fine,' said Luke. 'Let me finish up what I'm doing here and I'll be with you in about ten minutes.'

'Thank you, Luke. I don't know what I'd do without you.'

'Everything OK?' asked Alice as Luke hung up the phone.

'Sorry, I'm going to have to go. A friend needs me.'

'A friend?' Alice paused her painting and looked at him with an eyebrow raised.

'Yes,' said Luke, 'a friend. I probably won't have time to come back here again before my lunch hour ends.'

'Of course,' said Alice. 'You've already done more than enough to help me.'

Luke appreciated her smile, even if it didn't reach her eyes. 'Great, well, I'll see you soon.'

'See you,' said Alice, turning her back on him and pushing the paint-covered roller up the wall.

When Luke arrived at the café, he was surprised to find Tricia at a table in the farthest corner of the room. Usually she enjoyed an audience, so perhaps whatever was upsetting her was genuine. Another surprise was seeing her makeup-free face. It made her seem prettier, and far younger than when fully made-up. Luke's heart lurched as he looked at her, and he was taken back in time to when he thought she was *the one*. How wrong he'd been.

'Thank you so much for coming,' said Patricia as he took a seat. 'Here, I ordered you a latte.'

'Thanks,' said Luke, not having the heart to tell her he only drank Americanos these days. 'So, what was it you needed to talk to me about?'

Patricia sighed and dabbed her eyes with the corner of a napkin. 'It's Paige. I don't know what I'm going to do about her.'

‘Paige?’ Luke sat up straighter in his seat. Patricia’s daughter had been a little girl when they’d been together. For a couple of years, he’d been the closest she had to a father figure. Luke had even spoken about adopting her at one point. But that was a long time ago, and the little girl he remembered was now a sullen teenager who ignored him if he passed her on the street.

‘She’s just so sad. Nothing I do seems to help. Ever since Duncan left, she’s been vile to me. Either she doesn’t speak at all, or shouts at me as though everything is my fault. I don’t know what to do, Luke.’

‘I’m sure she’ll be alright, she just needs time.’

‘But it’s been six months since me and D split and there’s been no improvement.’

Luke’s fingers gripped his cup tighter, and his jaw clenched. Something about the way Tricia referred to her ex as *D* set his teeth on edge. ‘Six months isn’t a long time in the grand scheme of things. Is Paige still in touch with Duncan?’

‘No, he abandoned us both, and now she doesn’t have any sort of male role model in her life.’ She dabbed her eyes again, even though Luke had yet to see any actual tears. ‘Listen, I know it’s a lot to ask, but could you talk to her?’

‘Me? Paige hasn’t wanted to talk to me for at least two years. I don’t see why she’d suddenly want to now.’

‘But she’s so sad.’ The whine in Patricia’s voice caused several other customers to turn and stare, and Luke patted her hand to calm her. Patricia grabbed his hand and clutched it tightly in her own. 'Please, Luke. I've no one else to turn to.'

Luke sighed and tried to ignore the voice in his head, telling him that taking on everyone else's problems wouldn't help block out his own. 'Fine. When would be a good time to talk to her?'

'It's best if it seems natural. If Paige gets wind that I've planned anything, she'll hate me even more. Could you come round and pretend you're scouting for work? I can let you know when I'll be out of the house and Paige will be home.'

'I suppose I could, so long as it fits with everything else I've got going on.'

'What, like that new girl in Seashell Cottage?' Patricia's tone was light, but her smile was too tight, too artificial for Luke to be fooled.

'As far as I'm aware, I'm allowed to make friends without asking your permission first.'

Patricia gave a tinkly laugh. 'What are you talking about, Luke? Of course you can have friends!'

Luke took a sip of his coffee to avoid saying something he'd regret. It hadn't been too bad living in the same village as Patricia when she was married to Duncan, but since the divorce she seemed hard to avoid, and he was wise enough to know he couldn't move forward while chasing feelings he'd left well in the past. 'I'd better get back to work.'

'Alright. Thanks for the chat. I'll message you when it's a good time to come round.'

Luke answered with a wave, not looking back as he walked through the café and ignoring the curious glances of other villagers, who would be wondering if Saffron Bay's erstwhile golden couple were about to regain that title.

Chapter 26

As her toes nestled into the sand, cold travelled up Alice's legs, causing her whole body to shiver. Considering she was effectively trapped in a life not of her choosing, Alice knew there were worse prisons. Her new home may not be up to much, but perched on the sea wall, looking out toward the horizon, there was no denying the beauty of Saffron Bay.

The tide was at its lowest for the day, and Alice stuffed her socks into her boots and left them behind on the wall. She inched her way across the sand on tiptoes, squealing as the cold bit her skin and sharp-edged pebbles pricked her like pins. The water itself was no better. People sometimes compared Cornwall to the Mediterranean, but Alice decided those people had never visited the Duchy in March.

The water was crystal clear as it swirled around her toes. The winds from earlier in the week had blown themselves out, and the water, like the air, was millpond still. Further out, two kayakers in bright orange life vests were manoeuvring between rock-pools. In the distance, the headland jutted out, woodland clinging to the cliff right up to the point where water met land.

Alice had been on a school trip to North Cornwall once, but whilst the dramatic coastline impressed her, she felt more comfortable on the gentle south coast. What it lacked in dramatic granite rock formations it made up for with aquamarine bays, abundant wildlife and forests that guarded sprawling villages like Saffron Bay.

A sudden bark and splash of water startled Alice from her thoughts. She cried out as a dog jumped up against her legs, spraying her with salty water.

'Sorry, sorry,' said a petite woman with a long grey plait as she waded into the water. 'Milo, you naughty boy. Come back here at once!'

Milo, who Alice assumed was the Golden Retriever currently trying to lick her face, cast a quick glance at his mistress, then set off at a gallop through the shallows of the bay.

'Oh God, it's going to take me bloody ages to get back now,' said the woman. 'Sorry, by the way. He gets so excited when I bring him to the beach. We rarely meet anyone at this time of year, which is why I had him off the lead. Are you OK?'

Alice smiled. 'Yes, no harm done. My jeans are soggy, but I'll live.'

'Your feet must be freezing,' said the woman, glancing from her own wellington boots to Alice's bare feet.

'I may have underestimated how cold the water would be,' said Alice, wiggling her toes to bring back some feeling to them.

'You're obviously not from around here?' laughed the woman. 'Sam, by the way.'

Alice shook the outstretched hand. 'Alice. And in answer to your question, yes and no.'

'Sounds intriguing. Tell you what, to make up for Milo's rudeness, how about I share some of my hot chocolate with you? It'll warm you up a bit.'

'Thank you, that's very kind, but I'll be fine.'

'I've got two cups on my flask, so we won't need to share germs. Where are your shoes?'

Alice pointed behind her to where her trainers and socks lay on the sea wall.

'Perfect. We can perch there and warm up with some hot choc while Milo does his thing.'

With the offer of hot chocolate not up for debate, Alice picked her way back up the beach, following in Sam's wake. When they reached the seawall, Sam pulled an old towel from her bag and offered it to Alice.

'I'm afraid it's Milo's towel, but it's better than nothing.'

'Thanks,' said Alice, drying off her numb toes before pulling on her socks and shoes.

'What did you mean, you know, when I asked if you were from here?'

'My family used to live here, but they left years ago. I moved here last weekend with my sister, May.'

'I see.' Sam took a flask from her bag and poured out two steaming cups of hot chocolate.

'Thanks,' said Alice. 'How about you? Do you live in the village?'

'Yes, I run the general store with my husband, Steve.'

'Oh, right, so have you lived here long?'

'All my life, except for five years in Australia. We thought we'd have a better quality of life over there, but as soon as we got there we realised what idiots we'd been to leave this place. We only stuck it out for five years to save face.' Sam laughed and took a sip from her cup. 'You said your family used to live here? What were their names? I might know them.'

'My dad was called Daniel Loveday.'

Sam choked on her hot chocolate. 'Sorry, it was hotter than I thought.' She turned her back on Alice and began shouting to Milo, who seemed quite content pottering among the rock pools. 'Milo, Milo, here, boy!'

'So, did you know my dad?' asked Alice.

'I recognise the name,' said Sam, not meeting Alice's eye. 'I think we might have gone to school together. How old is he?'

'I… um… I think he's around mid-forties, maybe early fifties. I'm not completely sure.'

'Right.'

Alice waited for Sam to say more, but nothing was forthcoming.

'I've heard something happened while he was living here. Something bad, but no one will tell me what.'

'Is that right?'

Alice got the impression Sam was being deliberately vague. 'Surely you'd know if something serious had happened, given you've lived here most of your life?'

'Hmm, if your dad's in his fifties, he'll be a few years older than me. We must've moved in different circles. You know how it is.'

No, thought Alice, *I don't know how it is, and I don't understand why no-one will tell me what the hell happened all those years ago.*

'Come on, Milo, home time,' shouted Sam. This time, Milo showed his obedient streak, trotting towards his mistress as though he always obeyed her commands. 'I'd best get back to the shop, but it was nice to meet you, Alice.'

'It was nice to meet you, too.'

'See you around,' called Sam, as she strode back along the beach with a compliant Milo at her heels.

Chapter 27

'You'll have heard about all the fuss with that young lady, I suppose?'

Luke, who was in a hurry and hoping Solly wouldn't engage him in conversation, stopped beside the bench. 'Sorry, Solly, I'm in a bit of a rush.'

'You youngsters are always in a hurry.'

'Yeah, sorry.'

'But you know about her, yes?'

'You're talking about Alice Loveday?'

'Hmm, yes, the Lovedays. I thought we'd all seen the back of them for good.'

'You've met Alice?'

'Yes, lovely girl. But lovely girl or not, she's caused one heck of a stir up on the hill.'

'With Jack?'

'Yes. I had to call an ambulance last night he'd got himself that worked up.'

Luke gave up on the idea of getting to his next job on time and sat down beside Solly on the bench. 'What happened to Alice's dad, Solly? Everyone seems so shocked about Alice moving here, but no one will tell her why. She's putting on a brave face, but it can't be easy for her or her sister.'

'Another Loveday?'

'No, May has a different father.' Luke instantly regretted letting slip a piece of personal information, but Solly wasn't known as a gossip, so Luke hoped he'd keep the information to himself.

'Of course, it's not the poor girl's fault. She can't help her parentage.'

'What did her dad do to Jack, Solly?'

'I'm sorry, Luke, but it's not my place to say.'

'That's all very well, but it seems half the village already knows, so I can't see what harm telling me would do.'

'Actually, only a handful of people know what really happened all those years ago. It's not my place to go telling tales, but you could try asking your grandmother, she knows.'

'I've tried already, and her lips are sealed as tightly as yours are.'

Solly sighed. 'All I'll say is that Jack hasn't always lived the way he does now. Once upon a time he was effectively the head of the village, living in a big house with his wife and children. It was Daniel Loveday's actions that put paid to all that. It would be best for that young woman to do up the cottage and sell it on. If I know one thing about my brother, it's that he can hold a grudge like no one I know.'

'Doing up that cottage will take time and money, and Alice and May have nowhere else to go. Even if they eventually sell, it will take months before the cottage is in a market-ready condition.'

'Then it's best she keeps her head down. Mind you, after what happened last night, I doubt my brother will be out and about for a while.'

'Sorry,' said Luke, 'I didn't ask how he is.'

'Ah, he's fine. I was worried it was a heart attack, but when they checked him over, his heart was fine. It's a miracle, really, given his lifestyle.'

'And what is his lifestyle? From what I can make out, he lives like a hermit, tucked away behind those big stone walls. At least he's got a big house, I suppose.'

'You've seen the house?'

'Only from the water when I've been kayaking. It looks like an impressive building.'

'Don't let Jack catch you on his private beach or they'll be hell to pay.'

'I won't. Does he let you visit him up there?'

'I'm the only one he lets through the gates. I don't think anyone else has stepped foot on his land for the past twenty-five years.'

'Twenty-five years? Wow, that's a long time. Hasn't he seen his children for that long?'

'Not all of them, no. Mary, his ex-wife, brought the two youngest girls down to visit one summer, but Jack wouldn't let them in. He sees Clara and Amelie every few years, and gets a train up to London to meet them. He doesn't want them coming back down here, not after what happened.'

Luke sighed, frustrated with Solly talking in riddles. It didn't seem as though keeping secrets was doing Jack much good.

'How's that cottage coming along?'

'What cottage?'

'The Loveday residence, of course.'

'Alice is putting in a sterling effort to get the place habitable, but it's a big job. She and her sister have been camping out at Gran's until their new boiler arrives. Her sister was staying with a friend in the city, but the arrival of the boiler was delayed, and there was only so long she could stay with her friend, so Gran has had a house full.'

Solly let out a quiet chuckle. 'I bet Sylvie couldn't resist the chance to step in and help them.'

'You know what Gran's like.'

'I do. Any chance to step up and help someone, and she'll be there like a shot. If only Sylvie would...' Solly stopped talking and began picking a weed from between two paving slabs with the end of his walking stick.

'What were you saying?'

'Oh, nothing, nothing. I lose my train of thought sometimes in my old age.'

Luke frowned and studied Solly. As far as he was concerned, Solly could keep all the secrets he liked, but if he was hiding something about Sylvie, that was a different matter. Why was Solly suddenly looking so shifty? Was Sylvie more involved with the Tyler's business than Luke realised?

'Don't you have work to be getting on with?' asked Solly.

Luke sighed and stood up. 'I'll see you around, and I hope your brother feels better soon.'

Solly nodded and continued fiddling with his walking stick. As soon as Luke was out of sight, he stood up and began making his way towards Sylvie's house.

Chapter 28

'I love it here,' said Sylvie, standing with her back to the café and staring out across the sea.

'You say that every time,' said Solly with a smile. He reached out and took Sylvie's hand in his.

'Our special place,' said Sylvie, leaning against Solly as he wrapped an arm around her.

'Don't you think we're getting a bit old for all this sneaking around?'

'You know I don't want to be the subject of village gossip.'

'Yes, but at our age, would folk really begrudge us some happiness?'

'Then there's Luke to think about. He adored his grandfather.'

'Everyone loved George, but Sylvie, he's been gone ten years. We've only been courting for five. It's not as though we've committed adultery.'

Sylvie smiled and nuzzled into Solly's neck. 'Can you imagine their faces if we walked into the pub hand in hand?'

'Promise me we'll do just that one day.'

'Maybe.'

'Maybe is better than no. Shall we walk? How are your knees today?'

'Not as sore as they have been. I don't need to watch the weather forecast on TV, I can feel the change of seasons in my joints. A walk sounds lovely. You can tell me all about what's going on with Jack.'

'Urgh, where do I start?' said Solly, taking Sylvie's hand and leading her towards the coast path. 'Are you warm enough?'

'I'm fine, there's no need to fuss.' Sylvie adjusted her scarf and then linked arms with Solly. The coast path was deserted, with locals at work or school and the tourists not yet having escaped for their Easter holidays. A hearty breeze tickled the gorse that framed the path, tall spindles of wild grasses dancing around their shins as they walked. 'So,' said Sylvie. 'Jack?'

'You know, Sylvie, I'm at a loss for how to help him.'

'It's that bad?'

'It's been bad for the past twenty-five years, but since that girl and her sister moved to the village, well, it's as though he's reliving the whole dreadful debacle.'

'Surely he knows Alice and May are innocent bystanders in all of this? Poor May isn't even a blood relation of the Lovedays, and Alice wasn't born when everything happened.'

'I don't think my brother is capable of rational thought. He seems to have taken it as a personal affront, as though they've moved here to spite him.'

'Perhaps I should talk to him.'

'Hah,' said Solly, 'you'll be lucky to get past his gates. You know he's not been down into the village since he found out about Alice? He's making me take food up to him. You should see the conditions he's living in...'

'I would help him if he'd let me in.'

'Don't take it personally. Jack's a proud man.'

'He's not the only one,' muttered Sylvie, watching as Solly struggled on the uneven terrain, even with his walking stick for assistance. 'There must be something we can do to help Jack.'

Solly shook his head. 'I'm afraid he's planning some sort of vendetta against those poor girls. He's up on that hill, working through all the ways to get them to leave the village.'

'He'll have a job doing that. They've nowhere else to go.'

'How much does Alice know about her father?'

'Very little.'

'You've not told her what happened?'

'You made me promise I wouldn't,' said Sylvie, offended that Solly needed to ask the question.

'I know, and I'm sorry. I've tried persuading him to move into the cottage with me, but he won't leave that damned house.'

Sylvie looked at Solly from the corner of her eye. She still saw him as the young man she'd once known and usually looked past the signs of age that had worn into his skin. But today, Solly was looking every one of his seventy-five years. 'Would he accept food from me, do you think?'

'He would if I took it up to the house for him.'

'I'll prepare some meals for him later. There's nothing like a bit of home-cooking to lift the spirits. And please, Solly, have another think about whether I can speak more freely to Alice. She'd be as horrified by her father's actions as the rest of us, and I'm sure she'd want to make amends. There's no hope of Jack reconciling with Daniel, but perhaps he could at least find it in him to forgive Alice. Although personally, I don't think holding the Loveday name is much of a crime.'

'I'll talk to Jack again.'

'You do that. Now, I can see you're dragging your left foot.'

'I'm not.'

'You are. Come on, let's sit down here for a moment to catch our breath, then we'll walk back to the car.'

'If I sit down, I might not get up again.'

Sylvie laughed, easing her way to the ground and pulling Solly gently down beside her.

'You know,' Solly said, once he'd found a comfortable position, 'I sometimes forget I'm old.'

'So do I until I look in the mirror.'

'We might not have many years left together.'

'Speak for yourself.' Sylvie took Solly's hand and lifted it to her lips, planting a light kiss on his weathered skin. 'We've got plenty of years left, don't you worry.'

'I hope you're right. I've loved you for half a century. I hope we can manage at least a decade together before one of us kicks the bucket.'

'One of us? Men are usually the first to go.'

'Is that so?' asked Solly. 'Then I'd best make the most of the time I have left.' He leaned over and kissed Sylvie deeply.

When Sylvie pulled away, her eyes were sparkling. 'Come on, you old romantic, we'd best be getting back. I need to get cooking for that stubborn-headed brother of yours.'

Chapter 29

Alice finished the final bar of Liszt's *Transcendental Études* and closed the lid of the piano. She was exhausted from the effort of moving her rusty fingers across the keys, but the music had soothed her soul. She jumped as someone coughed and turned to see Sylvie in the doorway watching her.

'Please don't stop on my account,' said Sylvie. 'Your playing is remarkable.'

'Thank you,' said Alice, feeling suddenly shy. 'But there's only so much Liszt I can play before my fingers seize up. How was your coffee?'

Sylvie pulled off her coat and hung it on the back of a chair. When she turned back to Alice, her cheeks were flushed. 'My coffee?'

'Didn't you say you were meeting a friend for coffee in the next village?'

'Oh, yes, that,' said Sylvie.

Alice watched as two delicate red circles appeared on Sylvie's cheeks. Had she caught the old woman out in a lie? But what need was there to lie about meeting an old friend? 'Did you have a nice time?'

'Lovely, thank you. It's wonderful to see you making use of the piano. The last person to play it was my daughter.' Sylvie smiled, and Alice breathed a sigh of relief when she added, 'It brings back happy memories.'

'I only popped in to pack up our things, but I couldn't resist a quick play. The new boiler's finally arrived, and there are men fitting it as we speak, so we'll be out of your hair by this evening.'

'There's really no need. You can stay longer if you'd like to.'

'We've loved being here with you, but honestly, I wouldn't want to impose any more than we already have. I would, however, like to cook you dinner as a thank you.'

'That sounds marvellous.'

'Would seven o'clock be alright? It might take me a while to get the hang of the new oven.'

'Of course. A meal cooked for me sounds just the ticket, whatever time it's served. Thank you, Alice.'

'No, thank you for hosting us for far longer than you'd originally anticipated.'

'It's been my pleasure. Is May at school?'

'Yes. She should be home in a couple of hours. I feel so dreadful that she has to get up so early, but buses are few and far between. At least once her exams are over, she'll have a nice long holiday to look forward to.'

'From the little I've seen of May, I've decided she's a sharp cookie. She'll do well in those exams, you mark my words.'

A flush of pride rushed through Alice. Afterall, when it came to raising May, she'd taken the number one spot for caring. Beneath the mad clothes and teenage angst, May was developing into a powerful young woman, and Alice prayed the move to Saffron Bay wouldn't knock her sister off course.

A heavy knock sounded on the door, and Alice opened it to be greeted with the good news that her new boiler was up and running. After thanking the workmen, she packed up the last of her things and handed Sylvie a box of chocolates and a bunch of flowers she'd bought as a thank you. 'Oh, and if you happen to speak to Luke, he's welcome to come to dinner as well,' said Alice. She ignored the smirk on Sylvie's face, picking up the two overnight bags and heading back to the cottage.

The first thing Alice noticed on walking through her front door was the warmth. It transformed the atmosphere of the cottage, and for the first time, Alice felt as though she were arriving home. She walked through to the kitchen and flicked the kettle on.

Luke had been round the previous day to fit the new oven and re-hang the last of the kitchen cupboards. They needed a fresh coat of paint, but they didn't look too bad. Luke had offered his van the following day for Alice to collect a second-hand fridge-freezer and washing machine she had found online. Alice shook her head. She was spending far too much time thinking about Luke.

The afternoon passed quickly, with Alice consumed by preparing a lasagne with a trifle for pudding. To cook was to go to a happy place. Maz had never been particularly interested in food, so Alice had learned to cook from a young age, despite being the envy of the other kids at school when she'd told them her mum cooked fish fingers every night.

By the time May arrived home, the lasagne was in the oven and Alice was laying the table in what would eventually become their living room.

'This looks posh,' said May, throwing her bag and coat down onto the floor.

'I've invited Sylvie and Luke over for dinner to say thank you for all their help. Have you noticed how warm it is in here?'

'Yeah, it makes a nice change.'

'How was school?'

'Good, but that journey's a real ball-ache.'

'Please watch your language when our guests are here.'

'Please stop acting so middle-aged.'

Alice sighed. 'Sorry. And I'm sorry you've got such a long journey.'

May shrugged. 'It's OK. I met some local girls at the bus stop. They seemed alright.'

'That's great.'

'Maybe.'

'Could you fetch the candles we found in the cupboard under the sink? They might help distract from how unfinished this room is.'

'We've barely moved in yet,' said May. 'Cut yourself some slack. Sylvie and Luke won't be expecting miracles.'

'I know. I just want it to look nice.'

'Yeah, well, this weekend we're tackling your bedroom.'

'There's nothing wrong with my bedroom.'

'There's nothing right with your bedroom. It's depressing, Alice, and after all you've done to get this place ready, you deserve to sleep somewhere nice.'

Alice's eyes filled with tears, and she wiped them with her sleeve. 'Who are you and what have you done to my grumpy sister?'

May smirked. 'I'm not grumpy all the time.'

'I know.'

'To be honest, it's a relief not to be living with Mum.'

'Really?'

'Yeah, I mean, she was a total cow leaving you to look after me, but it's kind of... I don't know... more relaxed somehow, now she's gone.'

Alice laughed. 'More relaxed? Really?'

'Don't get me wrong, I love Mum, but she can be a bit... erratic. Do you know what I mean?'

'I know exactly what you mean.'

'And as for those gross men she kept bringing round.' May shuddered. 'At least you've got better taste.'

'What? I don't know what you're talking about.'

'Yeah right, I've seen how soppy you get when a certain builder is around.'

'I do not get...' Alice was interrupted by a knock at the door. She glared at May as a warning to behave, then went to welcome her guests, determined not to exude an ounce of soppiness and to prove her sister wrong.

Chapter 30

'Well, that was utterly delicious,' said Sylvie, pushing away her plate. 'Was that a family recipe?'

'It was a Delia Smith recipe,' said Alice with a smile. 'I learned from the best.'

'Your mother didn't teach you to cook?'

'No, Mum was never very... motherly. Not in that way, anyway. Don't get me wrong, she could be great fun, but cooking and cleaning and the mundanities of life weren't her thing.'

'Let's raise a toast to Delia, then,' said Luke, raising his glass and rubbing his full stomach.

Candles flickered, spilling yellow puddles of light onto the table and adding to the cosiness of the room. Alice pinched herself as the romantic lighting messed with her head. It was impossible not to notice how good Luke looked in the cotton shirt he was wearing. He'd brushed his wavy hair back from his face, but a lock kept falling across his eyes, and Alice had to fight the urge not to reach up and brush it away. To her horror, Luke caught her staring, but rather than look away, he held her gaze. Her heart raced, and her mouth felt dry, but although it was almost painful to look, she couldn't drag her eyes away. The corner of Luke's lips curled in a half smile, and Alice's mirrored the expression. Then May sniggered, and the spell was broken.

'Do you like cooking, May?' asked Sylvie as Alice hid her embarrassment by filling her glass with water and taking a long drink.

'No, I prefer eating.'

'And drinking,' muttered Alice, who received a kick under the table from her sister.

'How have you found the commute from here to school?'

'It's a real b… pain, but I'm sure I'll get used to it.'

'May met some local girls at the bus stop earlier, didn't you?' said Alice, trying to sound normal while feeling anything but.

'Yeah, they seemed alright.'

'What were their names? We probably know them.'

May screwed up her face. 'One of them was called Paige. I can't remember the others.'

'Let's hope Paige doesn't turn out like her mother,' said Sylvie.

'What's wrong with her mum?' asked May.

'We used to be a couple,' said Luke. 'Gran was never a fan.' He smiled at Sylvie, then took a sip of his wine.

'Do you currently have a girlfriend?' asked May.

Alice felt her cheeks redden and tried to hide her blush by clearing the plates. She could kill her sister.

'No, I'm happily single at the moment.'

Alice managed a subtle glare at May.

'What are your plans for next year?' asked Sylvie. 'Will you stay on at school once you've finished your GCSEs?'

'Dunno.'

'She does know,' said Alice, stacking the empty plates on top of each other. 'She won't tell anyone, as she doesn't think it's cool, but May is top of her year in all the sciences and on track for top grades in maths. She must have gotten good genes from her dad, as they certainly didn't come from our mum.'

'You're clever too,' said May, 'just in a different way.'

'Like cooking,' said Sylvie.

'Exactly,' said May. 'And have you heard her play the piano yet?'

'As a matter of fact, I have,' said Sylvie with a wide smile.

'Sylvie's kindly letting me practice on her piano, so if anything, she's probably heard too much of my playing.'

'No one could get sick of your playing,' said May. 'I used to listen through the floorboards when you were practicing. Even on old Mr Butterworth's rubbish piano, you sounded amazing.'

'Do you know, it's so lovely to meet two sisters who get on as well as you two do?'

'We're on our best behaviour in front of our guests,' laughed Alice. 'Right, I'll grab pudding.'

Luke groaned. 'I didn't realise there'd be dessert. I shouldn't have had second helpings of my main course.'

'I'm sure you'll squeeze it in,' said Sylvie, 'especially given how hard you work.'

Just as Alice was serving the trifle, someone knocked on the door. 'Can you finish up here please, May?'

'Sure,' said May, taking over as Alice went to answer the door.

'Oh, Margot, this is a lovely surprise.'

'I won't keep you, but I wanted to welcome you properly to the village, so I baked you a cake.' Margot held out a metal cake tin. 'It's carrot cake, I hope that's alright.'

'It sounds delicious. Why don't you come in and have some with us? We've got Sylvie and Luke round for dinner and were about to start on pudding, so this is great timing.'

'I wouldn't want to intrude.'

'You won't be intruding. Come on in.'

Before Margot could argue, Alice turned and walked back into the cottage. 'Margot's joining us for dessert.'

'Oh, hello, Margot,' said Sylvie, shuffling her chair along to make space.

'I really don't want to intrude.'

'Don't be ridiculous,' said Luke. 'We'll always make room for the Queen of Saffron Bay.'

Margot gave Luke a playful tap on the arm before removing her fluffy coat to reveal a crimson cashmere sweater and skinny jeans. Alice noticed May's eyebrow raise in approval. Alice took Margot's coat from her and said, 'You sit in my place, Margot. I'll fetch another chair from the bedroom.'

'Thank you, love. You're very kind. It's lovely to see you again, May. I hope you enjoyed your milkshake?'

'It was delicious,' said May.

'I'm pleased to hear it. Do you know, it's wonderful to have another young person in the village. You'll have to come along to one of the groups we run at the community centre.'

'Margot doesn't just run the café,' said Sylvie. 'She also runs every group and society in the village. This woman's a machine, and she'll have you signed up to all sorts of weird and wonderful new hobbies if you're not careful.'

'You sound very busy,' said May.

'Ignore them, love. Sylvie likes to exaggerate.'

'Knit and natter, amateur dramatics, line dancing, men's club, cinema club, book club...' As Luke counted the clubs off one by one on his fingers, Margot laughed.

'Don't forget the rambling club,' added Alice. 'We first met when I was lost and Margot was scoping out a route for their next walk.'

'Do you ever sleep?' asked Sylvie.

'Staying busy keeps me out of trouble,' said Margot with a smile. Alice realised May had been right. Margot's smile didn't reach her eyes.

In the end, everyone opted for both trifle and cake. When everyone had bowls of sweet treats in front of them, Alice fetched a seat from May's bedroom and tried to find space for it. The table she'd found on Marketplace had seemed perfectly adequate for her and May, but with the addition of Margot, it now felt quite a squeeze.

'Here you go,' said May, shuffling her chair closer to Margot's, leaving a gap next to Luke.

'Thank you,' said Alice with a forced smile. As she squeezed her chair into the small space and sat down, she decided the situation couldn't get any more awkward. She was so close to Luke her arm kept brushing his, causing her cheeks to flame each time their skin met. It was a painful experience, and one she hoped wasn't obvious. When she risked looking up, May caught her eye and smirked.

The rest of the meal passed in a blur of friendly chatter. Margot was good fun and had a bank of funny stories to tell from her many clubs, keeping them all well entertained.

'Coffee?' said Alice, standing to clear the empty bowls. Away from Luke, she could finally breathe freely.

'Yes, please,' said Sylvie.

'Not for me,' said Margot. 'I'd best be getting back. Is it alright if I pop to the bathroom before I leave?'

'Of course.'

'Thanks, Alice.'

Alice opened her mouth to tell Margot where to find it, but Margot had already left the room and opened the correct door. Was it a lucky guess, or had Margot been in the cottage before? Alice remembered the comment about the kitchen cupboards. She glanced at Luke, but he seemed oblivious to anything out of the ordinary and was deep in conversation with May about the local water-sports on offer.

Alice was filling the kettle in the kitchen when Margot appeared to say goodbye. 'You found the bathroom OK?'

Did Alice imagine the flicker of guilt that crossed Margot's face? 'Yes, no problem. These bungalows are so similar in layout. My grandparents had one just like it. In fact, this cottage feels like a home from home.'

Ah, so there was an innocent explanation. Alice breathed a sigh of relief. She had enough secrets to unravel without adding more. 'Thank you so much for the cake. It was very thoughtful of you.'

'You're most welcome.' Margot leaned forward and kissed Alice on the cheek, then said her goodbyes and let herself out of the cottage.

'It was a nice surprise seeing Margot again,' said Alice when they were settled on her new three-piece suite in the living room, nursing their cups of coffee.

'The woman's a whirlwind,' said Sylvie. 'I've never known someone to do so much for other people.'

'Does she have a family?' asked May. 'She didn't talk about herself at all.'

'Well spotted,' said Sylvie. 'There's never been a partner on the scene that I'm aware of, but she had a son.'

'What happened to him?'

'May, don't be so nosy,' said Alice.

'What? Sylvie said *had*, which suggests she doesn't have a son anymore.'

'Very perceptive of you, young lady,' said Sylvie. 'Margot's son was called Marty, and he was a lovely young man. Sadly, whilst at university, he was involved in a fatal accident. I think Margot's busyness is her way of coping with the grief. It's a hard thing to cope with alone. At least when my daughter and son-in-law died, I had George and Luke. As far as I'm aware, Margot has always been alone, although if she has a secret boyfriend I'd be delighted for her.'

'Do you think she does?' asked May.

'No, but everyone's allowed some secrets, aren't they?'

Luke laughed. 'As if you have any secrets, Gran.'

Alice noticed a pink tinge form on Sylvie's cheeks and wondered what she was keeping from her grandson. It seemed remarkable anyone could have any secrets in a place like Saffron Bay, but it seemed everywhere she turned, someone was keeping something close to their chest. Alice took a sip of her coffee. It didn't matter what secrets Sylvie, Margot, or anyone else were keeping. All she cared about was finding out why Daniel Loveday was such a pariah in the village, and she'd start investigating that mystery tomorrow.

Chapter 31

'Hello, what can I get you?'

Alice smiled at the glamorous woman behind the bar and tried to ignore her nerves. 'Hi, I've just moved to the area and wondered if you have any work going?'

The woman frowned and pushed her pink-rimmed glasses down her nose. 'Alice, right? Just moved into Seashell Cottage?'

'Good news travels fast,' said Alice, wondering how much more of her life had been subject to village gossip.

The woman laughed. 'Rita, pleased to meet you. Don't worry, people will get used to you soon enough. It's just that so little happens around here at this time of year, and as for someone actually moving here. Well, let's just say there's not much hope of our local young people sticking around. It's caused great excitement getting some more young blood around the place.'

'I see. So...'

'Ah, yes, work. Hmm, we're pretty dead at this time of year, but come the season, we'll need all hands on deck. It goes absolutely mental around here once the tourists descend. How about I throw you a couple of shifts a week to get you trained up, then come the school holidays we can up your hours to closer to full time?'

'That sounds brilliant.'

'Do you have any bar or kitchen experience?'

'Yes, both.'

'Brilliant, then how about we employ you as a general dogsbody? You can do a bit of bar work, help in the kitchen when needed, maybe even a bit of chambermaiding once the season gets going?'

'That sounds great, thank you.'

'Let's start you on a Friday, as it's quieter. Are you free this Friday?'

'Yes, I am.'

'Perfect. Provided things go well this week, we could roster you on for Fridays and Saturdays, then take things from there?'

'That's amazing, thank you so much,' said Alice.

'Fancy a drink to celebrate?'

Alice had a million and one things to do back at the cottage, but felt after receiving the job offer it would be churlish to refuse. 'Thanks, that would be lovely, but just a Coke, please. I'm driving to meet my sister later.'

'Oh yeah, she's moved here too, hasn't she?'

'Yes, she's visiting friends in Plymouth today, but I said I'd pick her up so she doesn't have to sit on a bus for hours.'

'Good for you. Ice? Lemon?'

Alice nodded to both.

'How old is your sister?'

'Fifteen.'

'Urgh, what a horrible age. I remember it too well. There are a few other kids around that age in the village. Is your sister going to the local school?'

'No, she's got her GCSEs this year, so it didn't seem wise to move her.'

'No, I get that. I'm sure the local kids will welcome her into their gang anyway. My son's only fourteen, and would hang around with the older kids all the time if they'd let him.'

Alice smiled. 'Fourteen, another tough age.'

'Tell me about it, although I reckon boys are way easier than girls. I've managed to hold back the grey hairs despite turning forty-three last month, so my Ted can't be that bad.'

'Do you live at the pub?'

'Yeah, I bought this place with my husband, then a couple of years back he ran off with one of our regulars, so now it's just me and Ted here.'

'Goodness, that must have been awful.'

'It was. I'm used to hearing all sorts of village gossip in here, but it was a shock being the subject of it. Took months for the scandal to blow over.'

'I bet. Have you ever heard anything about my dad?'

'Your dad?' Rita turned her back on Alice and began fiddling with some glasses on a shelf.

'Yes, his name was Daniel Loveday.'

'Was?' asked Rita, spinning round sharply. 'You mean Dan's dead?'

'You knew my dad?'

Rita flushed, then sighed. 'I did back in the day.'

'So you know why he left?'

'I've heard rumours, but they're only that. I was here the summer everything went wrong for your dad. I used to come every summer with my family and stay in a hotel on the cliff. The hotel's not there anymore, turned into flats years back. Anyway, I should have been here until the end of August, but my sister came down with chicken pox, so we ended up going home a week early. The next summer we came, Dan wasn't around. In fact, the entire group seemed to have broken up.'

'They didn't tell you what had happened?'

'No, everyone was tight-lipped. Even when they got drunk.'

'What rumours have you heard?'

Rita sighed again and began polishing a glass.

'Please,' said Alice, 'no-one will tell me anything.'

'Is he dead, your dad?'

'I don't know.'

'How can you not know?'

'I don't remember ever meeting him. According to my mum, he came to visit me in hospital when I was born, then he ran off, never to be seen again.'

'That's awful.'

'Yes, just what I think,' said Alice with a wry smile. 'I've managed without him all these years, but it would have been nice to know something about him.'

'Your mum never said anything?'

'She told me she didn't know him very well. Apparently, he was a holiday fling.'

'What's your mum's name?'

'Maz Green.'

'Maz... Maz... Oh, wait, long dark curly hair, Maz? Beautiful in an exotic way, like a fortune teller or something?'

'You know my mum?'

'I knew of her. She was here that summer. That must have been when she met your dad.'

Alice frowned, aware they'd somehow skipped talk of rumours, and yet this new tangent was almost as interesting. Maz in Saffron Bay? Why wouldn't her mum have told her something like that? When she'd handed Alice the letter about Seashell Cottage, Maz had acted like she'd never heard of the place.

'You didn't know your parents met in Saffron Bay?'

'No, I didn't. Like I said, Mum never told me much. Listen, I don't care if the rumours you've heard are unfounded. I'd just be so grateful to hear anything, you know.'

Rita leaned against the bar. 'OK, but please don't set too much store by this. Like I said, everyone was tight-lipped about what went on that summer.'

'OK.'

'It had something to do with Jack Tyler up on the hill. He was sort of like the lord of the manor. Lived in a massive house overlooking the bay. His wife was lovely, Mary, I think she was called. I know he had three daughters, but we never met them. They went to a fancy private school miles away and spent most of their holidays with their aunt somewhere up country, or maybe it was Ireland, I can't remember. I think I saw the youngest two on the beach once, but Jack Tyler didn't like his precious daughters mixing with the likes of us. Anyway, Jack was a real big-shot, self-made millionaire. He used to drive around in a Mercedes like he owned the place. Mind you, he also did a heck of a lot for the local community. People often used to badmouth him, but a lot of that probably came from jealousy. You know, that feeling of a local lad doing good, then leaving everyone else behind? When I left the summer my sister got ill, everything was as it had always been, but when I came back the next year, everything had changed.'

'In what way?'

'It's hard to say. The Tyler house had amazing views down to a private beach and across to the village, but with trees all around it, you can only catch glimpses from down here. Jack was also very hot on security, with big stone walls and iron gates. You know the kind of thing. Something happened in that house, and I think it had something to do with your dad. Whatever it was, by the time I came back here, there was no Mrs Tyler or her children.'

'They died?'

'Oh, God, no. Rumour had it they'd emigrated to Ireland, which is where she was originally from.'

'Without Jack?'

'Yep. I only saw him once that summer, but he was like a different man. The Mercedes had gone, so had the waxed jacket and flatcap. He looked like he'd picked his clothes up at a jumble sale and was shuffling around the village like a broken man.'

'He never told anyone what happened?'

'No. There were all kinds of wild theories, especially after your dad did a flit and his parents moved away, but that's all they were–theories. If you ask me, only a handful of people know what really went on, and they've chosen to keep quiet about it.'

'What makes you say that?'

'There was a really tight-knit group that summer, four or five teenagers, getting up to mischief. Kids like me could join in their parties, but there was definitely an inner sanctum thing going on that we weren't part of. It felt different from previous years. There was this weird, excitable tension, like they were up to something secret. I'm sorry, but that really is all I know.'

'Thanks. You've told me a lot more than anyone else in this village.'

'I'm pleased I could help. Anyway, I'll see you on Friday. Come in after lunch, around two-ish.'

'Great, see you then.' Alice left the pub, her mind whirring and with a new determination that she needed to get to the bottom of whatever had gone on.

Chapter 32

Luke saw Alice leaving the pub and ducked behind the old boathouse. The dinner at her cottage had been torture. She'd clearly been embarrassed when he and his gran turned up in their smart clothes, but she shouldn't have been. In her old jeans and jumper with her hair pulled back in a ponytail, she still lit up the room. The fact that she was so unaware of her own beauty only made her more attractive.

He had spent the entire evening sitting opposite her, trying not to stare. Then their eyes met, and all he'd wanted to do was kiss her. But he couldn't. How could he get involved with someone going through so much? Commitment was the last thing he could give, especially now he'd received the letter. No, the best thing to do was stay out of Alice Loveday's way, and wait for this stupid crush to fizzle out as it inevitably would.

'What are you doing hiding behind there?'

Luke jumped and spun around to see Nick frowning at him.

'I thought I heard kids messing around behind here, so came round to check it out. It must have just been birds.'

'Really? You look like you're hiding from someone.'

Luke laughed, joined Nick on the seawall, and gave him a playful punch. 'Don't be ridiculous. Come on, I thought you were thirsty?'

'Alright, lads?' said Rita when they walked into The Ship. She was behind the bar, polishing the wooden ship's wheel salvaged from a wreck centuries earlier. 'The usual?'

'Just a Coke for me, please,' said Luke. 'I'm working this afternoon.'

'I'll have a pint,' said Nick.

'Of course you will,' said Rita, rolling her eyes.

'Oi, don't be rude to your customers. It's hard to find work around here out of season.'

'You seem to find it hard to get a job at any time of year,' said Rita, clearly enjoying the chance for a bit of banter. 'You just missed the new girl.'

'New girl?' asked Nick, taking a sip of his pint and handing over his credit card.

'Alice, the girl who's moved in to Seashell Cottage.'

'She was here, was she?' asked Nick, smirking at Luke, who refused to catch his eye.

'She's going to be working for me, just a couple of shifts a week to start with.'

'I've yet to meet this mystery woman,' said Nick. 'Luke's been spending all his spare time with her, but won't tell me anything about her.'

'That's a massive exaggeration,' said Luke. 'I've been doing a bit of building work at the cottage, that's all. Come on, let's find a table or my lunch break will be over and I won't have sat down.'

They had their pick of tables, with a handful of local men propping up the bar, but a group of walkers were the only other people wanting a table. Over the years she'd been there, Rita had done a great job sprucing up what was once a dive of a pub that locals avoided and which catered only to tourists. These days it was a hub of the community, and its grey and navy colour scheme reflected its beachside setting, whilst giving a cosy atmosphere when the weather was too bad to enjoy the nature outside.

'What's all this about, then?' asked Nick. 'You never usually want to meet up during the day. Are you going to tell me about the mysterious Alice Loveday? Is that it?'

'No,' said Luke, 'this has nothing to do with Alice.' He pulled the letter from his back pocket and pushed it across the table to Nick.

'What is this?'

'Read it.'

Nick pulled the letter from its envelope and scanned through. When he looked up, his eyes were wide and his face broke into a smile. 'Mate, this is fantastic!'

'Is it?'

'Isn't it? I thought you'd be jumping for joy. This is just the opportunity you've been waiting for, and it shows how much your customers value your work.'

'Yeah, I get that. It's a massive compliment.'

'You've said yes, I take it?'

'No, I haven't replied yet.'

'Why not?'

'What about Gran?'

'Sylvie would be all for it, you know she would.'

'Which is why I haven't mentioned it to her yet. She needs me.'

'Does she? It's always seemed to me like the other way round.' Nick took a sip of his pint, a line of foam resting on the moustache he'd recently been sporting to go with the dreadful mullet he thought looked cool.

'That's not true. She's getting frailer by the day. What about the falls she had? I was the one who had to take her to A&E.'

'Sylvie has plenty of people in the village who'd look out for her, and I don't think she's as frail as you think. She looked very sprightly when I saw her up on the cliff with Solly the other day.' Nick raised an eyebrow, and Luke frowned.

'What were she and Solly doing up on the cliff?'

'Walking, drinking coffee... enjoying each other's company.' This time, Nick's raised eyebrow wiggled.

'Enjoying each other's company?' Luke frowned, then his eyes widened and his mouth fell open. 'You don't mean...'

'Yep,' said Nick, laughing. 'They looked like proper love-birds smooching away up on that cliff.'

'Gran and Solly? I mean, I know they've been friends forever, but why wouldn't she tell me if they're a couple? I don't get it.'

'She's probably worried about how you'd react.'

‘I mean, it’s a bit gross to think of them kissing, but apart from that, I’m happy for her. Solly’s a great guy, and it’s been years since Granddad died.’

Nick picked up the letter and held it in the air. ‘I’d say you and Sylvie have a lot you need to talk about.’

Luke snatched the letter from Nick and shoved it back in his pocket. ‘I just need to find the right time.’

‘Mate, if you wait too long for the right time to present itself, you’ll miss the opportunity. See Sylvie after work and talk all this through with her.’

Luke downed the last of his Coke and stood up. ‘I’ll think about it. Cheers for meeting me. I’ve got a lot to think about, especially thanks to your revelation about Gran’s love life.’

‘Anytime, mate,’ said Nick. ‘Anytime.’

Chapter 33

May replaced her brush in a pot of paint and stepped back to admire her hard work.

'It looks so much better, thank you,' said Alice, walking into the room with two cups of tea. 'I've seen a bed on Marketplace, and Luke says I can borrow his van to pick it up tomorrow.'

'Your knight in shining armour,' said May, taking a cup and sitting down on the floor.

'Don't start on that again. We're just friends.'

'Are you going to get carpet in here?'

'Eventually, but for now, I'll just mop the floor and throw a rug down.'

'These floorboards might be alright if you sand them down.' May stood up and kicked her toe against a floor-board. 'That's weird,' she said, kicking it again.

'It's probably rotten.'

'No, I don't think so. I think it's just loose. Here, take this.' May handed Alice her cup and got down on her hands and knees. 'Ah, my nails are too long and I can't get a good grip. Do you have a screwdriver?'

'Yes,' said Alice, pulling one out of her back pocket. 'I've been using it to put together the flat-pack coffee table.'

'Right, let's see what we've got here.' May levered the plank of wood, which popped up, revealing a small cubby-hole beneath the floor.

'Is there anything in there?' asked Alice.

'Yes, I'm guessing this was your dad's room.' May rummaged through the hole and produced a dust-covered pouch of tobacco. 'Naughty Daniel,' she said with a grin. 'I wonder if it's still OK to smoke?'

'Don't even think about it,' said Alice with a glare.

'There's a bunch of photos in here, but no money, unfortunately.' May replaced the floorboard and spread the photos out on the bed. 'Wow, people were rubbish at taking photos in the olden days.'

'For starters, these weren't taken in the olden days, but they would have been taken before there were camera phones, or digital cameras, for that matter.'

'See,' said May.

The two sisters leaned over the blurry shots of a group of teenagers hanging out at a beach.

'These were taken in Saffron Bay,' said Alice. 'Look, this one's not too bad. That's my dad there... I think. And I'm sure this was the woman I met on the beach the other day. Sam, her name was. She claimed not to have known my dad well, but look at this, they've got their arms around each other.'

'Oh my God. Is that Mum?' May handed a photo to Alice.

'Yes, I think it is.'

'Mum was here in Saffron Bay?'

'Yes, Rita from the pub told me when I went there looking for work. I think she must have met my dad here.'

'I remember her saying you were the result of a holiday fling, but I assumed she meant she'd gone to Spain or somewhere like that.'

'You didn't assume, May, she told us it happened in Spain. She always said that's why she wouldn't be able to find my dad even if she wanted to.'

'What a cow! He was living less than an hour from you the whole time!'

'No, he must have left the village soon after this photo was taken. I know Mum lied, but it wasn't much of a lie. She probably couldn't find him.'

'You always think the best of people,' said May. 'You should learn to be more cynical.'

'And you should learn to be less cynical. I know Mum had her faults, but it can't have been easy being a single parent to two girls born ten years apart.'

'Maybe not, but she chose which men to sleep with. It wasn't our fault we were born. You know what? You were probably conceived in this very room.'

Alice pretended to retch. 'Can we please change the subject?' She turned back to the photographs. 'It's this photo that interests me the most.' She studied a picture taken in what looked like the golden light of a sunset. There were four friends with their arms around each other. Alice now knew the identity of three out of the four, but had no idea who the second man was.

'Why don't you show the photo to Luke?' suggested May.

Alice rolled her eyes.

'I'm serious. He's lived around here for years, so if those guys are local, he'll know them.'

'True, but the same could be said for Sylvie.'

'She's not as good-looking though, is she?'

Alice scowled at May. 'Don't you have painting to be getting on with?'

'Oooh, looks like I hit a nerve,' said May with a grin.

Alice ignored her sister and carried the photos through to the kitchen. She propped the handful that weren't blurry up on the windowsill and put the kettle on. When she opened the fridge, she found it empty, other than a pack of cheese and half a bar of chocolate.

'Did you use the last of the milk?' Alice called to May.

'Yeah, sorry, I meant to replace it but forgot. Do you want me to go down to the shop?'

Alice walked through to May, carrying one of the photos. 'Why don't we both go and take this photo with us? When I met Sam, she told me she ran the general store. There's no way she can deny knowing my dad or this mystery man now that we have photographic evidence.'

'Ooh, we'll be like a pair of detectives.'

'I wouldn't go that far, but does that mean you'll come with me?'

''Course.'

'Great, grab your coat.'

Chapter 34

There was no one behind the counter when Alice and May walked into the general store.

'Wow,' said May, picking up a bucket and spade set in one hand and a box of leg wax in the other. 'This place sells everything.'

'I guess the clue's in the name,' said Alice, browsing the shelves. 'I know we're here for answers, but as we've no food in the house, we may as well kill two birds with one stone. Grab a basket, will you?'

As May was collecting a basket, a voice from behind a door called, 'Be with you in a tick. We've just had a delivery.'

'No problem,' Alice called back.

The two sisters ambled along the shelves, filling their basket with a mixture of dried goods and fresh vegetables.

'Can we get some treats?' asked May.

'You sound like you're ten.'

'You're never too old for treats.'

'Fair enough. But not too many. We're on a tight budget, remember?'

'I've still got some money from Dad left over, so this is my treat.'

'No way. I'm not taking your money.'

'Why not? I'm happy enough to take yours. Anyway, it isn't my money, it's my useless dad's. I don't see him stepping up to provide a home for me now Mum's gone.'

'Does he even know Mum's done a runner?'

'Yeah, I called him.'

'What did he say?'

'Well, he still wouldn't tell me where he lives, if that's what you're wondering. And he didn't offer for me to move in. But he popped a hundred pounds into my account to ease his guilt.'

'Treats are on Phil then,' said Alice with a smile. 'Would you have wanted to live with him if he'd offered?'

May linked her arm with Alice's. 'Of course not. I want to live with you.'

Alice smiled and swallowed the lump in her throat. She'd had to sacrifice a lot for May, but it was a sacrifice she'd make a hundred times over.

'Sorry,' said a bald man in a checked shirt, rushing through the shop. 'We had a delivery of frozen goods, so I couldn't leave it. Do you need any help, or are you happy browsing?'

'We're happy browsing,' said May, dragging Alice behind a shelf. 'That's him,' she whispered. 'The man in the photo.'

'Are you sure?' Alice pulled the photo from her pocket. 'I don't think it's the same man.'

'It is, I swear. You need to look past the hair and imagine this guy bald with glasses.'

Alice studied the photo, then poked her head above the shelf. 'I think you're right,' she whispered.

'What do we do?'

'Pay for our shopping and hand over the photo along with our money?'

'Good plan, come on.'

'Sorry about that,' said the man as Alice loaded her shopping onto the counter.

'Honestly, it's no problem.'

'You two on holiday?'

'No, we've just moved here.'

'Right.' The change in the man was instantaneous. The friendliness was gone, and in its place was a tension that showed in the tightness of his jaw and the speed with which he scanned the barcodes on their groceries.

'Actually, we were hoping to ask you some questions,' said May.

'I see, want to know about the local area, do you? I'm afraid you've not arrived at the best time of year. There's a lot more going on in the summer.'

'No, we were hoping you could tell us about this man,' said May, taking the photograph from Alice and sliding it across the counter. 'That is you, isn't it?'

The man coughed and wiped his sleeve across his damp brow. 'Um, yeah, I guess so. I've changed a bit.'

'Not that much,' lied May.

Alice smirked at her sister's attempts at flattery. 'I met this lady at the beach the other day. She told me she runs this place.'

'Yeah, that's my wife, Sam.'

'So you're Steve?'

'That's right.'

'You know, Steve, the weird thing is when I spoke to Sam, she told me she didn't know my dad. But you all look very cosy in this picture.'

'The camera can lie.'

'Not as well as people,' said May, and Alice wanted to give her a high five.

'Please, all I want is to know more about my dad. I'm not looking to get anyone into any trouble.'

The bell above the shop door rang, and a young woman walked in with a buggy and a toddler in tow. 'Hi, Steve,' she called.

'Hello Dawn, hello Lily.' When the woman moved further into the shop, Steve turned back to Alice and May. 'Listen, now isn't a good time to talk about this. I can see how badly you want answers, but to be honest, I'm not sure how many we can give.'

'Still, you knew my dad, which is more than I can say.' Alice struggled to contain the wobble in her voice.

'Alright. Why don't we meet later at the pub? This place closes at seven, so would eight be OK?'

'Fine by us,' said Alice. 'Will your wife come too?'

'I'm sure she will if I speak to her.'

'OK, we'll leave you in peace for now. See you at eight.'

'See you then.'

Alice and May let themselves out of the shop and began walking back towards the cottage.

'I think we really freaked the poor guy out,' said May.

'Yeah, he seemed really rattled. I almost felt sorry for him. You were amazing, by the way. Where did you learn to be so direct?'

May shrugged. 'You learn how to take care of yourself at school, I guess. I've had a few lads try to take things too far, and you have to learn how to put them in their place. You must have had the same when you were at school?'

Alice shook her head and kept her eyes on the pavement. She'd never been bothered by any lads at school. In fact, she'd never been bothered by anyone. Alice may have been wearing an invisibility cloak throughout her teenage years for all she was noticed.

'Tonight will be interesting,' said May. 'Are you sure you want me there, it's not like Daniel Loveday is anything to do with me?'

'Of course I want you there. Safety in numbers and all that.'

'Will you buy me a pint?'

'Don't push your luck.'

Chapter 35

'Couldn't keep away, hey?' asked Rita as Alice and May walked towards the bar.

'Something like that,' said Alice, pleased to see how quiet the pub was. The last thing she wanted was locals eaves-dropping on their conversation.

'Is this your sister?'

'Yes, Rita, May, May, Rita.'

'Lovely to meet you, May. What can I get you lovely ladies to drink?'

'I'll have a glass of merlot, please, and a Coke for May.'

'With a splash of Jack Daniels,' said May.

'Unfortunately for you, your sister's already told me your age,' said Rita with a grin. 'But I can offer you ice and lemon.'

'Both, please.'

'Coming right up.'

The pub door opened, and a gust of cold air blew into the warm room.

'More customers!' said Rita. 'And on a Wednesday night, too. This is a turn-up for the books.'

'Hi, Rita,' said Steve, nodding to Alice and May as he reached the bar. Behind him, Sam kept her eyes lowered, fiddling with the buttons on her coat as an excuse not to look up.

'I'll grab us a table,' said Alice as Rita handed over the drinks.

'Oh, you're all here together? Isn't that lovely?' said Rita. 'I'm pleased you're settling in so well, Alice. Did you know Alice is my newest employee?' Rita asked Steve as she pulled his pint.

'No, I didn't.'

'And how are you, Sam?' asked Rita.

'Fine, thanks. Oh, I'm not actually drinking tonight,' said Sam as Rita grabbed a bottle of cider from the fridge. 'Can I just have a lemonade, please?'

'Sure. Everything alright?'

'Yes, fine, I've got a nasty headache, that's all.'

From her table in the corner of the room, Alice noticed Rita's furtive glances between her customers. She must have sensed the awkwardness and figured out this was no ordinary drink with friends.

Once Steve and Sam had taken their seats, May reached out a hand across the table. 'Hi, I'm May.'

'Sam,' said Sam, looking up for the first time as she took May's hand. 'Pleased to meet you.'

'Thanks for coming,' said Alice. 'And before we get going, I just wanted to say that we're not looking to cause any trouble. I know you probably felt strong-armed into meeting us, but I know nothing about my dad. To meet people who knew him, well, I couldn't let that opportunity slip by.'

'I understand,' said Sam, lifting her eyes to Alice and managing a small smile. 'And I'm sorry for lying to you when we first met. That last summer with Dan feels like a different lifetime, and it was such a shock hearing his name again after all these years.'

'That's OK,' said Alice. 'Would you like to see the photo I found?'

Sam nodded, and Alice slipped the photograph across the table.

'Wow, we look so young. I'd forgotten you used to have hair.'

'Oi,' said Steve, nudging his wife. 'We don't just look young, we were young. Still teenagers, if I remember rightly.'

'Yes, we were. Dan was a couple of years older, though. I think he'd reached twenty by the time this photo was taken.'

'That's my mum,' said Alice, pointing to the photograph. 'You must have known her too.'

'God, I never expected Dan and Maz to have a kid together,' said Sam.

'Why not?'

'Maz was a bit of an enigma. She just appeared one day at a beach party. We assumed she was in Saffron Bay on holiday with her family, but she was really vague whenever we asked her about it. She wouldn't even tell us where she was staying. From the minute she laid eyes on Dan, it was obvious she fancied him. She made no secret of her plan to seduce him. Dan though... well, let's just say Maz wasn't his usual type.'

'What was his type?'

'He only had a couple of girlfriends that I knew of, but they were both sensible, homely girls. Maz was a whirlwind of energy and mischief and, to be honest, I think she scared Dan a bit.'

'Why should he be scared of a strong woman?' asked May, pouting and folding her arms.

'I'm not suggesting there's anything wrong with being a strong woman, and that wasn't what put Dan off. No, it was more... um...'

'Her recklessness?' asked Steve.

'Exactly. Like I said, she sort of appeared out of nowhere, and it was obvious she wasn't planning to stay in Saffron Bay for long. She didn't care if she annoyed a few locals. But it was different for Dan. He had to stay in the village long after the tourists had left, and he was trying to establish a business in the area. He couldn't afford to have his reputation dragged through the mud.'

'Why did he get together with my mum then, if they were so incompatible?' asked May.

'For starters, it would have been her looks. She was beautiful,' said Sam. 'Actually, she was the spitting image of you, May.'

May blushed and fiddled with her glass.

'It wasn't just her looks though,' said Steve. 'Although she was wild, there was something magnetic about her, like you'd be missing out on an amazing time if you weren't with her.'

'If it's not too intrusive,' said Sam, 'I'm really curious what Maz is like as a mum?'

Alice and May exchanged a glance.

'Unconventional,' said May.

'Unreliable,' said Alice.

'Sorry.'

'Don't be,' said Alice. 'There's no question she loves us, but I always felt a bit of an inconvenience. Like I was stopping her from living the exciting life she'd dreamed of.'

'Same,' said May.

'It's why we're here,' said Alice, 'because she finally had enough of motherhood and ran off to the other side of the world.'

'I'm so sorry,' said Sam, 'but unfortunately, not surprised. I didn't know your mum long, but she wasn't someone I could imagine being tied down.'

'No. Anyway, what about my dad? What happened between him and Jack Tyler?'

'Oh, God,' said Steve. 'I don't imagine you'll believe us, but we actually don't know. We were with him that night, but...'

'But I got myself in a real state and ended up in hospital,' said Sam. 'Alcohol poisoning. Something went down that night, but I was too out of it to remember, and Steve was stuck looking after me.'

'When we got back from the hospital, we found out there'd been a fire up at Tyler's place. Several locals had seen smoke and heard the fire engines. Then it all went quiet.'

'What do you mean?'

'I mean, quiet in a way you wouldn't expect from a village where everyone knows everyone else's business. I don't know how he did it, but Jack Tyler shut down any gossip by threatening lawsuits. There was nothing in the press, no one knew what was going on.'

'I tried asking Dan about it,' said Steve, 'but he wouldn't tell me anything. Then one day, I went round to his house, and he and his parents were gone.'

'He left without telling you?'

'Yes. I mean, the neighbours must have seen the removal van, but from what I heard, they left under the cover of darkness. I was really hurt, to tell the truth. All those years of friendship, and your dad didn't even leave me a note. I thought I'd hear from him when he was settled somewhere new, but nothing. So, you see why hearing his name again was a shock? It's been twenty-five years since I've seen or heard from Daniel Loveday.'

'What about our mum?' asked May. 'Did you see her again after that night?'

'No,' said Sam. 'By the time I left hospital, your mum had gone. I don't know where she went, when or why she left.'

'Could my parents have left together?'

'It's possible,' said Steve, 'but I'd say highly unlikely. Mind you, if he knew Maz was pregnant, I suppose there's a chance they did.'

'Hmm,' said Alice. 'I know by the time I was born Dad wasn't on the scene, and I can't see he'd run away with Mum then abandon her before the birth.' Alice sighed and finished her glass of wine. She'd hoped that talking about her dad with former friends would provide some answers. Instead, Alice was more confused than ever.

Chapter 36

'Hello?'

'Sylvie, it's me.'

'Solly? What's the matter? Are you ill?'

'No, no, I'm fine. It's Jack.'

'What's happened now?'

'He's very unwell, but won't listen to sense. He needs a doctor.'

'You need my help?'

'He'll hate me for it, but yes. I can't think what else to do. He's told me if I call a doctor, he'll lock himself in his room. But you know how proud he is. He won't be able to help being polite to an outsider, especially a woman.'

'If you think it'll work…' Sylvie had serious doubts about Solly's plan. Jack Tyler hadn't spoken a word to her in years, and now Solly expected her to be allowed into his home?

'I can't think of anything else. You know where to come?'

'The big Keep Out signs are a bit of a clue. I'll be there as soon as I can.'

Sylvie put down the phone and thought about her next step. She hadn't owned a car in years, and despite her own stubbornness, she knew there was no way she'd get up the hill on her own two feet. She picked up the phone and dialled Luke's number.

'Sorry, Gran, I can't really talk. I'm in the middle of a job. Are you OK?'

'Oh, yes, fine, nothing to worry about. I'll leave you to it.'

'Was there a reason you called?'

Sylvie knew if she told Luke the truth, he'd drop everything to help her. But he had a business to run. 'I was only calling to invite you round to dinner later.'

'Sounds great. See you later.'

Luke hung up, and Sylvie stared at the phone in her hand. One by one she trawled through her address book, calling all her friends and acquaintances, but most were out, and those who answered were too busy to help. There was one other person she could try. Sylvie replaced the receiver and pulled on her coat. She walked the few short paces to Seashell Cottage and knocked on the door.

'Hello?' Alice answered the door, looking frazzled. Her blond hair was pulled up in a headscarf, and she was wearing an old pair of overalls that were covered in splatters of paint.

'Sorry, I can see you're busy,' said Sylvie, pointing to the paintbrush in Alice's hand.

'Oh, don't worry about this. There's enough work to keep me busy for months. It won't hurt to stop for a cuppa, or was there something else you needed?'

'A cup of tea would be lovely, but I'm afraid I don't have time. Actually, I came round to ask you a favour.'

'Fire away.'

'I need a lift up the hill. I've tried Luke, but he's in the middle of a job. But I can see you're busy, so forget I asked.'

'Don't be silly. Of course I'll help. When do you need to go?'

'Now,' said Sylvie with a wince. 'And before you say yes, you should know that I'm going to see Jack Tyler. I don't expect or want you to come in. The sight of you would probably finish the poor man off, but if you could drop me at the gates, I'd be very grateful.'

'Of course, but why are you going to see Jack Tyler?'

'He's not very well.'

'And he asked for your help?'

'Not exactly. His brother called me.'

'Solly? Oh, I didn't realise you two were friends.'

Sylvie felt her cheeks redden like a teenager. She pinched the skin on her hand to get a grip. 'Are you able to help me?'

'Give me a second to get out of these overalls, then I'll be right with you. Here you go,' said Alice, handing Sylvie a set of keys. 'The car's just a little way down the road. Make yourself comfortable, and I'll be as quick as I can.'

Sylvie had only been waiting a couple of minutes when Alice climbed into the driver's seat. 'You'll have to give me directions,' she said, turning on the engine.

'Head straight up this hill, then follow the road round to the left. After a sharp bend, you'll see a very narrow road to your right. It's a little overgrown, but the car should get through.'

'Sorry for the mess,' said Alice as they drove.

'I hadn't noticed,' lied Sylvie, discreetly kicking an empty crisp packet off the toe of her shoe. 'Slow down,' she said as they reached the top of the hill. 'There, see that sign?'

Alice leaned forward and turned the car sharply to the right. The sign was almost impossible to see, the post it was attached to having fallen into the nearest bush quite some time before, if the rust was anything to go by. 'Saffron Manor,' muttered Alice.

'In about half a mile, we'll reach a set of gates. If you could drop me there, that would be lovely.'

'Half a mile? Wow, this place is enormous.'

The car scraped and groaned its way along the narrow lane. Sylvie squirmed every time a wayward branch scraped against the car's paintwork. 'I'll pay for any repairs needed to your vehicle.'

Alice laughed. 'Sylvie, you've seen the state of my car. I don't think a few scratches will make much difference, do you?'

'Even so. Goodness, it's been so long since I came up here. I can't believe Jack's let it get into such a state.'

'These bushes could certainly do with a prune,' said Alice. 'I'm surprised he doesn't have a gardener for an estate this size.'

'He did once,' said Sylvie, picturing Daniel Loveday in his uniform. He'd been so proud when he bought his first van with *Loveday's Landscaping* painted across the side.

'Are you sure you'll be alright from here?' asked Alice, pulling the car to a halt beside two large, rusting gates. Strings of ivy had entwined themselves around the railings, making the entrance look like something from a Gothic novel.

'Quite sure.'

'I'll wait here for you, if you like.'

'There's really no need.'

'I was due a break. Besides, it's a treat to read my book for a while,' said Alice, tapping her coat pocket where a paperback was poking out.

'Alright, but please don't wait too long. If I'm not back in half an hour, you head home and I'll make my own way back.'

'I'll give it an hour,' said Alice, 'and no arguing.'

Sylvie smiled and climbed out of the car. Alice helped her yank open the gates, then with a deep breath she began walking along the overgrown driveway, unable to imagine what she might find at the end of it.

Chapter 37

Sylvie had only been walking for five minutes, but already her knees were throbbing in protest. It didn't help that twice she'd tripped over roots hidden by layers of debris that lay strewn across the driveway. Ancient trees blocked any view of her destination, and as Sylvie tried to glimpse the house, her toe caught on another tree root and she fell to the ground, her hands tearing against gravel as they flew out in front of her.

Tears pricked Sylvie's eyes as she lay with her face in a pile of rotten leaves. She lifted her head and scanned her body, checking that nothing was broken. All her limbs seemed intact. The worst damage was to her pride. Sylvie pulled herself up and crawled to a tree stump, where she sat down to survey the damage. Her hands were grazed and dirty, her stockings torn, blood pooling on the fabric around her knee. Her patent court shoes now housed large scuffs that no amount of polishing would hide.

'You silly old woman,' Sylvie said to herself. With the last of her energy, she climbed to her feet and slowly edged her way forward. When she turned the last corner, it took all her strength not to collapse to the ground once more. Of all the times she'd imagined Saffron Manor, nothing could have prepared her for the sight that greeted her.

The once-bowling-green-smart lawn was now a meadow, peppered with sprawling bramble bushes. Someone had cut a narrow path among the weeds, which led past a crumbling water feature to the door of a building almost unrecognisable from the home Sylvie had visited in her youth.

Of the hundreds of windows, only a handful held any glass, and even the remaining panes were streaked and opaque. Around the gaps where windows were once housed, the granite was blackened. Birds perched on singed roof joists, swooping down into the void where tiles once lay.

Sylvie's head throbbed as her pulse surged at an alarming rate. She stepped towards the front door, her fingers sinking into soft wood as she gave a tentative knock. When after a few minutes there'd still been no answer, Sylvie turned the handle and pushed the door open. She gasped at the sight of a once-grand entrance hall, now like the set of a horror film. Checkerboard tiles sat discoloured and covered in dust. A circular walnut table was grey with dirt, with a vase containing what must once have been flowers at the centre.

Sylvie leaned a hand against the wall, and it came away black. In front of her, a once-sweeping staircase now led to nowhere, a gaping hole in the blackened wood where the fifth to eleventh treads should have been. A charred picture frame still hung on one wall, the possibly priceless artwork it once housed now long gone.

From somewhere in the building came the sound of raised voices. Sylvie shivered at the thought of walking through the ruined house alone and regretted not buying a mobile phone when Luke had suggested it. Picking her way through debris and rubble, Sylvie followed the sounds of shouting. She passed the staircase on her left, moving further into the bowels of the building toward what must once have been servants' quarters.

Sylvie paused outside a thick wooden door, which, unlike the others she'd seen, was sturdy and free of burn marks. She knocked, but no-one heard her above the low male voices shouting over each other. Taking a deep breath, Sylvie pushed open the door.

'What the...'

'Hello, Jack; hello, Solly.' The two men stared at Sylvie, Solly with relief in his eyes, Jack with disbelief.

'What the blazes are you doing here?' Jack's voice boomed across the room, making Sylvie jump.

'I'm sorry, Jack...'

'Get out of my house!'

Sylvie stood pinned to the spot, struggling with the anathema of Jack's words. He may still own what once was a fine house, but it was obvious within seconds of opening the door that Jack lived in one room.

'Jack, hang on a minute.'

Solly stepped in front of Jack, his back to Sylvie, and began muttering in a low voice. Sylvie took it as an oppor-

'Lucky for you, the NHS is rather stretched these days and GPs don't do house calls like they once did. We'll need to get you down to the surgery.'

'How?' asked Solly. 'My car's in the garage for its MOT and neither you nor Jack has a car.'

'I know someone who can take us,' said Sylvie. 'You're not going to like it, Jack, but if you don't come with us now, you could end up in hospital, or worse. So, what's it to be?'

'I'll get my coat,' muttered Jack.

Chapter 38

Alice glimpsed an unlikely-looking group in her rearview mirror and jumped out of the car. She ran to the ancient iron gates and dragged them open. The sound of hinges creaking caused one of the group to lift his head. A look of horror passed across his face as he saw Alice waiting at the gates. He fought against his friends, and Alice ran to Solly and Sylvie's aid.

'You didn't tell me she'd be here. You tricked me!'

'Jack, please,' begged Sylvie. 'We need to get you to the doctor, and Alice is the only one of us around here with a car.'

'I won't go within three feet of a Loveday.'

'Then your choice is to crawl into the village or crawl back home where the infection will most likely get worse and you'll either lose that leg or your life.' Sylvie stood back and folded her arms.

Solly, struggling under the weight of his brother, tried a different tack. 'Please, Jack, do this for me. I've met Alice, and I promise you she's no ogre.' Solly turned his attention to Alice. 'I'm sorry, Alice, we haven't even asked if you'd mind driving us all to the surgery in the village? My brother has an infected wound, and we think he's going to need some antibiotics.'

'Of course I don't mind. Listen, Mr Tyler, I know you've got a problem with my family, especially my dad, but given I have never met the man, and have no idea why or what happened, perhaps you could cut me some slack?'

Jack muttered something under his breath.

'Pardon?' asked Sylvie.

'I said OK, I'll go with her.'

'How generous of you,' said Solly, helping his brother through the gates and into the car.

'Are you alright?' asked Alice, placing a hand on Sylvie's arm. 'You look rather pale yourself.'

'I'm fine,' said Sylvie, 'just worried about Jack. And it was a bit of a shock seeing the house after all this time.'

As Sylvie climbed into the car, Alice strained her neck to see beyond the trees, but no matter how hard she tried, she couldn't get a glimpse of Saffron Manor. After checking her passengers were comfortable, Alice turned on the ignition and headed back towards the village.

The passengers in the car remained quiet, and Alice fought the urge to turn on the radio to cover the awkward silence. She risked a glance in the rearview mirror and found Jack Tyler's eyes boring into her. Alice flushed and looked away, then cursed herself for feeling guilty. She had done nothing wrong and would do well to remember that fact.

As they approached the village, Sylvie directed Alice to a row of Victorian three-story terraced houses.

'The doctor's surgery is in the end house,' Sylvie explained.

'Yes, I've walked past it, I think. It's an unusual place to have a surgery.'

Sylvie glanced behind her, then back at Alice. 'Years ago, the council was going to close our doctor's surgery due to the supposed running costs of the building. A mysterious benefactor stepped in and donated the house for use as a surgery, with the offer to cover all running costs for a period of ten years.'

'What? But who would do something like that? That's beyond generous!'

'Isn't it just,' muttered Solly from the back seat.

'Look, dear, there's a parking space right outside. Will your car fit in there?'

'Yes, I'm used to tricky city parking, don't worry.' Alice expertly manoeuvred the car into the tight space and turned off the engine. She climbed out and opened the door for her passengers. 'Do you need some help to get up the slope?'

'No,' barked Jack.

'Thank you for the offer,' said Solly, 'but between us, we'll manage.'

'Alright. I'll wait here until you're done.'

'There's no need,' said Solly. 'You've been a tremendous help already.'

'And with little thanks,' said Sylvie, glaring at Jack. 'Get back to your cottage, Alice. You've given us enough of your time.'

Whilst spending any more time in the company of Jack Tyler wasn't a prospect to relish, Alice wanted to show she was the bigger person. 'It's fine. As I said before, I've got a good book with me, and I've not taken any time off since I arrived, so it's nice to have a break.'

Sylvie reached over and patted Alice on the arm. 'You're a kind girl,' she said under her breath. 'Other people could learn a thing or two about manners from you.'

'It's OK,' mouthed Alice, climbing back into the car. She watched as the three friends shuffled up the slope, Sylvie and Solly supporting Jack on either side. Alice wondered if Jack knew how lucky he was to have friends who'd put up with his grumpy nature. After being on the receiving end of his ungratefulness, Alice decided Solly must be a hero to have put up with his brother for years.

Alice was engrossed in her book when a knock on the car window made her jump. She looked up to see Luke's face peering down at her. Alice wound down the window and folded the corner of her book.

'Is everything OK?' asked Luke.

'Yes, why?'

'You're sitting in your car outside the doctor's surgery.'

'Oh, yeah, no, everything's fine. Well, I'm fine at least. I'm here waiting for your gran.'

'Gran? What's wrong with Gran? Why didn't you call me? I need to get in there.'

'Calm down,' said Alice. 'There's nothing wrong with Sylvie. She's fine.'

'Then what's she doing visiting a doctor?'

'It's not for her. She's in there with Jack Tyler.'

'What? Now I'm really confused.' Luke walked around the car, opened the passenger door, and climbed in. 'So you're here, waiting for my gran and Jack Tyler?'

'And Solly.'

'Wow. How on earth did you get roped into this?'

'Solly called your gran needing help with Jack, and she called you, but you were busy, so then she asked if I could help. She needed someone to drive her up to Jack's house. Then, when we got there...'

'You've been to Jack Tyler's house?' Luke looked at Alice as though she'd just announced she'd been to the moon.

'Not inside, no. In fact, I didn't even get down the drive. Sylvie made me wait in the car by the gates.'

'But now you're here?'

'Yes, it seems Jack's in a bad way and needed someone to check him over. Sylvie thinks he'll need antibiotics. It was too far for them to walk, given they're practically carrying Jack, so I drove them, and now I'm waiting to take them home.'

'That sounds like quite a day. How has Jack been with you?'

'Rude. Sullen. Ungrateful.' Alice winced, then laughed. 'It's OK though. I'm on a mission to clear the Loveday name, so if that means playing taxi for an afternoon to an ungrateful passenger, so be it. And to be fair to him, I think he's in a lot of pain, and I get terribly grumpy when I'm ill.'

'Thanks for the warning. I'll stay well clear the next time you get a cold.'

Alice laughed. 'Aren't you supposed to be at work?'

'I started early, so I'm done for the day. Would it help if I stuck around?'

'You know what, it actually would. Jack doesn't want me anywhere near him, so Sylvie and Solly are having to manage him by themselves, and he's not very mobile.'

'Right, you stay here, and I'll find out what's going on.'

Chapter 39

Luke kicked the front door closed, grabbed a beer from the fridge, and flopped down in an armchair. What a day. He ran his hand through his hair and tried to process what he'd seen up at Saffron Manor. How had Jack Tyler lived like that all these years? Was he now so poor that he had no choice? Surely Saffron Manor could still command a decent price, even just for the land and views.

Luke closed his eyes and pictured Saffron Manor through his builder's eyes. It would be a huge undertaking, but he was certain that something could be salvaged from the wreckage. The stone outer walls had a little water damage, but nothing that couldn't be rectified. The interior would need ripping out and starting again. The time and cost of such a renovation would be enormous, and any prospective buyer would probably knock down the original building and begin again. Perhaps that was why Jack had never put it on the market. Perhaps Saffron Manor meant so much to him he'd rather sleep among its ruins than see it razed to the ground?

'Alright, mate?'

Luke opened his eyes to see Nick standing in his living room. 'What are you doing here?'

'Door was unlocked. What are you doing sitting there with your eyes closed? Have you found God? Meditation?'

'No, I was thinking.'

'About what?'

'How sad some people's lives are and the strange choices people make.'

'Sounds a bit deep to me. I came to see if you fancy a pint?'

Luke yawned. 'I don't know, mate. I'm pretty knackered.'

'I thought you had an early finish today?'

'I did, but then...'

'Then?'

'Nothing.'

'Come on, just a quick one.'

'Alright,' said Luke, downing the dregs of his beer and pulling his boots back on. 'Just one, though. I really am done in.'

'Yeah, whatever you say.'

It was only as they walked into the pub that Luke realised his mistake. He'd forgotten tonight was Alice's first shift. Would she think he was checking up on her? She was standing behind the bar, her back turned to Luke as Rita showed her the different spirits the pub offered.

Nick walked up to the bar and rapped his knuckles against it. 'Any chance of a drink, Rita?'

Rita spun around and smiled at Nick. 'It's what we do. Pint of Ghost Ship?'

'You know me too well.'

'Hi,' said Luke, as Alice turned around. 'Sorry to gate-crash your first shift. I forgot you were working tonight.'

'It's fine,' said Alice, her cheeks turning pink. 'What can I get you?'

'I'll have a Guinness, please.'

'Sure.' Alice pulled a pint glass off the shelf and began filling it with dark liquid.

'Woah,' said Rita, stepping in and taking the pint from Alice. 'Take it slowly and don't forget to let it sit for a minute.'

'Sorry,' said Alice, the red of her cheeks deepening.

'Can you remember how to work the till?'

'I think so.'

Luke handed over his bank card, and Alice took the payment, keeping her eyes fixed on the till in front of her. As she returned his card, their hands brushed against each other, and Luke felt an unexpected jolt of electricity pass through him. He felt his own cheeks redden and said a hasty thank you to Alice before turning to find a table.

'I reckon that new barmaid likes you,' whispered Nick when they sat down. 'Did you see how red she went?'

'She has a name,' said Luke. 'That's Alice, the girl I've been helping. Gran's new neighbour.'

'Oh, the famous Alice! So she definitely likes you then,' said Nick with a smirk.

'It's not that. She's probably just nervous as this is her first shift.'

'Yeah, whatever you say.'

The pub began filling up, and as Nick prattled on about a film he'd recently watched, Luke studied Alice from the corner of his eye. Her nerves soon evaporated, and by the time she'd served her fifth customer, she looked like she'd been working behind the bar for years. Luke felt a rush of pride on his friend's behalf. He'd only known her for a matter of weeks, but he admired Alice's courage and persistence. The way she tackled every and any job in the cottage showed determination, and there was no doubt she was a quick learner. And then there were the events of the day, which spoke of kindness and generosity, which were more than Jack Tyler deserved.

'Earth to Luke.'

'Sorry. I was listening, I promise.'

'Yeah? So what film was I talking about?'

'The one with robots? I've forgotten the name.'

'I knew you weren't listening. They were aliens, not robots. Seriously, mate, you need to stop staring at the new barmaid.'

'Alice.'

'Yeah, whatever. I get it, she's fit, but I wanted to spend some time with my best mate, not some lovesick teenager.'

'I'm not lovesick,' said Luke. 'Tell me about the film again, and I promise I'll listen this time.'

Luke forced himself to listen to Nick as he analysed the movie plot in depth, but was relieved when the monologue reached its conclusion and he had an excuse to go back to the bar. 'Same again?'

'Cheers, mate.'

The other customers were settled at their tables, and Rita had left Alice to man the bar. Luke handed her his empty glasses and ordered the same again.

'That was quite a day,' said Alice, smiling at Luke as she filled a pint glass. 'Thank you for helping this afternoon.'

'Honestly, I wish I could have done more. I'm sorry you wasted an entire day.'

'It's fine,' said Alice. 'At least Jack got his antibiotics, and Solly's car will have been fixed before Jack needs to go back to have his dressings changed. So, come on, what was the house like?'

'Not what I'd been expecting,' said Luke.

'In what way?'

'I've only seen it from the water before and it looks amazing, but up close... well... let's just say it's in a bit of a state.'

'It must be lovely seeing the village from the water. I've always fancied having a go at stand-up paddle boarding.'

'Ever tried kayaking?'

'No, but it's something I've always wanted to do. I even got as far as booking myself a sea safari for my birthday, but then Maz left and I ended up getting a refund.'

'That's a shame. Would you like to try kayaking in Saffron Bay?'

Alice handed Luke his pint. 'Yes, I would.'

'How are you fixed tomorrow?'

'I'm working here in the evening, but I'm free all day.'

'Fancy a couple of hours out on the water? I've got a double kayak, so I could ease you in gently.'

'Won't it be cold?'

'Yes, but the forecast is for sunshine. I've got a spare winter wetsuit you can borrow, although I don't plan on actually getting wet.'

'That sounds great. Would ten suit you?'

'It's a date,' said Luke, 'I mean...'

'It's OK,' said Alice, her eyes twinkling, 'I knew what you meant.'

As Luke walked back to his table, he couldn't wipe the grin off his face.

Chapter 40

It had been a while since she'd done any bar work, and by the time Alice arrived home after her first shift, she was exhausted. The last thing she was expecting on walking through the door was blaring music and high-pitched giggling.

'Alice?'

Alice was almost knocked off her feet as May hurled herself against her, wrapping her arms tight around Alice's waist.

'Woah,' said Alice, 'what's happened?'

May's body began shaking with sobs. 'I'm so, so sorry. I tried to stop them, but they got more and more wasted and refused to leave.'

'What are you talking about? Are you drunk?'

'No! I only had two vodka tonics, then I saw the way things were going and stuck to tonic. Oh, God, Alice, I really am so, so sorry.'

Alice peeled May off her and marched along the corridor, the music growing louder the closer she got to May's bedroom. With a deep breath, Alice turned the handle and let the door swing open. 'What on earth?'

Three teenage girls were twirling round, swinging May's clothes above their heads like scarves. Their faces were a riot of colour, matching the once-white walls, which had been given a makeover in Alice's absence. Unable to contain her anger, Alice walked over to the stereo and pulled the plug from its socket. The girls paused mid-spin and stared at Alice.

'Get out of my house,' said Alice, her voice ominously quiet.

'No need to be like that,' said a pretty blonde. 'Haven't you heard of having fun?'

'You... you've trashed my house!' squealed Alice, her voice rising. 'Look at the walls! I only painted them last week! How dare you come in here and...'

'May told us you said she could redecorate however she wanted. We were giving her a helping hand.'

'By covering the walls in makeup?'

'It's modern art,' drawled the blonde. There was now no doubt in Alice's mind she was the ringleader.

'What's your name?'

'None of your business.'

'I need to call your parents.'

'Why? We've not broken the law. May invited us in and gave us permission to decorate.'

'Deface more like. Now I'm going to ask you one more time. Get. Out. Of. My. House.'

With no sense of urgency, the three girls gathered up their belongings, stumbling around and giggling intermittently. Alice fought the urge to push them out of the door herself and tried equally hard not to cry. All the work she'd put into the room, and this was how May repaid her?

'I don't feel well,' said a small brunette who had turned an alarming shade of grey.

Alice grabbed the girl's arm, dragging her through the house and shoving her through the front door. She had enough to clear up already without the reappearance of half a bottle of vodka.

'You'd better check on your friend,' said Alice, shepherding the other girls along the corridor and out of the front door. 'And never think about coming around here again.' Alice slammed the door and walked through to the kitchen, where a white-faced May was rocking on a hard-backed chair. 'Go and wait for me in the living room,' said Alice, unable to look at her sister.

'Alice...'

'We'll talk when I've made a coffee. You look like you could do with one.'

'I'm not drunk, I...'

'Go to the living room and wait.'

'OK,' whispered May, her head hanging low, her feet shuffling as she left the room.

Alice took her time making a pot of coffee, taking long, deep breaths to calm some of her anger. Given May's earlier tears, shouting wouldn't achieve much. The calm approach would be best, Alice decided. She poured milk into two mugs and placed them alongside the coffeepot on a tray. With a sigh, she lifted the tray and went to find her sister.

Alice found May curled up in a ball in an armchair. 'Alice, I'm so sorry.'

'Here,' said Alice, handing May a cup of coffee. 'You've already said you're sorry. But what I can't understand is how you could let this happen? You know how hard I worked to make your bedroom nice for you. Why would you let those girls trash it?'

'I didn't mean to. It sort of... well, I guess things got out of hand.'

'Start from the beginning,' said Alice, sipping her coffee in the hope it would banish some of her tiredness.

'I met them at the bus stop when we first moved here. They seemed really nice. It's been hard, you know, my friends being so far away? I thought if I could make some new friends in the village, I wouldn't be missing out so much.'

'May, you've spent more time in Plymouth than in Saffron Bay since we moved in. I'm sorry, but I find it hard to believe you're missing out.'

May pouted and pulled her knees up to her chin. 'I miss hanging around with my friends after school. The bus takes so long I can't risk missing it.'

'Fair enough. So, tonight. What happened?'

'I bumped into the girls on my way home from the bus stop. They asked if they could hang out here. I didn't know they had booze with them, I promise. It was cool at first, listening to music, chilling out. Then they went all weird and started saying this house was haunted.'

'Haunted?'

'Yeah, stupid, I know. They started teasing me about your dad, saying he was a murderer and all sorts. Even when I told them I have a different dad, they wouldn't shut up about him. They said everyone in the village knows the Lovedays are weirdos.'

'If that's the case, I'm surprised they wanted to come round to our house.'

'That's what I said. I tried to change the subject and asked for advice about decorating my room. That's when things got really crazy. At first, it was kind of a joke. They got their makeup out and started doing little doodles on the wall. I didn't think it was a big deal. They were so small I could have covered them with posters. But the more they drank, the crazier they got. I tried asking them to leave, but they just laughed at me. I'm sorry, Alice. I know this is all my fault. Honestly, I never thought it would get so out of hand. I really thought they liked me.'

'Tell me their names and I'll speak to their parents tomorrow.'

'No, please don't!'

'May, what they've done tonight amounts to bullying.'

'Please, Alice. They're the only people my age in this village. If I get on the wrong side of them, my life will be a misery.'

'Fine,' said Alice, letting out a long sigh. 'But I want you to steer clear of them. Be polite, friendly even, but I don't want you getting too embroiled with them. If tonight's taught us anything, it's that they can't be trusted. Understood?'

'Yes.'

'Good. Now let's get to bed, and tomorrow I'll help you clean up the mess.'

May climbed out of the armchair and crossed the room, pulling Alice into a tight hug. 'Thank you. I love you, sis.'

'I love you too.'

Chapter 41

It took Alice a moment to remember why she was so tired. Then the events of the previous day came flooding back; a strange afternoon spent helping Jack Tyler, her first shift in the pub, and finding a group of feral teenagers destroying her home. Alice pulled her covers over her head and closed her eyes.

With a jolt, she sat up. Luke was taking her kayaking. In all the drama of the previous evening, she'd completely forgotten. Alice grabbed her alarm clock from beside the bed and checked the time. With a groan, she saw it was already nine-thirty, which left very little time to get ready and get down to the beach. Alice had hoped to have time to do her hair and put on a little makeup, but in the event, all she had time for was a quick shower, a gulp of tea, and grabbing the only clean clothes to hand, a pair of leggings and an old hoodie.

Alice didn't bother looking in the mirror, as she knew it would be depressing. After tossing and turning half the night, there was no way she'd be looking her best. *It doesn't matter*, Alice told herself. *This is just a fun day out between two friends, nothing more.* But as she left the cottage and headed for the beach, the hammering of her heart and sweaty palms betrayed her true feelings about the day.

As Alice reached the bottom of the path and scanned the beach, her heart sank. Luke was there, waiting next to his kayak, but he wasn't alone. Beside Luke stood Patricia, looking like Lara Croft in her tight black wetsuit. Unlike Alice, Patricia had left plenty of time to get ready, her glowing skin was easily mistaken for natural if you didn't know better. Likewise, her hair had been pulled into an artful messy bun, giving off a low-maintenance-natural-beauty vibe, despite the hours it must have taken to achieve.

Luke spotted Alice and waved. She waved back, forcing a smile on her face as she trudged across the beach.

'Ah, Alice,' said Patricia, 'I hope you don't mind, but I heard Luke was going out on his kayak and he's been promising to take me out for yonks, so I asked if I could tag along.'

'The more the merrier,' said Alice, smiling at Patricia but refusing to look at Luke.

'Right, yeah, so I thought I'd take Alice in the double kayak with me as this is her first time, and you could take the single kayak, Patricia?'

'Oh, but Luke, I'm really suffering from tennis elbow. Manning a kayak alone could be very tricky.'

'Perhaps you shouldn't be coming at all if you're injured?' asked Luke.

'I'll be fine as long as I don't have to do all the paddling. That is alright, isn't it?' Patricia pouted and fluttered her eyelashes. Alice risked a glance at Luke and was pleased to see him looking more annoyed than excited by Patricia's obvious flirting.

'It's fine by me,' said Alice, 'as long as you don't get too far ahead.'

'Are you sure?' asked Luke.

'Yeah, honestly, it's fine.' If it was a choice between a kayak on her own or sharing with Patricia, Alice knew which she'd rather.

'OK. Here's a wetsuit for you.'

'Thanks. Is there somewhere I can get changed?'

'Yeah, if you go behind the old boathouse you'll be safe from prying eyes.'

'Thanks.'

Alice carried the wetsuit behind a concrete wall and, after making sure the only voyeurs were a pair of seagulls, began the arduous job of pulling it on over her swimming costume. Being a good deal shorter than Patricia, Alice suspected she looked more penguin than Lara Croft, but given there was no way she could compete with Patricia's glamour anyway, Alice tried to push any self-consciousness to the back of her mind.

'Could you help with the zip?' Alice asked Luke after waddling her way back across the sand.

'Sure, stay still.' Luke pulled the zip, but before reaching the top, he brushed a handful of hair from the nape of Alice's neck. Heat flooded through her at the gentle touch of his fingers against her skin.

'Let me help,' said Patricia, barging Luke out of the way. 'I think this wetsuit is a bit small for poor old Alice. Perhaps you should have gone up a size.'

'I'd say it fits like a glove,' said Luke, throwing a smile Alice's way.

'Thank you,' she mouthed. 'Ow!'

'Oops, sorry,' said Patricia. 'I caught you with my nail.'

'Come on, let's get going,' said Luke.

Between the three of them, they hauled the kayaks to the shoreline. Luke pushed the double kayak a few feet into the water and held it steady as Patricia climbed in. She squealed and made a show of wobbling and holding onto Luke to steady herself.

'Oh, no, Luke, please don't leave me,' she said as Luke began walking back to the beach to help Alice. 'I might float away.'

'You've got a paddle there. If you think you're going to float away, paddle back to shore.'

'But my shoulder!'

'You'll manage.'

Luke reached Alice and lifted the front of the kayak.

'I can manage if you need to get back to Patricia,' said Alice.

Luke shook his head. 'I'm really sorry about her,' he whispered. 'She cornered me on the street, and I didn't feel I could say no when she asked to come, as I know she's been having a tough time lately. But I was hoping it could just be the two of us.'

Flustered, Alice quickly changed the subject. 'Perhaps we could abandon our plan to see Jack Tyler's house from the water?'

'Really?'

'Yes, there's enough speculation about the Tylers and Lovedays without Patricia adding fuel to the fire.'

'Good thinking. OK, we'll still head that way, but I won't point out the house. Just keep your eyes peeled, and you should be able to spot it.'

'Thanks.'

'Here you go,' said Luke, holding the kayak steady. Once she was safely in, he handed Alice the paddle and gave her a quick lesson on technique.

'Luke? Luke, I'm floating away, and my shoulder's too sore to paddle. Luke!'

Alice looked over at Patricia. From her hysteria, she sounded like she was on the Titanic, not floating in two feet of water.

'I'd better go,' said Luke. 'And I am really sorry.'

'It's OK,' said Alice. 'Just make sure you don't leave me behind.'

Chapter 42

Sweat beaded on Alice's brow as she tried to keep up with Luke and Patricia's kayak. Patricia's tennis elbow seemed to have miraculously healed, and any attempts Luke made to slow down were hampered by Patricia's yoga-toned muscles.

'Are you alright back there?' called Luke, his voice carrying easily over the millpond still water.

'Fine,' panted Alice, a torrent of icy water hitting her in the face as her paddle landed awkwardly. Alice was aware of shoals of tiny fish swimming below in the crystal clear water, and would have liked the chance to appreciate the beauty of the underwater world. Instead, her sharp paddle strokes scattered the wildlife beneath, and it was all she could do to stay on course, never mind admire her surroundings.

Half an hour into their excursion, Patricia seemed to lose interest in paddling, resting her paddle across her lap and leaning back, her face tilted towards the weak spring sun. Alice took the opportunity to catch up. By the time she reached them, Luke was holding the kayak steady while Patricia dangled her manicured fingers in the water below.

'You OK?' asked Luke as Alice drew level.

'Fine,' she said, wiping her brow with her arm.

'Sorry we got so far ahead.'

'It's fine.'

'Oh, Alice, I almost forgot,' said Patricia, lifting her sunglasses to fix Alice with a glare. 'My daughter encountered your sister last night. Apparently, she's quite a handful.'

'Your daughter or my sister?'

'Your sister. Poor Paige was quite shaken up when she got home. She had to go straight to bed.'

'Right. The girls I found in my house last night wouldn't give me their names, and May wouldn't tell me either. Is your daughter blonde or brunette?'

'Blonde and very beautiful,' said Patricia.

'OK, so she was one of the girls trashing my home last night. In fact, I'd go as far as to say she was the ringleader.'

'How dare you!'

'More like how dare *you*.' Exhaustion fuelled Alice's anger. Not only had this awful woman gatecrashed what should have been a lovely time with Luke, she was now trying to cover her own daughter's misbehaviour by pinning it all on May. Alice could bite her tongue most of the time, but not when it came to her sister.

'What's this all about?' asked Luke.

Patricia tried to speak, but Alice raised her voice and talked over her. 'I got home from the pub last night to find May distraught. There were three teenage girls in her bedroom, completely wasted on vodka, drawing all over the bedroom walls with makeup.'

'What? You mean the walls you'd just painted?'

'The very same.'

Luke spun around to look at Patricia. The kayak wobbled, and Patricia screamed.

'You're telling a very different story from the one I've heard,' said Patricia. 'According to Paige, your sister went mad, drinking neat vodka from the bottle before graffitiing the walls of her own bedroom.'

Alice laughed. 'Seriously? Patricia, I saw it all with my own eyes. And to be honest, I don't know how you could have missed the fact that your daughter was completely wasted. She couldn't even walk straight by the time she left my house.'

'And whose fault is that?' snapped Patricia. 'Where did she get the vodka from? Your sister, of course. My Paige has never touched the stuff before. I've told her to stay well clear of May, as she's obviously a terrible influence. Unsurprising given the Loveday genes.'

'For starters, May doesn't have any Loveday genes, and second...'

'Ladies, please. Now, this isn't the time or the place. Why don't we head back to the beach so you can discuss this calmly when we're on dry land?'

'Fine by me,' said Alice, turning her kayak round. At least all the anger coursing through her helped with paddling, her kayak cutting through the water much faster than it had previously.

It was when they were almost back at the beach that Patricia struck up her accusations once more. 'And another thing,' she shouted. 'Your sister was putting all sorts of awful ideas into Paige's head about boys. I know things are different in the city, but in Saffron Bay we prefer our daughters not to behave like women of the night.'

'Women of the night? May's never even had a serious boyfriend!'

'That shows how little you know about your sister then, doesn't it? To be honest, it's a wonder she hasn't got herself pregnant. The stories she told Paige, well, hearing them made me blush.'

Alice dug her paddle into the water, sending a torrent of seawater in Patricia's direction. Patricia screamed, her face turning purple as a stream of very unladylike words flew from her mouth. She dug her own paddle into the water to retaliate, but the sudden movement caused her kayak to lurch.

'Careful!' shouted Luke, but it was too late.

With a scream, Patricia and Luke fell headfirst into the water, the kayak turning upside down. Alice's concern turned to amusement as she realised the water was only waist-deep and the danger of drowning minimal. Patricia emerged coughing and spluttering, and Alice couldn't stop the laughter bubbling up in her throat.

'Don't you dare!' yelled Patricia, wading towards Alice's kayak with a murderous look on her face.

By now, Alice had had enough opportunity to perfect her technique, and moved the kayak safely out of Patricia's reach.

'Just like your sister!' screamed Patricia, her makeup sliding down her face like a piece of modern art. 'Not to mention your father!'

'Come on,' said Luke. He grabbed hold of Patricia's arm and pulled both her and the kayak back towards the beach. Only when Patricia was sitting on the seawall wrapped in a towel did Alice venture back to shore. Luke met her at the water's edge.

'I'm really sorry about all that,' said Alice. 'It wasn't true, you know, what she said about May.'

Luke raised his hands in the air. 'I'm staying out of it.'

A rush of disappointment flooded Alice. She'd hoped Luke would take her side, but then he had history with Patricia, so his reaction shouldn't have surprised her.

'Listen, I'm not saying Patricia's accusations are true. To be honest, it's so long since I spent any time with Paige I don't know what she's like anymore. But regardless of who's right or wrong, I don't want to get involved in a dispute.'

'Fair enough. I am sorry. I should have ignored her. If she had been slagging me off, I probably could have done, but I felt I had to defend May. It's not been easy for her moving here, and you should have seen what those girls did to her bedroom.'

'Come on,' said Luke, helping Alice carry the kayak up the beach. 'I need to get the kayaks packed away, but how about I come to yours after and see what we can do about May's room?'

'Thank you,' said Alice, feeling ashamed of her behaviour and grateful to have such a good friend in equal measure.

Chapter 43

'It looked like you had your hands full with those two.'

'Oh, hi, Margot.'

Luke paused beside the seawall and dropped the deflated kayaks onto the sand. He jumped onto the wall and perched beside Margot, who was smiling up at the sun. She looked ready for summer with her sunglasses holding back her silver hair and sandals dangling from her feet. The only concession to the true season was the thick purple cardigan draped over her shoulders.

'You want to be careful around Patricia.'

Luke frowned at Margot. 'Don't you think I already know that? Her leaving me standing at the altar like the village idiot was enough to warn me off her.'

'Of course, I'm sorry for being insensitive. She's been a mess since her divorce. You deserve better and, to be honest, I can't believe she has the nerve to even speak to you after what she did.'

'That's Tricia for you. Don't worry, though; I have no intention of revisiting the past. She invited herself along kayaking.'

'You could have said no.'

'Have you tried saying no to Patricia Morris?'

Margot turned her head and smiled. 'As it happens, I have.'

'Of course you have,' said Luke, shaking his head.

'Alice seems nice.'

'Yes, she is.'

'You like her?'

'I just said she's nice, didn't I?'

Margot smiled a knowing smile, and Luke looked away. It was impossible not to like Margot, but she could display busybody tendencies as well as the best of them, and he wished she'd mind her own business.

'She's been through a lot, has Alice. And she's more fragile than she looks.'

'What do you mean? Has she said something to you?'

'No, but it's obvious. She's prepared to put all her dreams on hold to take on the role of mother to her younger sister. She picks up the pieces of everyone else's mess without a thought for herself. Alice Loveday strikes me as a woman who could use a good friend.'

'Do you know something about Alice I don't?'

'Not about Alice, no...' Margot picked up a handful of sand and watched as it ran through her fingers.

'Margot, I need to get the kayaks back. What is it you're trying to tell me?'

Margot folded her hands in her lap, and Luke wondered if she was going to clam up. When she spoke, her voice was quiet, her tone serious. 'I should probably start with the fact that I've been a friend of Daniel Loveday's for the past thirty years.'

Luke's mouth fell open. 'So he's alive then. Wow.' He frowned and shook his head. 'Hold on a minute. Are you the fairy godmother?'

'The what?'

'Did you clean the cottage before Alice arrived?'

Margot raised her palms in the air. 'Guilty as charged.'

She didn't look very guilty. 'How did you know when she'd be arriving?'

'I didn't. Not exactly. But I knew her date of birth, and Dan had told me she'd probably come to claim the cottage as her own soon after. The amount of sneaking about I had to do, keeping that place dust free.' Margot shook her head and sighed.

'You've been in touch with Daniel Loveday recently?'

'He writes to me once a month.'

'Don't you think Alice should know?' asked Luke, his voice rising. 'The woman doesn't even know if her dad is dead or alive!'

Margot sighed again. 'It's not as simple as that. She needs to hear his side of things, from the horse's mouth. I've written to Dan to let him know she's here. I'm hoping he might come and meet her, but I've not had a response from him yet.'

'Are you surprised?' asked Luke. 'He's ignored her for twenty-five years. What makes you think he'll be interested now?'

'Because I know him. I know what he's like. He was Marty's best friend.'

Luke frowned again, then realisation dawned. Marty. 'Your son?'

Margot nodded and tilted her head back to stop tears from falling. 'From the moment Dan moved to Saffron Bay, he and Marty were inseparable. Even when Marty went off to uni, their friendship remained intact. Marty loved the ocean and was studying marine biology. He died overseas in a diving accident during his second year of uni. You can imagine how hard his death hit me. Dan was the only person in this village who could understand the depth of my loss. He'd loved Marty almost as much as I had. We grew close through our grief, and he became a sort of surrogate son to me. Not that I was trying to replace Marty; no one could ever replace my beautiful boy. But Dan was the closest I was ever going to get to Marty, and I think he felt the same about me.' Her eyes had a faraway look, and she smiled as though reliving precious memories. Luke coughed, and Margot's attention returned to the present.

'That summer before Dan left, he'd been acting out, trying to block his grief with booze and girls. It was so self-destructive, but all I could do was watch from the sidelines and pray he'd be OK.' Margot used a finger to make patterns in the sand, and Luke could tell she wasn't finding the conversation easy.

'What happened between Daniel and Jack Tyler, Margot?'

'I honestly don't know. Don't get me wrong, I've asked, but Dan wouldn't say. When he left the village, he didn't say goodbye, and I heard nothing from him for the best part of two years. It was like losing Marty all over again, and I hated Dan for that. Then, out of the blue, one day I had a letter from him. It was full of apologies, and he said he'd been in therapy and realised how hurt I must have been by his lack of contact. He said there had been mistakes made that summer, which meant he couldn't come back to Saffron Bay, but that he'd like to stay in touch. At first, I didn't think I'd be able to forgive him, but in the end, I don't think either of us could bear to cut that final tie to Marty. Do you understand?'

'I do, up to a point, and I'm so sorry you've suffered such a loss in your life. After what happened to my parents, I get how hard it is to move on. I suppose Sylvie is to me what Daniel was to you. What I don't understand is why you're sharing this with me, not Alice.' Luke jumped off the seawall and ran his hands through his hair. 'What am I meant to tell her?'

'Nothing, not yet. Shortly after initiating that first contact, Dan wrote to me and told me he had a daughter. He said he wasn't able to be part of her life and left it at that. He said he hoped they'd one day reconnect and that he'd put the cottage in a trust for her, ready for when she turned twenty-five. It was all done through a solicitor, but he asked if I would become the unofficial caretaker.'

'Didn't you ask him about Alice, about why he abandoned her?'

'I tried, but all he'd say is it was best I didn't know. Yes, I probably could have pushed harder, but I was scared he'd cut contact with me again. It's why I want to leave it up to Dan to contact Alice.'

'It sounds like he's emotionally blackmailing you.'

Margot laughed. 'Not at all. He's not like that, but he is my only link to Marty, and I'm not prepared to do anything to jeopardise that. You're closer to Alice than anyone else in Saffron Bay, including me. I've told you because you're her friend, and I need to know someone is looking out for her. But the truth is neither mine nor yours to tell. Dan needs to come back here and explain himself to his daughter. It's the least he owes her. I know keeping this from Alice will be hard, but I honestly think it's for the best.'

'So where's he been all this time, then?'

Margot brushed her hands together to rid them of sand, jumped down from the wall and smoothed down her skirt. 'I've said too much already. Just look out for Alice, Luke. I'll let you know when I hear from Dan. If, or rather when, he comes back, it's going to turn Alice's life upside down. Dan's got me to lean on, and I hope Alice will have you.'

As Margot walked away, Luke felt as heavy as the water-logged kayak he was holding. She had just put him in a terrible situation. Why tell him Daniel Loveday was still alive if he couldn't share that information with Alice? Now he'd have to keep secrets from her, just when he thought they were getting close. For all Margot's insistence that she had Alice at the front of her mind, Luke felt the revelation was selfish. Margot had unburdened herself of a secret that no doubt was weighing heavily on her. He needed to think. What if Daniel didn't come back? How long would he keep this from Alice?

'Thanks a lot, Margot,' muttered Luke as he began hauling the kayaks back to the boathouse.

Chapter 44

Alice crept into the cottage and flicked on the hallway light. As she hung her coat on the hook, she paused and listened. It was unusual for May to be asleep already. Most nights, May considered midnight an early night, and it was only just gone ten. As much as Alice could have done with the money, she'd been happy to finish her shift early. There were only a handful of customers in the pub all evening, and one of them was Patricia Morris. Alice would rather never see the woman again, never mind having to keep a smile on her face as Patricia changed her drinks order multiple times and did her best to make Alice's shift as difficult as she could.

But without a doubt, the worst part of the evening had been when Luke turned up. Patricia had been all over him and, unless Alice was mistaken, he seemed to enjoy the attention. Her heart had sunk into her boots as she watched them flirting. Alright, so maybe he wasn't exactly flirting, but he also wasn't doing anything to discourage Patricia as she fawned over him. Perhaps Luke Richards was no better than any of the other men who'd crossed her path over the years, not that there'd been many.

'May?' whispered Alice, pushing open her bedroom door. 'May?'

Enough moonlight flooded through the windows for Alice to see the room was empty. Where was May? She checked every room in the cottage, despite knowing there was little point. Could May have got on a bus to Plymouth? Not without telling Alice, surely. Alice tried calling May's phone, but it went straight to voicemail. Her heart was hammering, and although she told herself she was over-reacting, Alice couldn't shake the feeling that something was terribly wrong.

Alice grabbed the coat she'd only just hung up and pulled it back on. She shoved a hat over her hair, wrapped a scarf around her neck, and stepped back into the cold of the night. *Think logically*, Alice told herself. *What if May has gone for a walk to look at the stars?*

Alice jogged down the hill towards the beach. She had just passed the café and was about to turn onto the path that led to the beach when a dark figure came rushing towards her.

'Hello? Hello, who's there? Is that you, May?'

'Alice?'

The voice in the darkness didn't belong to May. Alice breathed a sigh of relief as recognition struck. 'Solly? What are you doing out at this time?'

'It's Jack. I need to help Jack. I've tried calling Luke, but there's no answer.'

'Solly, calm down. What's happened to Jack?'

'I can't talk to you about this. I need Luke.'

'I'll get Luke for you,' said Alice. 'I know where he is, but first you need to tell me what's happened.'

Solly lifted his cap from his thick white hair and wrung it between his hands. 'Jack found a group of kids in his house. He's... he's...'

'He's what, Solly?'

'He caught one of them, a teenage girl, he said.'

Alice's heart sank. No, please, no. 'Solly,' she said, hearing the shake in her voice but unable to do anything about it. 'What has Jack done to the girl?'

'I don't know,' wailed Solly, 'but he's been in such a bad way lately, and I know he's blocked the door and won't let her leave...'

'Wait here.' Alice sprinted back towards the pub. She barged through the door, ignoring Rita's greeting and running through to the back, where Luke and Patricia were looking very cosy, sharing a bottle of wine.

'Alice?' said Luke, flushing and standing as she reached their table.

'I need your help,' said Alice. 'It's urgent.'

'In case you haven't noticed, we're in the middle of something,' said Patricia.

Alice ignored her. 'Please, Luke.'

'Um, excuse me,' said Patricia, her voice slurred. 'You can't just barge in here and demand Luke comes with you. He's with *me*, get it, *me*.'

'Sorry, Tricia,' said Luke, pulling on his coat. 'We'll have to have a catch-up another time.'

Patricia protested, but Alice was already making her way through the pub.

'Is everything alright?' called Rita.

Alice paused with her hand on the door. 'Yes, sorry, I'll explain tomorrow.' Then she was out in the night air, stamping her feet in impatience as she waited for Luke to join her.

'Sorry,' he said, as he emerged from the pub. 'What is it? What's wrong?'

'May's disappeared,' blurted Alice, 'and I bumped into Solly, who said Jack's found a teenage girl in his house, and Luke, he's blocked the door and won't let her out. It's got to be May in there. She'll be so scared. Oh, God, I don't know what to do!'

'OK,' said Luke, taking hold of Alice's arms, 'don't panic. For starters, it could be anyone. You don't know it's May, and also, does Solly have any reason to think Jack intends to hurt anyone?'

'No, but...'

'Then let's not panic. Where's Solly now?'

'Waiting outside the café. I told him I'd come and get you.'

'Good. We'll drive up there in my van.'

'But you've been drinking.'

'No,' said Luke as they hurried along the path, 'Patricia has been drinking. I had one small glass to be polite, but she drank the rest of the bottle. I'm well within the limit to drive.'

'OK.'

'You wait with Solly and I'll be there in a minute.' With that, Luke sprinted off towards his cottage.

Alice found Solly pacing up and down outside the café. 'Luke's gone to get his van,' she said. 'Come here.' Alice took Solly's hand and led him to the bench. 'You said Jack has locked someone in his house. Do you have any reason to think he might hurt that person? Because if you do, we need to call the police.'

'No,' said Solly, flopping down on the bench. 'He would never hurt anyone. But... but... he might scare someone.'

'I see.'

'If we call the police, all hell will break loose. He's barely coping as it is. The shame of being arrested would break him.'

'Fine, we'll drive to his house and see what's going on. But if there's even a whiff of violence, we're calling the police straightaway. Alright?'

Before Solly could answer, Luke's van screeched to a halt beside them. 'Get in,' he said, and they did as they were told.

Chapter 45

When they reached the gates of Saffron Manor, Alice jumped out of the van and hauled them open. 'I'm not closing them,' she said as she climbed back into the cab, 'just in case the police need to get through.'

Solly groaned. 'Please, Alice, no police.'

'I'm not promising anything, Solly. Not until we know what we're dealing with.'

Luke drove as fast as he could along the driveway, but with all the potholes and fallen branches, their progress was painfully slow. Alice tapped her fingers against the window, her stomach churning at what they might find.

When they reached the house and climbed out of the van, Alice peered through the darkness. No lights were on, and the whole place felt eerie. Then the moon came out from behind a cloud, and she gasped. 'Oh my goodness. This place is... is...'

'A wreck?' asked Luke. He moved closer and took Alice's hand. 'Everything is going to be alright,' he murmured.

Tears burned at the back of Alice's eyes, and the feel of her hand in Luke's was almost her undoing, but she refused to let the tears fall. Instead, she gave Luke's hand a quick squeeze, then turned to Solly. 'You know this place and your brother best. Where do you think they might be?'

'There's only one part of the house he uses,' said Solly. 'Follow me.'

Without thinking, Alice grabbed Luke's hand as they entered the eerie building, the only light coming from the torches on their phones. Solly moved with confidence, and Alice was glad he was with them. He led them to a thick oak door and paused, his ear pressed to the wood. Then, with a nod of his head, he started hammering on the door, shouting Jack's name. They breathed a collective sigh of relief at the squeal of a key being turned in a lock.

The door creaked open, and they stepped into the gloom. A single lamp on a long wooden table lit the room. As soon as she spotted May whimpering on the floor, Alice wanted to run to her. But Luke put an arm out and held her back. Alice followed his gaze to where Jack Tyler stood, a baseball bat resting on his shoulder.

'What on earth are you doing, Jack?' asked Solly, sounding exasperated rather than scared. 'That poor girl is terrified.'

'She was trespassing in my house!' barked Jack, adjusting the bat as if his arm were tiring.

At the sight of the bat moving, May yelped and pulled her knees closer to her chest.

'Whether or not she was trespassing, you don't hold a child hostage.' To Alice's amazement, Solly stepped up to his brother and grabbed the baseball bat from him. 'What on earth were you thinking, Jack? I doubt you've even got the strength to swing this damn thing.' He turned to May, then seemed to step back in shock. 'Oh my God.'

'Tilly,' said Jack, gripping onto Solly's arm. 'I'm not imagining it?'

'No.' Solly stared at May again. 'Bloody hell, Jack, no wonder you're shaking.'

Alice watched open-mouthed as Solly helped Jack into a seat. Jack should be in handcuffs, not treated with kid gloves. May jumped to her feet, ran across the room, and flung herself at Alice. Alice wrapped her arms around her sister and held her close as her body shook with sobs.

'Let's all calm down,' said Luke, stepping further into the room. He pulled a couple of old chairs out from under the table. 'Come and sit down,' he said, but May refused to budge.

'I'll have a seat if no one else wants one,' said Solly, flopping down into a hardbacked chair with a sigh.

'What's she doing here?' said Jack, shaking his head. 'Why is she here?'

'Jack,' said Solly, placing a hand over his brother's. 'It's not Tilly. This is May, Alice's sister.'

'I should have known something like this would happen with the Lovedays back in town.'

'May isn't a Loveday,' said Alice. 'And aren't we ignoring the elephant in the room? How dare you lock my sister in a room whilst wielding a baseball bat!'

'It wasn't as if I was going to use it,' said Jack, showing no sign of remorse.

'But she didn't know that! You've scared her half to death!'

'And what about me, eh? Waking up in the middle of the night to find someone creeping about my house?'

'May,' said Alice, pushing her sister back and brushing tears and damp hair from her face. 'What were you doing in Jack's house?'

May tried burying herself in Alice's shoulder once more, but Alice wouldn't let her.

'I'm sorry, May, but however appallingly Jack has behaved, you owe him an explanation.'

'Th... they... s... said... it... was an... initiation.'

'What? Who said that?'

'The girls,' said May, breaking into noisy sobs. She wiped her eyes and nose on her sleeve and tried again. 'They said if I wanted to be in their group, I had to come in here by myself.' May took a deep breath and turned to Jack. 'I didn't think anyone lived here, I promise. I'm so sorry.'

'A likely story,' said Jack, pushing himself to his feet and pointing a finger at May. 'Were you here to steal from me? Is that it? Or did you want to give me a heart attack, finish the job your father and mother started?'

'Phil?' asked May, screwing up her face. 'What's he got to do with this?'

'He's talking about my dad,' said Alice. 'As you know full well, Mr Tyler, May is no relation to Daniel Loveday. I am. Not that I've ever met the man.'

'Who were the girls who told you to come in here, May?' asked Luke.

May shook her head, so Alice replied for her. 'Paige Morris and her pals, am I right?' May nodded.

'Jack, May has apologised to you. I know you're still angry, but I'm sure Alice will think of a fitting punishment. Now I think it's your turn to apologise.'

'Don't you tell me to apologise, boy! I've done nothing wrong.'

'I think the police would take a very dim view of you holding a child hostage,' said Luke. 'What if someone had done that to one of your daughters?'

'Now, Luke, there's no need for that,' said Solly. 'She can't have been in here longer than half an hour and Jack called me almost straight away. It's not as if he intended to keep her prisoner up here, is it?'

Luke didn't reply and let the silence stretch out into the room.

'Fine,' said Jack. 'I'm sorry for frightening the girl. I just wanted to teach her a lesson.'

'You certainly did that,' said Alice. 'I think the best thing is for me to get May home. Jack, I promise May's trespassing won't go unpunished.'

Jack nodded, but refused to look at her.

'Luke, why don't you get the girls into your van,' said Solly. 'I'd like a moment with my brother, then I'll join you.'

'No problem.'

Solly was quiet when he joined them in the van, and no one spoke on the drive home. After dropping Solly off, Luke insisted on helping Alice get a trembling May into the cottage.

'You see to May, I'll put the kettle on,' he said when they got inside.

Alice led May through to her bedroom and turned on the lamp.

'Alice...'

'No, let's talk about this in the morning.'

'But...'

'You've had a nasty shock, and need to get to sleep.'

Alice helped May out of her clothes like she had when May was little, tucked her up in bed and sat stroking her hair until she finally fell asleep.

'Sorry that took so long,' said Alice as she joined Luke in the living room. 'And thank you for your help.'

'Here,' he said, handing her a cup of tea. 'If you want me to leave you in peace, I will.'

'No,' said Alice, her eyes filling with tears, 'please stay.'

Luke stood up from the armchair he'd been sitting in and joined her on the sofa. 'It's OK,' he said, putting his arm around her shoulders.

On reflex, Alice leaned into him, but the feeling of someone looking after her was too much, and she pulled away. 'I'm sorry,' she said, shaking her head and pushing back her shoulders. 'This mothering lark gets a bit much sometimes.'

'Don't you ever get angry?' asked Luke.

'Of course. May can be very difficult sometimes. But tonight...'

'I don't mean with May. Don't you ever feel anger towards your mum?'

Alice laughed, surprised by his question.

'I'm serious. In your position, I would be.'

Alice took a sip of her tea. 'I suppose it feels there's not much point. I resigned myself to my responsibilities a long time ago.'

'But that's just it, Alice. May shouldn't be your responsibility.'

'I'm her sister.'

'But not her mother.'

Alice leaned back in her chair. This conversation felt too personal, and if she was honest, dangerous. She could cope with her situation as long as she didn't give it too much thought. What was the point of being angry or frustrated? Her time would come, even if it took another ten years before she finally made it to university.

'You're amazing, you know that?' Luke reached out to take Alice's hand, but she moved it into her lap. She'd let her defenses down too much already. 'I'd better let you get to bed,' said Luke. He tried to sound upbeat, but Alice could hear the disappointment in his voice.

'Thank you so much for your help.'

'Anytime.' Luke leaned over, kissed Alice on the cheek, then left.

Rather than going straight to bed, Alice stayed on the sofa, aware of the tingle of her skin where he had kissed her.

Chapter 46

Alice knocked on the front door. It was pointless, as the knock wouldn't be heard, but it felt rude walking straight in. She gave it a couple of minutes before opening the heavy front door and stepping into the wreck of what would once have been an impressive home. It was shocking seeing the shell of a grand entrance hall in the daylight and made Alice even less sure she was doing the right thing.

Alice marched to the door of Jack's living quarters, not allowing herself the chance to back out. She knocked hard on the door and heard shuffling footsteps from the other side. When Jack opened the door and saw her, his face fell.

'I thought you were Solly. What are you doing here? Do you think it's acceptable to barge into someone else's home?'

'I knocked on the front door, but there was no answer.'

'Because I don't want visitors. Now please leave my property.'

'Not until we've talked.'

'I don't want to talk to you.'

Alice sighed, wondering if she should do as Jack wanted and leave. But what would that achieve? 'Listen, Mr Tyler, even if I wanted to leave Saffron Bay, I can't. Through no fault of my own, I am stuck living here, and as we're both going to be living in the same village for the foreseeable future, surely it would be best if we sorted things out between us?'

'I don't talk to Lovedays.'

'How many times do I have to tell you?' asked Alice, her voice rising in frustration. 'I've never even met my father. And anyway, I'm not here to talk about him. I'm here to apologise for my sister, and discuss a suitable punishment for her behaviour.'

Jack's eyes snapped up, his curiosity piqued. He turned and walked into the single room he lived in, and Alice took it as an invitation to follow. The scruffiness of the space was highlighted by the light streaming in from an enormous window. Alice tried to hide her shock at the state of Jack's living conditions and sat down at the table covered in mounds of paperwork. There weren't, she noticed, any dirty dishes lying around, and she realised the chaos of belongings was an organised chaos, and the space, although basic, was clean.

Jack sat opposite Alice, a cup of steaming tea in his hands. He didn't offer to make Alice one, not that she was expecting him to. 'Here,' she said, pulling an envelope from her bag and pushing it across the table. 'It's a letter of apology from May.'

Jack grunted and chucked the envelope on top of one of the piles of paperwork.

'May knows what she did last night was awful, and she is truly sorry. I've grounded her, but I wondered if you had any jobs you'd like to give her.'

'What are you talking about, woman?'

'I don't know. Perhaps she could do some gardening or something?'

Jack surprised Alice with a laugh. Although his smile didn't reach his eyes, Alice noticed how it transformed his face. She could see the handsome man lurking behind the gruffness, and realised he wasn't as old as he'd first seemed.

'What's the point of sending her up here to pull out a few weeds?'

'I don't know, I just thought she could help somehow.'

Jack leaned back in his chair and took a sip of his tea. 'Help?' he said, mulling over the word.

'Yes, to make up for her behaviour.'

'Talk to Margot.'

'Pardon?'

'Talk to Margot. There's nothing your sister can do up here, but once... well, let's just say I can't help the villagers as I once did. Margot will find her something to do.'

'You want May to help the villagers?' asked Alice, confused.

'Yes, get her to help with one of Margot's clubs.' Jack stood up and carried his mug to the sink.

Alice waited a moment, then realised this was her sign the conversation was over. 'I know I said I wasn't here to talk about my dad, but...'

'You've got what you came for,' said Jack, not turning round. 'Now I've got things to be getting on with.'

Alice left Saffron Manor and made her way straight to the café. When she walked in, noisy chatter assaulted her ears coming from a table surrounded by customers and covered in colourful balls of yarn.

'Oh, hello, Alice,' said Margot, her face flushed as she carried a tray groaning with tea and cake. 'Have you come to join our knit and natter group?'

'No, not today. I wondered if I could have a quick word?'

'Sure, just let me serve these customers, then I'll be right with you.'

Alice settled herself at the only free table in the corner of the room. The laughter coming from the knitting group made her uncomfortable. With a start, she realised why. When was the last time she had laughed like that? She'd only ever had a handful of friends, and they'd soon lost interest and drifted as her responsibilities had grown and she hadn't been able to join them on days out or nights clubbing.

'Sorry about that,' said Margot, sitting down opposite Alice. 'This is our busiest time of the week.'

'I can come back another day if it would be better?'

'No, now's fine, though I'll probably be called away soon. What can I do for you?'

'May's got herself into a bit of trouble. Last night some girls dared her to go into Saffron Manor.'

'Oh no!'

Alice grimaced. 'In her defence, she hadn't realised anyone still lived there, but even so.'

'I can imagine how well that went down with Jack.'

'He wasn't best pleased. I've been to see him this morning to ask how May can make it up to him, and he suggested I talk to you.'

'You went to see Jack Tyler?'

'Yes.'

'Wow. Why did he suggest you come to me?'

'He thought May could volunteer some time to help the local community. Do you have any bright ideas about how she could do that? She's at school all week but has Saturdays and Sundays free.'

'Residents from the local care home come here for tea and cake every Saturday morning. I'm sure they'd be delighted to see a youthful face around the place. Would that work?'

'That sounds perfect. You can expect her bright and early on Saturday morning.'

'Wonderful. Well, I'd best get back to it.' Margot stood to leave, then turned back to Alice. 'You know, your dad would be so proud of the young woman you've become.'

'What...' began Alice, but Margot had already walked away.

Chapter 47

Luke walked up the driveway of the fancy new build and steeled himself for what he was about to do. When Patricia opened the door, she was wearing a satin dressing gown but little else. Her face was fully made up, and Luke wondered if she ever took her makeup off.

'Luke, what a lovely surprise. Do you want to come in for a coffee?'

'No, thanks, but I'd like a quick chat, if that's alright.'

'Come in,' said Patricia. She stepped aside to let him across the threshold, and as he brushed past, she loosened the tie on her robe to expose more flesh. 'I need to get dressed, so you may as well have a coffee while you wait.' Patricia led him through to a marble-topped kitchen and began fiddling with a fancy coffee machine.

'There's no need to get dressed,' said Luke. 'This won't take long.'

Patricia turned around, her lips curled and eyes twinkling. 'Are you saying you like me like this?' she asked, pushing out her chest and giggling as the silk slid even lower down her skin.

'No,' said Luke, turning his head, 'that's not what I meant. I'll have that coffee after all, and you can put some clothes on.'

Patricia made a coffee and pushed it across the breakfast bar. 'Here,' she said, 'I won't be long.'

It was a further fifteen minutes before Patricia reappeared, and Luke wondered what she'd been doing, as in her skin-tight vest and shorts, she seemed to be wearing little more than before.

'Is Paige here?' he asked.

'No,' said Patricia with a smile. 'We've got the house all to ourselves.' She dragged a bar stool so close to Luke's that when she perched on it, they were almost sitting on top of each other.

'I came to talk to you about Paige,' said Luke, shifting his stool back, hating the way his body instinctively responded to her proximity. 'She needs to stay away from May.'

'May?'

'May Green, Alice Loveday's sister.'

'Oh, her,' said Patricia. 'I'd be delighted if she could, but that wretched girl won't leave Paige alone. She seems rather desperate if you ask me.'

'That's not the impression I got,' said Luke. 'Last night, Paige and her friends took May up to Saffron Manor. They told her it was an initiation into their group and made her go in.'

'Made her?' asked Patricia, with an eyebrow raised. 'We're not talking about five-year-olds, Luke. The girls are fifteen. If May went trespassing into Jack's home, it was of her own accord. If anything, she's the bad influence. Poor Paige has tried asking her to leave them alone nicely, but May won't get the message.'

'Come on, Patricia, drop the act. You know as well as I do what Paige is like.'

'What are you implying?' asked Patricia, jumping off her stool and placing her hands on her hips.

'I'm saying Paige is the ringleader, and the other girls in the village do as they're told.'

'How dare you come into my home and criticise my daughter and, by implication, my parenting? What would you know about raising children? You can't even keep hold of a girlfriend, let alone start a family.'

'I'm not claiming to know about parenting,' said Luke, trying to stay calm, 'but I'm telling you what Paige has been up to so you can put a stop to it. I'm here as a friend.'

'A friend? Oh, you're no friend of mine, Luke. You're here because you've taken a fancy to Alice Loveday and are trying to be her knight in shining armour. I'd stay well clear of that little witch if I were you. Lovedays have a habit of causing trouble around here.'

'The only person causing trouble around here is your daughter.'

Patricia stared at him and shook her head. Luke was surprised to see tears filling her eyes. 'You talk about Paige as if she's a stranger. Doesn't it mean anything that you loved her once?'

'Of course it does,' said Luke, 'but that doesn't mean I can ignore her behaviour.'

Patricia walked across to a plush white armchair and sat down, perching on the edge of the seat, fiddling with one of her long nails. When she spoke, her voice was slow and deliberate, but Luke knew her well enough to know she was trying to hold back tears. 'I asked for your help with Paige. Did you ever even speak to her?'

When Patricia looked at him, it was like a mask slipped, and Luke saw the vulnerability behind her bolshy persona. He saw a frightened mother, and the woman he'd once loved. When he shook his head, a rush of shame flooded through him. Should he have tried harder to stay in Paige's life? Duncan made it clear Luke was no longer needed, but maybe it gave him a convenient way out. 'I'm sorry.'

'It's not your fault. She's not your daughter. But please, Luke, it's one thing not to help when I ask for it, it's another to come around here criticising my parenting. I'm trying my best.' Patricia stood up and brushed invisible fluff from her clothes. She pushed back her shoulders and when she looked at Luke, the mask was firmly back in place.

'I'll try to speak to Paige about what's happened.'

'Don't bother,' said Patricia with a shake of her head. 'You've already made up your mind about what happened. The last thing Paige needs is you coming in all guns blazing. I think you should go now, Luke. And please tell your girlfriend to keep her sister away from my daughter.'

'She's not my...'

'Just go.'

Luke held his hands up. 'OK, I'm going.'

As Luke walked away from Patricia's house, he cursed his good intentions and couldn't shake the feeling he'd just made everything ten times worse.

Chapter 48

'Hey, Milo,' said Alice, as the Golden Retriever raced towards her, jumping up and covering her jeans in the sand from his paws.

'I'm so sorry, Alice,' shouted Sam, running across the beach, a lead in her hand. When she reached Alice, she bent over, trying to catch her breath. 'He's such a naughty dog. Look at what you've done to Alice's clothes, Milo!'

'It's alright,' said Alice. 'I don't mind. It's nice to be greeted so warmly by a villager, even if he isn't human.'

'Have you got time for a walk?' asked Sam. 'Milo could do with a bit longer to burn off some of his excess energy, and it would be good to have a chat.'

'Sure,' said Alice. 'The work on the cottage is never-ending, so an extra half an hour away from it won't make much difference. What did you want to talk to me about?'

Sam threw a stick for Milo, and they began walking along the beach. 'I feel you've not had the best start in Saffron Bay, and I want to apologise for any part I've played in that.'

'It's fine, I get it. My dad is a persona non grata in Saffron Bay, even though no one seems to know what he did, and by default, that means everyone's suspicious of me.'

'No!' said Sam. 'No one's suspicious of you, and deep down, I don't think anyone hates Daniel. Everyone loved him when he was living here.'

'Come on, Sam. The Loveday name is mud around here.'

Sam kicked up sand and pebbles as she walked, and seemed unsure of what to say.

'Perhaps I should leave you in peace?'

'No, Alice, please don't. Listen, you deserve an explanation, and I'll try to give you one. I was honest when I said I didn't know what happened that night, but I know what happened after with Jack.'

'What do you mean?'

'If Saffron Bay had ever had a king, Jack Tyler would have been it. Yes, he could be a grumpy sod, but everyone knew what he did for the village. He was a good man, Alice, a very good man. Beneath the gruff facade lay a man generous to a fault. It was as if he owed the village, or couldn't reconcile his personal success and humble beginnings. He gave to the village to the detriment of his own family.'

'In what way?'

'He never admitted it, but we all knew the anonymous donations came from him. When the church roof needed repairing, someone put an envelope through the vicar's door containing a thousand pounds. When the village hall was destroyed in a flood, an anonymous donor funded a complete rebuild of the community centre you see today.

Likewise, the school, doctor's surgery, even the pub were all kept on their feet by the village's guardian angel.'

'When you say to the detriment of his own family, what do you mean?'

'I can't say for sure, and this is all based on rumour, but from what I've heard, Jack became careless with his money. He was falling deeper into debt, but spending just as much as before. The irony is, whatever happened with Daniel, it's unlikely Jack would have been able to keep propping up the village financially.'

'But my dad made for an easy scapegoat.'

'Exactly. What happened the night of the fire is still hazy, but it was obvious Dan was involved in some way and at least partly responsible for what happened next. One minute Jack's family moves away and the man himself disappears from village life, the next your dad and his parents leave the village suddenly. The rumour mill got to work, and people put two and two together.'

'I'm still not sure I understand why there's such a grudge being held.'

'A seaside village is hard to keep going. Businesses don't last long around here.'

'But what about all the tourism?'

'The tourist season is short and unreliable when it's cheaper for families to get guaranteed sunshine on the continent. And with so many properties being sold off for second homes, you end up with an unstable community and an even less stable income.'

'You manage alright in the shop though, don't you?'

'We don't make a profit in the shop. Steve does graphic design work on the side, and I work part-time as a teaching assistant at the school. We keep the shop going for the sake of the community, but it's more like running a charity than a business.'

'I didn't realise things were so hard around here.'

'Not many people do. People look back and see the past as a golden age. In that context, you can see how some may lay the blame for the village's struggles at your dad's door. I'm not saying they're right, or that it makes sense, just trying to help you understand.'

'Thank you,' said Alice. 'I appreciate it. Hey, can I ask you something?'

'Go ahead.'

'Were Margot and my dad close?'

'What, like romantically?' asked Sam, laughing. 'Not that there's anything wrong with an older woman hooking up with a younger man.'

'No, I don't mean romantically. I mean, were they friends?'

'I'm really not sure. Why do you ask?'

'Something she said to me earlier. It made me wonder if she knew my dad better than she's let on. And there's something else, although this is a bit weird...'

'Now I'm intrigued.'

'Someone had cleaned the cottage before we moved in.'

'What? Who knew you were coming?'

'That's just it. No one knew. I didn't even know until a few days before.'

'I'm really confused.'

'Same,' said Alice, picking up a piece of driftwood and throwing it for a delighted Milo. 'The only explanation I can think of is someone in the village knew I'd inherit the cottage when I turned twenty-five, which means they must also have known my birthday, and been in contact with Dad after he left the village.'

'And you're wondering if that person is Margot?'

'I can't think who else it could be.'

'Yes, alright,' Sam told Milo, taking the saliva-covered stick from his mouth and throwing it further down the beach. She turned back to Alice and frowned. 'You might be right, you know. I'd forgotten, because it was so long ago now, but Daniel was best friends with Margot's son, Marty. You know Marty died young?'

Alice nodded.

'I was still quite young when it happened, but it must have affected both Margot and Daniel deeply. I don't remember them being friends as such, she's much older than him. But it's possible they were drawn to each other from a shared sense of grief. If she did clean the cottage, I can't see why she'd keep that from you. Are you going to talk to her about it?'

'I don't think I have much choice.'

Chapter 49

'Whatever you do, don't knock the hatch. The lock's broken and only works from the other side. I'll prop it open with this.' Luke rested an old cricket bat against the hatch door.

'Are you sure it's safe up there?'

'It is as long as you're not scared of spiders.'

'Not at all. I actually rather like them. It's whatever's scampering around up there at night I'd like to get rid of.'

'Your wish is my command,' said Luke, pulling himself up into the dusty attic and picking up his torch. It felt good to help Alice again. With the cottage in a liveable state, there'd been little call on his skills lately. He could think of ways he'd rather help than exterminating whatever critters were keeping Alice and May awake at night, but you had to take an opportunity when it presented itself. 'Are you OK getting up here? Do you need a hand?' he offered out his arm, but Alice shook her head.

'I'll be fine,' she said, holding tight to the metal sides of the ladder. The ladder wobbled, and Alice closed her eyes, taking a few deep breaths before climbing higher. Luke fought the urge to reach down and help.

'The wood around the hatch opening is in reasonable condition and should support your weight. Put your hands here and pull yourself up.'

Alice lifted her shaking hands from the ladder and onto the loft hatch. 'Before moving here, I spent a few months working in a warehouse lugging around heavy boxes,' she said, pushing herself up from the elbows. 'I'm glad the muscles I gained there are coming in handy.'

Luke laughed. 'It doesn't sound like the best job in the world.'

'It was OK,' said Alice, tentatively standing up on a wooden board. 'It paid the bills.'

'Careful where you step,' said Luke, bending his head to avoid the sloping ceiling. 'You can see where the beams run. Stick to those if you can. So what will you do when you finish your degree?' He held out a hand as Alice wobbled, and she took it.

'If I get a degree,' she said. 'I don't know. I'd like to teach, I guess. A bit of a cliché, I know, but I had an amazing music teacher in high school, and I'd like to inspire kids like she inspired me. Life was pretty tough growing up, music brought colour into my world.'

Even in the torchlight, Luke could see the uncertainty in her eyes. He wanted to tell her she was amazing and could be whatever she wanted to be, but felt it would overstep an invisible mark. Instead, he bent down and examined the attic floor. 'The good news is these little poops are too small to belong to rats. It looks to me like you've had a family of mice living up here.'

'Yuck.'

'Mice are cute. I'll get some humane traps to put up here.'

'Thanks. You know, this is actually a great space.'

'Isn't it?' said Luke, waving his torch around. 'It might be worth thinking about converting it in the future. It wouldn't be too big a job to put some windows in, or you could go all out with dormers and maybe even a balcony looking out to sea.'

'Woah, now you're getting ahead of yourself. I'll start by getting some insulation in here. When I win the lottery, I'll think about attic conversions.'

'Fair enough.' As Luke inspected the space, the beam of his torch landed on a box in one corner. 'Can you see that?'

'Do you think it's the home of a certain mouse family?' asked Alice with a shudder. 'If it is, I don't want to go anywhere near it. Give me cobwebs and a family of spiders any day. There's something about rodent tails that freaks me out.'

Luke laughed and took Alice's hand. 'Come on, let's investigate.'

'Can you check it out first?'

Luke rolled his eyes. 'Fine.'

As he let go of Alice's hand, she stumbled back, knocking the cricket bat holding the hatch lid up. 'Oh no.'

'Hang on,' said Luke, bending down to lift it. After five minutes and no luck, he sighed, and sat down heavily on a beam. 'Looks like we're stuck.'

'I'm so sorry,' said Alice. 'Aren't you due at work? Can you ring them to let them know you'll be late?'

'I could if I'd brought my phone up here with me. It's down in the kitchen.'

'Oh.'

'Yes, oh. What time was it when we came up here?'

'About two, I think.'

'And when does May get back?'

'Five. And now I won't be able to meet her at the bus stop.'

'Is she still struggling with Paige and her gang?'

'It's mostly just name-calling, and she says it doesn't bother her, but she's so quiet these days. I wish I could make things better.'

'I could try talking to Paige.'

'You know her well enough to do that?'

'I was planning on adopting her once,' said Luke, disguising his discomfort with a laugh.

'What happened?'

'Patricia left me waiting at the altar. Turned out she'd been sleeping with someone else behind my back and ended up marrying him instead.'

'Oh, Luke, I'm so sorry.'

'Don't be. It was a lucky escape. I'm not sure I ever loved Patricia. I was in love with the idea of creating a family of my own. Ever since my parents died, it's all I've ever wanted, but there are limited options in Saffron Bay.' He swung his torch beam around the attic, suppressing a sigh. While part of him was delighted to be spending an entire afternoon with Alice, his client would not be. He'd only nipped out for half an hour and dreaded the reaction when he arrived back on site after all the other trades had left.

'I really am sorry about our being stuck up here,' said Alice.

'It's not your fault.'

'Well, it wasn't Mrs Mouse who knocked over the cricket bat.'

Luke laughed and held out his hand. 'Come on, if we're stuck in here, we may as well do something useful. Let's check out that box and see what's inside.'

'Fine,' said Alice, taking his hand and letting him guide her across the beams. 'But you're looking in there first.'

As they picked their way across the patchwork of beams, Luke felt a fluttering of nerves. He'd been waiting for the right time to talk to Alice about what Margot had revealed, and if they were going to be stuck up here for hours, surely, this was the perfect opportunity? But what if it proved a case of shoot the messenger? Did he really want to put himself in the firing line? And how would she feel to find out her dad had been alive and kicking, and ignoring her existence for the past twenty-five years? Perhaps it was kinder to say nothing, or wait until Margot heard from Daniel and let him explain himself?

'What's in it?' asked Alice when they reached the box.

Luke crouched down in front of it and held his torch between his lips. He peeled back the lid and had a rummage around. He took hold of the torch and lifted a tatty book for Alice to see. 'It's just a box of old books. There are no mice here that I can see, but there is evidence of them getting hungry.' He shone the torch onto the ragged edge of the pages, where something had been having a good nibble.

'Wonderful. And you're sure the mice aren't there now?'

Luke checked the box again. 'Certain.'

'I suppose that's something. And at least we'll have something to entertain us for the next few hours.'

Luke's heart sank. He'd been thinking of other ways they could pass the time, and none of them involved reading mouse-nibbled old books. 'Here,' he said, handing a musty-smelling paperback to Alice. 'Is Pride and Prejudice your thing?'

'Oh yes,' said Alice. She sat cross-legged on the beam, shuffling to get comfortable. 'You'll have to sit next to me so we can share the torch.'

'Of course.' Luke pulled a copy of Wuthering Heights from the box and sat on the beam beside Alice. Their thighs were touching, and his heart raced as her arm brushed against his. 'Is that enough light?'

'Great, thanks.' She turned to look at him, and he could feel the warmth of her breath on his cheek. Their noses were almost touching. He leaned forward a little, his lips inches from hers. The air in the attic seemed suddenly dense and warm, the light from the torch softer than before. Just as his lips scuffed hers, Alice jolted away. 'What was that?'

Luke inwardly groaned. Please say Mrs Mouse hadn't just ruined the moment. He risked placing his fingers on her cheek and guiding her face back to his. For a moment, Alice seemed to hesitate, then she tilted her head to one side, and with an apologetic smile said, 'Something just fell out of that book.'

Understanding the moment had passed, Luke directed his torch light between two beams. 'Looks like a photo,' he said, as Alice reached down to retrieve it. She held it up in the beam of light. 'Why's there a photo of May up here?' asked Luke, staring at the young girl in a summer dress smiling into the camera.

'That's not May,' said Alice, turning the photo over. On the back, someone had written *Tilly Tyler, Saffron Manor, July, 2000.*

'Tilly Tyler? I don't get it,' said Luke. 'She's the spitting image of May, if May had long hair.'

'That's because they're related,' said Alice, her voice hoarse. 'Tilly is short for Mathilda, right? Luke, this is Maz. This is my mum.'

Chapter 50

Luke stared at the photograph, then frowned at Alice. 'Your mum? How can that be your mum? I thought May's last name was Green?'

'It is. And so is Mum's.'

'Then how can Tilly Tyler be Maz Green?'

Alice shrugged. 'Could it have been her mother's maiden name? Or maybe she just picked out a random surname and adopted it as her own.'

'But why would she do that?'

Alice scrubbed her hands through her hair. 'How should I know? Luke, I'm as clueless as you are. We need to talk to Jack.'

'We should talk to Gran first.'

'We need to get out of here before we can talk to anyone,' said Alice, staring forlornly at the closed hatch. 'I don't get it. If Maz used to be called Tilly Tyler, does that mean she's Jack Tyler's daughter?'

'Maybe, or at least some relation.'

'But both Rita and Sam have told me Maz was here on holiday. Surely they'd have known if she was Jack's daughter?'

'You'd think, wouldn't you? This doesn't make any sense at all.'

'Either way,' said Alice. 'Someone has been lying to me. It's either Sam or Maz.'

'What did Maz tell you about her parents?'

'Nothing, except she was estranged from them and hadn't seen them in years. Given the way Maz lived her life and the way we grew up, I always assumed they'd done something terrible to her, so I never pushed it. And I never thought for a second she might have come from a wealthy background. We scraped through life by the skin of our teeth. We never had new clothes, shoes, or toys. The amount of stick I suffered at school for wearing hand-me-downs, and all the while, Maz could have gone to her parents for help?' Alice was fighting a losing battle against the anger welling up inside her.

'Hey,' said Luke, placing an arm around Alice. She felt her trembling limbs still and sucked in a deep breath, fighting the urge to rest her head on his shoulder. 'We don't know anything for certain right now. Let's stay calm until we have a few facts under our belt.'

'OK,' said Alice, rubbing the cuff of her jumper against her damp eyes. 'Everything's such a muddle and I feel like I've been flung into the middle of someone else's story without knowing the beginning or end. If only my dad were around and I could ask him what really happened.'

'Alice, there's something...'

‘What are you doing up here?’ The hatch flew open, and May stuck her head through the gap. ‘Oh, sorry, are you having a moment?’

Alice jumped up. ‘No, we were trying to deal with the rodent problem and got stuck. What are you doing home so early?’

‘There was a fire in the science lab, so we all got sent home. Just as well, from the looks of things. How long have you been up here?’

‘Only about half an hour,’ said Luke.

‘With the mice? Gross. What’s that?’ May pointed to the photograph in Alice’s hand.

‘Oh, nothing,’ she said, shoving the photograph in her pocket. ‘Just a postcard we found in a box of old books.’

‘Boring. So, are you coming down, or do you want to stay up here?’

Without answering, Alice picked her way across the beams, and Luke followed. She climbed down the ladder, relieved to be back in the daylight. ‘Why don’t you use the afternoon for revision?’

May rolled her eyes, picked up her backpack and trudged towards her bedroom.

‘I’m going to pop round to Sylvie’s for a bit,’ Alice called after her.

May kept walking, giving Alice a thumbs-up to show she’d heard.

‘Are you alright?’ asked Luke, folding up the ladder. ‘You’ve had quite a shock.’

'I'm fine, but I want some answers. I'm going to see Sylvie. Want to come?'

Luke glanced at his watch and pulled a face. 'I'd love to, but I'll lose the contract if I don't get back to work. Will you message me later so I know how you got on?'

Alice nodded. For a moment Luke paused, holding her gaze, and Alice felt her palms go sweaty. Despite herself, she'd grown fond of Luke, and it was impossible not to notice how attractive he was, but was she ready for this? He'd said it himself; he wanted a family. After years of being tied down with May, starting a family of her own was the last thing on Alice's mind. She'd be trapped for another god-knows how long. No, this wasn't right. She wasn't right. Luke deserved someone who could give him all he dreamed of. 'I'd better get going.'

Luke cleared his throat. 'Yes, OK. Message me, yeah?'

'Will do.'

Alice walked the short distance to Sylvie's front door and knocked. *Please let Sylvie be in*, she thought, unable to bear a moment longer smothered by the sludge of family secrets.

'Oh, Alice, how lovely to see you,' said Sylvie, answering the door with a flour-covered apron tied around her waist. 'Had we arranged for you to come over for some piano practice? I'm sorry, it must have slipped my mind.'

'No, I'm not here to play the piano. Can I come in, Sylvie? There's something I need to talk to you about.'

'Of course, but do you mind sitting in the kitchen? I'm making some cheese scones for Jack and Solly and have reached a crucial stage.'

'Of course not,' said Alice, following Sylvie through the house.

Sylvie filled the kettle, then checked the temperature of the oven. 'Sit down, love. What is it you wanted to talk about?'

Alice pulled the photograph from her pocket and slid it across the table. Sylvie picked it up with trembling fingers, then pulled out a chair, slumping into it, all thoughts of the scones she was baking forgotten.

Chapter 51

'Where did you find this?' asked Sylvie, frowning at the photograph.

'It was in an old book we found in the attic.'

'We?'

'Luke and I.'

'Ah.'

'It's my mum outside Saffron Manor. But the name on the back says Tilly Tyler. What's going on, Sylvie? Who was Tilly to Jack?'

The kettle whistled, and instead of answering, Sylvie stood up and made a pot of tea. To Alice, the seconds felt like hours as Sylvie laid out cups, saucers, a jug of milk, and finally the teapot on the table. She poured tea into the cups slowly, avoiding Alice's eye. Was she about to lie? Was she using the moment to get her story straight?

Alice needn't have worried. For after handing her a cup, Sylvie looked directly at her and said, 'I'll tell you the truth, Alice. At least, as much as I know of the truth.'

'Thank you.'

Sylvie picked up the photograph once more and twirled it between her fingers. 'You're right, this is your mother. Tilly Tyler, as she was known back then, is Jack's daughter.'

Alice had suspected as much, but the news came as a shock. She'd gone from having no family to having a grandfather who hated her guts. Great. 'So, Sam lied to me.'

'Sam probably didn't know. Jack kept his children away from the village. The younger girls sometimes went down to the beach, but Tilly was a few years older than the others. Mary, Jack's wife, had moved here from Ireland and, from what I've heard, it was a source of tension between the couple. The compromise they reached was that Mary and her daughters would spend the school holidays in Ireland with her side of the family. The girls never attended the local school, so never mixed with local children.'

'But why wouldn't Maz, Tilly, whatever her name is, have told her friends she was Jack's daughter?'

Sylvie shrugged. 'Your guess is as good as mine. From what Solly's told me, she was quite the tearaway. Jack ended up sending her to boarding school to instill some discipline, but it didn't work. When she came home that summer, she was even more reckless than before. She had a tumultuous relationship with her father, and I suppose didn't want to be associated with him. Or perhaps she just enjoyed playing the role of holidaymaker and keeping an air of mystery. Who knows?'

'When did you find out who she was?'

'The day before your father left Saffron Bay. I was good friends with Solly, even then. He came over here distraught one day, and it all came spilling out. Tilly was pregnant, and Daniel was the father.'

'Hang on, so all this has been about Maz being pregnant and not the fire?'

'It's about both. Mary was away in Ireland, staying with her parents, when Jack found out about the baby. Tilly was only sixteen. He was furious and forced her to admit who the father was. He demanded she end the pregnancy, threatening to disown her if she didn't. On the night of the fire, Jack had gone up to London to meet his lawyer. I don't know what happened that night, and neither does Solly. What we know is that the next day Tilly was gone. Jack called Daniel's parents up to the big house for a meeting, and the next thing we knew, they were packing up the house and leaving the village.'

'Did my mum see Jack again?'

'No. Never. He tried looking for her but never found her.'

Alice couldn't help laughing. 'Tried looking for her? He can't have tried very hard! She was in Plymouth the whole time!'

'I understand why you're angry.'

'Do you really? I've been lied to throughout my entire life. I've had to pick up the pieces of my parent's mistakes, take on responsibility for May, put my life on hold, and all the while Maz had a support network up the road she could have called on?' Alice stood and pushed back her chair. Her entire body was shaking uncontrollably, her vision blurred. Alice closed her eyes, and when she opened them, Sylvie was standing beside her. Without a word, Sylvie took Alice's hand and led her to the sitting room, giving her shoulders a gentle push until she was sitting on the piano stool.

'You've had a terrible shock,' said Sylvie. 'Playing might help.'

Alice didn't notice Sylvie slip out of the room. She didn't notice the sun filtering in through the window, the ticking of the grandfather clock, or the gurgling of the radiator. Her fingers spread across the keys of Sylvie's piano. With no conscious decision of what to play, her fingers decided for her, beginning the lightning runs of Chopin's *Revolutionary Etude*. The fingers of her left hand moved in a frenzy, loosening the threads of confusion inside her mind. As her left hand ran across the keys, the right hammered out her anger in aggressive minor chords. With each chord played, Alice felt the dome of anger inside her crack, fragments of rage giving way to calm and sadness.

The music became all-consuming. Alice was no longer a sister, a mother-figure, a downtrodden woman who should have been in her prime. It was just her and the music, her mind free from all that had filled it moments before. The experience of playing was as close to a trance as Alice had experienced, and she leaned into it, allowing the music to wash away her anger and tension.

She finished the piece, closed the lid of the piano, and collapsed onto it, exhausted. She allowed herself a moment, just lying there, head in hands. The smell of baking wafted in from the kitchen, and Alice remembered she was in someone else's home. Resting here was an indulgence she couldn't afford. With a sigh, she climbed off the piano stool and went to find Sylvie.

'You really are a marvel,' said Sylvie, as Alice appeared in the doorway. 'Did playing help?'

Alice managed a smile. 'Yes, it did. Thank you.'

'Would you like another cup of tea?'

'No, thank you. I need to get back. May needs to know what I've found out today.'

'Are you sure that's a good idea? You don't want to upset her too much with exams just around the corner.'

'That's true, but I've had enough of secrets and May deserves to hear the truth.'

'All right, but remember, I'm here if you need me.'

Alice surprised Sylvie by crossing the room and pulling her into a hug. Then she turned and left the house, dreading May's reaction to the news, but knowing she had no choice but to share it.

Chapter 52

Luke stretched and yawned. Spending an entire afternoon fitting insulation was not his idea of fun. On the whole, he loved his job, but the architect who designed the house he was working on had filled it with pretentious angles that made cutting the pieces of insulation fiddly and laborious. He needed to get out in the fresh air, and decided that rather than heading straight home, he would have a quick walk along the beach.

Seaview was unsurprisingly close to the sea, so Luke left his van in the driveway. He checked his phone before pocketing it, but there was no news from Alice. She must have spoken to Sylvie by now. Was she too upset to message, or had she forgotten? Not wanting to put pressure on her, Luke decided he'd call his gran when he got home.

The day was sunny, and although the breeze carried a chill, there was a hint of warmth in the air, the sea almost turquoise as the high tide stole much of the beach. Several families were out, school trousers rolled up the legs of children as they jumped, the waves slapping against the shore, jumpers turning yellow as sand sprayed from spades making sand-castles.

Luke felt a tug of longing deep inside him. Was a family of his own really too much to ask for? He wasn't ugly; he had a steady job, people seemed to like him, yet ever since Patricia, he'd struggled to find anyone he wanted to settle down with. Alice was the first woman he'd met who he could picture a future with, and yet the timing was awful. She had enough on her plate without being lumbered with his needs. And besides, what Alice wanted was to be free, not tied down. Maybe in five years she might be ready for the life he wanted, but could he really wait that long? Would she even want him to?

Luke carried on walking, his eye drawn to a solitary figure angrily chucking pebbles into the sea. He shielded his eyes and squinted against the sun before picking up his pace. By the time he reached her, he was out of breath, his shoes damp from a wave which had caught him unawares.

'Hi, Paige.'

The girl looked up at him and screwed up her pretty face. 'What do you want?'

'Just to say hi. I've been meaning to catch up with you for a while.'

'Mum told you to, is that it?' Luke felt his cheeks redden, and Paige must have noticed. 'Thought so.'

'Fine, your mum asked me to check in with you, but I wanted to anyway. It's been ages since we caught up.'

'And who's fault's that?'

'I don't know,' said Luke, 'but it's not mine.'

Paige spun around, oblivious of the water now soaking into her jeans. 'Not your fault? It was Mum who dumped you, not me. You were the one who turned their back on me. It wasn't fair. I had done nothing wrong!'

'I thought it was best you got to know Duncan without me hanging around.'

'Duncan never liked me.'

'I didn't know that.'

'You wouldn't, would you?'

'Listen, Paige, I'm sorry. I was really hurt by what your mum did to me, but I shouldn't have used that as an excuse to sever ties with you. I honestly thought it was for the best, but now I can see I got it wrong.'

'I wanted you to be my dad.' Paige's voice was tiny, childlike, and at first Luke wasn't sure he'd heard right. But the tears glistening on her cheeks confirmed it.

'And I wanted you to be my daughter.' The words caught in Luke's throat, and he coughed.

'I hate Mum,' said Paige, hurt replaced by anger in her voice.

'Everyone messes up and makes mistakes. I'm sure she means well. She's trying her best.' Why am I defending her? wondered Luke.

'Well, her best isn't good enough.' Paige picked up a large stone, hurled it into the sea with a shriek, then smirked as it landed near a little boy, sending a torrent of icy water onto his clothes. She turned to Luke, her hands on her hips. 'Now Duncan's dumped Mum, why can't you two get back together?'

Luke picked up a pebble of his own and threw it into the sea. 'Life doesn't work like that, Paige. Your mum and I are different people now.'

'Yeah, and you fancy that cow Alice Loveday.'

'Alice has nothing to do with my not wanting to date your mum.'

'Yeah, right. She's a stuck-up cow, just like her sister.'

'Stuck up? Is that what you really think of Alice and May? Honestly, Paige, I expected more from you.'

'More from me? What are you talking about?'

'The way you've been treating May. It's nasty, vindictive. She's had such a rough time of it lately. You may hate your mum, but at least she's there for you. May's mum has up and left just when she's about to sit her exams.'

'I don't think being left a house in Saffron Bay is such a hardship, do you?'

'You've been inside. You know it's not like that. May and Alice aren't entitled rich girls, and even if they were, what does it matter to you?'

Paige kicked at the sand.

'Look, I'm not here to fight with you, Paige. I'd love it if you could reflect a bit on how you've treated May, but as you've pointed out, I'm not part of your life anymore, so it's not my place to tell you what to do.'

'I'm glad we agree about something.'

'Can we start again?' asked Luke. 'Your mum and I don't have to be together for us to hang out.'

'Isn't that creepy? An old guy like you hanging out with a fifteen-year-old girl.'

'Probably, if you weren't almost my stepdaughter once upon a time. Anyway, I was only suggesting a coffee or hot chocolate from time to time, just to keep up to date on each other's lives. I never wanted to lose touch with you after your mum and I split, and I see now it was a mistake on my part.'

Paige stared out to sea. Sensing the conversation was over, Luke said his goodbyes and walked away.

'Luke!'

Luke turned around.

'I hate coffee, but I'd let you buy me a hot chocolate sometime.'

Luke smiled. 'Great, I'll look forward to it.'

As he walked along the beach, Luke felt lighter. His lack of contact with Paige had been nagging at him for years. He knew he'd let her down, whether or not he meant to, and to have the chance to put things right felt like a step in the right direction. His thoughts inevitably turned to Alice, and he hoped she had had as successful a day as he had.

Chapter 53

Alice wasn't surprised to find May in her bedroom studying. If nothing else, her sister was determined, and not about to let a few pesky things like a house move, being abandoned by her mother and some light bullying get in the way of her grades. Not for the first time, Alice had to push down envy. Somehow, May managed to remain cool and popular, whilst also being an A grade student who took her work seriously. Alice's own school days weren't so long ago that she couldn't appreciate what a hard balance that was to achieve.

'Can I come in for a minute?' asked Alice, knocking gently on the doorframe.

'Sure.' May closed the book she'd been writing in and signalled for Alice to sit on the bed. She'd added her own touches to the room over the past few weeks, and the room was a riot of colour with its Indian throws and dream catchers in the window. 'Are you alright?'

'Not really. I've had a bit of a shock.'

'Another one?' May raised a perfectly plucked eyebrow, and Alice couldn't help but smile. 'Come on,' said May, flopping down onto the bed beside Alice and hugging her favourite cushion. 'Tell me all about it.'

Alice handed May the photograph. 'What do you make of that?'

'Is that Mum when she was younger?' she asked with a frown.

'Yes, she's the spit of you, with longer hair, obviously.'

'Where did you find the picture?'

'Inside a book in the attic. I've just shown it to Sylvie, and she confirmed it was Maz, but not only that.' Alice took a deep breath. 'May, I think Jack Tyler is our granddad.'

'What?' May frowned, then spluttered with laughter. 'Our grandad? You're having a laugh.'

'I'm not.' Alice took back the photo and turned it around. 'See, Tilly Tyler. It's there in black and white.'

'That bast... *man* is our grandad?'

'It looks that way. Don't you remember him muttering something about Tilly while holding you hostage?'

'I've tried to block that whole evening from my mind,' said May with a shudder. 'What are you going to do about it? Can we call Mum and ask her?'

'No, she messaged a couple of days ago to say she's on a month-long silent retreat.'

May laughed. 'A silent retreat? Maz? Yeah, good luck with that one. You're not going to talk to Jack about it, are you?'

'That was one option I'd thought about.'

'Don't.' May threw her cushion down onto the bed and turned to face Alice. 'Please don't, Alice. I don't want anything to do with that man. If he finds out we're his grandchildren, he might come sniffing around. Please, I want nothing to do with him.'

'At the very least, he must suspect the connection. It's hard not to notice your resemblance to Maz. But if you're not ready to approach him, I'll respect that. It's not like it makes much difference to our day-to-day lives, is it? But at least we now know why he hates us.'

'I still don't really get that.'

'From what Sylvie said, he knew Maz was pregnant and told her to get rid of the baby, get rid of me,' said Alice with a shudder. 'Instead, she ran away from home and never spoke to him again. I can understand why he's angry, and why he'd blame my dad. She must have been sixteen when she got pregnant. If someone had done that to you, I'd want to kill them.'

'But it wasn't like he forced her.'

'No, but he was older. He should have known better. And then to abandon her and leave her to raise me alone? That's unforgivable as far as I'm concerned.'

'At least he gave you a house.'

Alice couldn't help laughing. 'True, and whilst I'm incredibly grateful to have a roof over my head, it's not exactly the lap of luxury, is it?'

'Look at that,' said May, pointing out of the window to where the sun was sitting like a ball of fire just above the horizon, turning the sky into a pastel watercolour painting. 'There are worse places to be. You know, as much as I hate Maz for lying to us all these years, I'm kind of glad you told me.'

'Why?'

'Because ever since we moved here, this has felt like your place. This was your dad's home, not mine. You were the one with links to Saffron Bay. I suppose I've felt like an imposter, clinging to your coattails, along for the ride. Knowing I'm a Tyler makes me feel more like I've a right to be here. And it makes me feel closer to you.' May took Alice's hand, and Alice had to blink away tears.

'You know, for a teenager, you're not half bad.'

'Thanks,' said May. 'But please, Alice, can we keep this revelation to ourselves for now, or at least until my exams are over? I can't face any more drama right now.'

'How's it been with Paige Morris and her friends lately? I've had a feeling you've been playing things down.'

May drew her knees up to her chest and hugged her arms around them. 'It's nothing I can't cope with. They call me names whenever I see them, but I just turn the volume up on my headphones, so they're wasting their breath. Once I'd given up on the idea of making friends here, things have felt easier.'

Alice swallowed the lump of sadness stuck in her throat. Her sister was putting on a brave face, but Alice knew how much it had cost her moving out to the sticks, and understood better than most how it felt to be alone, and lacking in friendship. At least they had each other.

'Do you mind if I get back to my revision now?' asked May.

'Of course not. Anyway, I need to get ready for my shift at the pub, but I'll make dinner first. What do you fancy tonight?'

'Anything so long as it's not fish fingers.'

Alice laughed and left her sister alone with her work. She'd cook Alice her favourite, shepherd's pie. After dealing with the latest revelation so well, it was the least she deserved.

Chapter 54

'Like this?' asked Alice, as she created a small hole in the earth. She'd hoped to have longer on the piano before Sylvie dragged her outside, but now she was out in the warm sunshine, she was pleased to have curtailed her practice.

'Perfect,' said Sylvie, handing Alice a Crocosmia bulb. 'Now make sure it's fully covered with soil. Yes, that's it. We'll make a gardener out of you yet.'

Alice smiled up at Sylvie. 'Wasn't my dad a gardener?'

'Yes,' said Sylvie, shifting on her folding stool. 'He'd just set up his own business, Loveday Landscaping, when he moved away. It's a shame, really. I know a lot of the locals were sorry to lose him from their gardens.'

'We never had a garden growing up,' said Alice, 'so I'm clueless about plants.'

'Then I'll have to teach you,' said Sylvie, handing Alice tea from a flask.

'She's got you working hard,' said Luke, walking into the garden. His warm smile made Alice's heart race, and she mentally scolded herself for being so susceptible to his charms.

'Get yourself a cup and you can have some of this tea,' said Sylvie. 'Isn't it wonderful to feel the first warm sun of the year? It feels like spring is here at last.'

'Perhaps I'll go for a walk along the cliff once I'm finished here,' said Alice. 'There's still so much of Saffron Bay I need to explore. I'm not working at the pub until this afternoon, and May's volunteering at the café all morning, so I may as well make the most of my free time.'

Luke rejoined them and held out an empty mug for Sylvie to fill. 'Alice was just saying she'd like to do some exploring this morning,' said Sylvie as she tipped tea from the flask. 'Why don't you go with her? You can act as a tour guide.'

'I'm sure Luke has better things to do with his morning,' said Alice.

'No, actually, I'm at a bit of a loose end this weekend. I'd love to come for a walk if you don't mind my joining you.'

'You should go now,' said Sylvie. 'We don't know how long this fine weather will last.'

'I'll finish planting this bed first.'

'Don't be silly. The plants will still be here when you get back. Go on, off you go.'

Alice felt like she'd been ambushed, but did as she was told and set off towards the village with Luke by her side.

'How's May been since you told her she's related to Jack?'

'She took it surprisingly well. I suppose after growing up with Maz, we're used to life being a bit of a rollercoaster.'

'Are you going to talk to Jack about it?'

'Not yet. I have so many questions, and if I only had myself to think about, I would have marched straight up to Saffron Manor to get answers. But May doesn't want any more drama ahead of her exams, and I need to respect that. Anyway, it's not like I'm going to bump into Jack around the village, so the questions I have will have to go unanswered for a while longer.'

'According to Solly, Jack hasn't left the house since the incident with May.'

'Good,' said Alice. 'What he did was completely out of order, and he's lucky we didn't call the police. I know May was wrong to enter his house without permission and it was right she apologise and make amends, but that experience has given her nightmares. Literally.'

'Don't worry, Solly told me he read the riot act to Jack. I hope May appreciates everything you do for her. She's lucky to have you fighting her corner.'

Alice smiled. They walked past the café, and Margot waved through the window. She pointed to where May was sitting beside a resident from the care home, chatting away. Despite the mixed feelings seeing Margot dredged up, and the reminder of the conversation they were yet to have about her father, Alice knew sending May to volunteer in the café had been a good call. Her sister had made some fairly major mistakes lately, but she had a big heart. Alice was tempted to nip in and grab two coffees, but didn't want May to feel she was checking up on her, so they continued walking.

When they reached the General Store, a shiny black four by four pulled up beside them and Patricia climbed out. Alice groaned inwardly, but instead of collaring Luke as she'd expected, Patricia completely blanked them, marching into the shop without a backward glance.

'What's wrong with her?' asked Alice.

'We had words,' said Luke. 'I went to speak to her about Paige's behaviour after what happened up at Jack's.'

'You didn't need to do that,' said Alice, mortified. 'I can fight my own battles.' She stomped off ahead, but Luke caught her up.

'I didn't do it for you,' said Luke. 'I did it for Jack. I doubt that's the first time Paige and her friends have been up there, and the poor guy's dealt with enough over the years without worrying about the local kids using his house as their personal playground.'

'Right,' said Alice, embarrassed that she'd assumed he was leaping to her defence.

'Actually, I bumped into Paige on the beach the other day. We had a good chat. Patricia's split with Duncan has messed her up, and I think she knows she's behaved really badly.'

'That's something, I suppose. But I'll believe she's sorry when she leaves May alone.' They walked side by side in silence for a few minutes, then Alice turned to Luke. 'I've been meaning to ask about Jack's house and the fire that destroyed it. My dad was involved somehow, wasn't he? Did he start the fire? Is that what all this local animosity is about?'

'I promise I don't know any more than you. This way.' Luke turned off along a narrow path hugging the cliff, and for a while they walked in silence, the incline stealing Alice's breath.

'Wow,' said Alice, when they reached the top of the hill and stopped to admire the view. 'It's beautiful.'

'Isn't it? Come with me. There's something I'd like to show you.' Luke turned his back on the sea and followed a gravel path, which cut inland through the bracken. He stopped at a small clearing, where a bench looked out onto spectacular views. He pointed to the brass plaque where two names and dates were written. 'My parents,' he said. 'We scattered their ashes up here. It was Mum's favourite spot.'

'What happened to them?'

'A drunk driver ran them off the road when they were on their way home from a night at the theatre. I was twelve when it happened.'

'That's awful. Are you an only child?'

'Yes, unfortunately. In fact, I'm quite jealous of you and May. I know it's a lot to take on looking after her, but whatever you go through in life, you'll always have each other.'

'That's very true, and I need to be more grateful for all we have. Shall we sit for a moment? I'm not used to these hills and wouldn't mind resting my legs.'

Luke laughed. 'We've barely left the village, but yeah, OK.'

They sat on the bench, watching a small sailboat making the most of the light breeze and sunshine, gulls swooping above the cliff top as though playing tag.

'Mum used to bring me up here whenever we visited Gran. I used to moan like crazy. I wanted to be out with Dad on the water, not hiking with Mum, but I'm grateful for those memories now.'

'What were they like, your parents?'

'Great,' said Luke, his voice catching. 'They were really great.'

Without thinking, Alice reached across and took his hand.

'They'd like you,' said Luke, his voice thick as he turned to look at Alice. 'Mum especially would have liked you very much.'

The air between them crackled. Alice wasn't sure who moved first, but before she knew what was happening, she was in Luke's arms, his mouth on hers, kissing her like she'd never been kissed before.

'I'm sorry,' he said, pulling away. 'I should have asked if you wanted me to do that.'

Alice lifted a hand and stroked his face with her thumb. 'I think I've been wanting you to do that since the moment you burst into the cottage without knocking.'

Luke laughed and pulled her closer. 'I thought you hated me when we first met.'

'Only a little bit.'

Luke's mouth met hers again, and every sensible thought left Alice's mind as she let herself become lost in the moment.

Chapter 55

Alice buried herself under the bedsheets and groaned. This wasn't like her. She didn't jump into men's beds without even a first date. Not only that, deep down, she knew she couldn't give Luke what he really wanted. What if they'd just made a terrible mistake?

'Are you hiding?'

Alice poked her head out and saw Luke wrapped in a towel, carrying two cups of coffee. His hair was damp and curly from the shower, and Alice couldn't stop staring at his body, toned from manual work rather than the gym. Luke laid a coffee cup on the bedside table beside her and leaned down to kiss her.

'When you said you'd show me the sights, I didn't realise this was what you meant,' she muttered, pulling him back into the bed.

Half an hour later, Alice lay with her head on Luke's chest, wondering how she'd found herself here.

'Are you alright?' asked Luke. 'You've gone really quiet.'

'Just thinking.'

'Nothing bad, I hope.'

'No, just how out of character this is for me.'

'You can't be sensible all the time.'

'You think I'm boring?' asked Alice, propping herself up on an elbow and frowning.

'I didn't say boring, I said sensible. And I meant it as a compliment.'

'How is being sensible a compliment?'

'You take life and your responsibilities seriously. I love that about you.'

Alice flinched at the L word. It was way too soon for any of that. 'What about you?' she asked, not really wanting to hear the answer. 'Do you do this often?'

'Bring girls back to my house and take them to bed in the middle of the day? No,' said Luke, laughing. 'You're the first.'

'We know almost nothing about each other,' said Alice, pulling herself up to sitting and leaning against the headboard.

'We know enough.'

'I'm a mess.'

Luke pushed himself up to sit beside her. 'Listen, Alice, this can be whatever you want it to be. I like you, really like you, but I don't want to push you into something you're not ready for.'

Was this Luke looking for a way out? Was he already regretting what they'd just done? 'Likewise,' she said.

'What do you want, Alice? From me, I mean.'

'I don't know.'

'You need time?'

Alice nodded. 'I like you, Luke, more than is probably sensible,' she smiled, 'but with so much going on, with May, with the cottage, trying to find out about my dad, the revelation about Maz...I'm not sure how much of myself I can give to you.'

'Then let's take it slow,' he said, twirling a lock of her hair between his fingers. 'We've jumped the gun today, but we can slow things right down. Get to know each other properly.'

'I'd like that.'

'Why don't we go on a date?'

'A date? Won't that be a bit... public?'

'You're worried about being seen out with me?'

'No, I suppose I've had enough of being the centre of village gossip, first by being the new girl, then once people found out I'm a Loveday.'

'I'll think of something,' said Luke. 'Oh, by way, speaking of secret romances, did you know about Gran and Solly?'

'What about them?'

'My friend Nick reckons they're a couple.'

'What? Wow, they've kept that well hidden.'

'I know, I didn't think me and Gran kept secrets from each other, but this is a pretty big one.'

'She'll tell you in her own time. I'd better be getting back. I'm due at the pub at three.'

'OK. Do you mind seeing yourself out? I'm going to get in the shower.'

'Again?'

'I've had quite a workout this morning,' said Luke, leaning over and kissing Alice gently. Their kisses deepened and intensified, but Alice pulled away, laughing.

'Don't,' she said, 'or I'll never get to work on time.' Luke groaned, and Alice batted him with a pillow. 'I thought we were going to take things slow?'

'This is going to be torture,' said Luke, covering his face with a pillow and groaning again.

Alice laughed, jumped out of bed, and pulled on her clothes. When she was ready to leave, she leaned over and kissed Luke one more time. 'Thank you for an interesting morning.'

'Interesting?' asked Luke, one eyebrow raised.

'OK, surprising.'

'A pleasant surprise?'

'The best.'

'Is it OK if I grab a quick drink of water on my way out?'

'Of course it is. When will I next see you?'

'Soon,' said Alice. She blew Luke a kiss and left him lying in bed, a soppy smile on his face.

The downstairs of Luke's house was open plan and petite. Alice wondered how tourists fared stuck inside on rainy days. She suspected they'd get cabin fever pretty quickly. She poured herself a glass of water and was drinking it when a letter on the kitchen counter caught her eye. Was it snooping if it was just lying there, waiting to be read? Alice scanned the letter, her heart pounding and dropping all at once. Anger swiftly followed disappointment. Why had Luke seduced her if he was going to be leaving Saffron Bay?

'Calm down,' Alice told herself. 'This is a job offer. It doesn't mean he's going to accept.' She replaced the letter on the counter just as she'd found it and washed her glass in the sink. Luke's phone was on the counter and buzzed with a message. The temptation to look at the screen overwhelmed her, and Alice reasoned that after reading his mail, reading a text message wasn't that big a leap. 'In for a penny, in for a pound,' she said, leaning over the phone.

The message was from an unnamed sender. *Have you told Alice about Dan yet? I shouldn't have said anything, Luke. Please keep things to yourself for a little longer.*

With tears burning the backs of her eyes, Alice stumbled backwards away from the phone. The sound of footsteps made her jump, and Luke appeared in the living room, towelling his wet hair.

'Oh, you're still here. I thought you'd already left.'

'Just going,' said Alice, forcing a smile. As she passed him, Luke bent down to kiss her, but Alice kept moving and the kiss landed on her ear. 'See you soon,' she called, forcing her legs not to break into a run as she let herself out of the house.

Chapter 56

Alice waited beside the bus stop, as she did every day her shifts at the pub would allow. Whatever Luke said about a change of heart, she didn't trust Paige Morris not to dream up some new scrape to drag May into. The day was cold and bright, but as Alice tilted her face to the sun, she could almost smell spring in the air.

In her old life, before Maz left and took Alice's dreams with her, spring was her favourite time of year. Even with all that had happened, a bright day with a hint of warmth would usually fill Alice with optimism, but after what happened with Luke, nothing could lift her spirits.

She still couldn't work out how she'd got him so wrong. He'd messaged her earlier, suggesting a date. Did he think she was stupid? Was she nothing more than entertainment to fill his time before he upped and left the village for the bright lights of London? But worse than any of that was that he knew something about her dad and had kept it from her. She'd shared everything with him and had told him all about Maz's relationship to Jack Tyler. But it seemed honesty and openness were a one-way street as far as Luke was concerned.

Alice mentally listed all the people who'd left her over the years. Her parents were the most obvious, but there were also a series of boyfriends she'd been hopeful about, until their lives moved on and hers, standing still by circumstance, was no longer compatible. Then there were the friends at school. A couple had moved away, but several moved on to more exciting girls when Alice had to stay at home babysitting instead of joining them on nights out.

Now here she was at twenty-five, with no real friends to speak of, no parents, no boyfriend, just a sister for company who was pressing full-steam ahead with a life of her own. There was no doubt May loved Alice, but she'd soon be obsolete in May's life, a bystander cheering her on and watching from the sidelines.

'Hi!'

Alice looked up to see Sam standing in the doorway of the general store, waving.

'Hi, Sam, how are you?'

'Good, thanks.' Sam looked both ways and then ran across the road. 'You waiting for May?'

'Yes.'

'How's she doing?'

Alice gave Sam a wry smile. 'As well as a teenage girl about to sit her GCSEs can be. She's holding things together pretty well, but I can tell she's stressed.'

'Teenage girls,' said Sam with a grimace. 'I remember what I was like at that age. My poor mum, the things I put her through! What about you? Were you a tearaway?'

Alice laughed. 'I never got the chance to find out. I was babysitting May every weekend so Mum could go out.' She looked up at Sam, hating to see the pity in her eyes. 'But it was fine,' she quickly added. 'I preferred music to people, anyway.'

'I'm sure May realises how lucky she is to have you,' said Sam. 'Hey, there's a cinema night at the community centre later. Do you fancy coming along?'

Alice felt a flicker of something deep inside her. Did this mean she was becoming accepted as part of the village? Could she call Sam a friend? Then she remembered her responsibilities and her shoulders sagged. 'I'd love to, but I need to stay in with May. She's got coursework due at the end of the week and might need some support.'

'OK, well, maybe another time. See you soon.'

Sam ran back across to the shop, and Alice stood up as the bus approached. As May stood up from her seat, through the window, Alice noticed her rolling down her skirt until it was a decent length. She had a scowl plastered across her face, and Alice wondered if the teasing from Paige Morris was getting to her more than she was letting on.

'Good day at school?' asked Alice as May climbed down the steps.

May shrugged. 'You don't have to meet me off the bus every day. It's embarrassing.'

'Yes, but what if Paige Morris and her cronies collar you again?'

'Cronies? What are you, seventy-five?'

Alice swallowed a sigh. 'Got much left to do on your coursework?'

'Tons.'

'I'll help if you like.'

'No thanks. What's for dinner?'

Alice bunched her hands into fists and tried to stay calm. 'Fish fingers and chips.'

May snorted. 'Fish fingers? That's like a meal Mum would have cooked.'

'It's all we have in the freezer and as I don't get paid until tomorrow, it's fish fingers or a cheese sandwich.'

'Fish fingers are fine.'

As soon as they walked into the cottage, May threw her bag and coat down in the hallway, kicked off her shoes, and disappeared into her bedroom. Alice walked into the kitchen and pulled a packet of fish fingers from the freezer. The oven was playing up again, and she wished she'd been able to buy a new one, instead of this one from a dodgy lock-up that either burned food to a crisp or cooked things so slowly they were at risk of contracting salmonella.

It took forty minutes for the fish fingers to cook through, long enough for Alice to rifle through the pile of bills that had been mounting up on the worktop. It was all very well being given a house, but Seashell Cottage was a money pit, the non-existent insulation meaning their electricity bills were through the roof as she tried to keep the place at a habitable temperature for May. It was still too early in the season to ask Rita for more shifts, and despite scouring the local papers and online job sites, there was nothing else out there.

'Dinner's ready,' called Alice, placing the plates of orange food on the table. She sat down and let the view of Saffron Bay ease some of the worry she was carrying. It was a priceless view. A priceless view? The cogs started whirring in Alice's mind, and as a sulky May joined her at the table, Alice started formulating a plan. It was ridiculous to think they could stay here. She would sell Seashell Cottage. The building might be worthless, but not the land. A property developer would snap up a plot with sea views. Alice forced her attention back to May.

'Good day at school?'

May shrugged.

'What subjects did you have?'

'The usual.'

Alice sighed and put down her fork, wincing as it clattered against the plate. May looked up, brushed the hair from her eyes, and frowned. 'What's wrong with you?'

'Nothing,' said Alice, picking up her fork and piercing a fish finger.

'It doesn't sound like nothing. You sound in a right grump.'

'And what if I am?' said Alice, pushing her plate away. 'Don't I ever get to feel angry, or sad, or scared? No, of course not. My job is to look after everyone else, pick up the pieces of everyone else's mess.' She stood up and marched to her bedroom, slamming the door behind her. She threw herself onto the bed and tried to control her breathing. The idea of selling the cottage had rattled her. What if her dad came back one day, and she wasn't there? Selling it would be to admit defeat, and if Alice was good at anything, it was keeping going, putting one foot in front of the other until she got where she needed to be.

The trouble was, deep down, Alice knew she'd never get to where she needed to be. Yes, May only had two and a bit years left of school, but then she'd go to university and Alice would need to support her through it. In five years' time, Alice would be thirty, and any hope of pursuing her own dreams would have passed her by.

Alice's phone buzzed, and when she saw it was another message from Luke, she threw it against the wall. As it thudded to the ground, Alice prayed it hadn't actually broken as she couldn't afford to buy a new one. She rolled onto her back and stared up at the ceiling. A few patches of damp were already appearing through the fresh paint. She closed her eyes, listening to the sound of May's footsteps in the hall. Alice expected May to knock on her bedroom door, but the footsteps continued through to the kitchen. Then came the sound of a sink filling with water, and the clink of plates as they were washed and dried. Alice managed a small smile. If it took a tantrum to get May doing the washing up, perhaps she should lose her cool more often.

Chapter 57

Luke picked up his phone, willing it to ring. Even a message would do, anything to let him know Alice didn't regret what had happened between them. It had been three days, and he'd sent five messages. Five too many, by the looks of things. He should have waited for her to get in touch first.

Work had been a good distraction, but now he was home with an entire evening stretching out and nothing to occupy his mind. He was in two minds about calling Nick. It would be good to speak to his friend, but Nick would suggest going to the pub, and the last thing Luke needed was alcohol. It was too risky, one pint too many, and he'd end up calling her. He knew he would.

Luke paced up and down the small living room, trying to work out what had gone wrong. Was he terrible in bed? Should he have taken her flowers? Or perhaps rather than inattentive, he'd been too full-on messaging to suggest a proper date night. The truth was, he was out of practice and, anyway, prior experience wouldn't help, as Alice was unlike anyone he'd dated before.

'Nick? Hey, it's Luke.'

'Alright, mate?'

'Not brilliant, actually. I've had a rough couple of days and could do with getting out of the house.'

'Fancy a pint?'

'No, I don't think alcohol would be a good idea.'

'No beer? You must be in a state. Has something happened at work?'

'No.'

'Is Sylvie alright?'

'Gran's fine.'

'OK, so by a process of elimination, it must be girl trouble. Am I right?'

Luke ignored the question. 'I wondered if you wanted to go out on the water?'

'In the kayaks?'

'Yeah, why not? It's a lovely evening.'

'It's a cold evening.'

'Cold but sunny.'

'Go on then, you've twisted my arm. But I'm very out of practice, and I reckon Sylvie has more upper arm strength than I do at the moment, so can we go for a gentle paddle? No racing?'

'Sounds perfect. Are you free now?'

Nick laughed. 'I'm always free. You know that.'

'Great, I'll head down to the beach and get set up.'

It took another hour before they were out on the water. Nick had arrived at the beach having forgotten his wetsuit, so had to go home for it. Then Luke's spare blow-up kayak wouldn't inflate, so he'd had to pack it away with no choice but to share.

'This is like old times,' said Nick, as they finally set off. 'Remember how we used to spend hours out on the water when we were kids?'

'I do. It was my happy place.'

'You were so quiet when you first moved here, but out on the water, I finally saw the real you. You weren't as boring as I first thought.'

Luke cut his paddle in at an angle, sending a torrent of water over Nick.

'Oi, what was that for?'

'I was grieving when I first moved here, you idiot.'

'Grief makes people boring. It's a well-known fact.'

'And you wonder why you're still single,' muttered Luke under his breath. 'You've got the empathy of a rock.'

'I heard that,' said Nick. 'And anyway, I know what I am. And not being in touch with feelings has its advantages.'

'Such as?'

'You don't see me moping around, do you?'

Luke thought back to the long winter months, when Nick would spend every pub trip bemoaning life in Saffron Bay. He smirked to himself, but kept quiet, choosing instead to enjoy the sight of the late afternoon sun rippling across the water. When he looked down, the sea was so clear he could watch a shoal of turquoise fish flitting between seaweed-covered rocks. He thought about the letter sitting on the kitchen counter at home. Could he really give all this up?

They paddled to the outer edges of the bay in silence, the only sound the gentle splosh of paddles hitting water, and the cries of gulls overhead.

'So,' so Nick when they stopped to catch their breath. 'Why did you really call me?'

'Like I said, I needed to get out of the house.'

'Yeah, and I'm grateful you did. It's been way too long since we came out on the water together. But you sounded depressed. Was I right? Is this about a girl?'

When Luke didn't answer, Nick took it as an affirmative.

'It's Tricia, isn't it? She's finally got her claws into you again.'

'Don't be stupid,' said Luke. 'I'm not that much of an idiot.'

'OK, so who is it?'

'Alice.'

'Alice Loveday? What's happened with her? I knew you liked her!' said Nick, thumping his fist into the water in triumph.

'We sort of got together.'

'Sort of? Sort of doesn't sound good.'

'I thought we had got together, but since we did, she hasn't been answering my messages.'

'Have you called her? Perhaps she's busy.'

'I suggested a date night. She read the message, but never replied. I don't know what to do.'

'Man up and talk to her,' said Nick, as though it was the most obvious thing in the world.

'She's a very private person. I'm not sure she'd appreciate being pushed into talking about things.'

'Mate, if you hooked up, she must be into you. If something has changed her mind since, it's better to get it out into the open. Apart from anything, you don't want an atmosphere between you when you both live in a village as small as Saffron Bay. Unless you've accepted the job offer?'

'I wasn't going to, but if things really have gone tits up with Alice, it might be best for both of us if I weren't around as much.'

'Talk to her,' said Nick, picking up his paddle. 'Now come on, let's head back to the beach. It's a gorgeous sunset and everything, but it's so cold I'm freezing my nuts off.'

As Luke paddled back towards the beach, he wasn't sure that meeting up with Nick had helped anything. He felt just as despondent as before.

Chapter 58

Alice was hot and sweaty after a busy lunchtime shift at the pub and was about to have a shower when someone knocked on the door. She opened it to a smartly dressed woman of about the same age as herself, holding a briefcase in one hand and a canvas bag over one shoulder.

'Hello, are you Alice Loveday?'

'Yes, that's me.'

'Hi, Alice. My name's Maisie Clark, and I'm from social services.'

'Social services? Sorry, what is this about?'

'Someone called us concerned about your sister's welfare.'

Alice felt her knees buckle, and she gripped the door for support. 'Has something happened to May?'

'Not that I'm aware of. Is May at home?'

'No,' said Alice, frowning in confusion. 'It's a weekday morning. She's at school. At least, I think she is. Perhaps I should call them?'

'Could I come in?' asked Maisie. 'It would be easier to talk inside.'

'Fine,' said Alice, distracted and barely aware of the woman following her inside as she dialled the school number. When she'd been reassured that May had turned up at the usual time and was currently in class, Alice's panic subsided. 'May's fine. Would you like a cup of tea?'

'That would be lovely, thank you.'

Alice didn't want to make the woman tea. She didn't want her in her home at all, but knew she needed to be at her best, as Maisie Clark would note everything down, if only in her head.

'Milk? Sugar?' called Alice from the kitchen.

'Just milk, please.'

Alice tried not to panic about Maisie's reaction to the cottage. She'd done the best she could on a tight budget, and the cottage was now as homely as she could make it without spending tens of thousands on more substantial renovations. If she had an endless pot of money, double-glazing and proper insulation would be at the top of Alice's list, but the fire kept them warm enough for now, and the two electric blankets Sylvie had gifted them had proved a revelation.

When Alice carried the mugs through to the living room, she found Maisie standing at the window, staring out at the view. 'Here you are.'

'Thank you. Your view is incredible.'

'We're very lucky,' said Alice. 'Would you like to take a seat?'

Maisie sat down on the sofa and pulled a notebook from her canvas bag. 'As I said, I'm here today because someone has raised a concern over your sister's welfare.'

'I don't understand,' said Alice. 'Who would do something like that?'

'I'm afraid I can't say who it was that called us, but I'm sure you understand we need to take such matters seriously.'

The formal language sounded strange coming from the mouth of someone so young and left Alice ill at ease. 'Can you tell me any specifics, though?'

Maisie ignored the question. 'I understand you have recently taken on an informal guardianship role of May.'

'Yes, that's correct.'

'And what led to this change in circumstances?'

'Our mother moved abroad.'

'I see. But she's still supporting you both financially?'

Alice actually laughed at the suggestion. 'No,' she said, and Maisie scribbled in her notebook.

'And you've recently moved into this cottage, I understand.'

'That's right. We had to leave our rented flat in Plymouth, but I found out I had this place to come to. I know it needs a bit of work, but...'

'Alice,' said Maisie, closing her notebook and taking a sip of tea. 'You have a lovely home.'

'I do?'

When Maisie smiled broadly, Alice felt her muscles relax. 'From what I've seen, yes, you do. I poked my head into what I assume is May's bedroom while you were making tea, and I can see the effort you've gone to to create a safe, welcoming space for her. I certainly have no concerns about May's living accommodation.'

'You should have seen it when we first arrived.'

'Do you have photos?'

Alice gulped. 'Photos?'

Maisie smiled again. 'I'm not trying to catch you out, Alice. I'm genuinely curious. My partner and I are currently renovating our first home together, and I'm obsessed with other people's houses.'

Alice smiled. She didn't fully trust the social worker, fearing she was trying to catch her out somehow, but it was hard to resist Maisie's warmth and what seemed genuine enthusiasm for the cottage. Alice sat beside the social worker on the sofa and began flicking through the photographs on her phone.

'I can't believe all you've done,' said Maisie, when they reached the last photograph. 'How long have you been here?'

'Six weeks.'

'Wow, that's amazing.' Maisie seemed to suddenly remember why she was there and pulled out her notebook once more. 'Sorry, I'm easily distracted. Better get back to business. So, Alice, are you currently employed?'

'Yes, I work at the local pub.'

'I see,' said Maisie, jotting the answer down. 'And do you see yourself being there for the foreseeable future?'

'Yes,' said Alice, the answer coming out as a sigh.

'But?' asked Maisie, her pen hovering over the notebook.

'But I was supposed to be starting university in September. Obviously, that can't happen now.'

'Why not?'

'Because I need to support May.'

Maisie closed her notebook again and leaned forward. 'Alice, there are options out there to support you. The first step is to assess you under a special guardianship order or as a kinship foster carer.'

'What? But I'm May's sister. I'm an adult. Why can't I just look after her? Surely there are thousands of siblings out there doing the same as me.'

'There are, and most stay under the radar, never coming to our attention. But as someone has contacted us regarding May's welfare, we are now involved. Don't view this as a negative experience. The purpose of an assessment is to make sure May is safe, and get you any support you're entitled to.'

'Such as?'

'Assuming the assessment results are positive, and I've no reason to think they wouldn't be, you'll be entitled to a foster care allowance. That should ease some of the pressure. I'll also need details of May's father. Does she have any contact with him?'

'Minimal.'

'But he pays child support?'

'No, not formally. He gives May money from time to time.'

'In that case, we'll need to speak to him about formalising the arrangement. I'd also like to schedule a time to come and meet May.'

'Of course.' Alice's throat had gone dry. Maisie seemed nice enough, but all this interference in their lives was unwelcome, not to mention the fact that someone had gone behind her back and reported her. The most likely candidate was Jack Tyler, and Alice wished she hadn't been so quick to apologise and try to make peace. Surely he was the only person who hated her enough to do something like this?

'Is that alright, Alice?'

'Sorry, what?'

'I'll come back tomorrow at five to speak to May.'

'Oh yes, that's fine. She'll be back by then.'

'Great. Well,' said Maisie, putting her notebook away and picking up her bag and briefcase. 'It's been lovely to meet you, and whilst I know this has probably all been a bit of a shock, we really want what's best for May, and to find the best way to support you. But, Alice, from what I've seen so far, May is lucky to have you.'

'Thank you.'

Alice showed Maisie to the door and breathed a sigh of relief when she closed it behind her. Her legs felt like jelly, and the effort of holding it together in front of the social worker had left her exhausted. She was about to retreat to the sofa to lick her wounds when a knock came on the door. Alice's heart sank. No doubt it would be Maisie Clark, back with more questions.

But when Alice opened the door, it wasn't Masie, but Margot. Her heart sank. She'd been meaning to confront Margot for some time, but after finding out Maz was Tilly, then everything that had happened with Luke, Margot had dropped down the list of priorities.

'Hello, Alice. I hope you don't mind my calling around. Is now a good time for a chat?'

'Actually, Margot, it isn't, not really. I've had a tough afternoon, and May will be home soon wanting her dinner.'

'I promise not to stay too long,' said Margot. 'But, you see, Alice, I haven't been completely honest with you. Please, can I come in and talk to you about your dad?'

Alice stepped aside to let Margot in, all thoughts of Maisie's visit forgotten.

Chapter 59

Alice followed Margot into the sitting room. She was almost too tired to care what Margot had to say. Almost, but not quite.

'I've actually been meaning to come and speak to you,' said Alice.

'Oh?' said Margot, drawn to the large window with its magnificent view, just as Maisie had been minutes earlier.

'It was you who came in and cleaned the cottage, wasn't it?'

Instead of answering, Margot pulled out a chair from beneath the dining table, sat down, and clasped her hands together on the table. 'How did you know?'

'A process of elimination. You were the most likely candidate. What I don't understand is why or how you knew I'd be moving to the village.'

'I didn't know you'd be moving to the village,' said Margot. 'But I knew the cottage had passed to you, and Daniel wanted to make sure it was in the best condition it could be when you first saw it.'

'You've been in touch with my dad?' Alice stayed standing, using all her control not to pace up and down.

'We've kept in touch over the years.'

'So he's definitely alive, then.'

Margot looked at the table and twirled her fingers together. 'Yes, and I should have told you that the moment you arrived in Saffron Bay.'

'Then why didn't you?' asked Alice, barely keeping her anger in check. She sat down at the table and tried to still her trembling body. 'Do you have any idea how stressful the past few weeks have been, then not to know if the man who left me this house is even alive? Well, that's just been the cherry on top.'

'I didn't feel it was my place. I was waiting to hear from Daniel to know what he wanted me to do.'

'And now you have?'

'No, but I felt I couldn't wait any longer to speak to you.'

'Right,' said Alice, her fingers drumming against the table. 'Let me get this straight. You told my dad I was living in Saffron Bay, and he ignored you?'

'It's not like that.'

'No?' said Alice, standing so suddenly her chair fell to the floor. 'Do you know, Margot, it was better when I thought he was dead? It's bad enough having one parent who doesn't give a toss about you, but now I know I have two parents who never wanted me. Thanks for that. You can leave now.'

'Alice, please let me explain.'

'No, I want you to leave.'

'Alice...'

‘Fine,’ shouted Alice. ‘If you won’t leave. I will.’ She stormed out of the house, slamming the door behind her, praying Maisie Clark was long gone and not out on the street, listening to Alice scream like a banshee.

Cliff Lane was mercifully quiet, everyone either at work or choosing to stay inside on such a grey day. The air held a light mizzle, which provided relief when it landed on Alice’s flushed skin. She heard the front door of the cottage open and close, but didn’t turn back. Instead, she increased her pace, turning left just before the beach and joining the coast path. The steep incline helped release some tension as she huffed and puffed her way onwards.

There was little in the way of a view, the slate grey sea barely distinguishable from the battleship grey of the sky. A thin layer of mist blurred the horizon, threatening to push its way landward. Alice followed the path Luke had shown her until she found the small clearing with the bench dedicated to his parents’ memories. Alice slumped down onto it, drawing her knees up to her chin and hugging her arms around her legs.

No matter how hard she tried to do the right thing, to be the best version of herself, to give everything she had to others, she was beaten down. Alice had thought social services turning up on her doorstep had been the final straw, but discovering her dad was not only alive, but choosing to continue the habit of a lifetime by ignoring her existence was one piece of bad news too many. Oh, and Luke was not only keeping secrets from her but about to up sticks and take up a job with a fancy construction firm in London. He was the one person she thought she could rely on, and he'd used her. The message on his phone must have been from Margot. There was no other explanation. How long had he known her dad was alive? What kind of person would keep that information to themselves?

Alice barely noticed the tears weaving their way down her cheeks. She'd used up all her fight, and couldn't even summon the energy to leave the bench and walk home. The sound of muffled laughter reached her, and she stiffened. As the voices drew closer, Alice knew there was nowhere she could turn. Thick bracken surrounded her on three sides, and the only route out of the clearing was the narrow path she'd already taken.

When Sylvie and Solly emerged into the clearing, their arms around each other, Alice's eyes opened wide. It took them a moment to realise they weren't alone, but once they did, Sylvie's arm dropped to her side, and Solly cleared his throat.

'Oh, Alice, um, how nice to see you. We, um, weren't expecting anyone else to be out today.'

'It's alright,' said Alice, pushing herself to her feet. 'I was just about to head home.'

'You're crying,' said Sylvie, stepping closer.

Alice lifted a hand to her face, surprised when it came away damp. 'Oh.'

'Sit down,' said Solly, 'tell us what's wrong.'

Alice didn't know where to start, and the last thing she wanted was to talk, but she didn't have the energy to refuse the request. She sat back down, with Sylvie and Solly on either side of her.

'What's happened, love?' asked Sylvie, taking her hand.

As much as Alice didn't want to talk, once she started, she found she couldn't stop. All her worries came pouring out, all, that is, except the shocking news of Luke's job offer and the fact he'd been keeping secrets. She doubted Sylvie knew about his plans to leave, and didn't want to be the one to break it to her.

'Someone called social services about you?'

'Margot has been in touch with Daniel all this time?'

Sylvie and Solly spoke simultaneously, and as Alice wasn't sure who to answer first, she nodded.

'I'll be having words with Margot,' said Sylvie, humphing and folding her arms.

'Solly,' said Alice, turning to face him. 'Do you think it was Jack who rang social services? I thought we'd cleared the air, but I can't think who else it could have been.'

'Do you want me to talk to him?' asked Solly.

'I don't think there's much point. His mind is made up about me, and there's nothing I can do to change it. Thank you, though. I'd better be getting back. May will be home soon.'

'As long as you're alright,' said Sylvie, rubbing Alice's arm. 'Remember, we're here for you if you need us.'

'I will,' said Alice. She walked along the path, then stopped and turned back. Sylvie and Solly looked up in surprise. 'You don't need to hide away, you know.'

'Hide what?' asked Solly.

'Your romance. Luke knows, and the only thing he disapproves of is that you didn't tell him yourselves and he had to find out from someone else.'

'Oh good Lord,' said Sylvie. 'Who told him?'

Alice shrugged. 'I'm not sure, but someone saw you together. Honestly, I think he's pleased for you. See you later.'

By the time Alice arrived back in the village, there was still almost an hour before May's bus was due, so she went home for a cup of tea, praying Margot wouldn't still be there, lying in wait. When she reached Seashell Cottage, she opened the front door slowly, poking her head through and listening. All she could hear were the usual creaks and groans of the old building. Alice stepped inside and checked the kitchen first. The mug Margot had used was clean, drying on the draining board. Alice let herself relax. She wandered through to the sitting room, and there on the table was a note.

Alice picked up the piece of paper and held it at arm's length, part of her scared to read whatever Margot had written. When she finally let her eyes rest on the paper, Alice gasped. Margot had written an address in a town about half an hour away. Underneath was written–*This is where your grandparents live. I'm sure they'd love to meet you.*

Chapter 60

Luke took a deep breath, bunched his fist and hammered on the door. When Alice answered and saw it was him, she tried to slam it in his face, but he stuck his foot in the gap just in time.

'Go away.'

'We need to talk. I need to know what I've done wrong.'

'What you've done wrong? *What you've done wrong?*' Luke took a step back as her voice hit him like a slap. 'Let's start with the fact you're leaving Saffron Bay. I saw the letter, so don't bother denying it.'

Luke laughed, relief flooding through him. 'Is that what this is about? I'm going to turn down the job, Alice. I'm not going anywhere.' If he thought Alice would be relieved, he was sorely mistaken.

'Do you know what, Luke? I don't care if you do. In fact, I'd be glad if you went.'

'Really? After everything that's happened between us? Everything I've done to help you?'

'I never asked for your help.'

'You did actually, several times.'

Alice scowled, turned her back on Luke, and said, 'I'm on my way out. I can't talk about this now.'

Luke followed Alice into the living room. 'Alice, I still don't understand what's going on between us.'

'If you're wondering why I've been ignoring your calls and messages, it's because I saw the message Margot sent to your phone.'

'What message?'

'The one asking if you'd told me my dad is still alive. You know, that tiny piece of information that could alter the entire course of my life? She came to see me and told me everything.'

As realisation dawned, Luke's heart sank. 'I'm sorry, Alice. I should have told you what I knew the second Margot told me. I know this sounds pathetic, but I was trying to protect you.'

'Protect me? Pull the other one.'

'It's true. Margot was waiting for a response from your dad, and it seemed crazy to upset you unnecessarily before she'd had a reply. I almost told you several times, but something always got in the way.'

'Such as?'

'I was going to tell you the day we found the photo of your mum, but then you had other things on your mind.'

'And how long were you going to let me wonder if my dad was dead or alive? Do you have any idea how that feels?'

'I know how it feels to lose someone. I know how it feels to be alone.' Luke hadn't intended to pull the sympathy card, but he wouldn't let Alice tell him what he did and didn't feel. 'I know how it feels to be desperate for a family you can't have, that doesn't exist.'

Alice pulled out a dining chair and slumped into it. 'Ever since I arrived in Saffron Bay, I've been surrounded by secrets, not knowing who I can and can't trust. You were the one person I thought I could rely on, and to find out you're no better than the rest of them really hurts.'

'I promise I was going to tell you.'

'Well, I know now.' Alice checked her watch. 'I need to go.'

'Where are you off to?' asked Luke, desperate to prolong the conversation.

Alice let out a laugh that held no joy. She pulled a piece of paper from her pocket and waved it in the air. 'Margot gave me the address of my grandparents.'

'Your grandparents? What, your dad's parents?'

'Are you seriously saying you didn't know I had grandparents living half an hour away? I thought you were Margot's confidante.'

'She didn't tell me about any grandparents, I promise.'

'I suppose that's something. Anyway, I'd better go.'

'Do you want me to come with you?'

Alice laughed, shook her head, and walked out of the cottage without saying goodbye. Luke let himself out of the cottage and fought the urge to turn left and go to Sylvie for comfort. He needed to get his thoughts straight and decide once and for all. Alice hated him, and if the rumours about Sylvie and Solly were true, there was nothing keeping him in Saffron Bay anymore.

He needed to clear his head, so headed for the beach, where he could stomp out his frustration at his own foolishness. He should have ignored Margot's warnings and gone straight to Alice as soon as he found out about her dad. Who was he to think he could protect her? She was right to be angry.

Luke kept his head down as he walked through the village, not wanting to be drawn into conversation with any locals. He practically ran down the path leading to the beach, the sound of the waves and big open skies calling to his troubled mind. As he reached the end of the beach and jumped the final meter onto the sand, his heart sank. Walking towards him was Patricia. Any hope of avoiding her vanished as she waved and called hello.

'Hi, Patricia,' he said as she reached him.

'Are you alright, Luke? You look a little pale.'

'I'm fine. It's been a stressful day, so I've come down here to clear my head.'

'Good idea. Hey, I've been hoping to bump into you. You deserve an apology for how I've been treating you, not just the flirting, I know that made you feel uncomfortable, but also the way I reacted when you came round. But most of all, I wanted to thank you for whatever it was you said to Paige.'

Luke frowned. 'I don't think I said anything very profound.'

'Well, whatever it was, it really helped. She came home and opened up to me about everything that's been on her mind. I've been so preoccupied with myself, I hadn't realised how much she's been struggling since me and D split. Oh, and she admitted to drawing all over May's bedroom and daring her to go into Saffron Manor. I feel such a fool for defending her.'

'It's what any parent would do.'

Patricia smiled, but her eyes were sad. 'I am sorry about how I treated you back in the day. You would have made such an excellent stepfather to Paige. I was an idiot to let you go.'

'Patricia, listen...'

Patricia interrupted him with a laugh. 'I'm not trying to get you back. Don't worry. Talking to Paige made me realise I need to stop chasing around after blokes and focus on my daughter for a change. I suppose I didn't think I could manage on my own, but I've been doing myself down. From now on, it will be me and Paige against the world. I don't need a man to hold my hand through life. After all, what kind of example does that set for my daughter?'

'I'm happy for you,' said Luke. He meant it, and not just because it took the pressure off him. Patricia said goodbye, and Luke took his shoes off, enjoying the jolt as his toes sank into the cold, damp sand. Everyone was moving on with their lives except him. With each step he took, Luke's resolve strengthened. How could he have judged Patricia for using men as a crutch when he was doing the same thing himself with Saffron Bay? For so long, it had been his safe space, his link to the family he'd lost, but now he needed to be brave and step out on his own.

Luke pulled his phone from his pocket and dialled the number his thumb had hovered over so many times over the past few weeks. The man answered after two rings. 'Luke, I hope you're calling with good news?'

'I am. I'd like to accept the job offer, if it's still going?'

'Of course it is. The work you did at our place down in Cornwall was first-rate. I'd love for you to head up the project here. How soon could you start?'

'I've got another month to finish the current house I'm working on. How does the beginning of June sound?'

'It sounds perfect. We should have all the planning in place by then, and you can move up here and hit the ground running.'

'Great,' said Luke, trying to sound as if his heart was in it.

'I think this will be the start of a beautiful partnership. This first development is only the start. We're rapidly building our portfolio of properties, so should be able to keep you in work for years to come.'

'Brilliant. Cheers mate. We'll talk soon.'

'Yes, look forward to nailing down the specifics over the next few weeks. Speak soon. Bye.'

Luke watched the screen go blank and questioned his decision. Either he'd just accepted an opportunity that would change his life for the better, or he'd just made the biggest mistake of his life.

Chapter 61

Alice sat in the car with the engine running, staring at a cul-de-sac of small bungalows. Some had been extended with dormer windows in the loft, but most looked just as they'd been when they were built. Every front garden housed neat beds with brightly coloured flowers. Garden gnomes and bird-baths nestled among the beds, and all the lawns were neatly trimmed.

Alice put the car into gear and trundled down the hill. She scanned the numbers on the sides of houses until finally spotting number sixteen at the end of the street. Her hands shaking, Alice turned off the engine, climbed out of the car and stood staring at the small bungalow. Was she doing the right thing in coming here? There was only one way to find out.

After pressing the doorbell, Alice heard the strains of *Greensleeves* reverberating throughout the house. Was anyone home? The small, practical car parked in the drive suggested the owners were in, but perhaps they had gone for a walk, or round to a neighbour's house?

Alice was about to turn back when a figure approached from behind the frosted glass. The door opened, and a tall, wiry man with a head of thinning white hair peered down at her over the top of his glasses.

'No cold callers.' He went to close the door, but Alice stuck her foot in the gap.

'I'm not a cold caller.'

'Then what do you want?'

What Alice really wanted was to run away, but now she'd made the journey, she had to see it through. 'It's... well... I suppose I'm here on a personal matter. Perhaps it would be better if we spoke inside?'

'Inside? Not on your nelly. Not until I know who you are and what your business is coming here.'

Something in Alice snapped. For the past few months, she'd been subject to stares, hushed conversations, or worse, rooms going quiet when she walked in. She was done with being the bad guy when she'd done nothing wrong. 'If you'd rather not speak to me, that's your prerogative. But my name is Alice Loveday, and I believe I'm your granddaughter.'

'My what?' The old man's cheeks had turned pink, his eyes bulging as though about to fall from their sockets. 'I don't have a granddaughter.'

'But you have a son, Daniel Loveday?'

'My son is dead.'

The old man's words hit Alice like a slap. Dead? That must be why Margot had received no reply to the letter she sent Daniel. 'I'm sorry for your loss.' Why did she say that? It was her loss too, wasn't it?

'Yes, well, as I'm sure you've gathered, given my son is dead, it is highly unlikely I have a granddaughter.'

'My father was called Daniel Loveday. This is a photo of him.' From her wallet, Alice pulled out the single dog-eared photo her mum had given her when she'd asked about the identity of her father. She held it up, and the old man pushed his glasses up onto the bridge of his nose. As he studied the photograph, all colour drained from his face.

'Where did you get this photograph?'

'My mum gave it to me.'

'And where's your mother now? How can I trust you? You could be one of those scammers.'

'I was worried you'd think that,' said Alice, pulling her passport and driving licence out of her bag and showing them to the man.

'These things can be faked.'

Alice sighed. 'Fine, well other than taking a DNA test, I can't see what other way I have to convince you. I thought you might be interested in meeting me, but clearly I was wrong. I'll leave you in peace.'

Alice was unlocking the door to her car, feeling utterly despondent, when an elderly lady came rushing up to her.

'Is it true?'

'Is what true?' asked Alice, fed up with being interrogated.

'That you're our granddaughter.'

'If you're Daniel Loveday's parents, then yes, I'm your granddaughter.'

'You'd better come in.'

'Your husband didn't seem to think that's a good idea.'

'Oh, ignore him,' said the lady. 'He fell foul of internet scammers last year and has been on high alert ever since. Do you know they stole three hundred pounds from him? I tell you, you can't even trust a call from your bank these days.'

The woman chatted all the way back to the house, and Alice observed her, trying to spot any features they might share. The woman's white hair was scraped back into a tight bun, but her blue-grey eyes sparkled, and were very similar in colour to Alice's. She was dressed in well-fitting jeans and a stripy jumper that gave her an ageless quality. Alice instantly warmed to her.

'Jerry, come out here and apologise to Alice. You almost scared off our only grandchild, for goodness' sake!'

Alice watched as Jerry slunk out from behind the door and muttered an apology.

'Honestly, I understand,' said Alice. 'It's not everyday someone turns up on your doorstep saying they're a relative. You were right to be cautious.'

'Thank you. That's very gracious. Celia, do you want to take this young lady through to the living room and I'll make us a pot of tea? She has me well trained,' said Jerry.

Alice smiled, hiding her surprise at how quickly her grandfather's attitude to her had thawed. After thirty seconds inside the house, it was clear to Alice who ruled the roost.

'Yes, love, you come through here and settle yourself down.'

Alice followed Celia into a large living room. A floral three-piece suite was positioned around a television, and a selection of porcelain dancers decorated the windowsill. It was just the type of room Alice had imagined when she'd daydreamed about visiting grandparents she didn't know she'd had.

'What brings you here, then, love? How did you find out about us?'

'I recently moved to Saffron Bay and...'

'You moved to Saffron Bay?' The sparkle left Celia's eyes and a muscle in her jaw twitched.

'Yes. It's a long story, but the short version is that my mum moved away and left me with the key to a cottage in Saffron Bay that apparently belongs to me.'

'Seashell Cottage?'

'Yes.'

'You know we used to live there?'

'Yes, I'd gathered as much. Which makes me wonder how my dad could put the cottage in my name? Surely it belonged to you?'

Celia let out a long sigh. 'Wait here while I pop through to the kitchen. I know Jerry's making us tea, but I have a feeling we're going to need something a lot stronger.'

Chapter 62

'Are you sure you don't want one?'

Alice looked longingly at the glass of gin in Celia's shaking hand. 'No, I'd best not. I'm driving.'

'Very sensible. So, you wanted to know about the ownership of Seashell Cottage?'

'Yes, if that's alright. I've got all the official paperwork, but I don't understand why the cottage is in my name.'

'Well, I can tell you with a hundred per cent certainty you're not squatting. Daniel never told us he'd given the cottage to you. I'd assumed he'd just left it to go to rack and ruin. I'll ask him about it the next time he calls.'

'The next time he calls? I thought he was dead!'

Jerry stiffened and took a swig of his drink. 'I'm sorry, Alice. Everyone around here thinks Daniel's dead, and I've got used to parroting the lie.'

'Jerry!'

'How was I to know she really was our grandchild, Celia? You're the one who started the rumour about Daniel's death, not me.'

'But why on earth would you say such a thing if it wasn't true?'

'Because it's easier that way,' said Celia, her voice catching. 'When he came out of prison, we...'

'Came out of prison? What are you talking about?'

Jerry reached across the sofa and patted his wife's hand. 'Cece, perhaps you should start at the beginning?'

Celia sighed. 'Yes, you're probably right.' She took a sip of her gin and glanced at Alice. 'Are you sure you want to know what happened?'

'Yes, I'm fed up with being at the centre of some scandal I know nothing about.'

'Believe me, love, you're very much the innocent party in all of this.' Celia set her drink down on the coffee table and folded her hands in her lap. 'It happened in the summer of 2000. Daniel was twenty and in the process of setting up his own landscaping business. Every summer, Saffron Bay would be flooded with tourists, and a group of youngsters would form and get up to mischief.'

'Mischief?' asked Alice.

'Partying on the beach, drinking too much, nothing too scandalous. Anyway, that summer Daniel was getting a bit old for all that nonsense, but there were regular visitors who came back year on year, so it was inevitable he'd slot back into the group. I suppose twenty is a funny age really, the start of adulthood, but so often you still feel like a child.'

Alice nodded. She didn't find being twenty-five particularly easy, either.

'There were some new kids in Saffron Bay that year. I say kids, but they were well into their late teens. I remember one girl, oh, what was she called, Jerry?'

'I don't know who you're talking about.'

'Yes, you do. She was always calling round for Daniel. She stuck to him like a limpet. I think he was flattered by the attention. Unfortunately, she wasn't a very savoury character, always drinking, yelling in the street, you know the type. Oh, come on, Jerry, you must remember her name?'

'I think it started with an M. Maddy? Marilyn?'

'Maz?'

Sylvie stared at Alice. 'How do you know that?'

'It could be a coincidence, but that's my mum's name.'

'Your mother is that awful little... sorry.'

Alice held her hands aloft. 'I lived with my mother for twenty-five years. I know what she can be like. Don't worry.'

'Even so, I don't wish to be disrespectful to your mother. Anyway, as I was saying, they were a wild bunch that year. I'm not excusing Daniel's behaviour. He was my son, and I loved him, but in some ways he was still an immature little boy. He allowed himself to be dragged along with the crowd. Many a night he'd roll in half-cut and I'd have a job getting him up for work the next morning. In a way, though, his behaviour was understandable. He'd lost his best friend not long before, and looking back now, he was struggling to cope with the grief. I'll never forgive myself for not seeing what was going on right under my nose.'

'Sorry to interrupt, but how come the cottage belonged to Daniel?'

'Seashell Cottage belonged to my father-in-law. We moved to Saffron Bay shortly before he died to care for him. He and Daniel were thick as thieves, so it came as no surprise when he left the cottage to Daniel in his will.'

'Wasn't that awkward?'

'No, not really. Saffron Bay was only ever meant to be a stopgap while Harry was ill. Jerry and I never enjoyed the extremes of the place, one minute nothing going on, the next overrun with tourists. Daniel, on the other hand, loved it. He was a true Loveday in that sense, wedded to Saffron Bay as generations of Lovedays before him had been.'

'I still don't understand what happened to Jack Tyler? Was it all because of Maz?'

'Sorry, dear, but what has she got to do with Jack Tyler?'

'She's his daughter. Tilly Tyler was the name she went by back then, but I've always known her as Maz Green.'

'Jack Tyler's daughter?' Celia let out a groan.

'You didn't know?'

'No. And I didn't think things could get any worse.'

'Why don't you tell me what it is you do know?'

'Well, Daniel worked for Jack. He was a hard taskmaster, but underneath all the puff and bluster, I think he was a good man. Full of himself, maybe, but I know he donated generously to village fundraising, and he was always looking for ways to improve the village for its residents.'

'It's hard to imagine him like that now.'

'He's still alive?'

'Yes, but something of a hermit.'

'That's no surprise. The fire devastated him.'

'What do you know about the fire? I've seen the state of the house now, seen the damage. And I know my dad was involved somehow, but no one seems to know the truth.'

'It was almost the end of the summer. By this point, Daniel had become embroiled in a relationship with Maz, Tilly, whatever her name was, and wasn't behaving like himself at all. The night before the summer holidays ended, the group went out for one last hurrah. Daniel told us they were going to the pub, but in fact, they went in boats and kayaks. If I'd known they were planning to go out on the water half-cut, I'd never have allowed it. Anyway, from what we later learned, they took their alcohol to Jack Tyler's private beach and drank themselves silly. Daniel had been moaning about how difficult Jack was to work for, and someone suggested they teach Jack a lesson.'

Alice held her face in her hands, part of her not wanting to know what was coming but knowing that she had to hear it.

'They climbed up the cliff and found themselves outside Saffron Manor. What happened next is hazy, and I'm not sure I believe the account we were told.'

'What were you told?'

'That they had a box of fireworks with them, and Daniel decided it would be fun to give Jack a fright. He set off a series of rockets, but positioned them wrong, and instead of going up in the sky, they flew through the window of

Jack's home. The police believed he positioned them at the house on purpose, but I can't believe that of Dan.'

'Oh my God. Was anyone hurt?'

'No, Mary was in Ireland visiting her family with her daughters, although by the sounds of things, not all of them. Jack was in London for a meeting with his solicitor, not that Daniel and his friends knew that. That's why what happened next is so unforgivable.'

'What did they do?'

'They ran away. For all they knew, Jack was inside the house, but rather than waiting to check, they ran. All they cared about was saving their own skins. No one even called the fire brigade. That's what makes the whole thing so tragic. The initial fire could have been easily extinguished had they stopped even for a moment to think about what they were doing. By the time the villagers noticed smoke up on the hill, the house was already destroyed.'

'I think I may have one of those drinks after all,' said Alice, reaching for a glass.

'Jack Tyler arrived home the next day to find everything he owned destroyed in the fire. Of course there was a police investigation, but Jack tried to keep as much under wraps as he could.'

'Why?'

'He'd been having money troubles and had cancelled their home insurance. When his wife found out, she was so angry. Their marriage never recovered. Jack didn't want the villagers to know his own part in the mess he'd made of things. He was a proud man back then, and probably still is.' Celia lifted the glass of gin to her lips with shaking hands and took a long draught.

'Daniel eventually admitted to the crime. To this day, I don't believe he did it. I knew when my son was lying, and he was lying about that night, of that I'm in no doubt. He was sentenced to an eighteen-month custodial sentence. Jack made it clear to us that the Lovedays were no longer welcome in Saffron Bay, not that we wanted to stay after what had happened. Within a month of the fire, we'd moved away. There were a few reports about the trial and sentencing in the newspaper, but given we were living elsewhere by then, I doubt anyone in Saffron Bay saw them.'

Alice let out a breath and sunk back in her chair. 'I don't know what I was expecting when I came here,' she said, 'but it certainly wasn't that. Did you know, Maz, Tilly, was pregnant?'

'We had no idea. Daniel never said a word about any baby.'

'Apparently, Jack told my mum to end the pregnancy. I suppose it's possible my dad thought she'd gone through with it.' Was she being too generous? It was far more likely Daniel had abandoned her. But Alice liked Celia and Jerry, and the hurt she felt was bad enough. There was no need to taint her grandparents' lives with the disgust she felt towards Daniel Loveday.

Chapter 63

Then

It was a smaller group than usual, with some hangers-on having left Saffron Bay already. The summer was almost over, with an autumnal crispness hanging in the air. Daniel was exhausted from a day digging out brambles ready to plant a vegetable garden and could have done with an early night. But, as it was the last night of the holidays and Maz would soon be gone, he felt he owed it to her to turn up.

'I don't understand why we need to go around the coast. We have a perfectly good beach here.'

'Stop being such a party pooper,' said Maz. She leaned closer to Daniel and whispered in his ear, 'Don't forget I've got a surprise for you later.'

Daniel hated the way his body reacted to the softness of Maz's skin and the tickle of her breath on his cheek. He didn't like her personality much, truth be told, but it was as though there were some force field drawing him to her, and he wasn't a strong enough man to resist.

'Yeah, come on, Dan, it will be fun.' Sam was already drunk, having announced on arrival that she and Steve had been preloading behind the general store.

'It's not safe to be out on the water while we're pissed,' said Daniel, but everyone ignored him, dragging kayaks and a small rowing boat across the beach towards the sea.

At least the sea was calm, and the tide was at its peak. Coming back would be more treacherous as rocks waited just below the surface, but for now, there was little danger. A bigger problem was the group's ability to move their crafts through the water with alcohol numbing their reactions.

Maz hooted in glee as she and Sam turned round and round in circles before finally settling on a stuttering rhythm with their paddles. Daniel kept on the far edge of the group in case anyone lost their bearings and began heading too far out to sea. The moon was only a sliver in the sky, and the water below was black as pitch. Only Steve had a torch, and had become the de facto leader as a result.

'Don't get too far ahead, Steve,' called Dan. 'We need your light.'

'Sure,' said Steve, slowing his pace and waiting for Dan to catch up. 'The girls are already rat-arsed,' said Steve when Daniel drew level.

'I know. It doesn't bode well for the rest of the evening.'

'Yeah, getting back could be a bit of a mission, especially once the tide has turned.'

'If the worst comes to the worst, we can head back on land and leave the kayaks behind.'

Steve laughed. 'Yeah, but imagine what a fit Jack Tyler would have if he found our kayaks abandoned on his private beach.'

'Jack's wrath would be far more pleasant than drowning.'

'Fair enough.'

It took the best part of an hour to reach Jack Tyler's private beach. It had been Maz's idea to come here, and despite his better judgment, Daniel had gone along with the plan. She was so evasive about her family and background, but seemed to have a strange fascination with Jack Tyler that he couldn't understand. He helped the girls drag their kayaks up the beach and removed their bags from the hold. They spread out the various cans of drink on the sand, and Steve set about lighting a small fire.

'What the hell are these?' asked Daniel, pulling several cardboard boxes from a canvas bag.

'Fireworks,' said Maz. 'I thought we could send me off into the sunset with a bang.'

'Jack will go mental if he catches us letting off fireworks on his beach.'

'What Jack doesn't know won't hurt him,' said Maz with a grin. 'Anyway, he'll only get what he deserves. Anyone else fancy having a snoop at the big house?'

'There's no need to go traipsing all the way up there,' said Daniel.

'Says the only one of us who's actually seen the place,' said Steve.

'Sam's seen it,' said Daniel. 'They hosted a garden party up there for all the villagers last year.'

'I wouldn't mind seeing it again,' said Sam.

Daniel found her eagerness to impress Maz embarrassing, but then, wasn't he just as bad?

'We won't be able to see much in the dark,' said Steve. 'Let's just crack open the beers and build a bonfire like we'd planned.'

'God, you're all so boring,' said Maz. 'Well, Sam, looks like it's just you and me going up to the big house.'

'Don't be daft,' said Steve. 'You'll get lost in the dark.'

'Says who?'

'Says anyone with any common sense.'

Maz stuck her middle finger up and displayed it to each boy in turn. Then she grabbed Sam's hand and marched across the beach to where a steep path cut through a wooded hillside.

'Wait,' called Daniel. 'You can't go up there alone. We'll come with you.'

'Bring the bags then, won't you?' called Maz without looking round.

The lads loaded themselves up with bags and crates of beer, and set off in pursuit of Maz and Sam, who'd already reached the gate with *Private! Keep Out!* Written in clear letters. It was a long trudge up the path that cut steeply into the hillside. After a tiring day of manual work, even Daniel was out of breath when they reached the top.

'Are you OK?' Daniel asked Sam, who was pale and shaking.

'Yeah, fine, it's just a touch of seasickness.'

'Seasickness?' laughed Steve. 'More like vodka sickness.'

'Shut up.'

'This way,' said Daniel, leading them through a small wooden gate and out onto the lawn he'd mown only the day before.

'Jack Tyler is loaded,' said Steve, awe in his voice.

'Appearances can be deceptive,' muttered Maz.

'He's put a lot of work into this place,' said Daniel, unsure why he was coming to the man's defence. 'It was a wreck when he bought it.'

'You sound impressed,' said Steve. 'I thought you hated the bloke.'

'Hate's a strong word. He's not great as a boss, but even I can appreciate the work he does for the village.'

'Hah, all self-promotion if you ask me,' said Sam.

'Actually, he does a lot more than you think. I know for a fact he's given to loads of local charities on the quiet.'

'And you know that how?' asked Sam.

Daniel shrugged, not wanting to admit he'd stumbled on Jack's office while looking for the toilet on his first day working there and hadn't been able to resist a quick snoop. After all, the papers were lying on the desk, it wasn't as though they'd been hidden away.

'Enough talking,' said Maz, 'let's get this party started.'

Chapter 64
Then

'Sam, I think you've had enough,' said Steve, as Sam cracked open another can of beer.

'Shut up, you're not my boyfriend.'

Steve looked at Daniel and shrugged. No one could keep up with the on-off nature of Sam and Steve's relationship, not even Steve.

'He's got a point,' said Daniel. 'We've got a long walk back to the beach, then a long paddle home.'

'Guys, it's my last night in Saffron Bay. Can you lighten up, please?'

Daniel noticed Maz was unusually sober. In fact, she'd only had a few sips from one can of beer since they'd arrived on Jack Tyler's lawn.

'What do we do now?' slurred Sam, spilling beer onto her T-shirt as she took another sip.

'Chill for a bit in our grand surroundings,' said Maz, lying down on the neat lawn.

'Sounds kind of boring,' said Steve.

'Look,' said Maz, pointing up at the sky. 'It's beautiful.'

'I never had you down as a stargazer,' said Daniel.

'Well, maybe my perspective on life has changed recently,' said Maz, throwing him an enigmatic wink.

Daniel felt his heart sink. Was Maz going to declare her undying love for him? Was that her surprise? He really hoped not. Their relationship had been nothing more to him than an ill-advised fling. The last thing Daniel wanted was to become embroiled in a long-distance relationship with a woman he didn't really know or like. He lay down beside Maz on the grass.

'Guys, the stars are pretty impressive,' Daniel said, looking up at his friends. Above him, Sam was swaying unsteadily from foot to foot. 'Are you alright, Sam?'

'I... I...' Sam slapped a hand across her mouth and ran back toward the woods.

'Oh God, she's going to throw up,' said Steve. 'I'd better help, even if she doesn't think I'm her boyfriend today.'

When both Sam and Steve were out of view, Daniel turned his head to Maz, wanting to get the moment he was dreading over with. 'So, what was it you wanted to tell me?'

Maz grinned. 'That can wait. I was thinking about giving Jack Tyler a bit of a fright. But as Steve and Sam are off in the woods, we could freak them out too. One last prank of the summer. What do you say?'

'What kind of prank?'

Maz sat up and began pulling the box of fireworks from her bag.

'Maz, no, that's a terrible idea.'

'I think it's a great idea. Help me set them up.'

'No.'

'Fine, I'll do it myself.'

'Have you ever even set off fireworks before? You need to be really careful. Besides, They'll wake the whole house up, and there'll be hell to pay if Jack Tyler finds us setting off fireworks on his lawn.'

'It's only Jack there.' Before Daniel could ask how she knew that, Maz jumped up and put her hands on her hips. 'Go back to looking at the stars, or head back to the beach if you're that scared.'

Daniel sat up and put his head in his hands. What was Maz thinking? He should try to stop her, but knew there was no point. Maz had proved throughout the summer that when she set her mind to something, there was no changing it. He was evidence of that.

Maz began haphazardly positioning fireworks on the lawn. 'I'll only do the rockets,' she said. 'I'll save the smaller ones for when we're back in the village.'

'Whatever.'

Maz giggled. 'Ready to give the Tylers, Sam and Steve, the fright of their lives?'

'Maz, please…'

But Maz was already lighting the fuse of the first firework. Without waiting or stepping back a safe distance, she lit the rest of the fuses. After a few seconds of fizzing, rockets began shooting up into the sky.

Suddenly, the sound of splintering glass cut through the noise of rockets.

'What the…' said Daniel, grabbing hold of Maz's arm.

Maz giggled. 'That will really teach Jack Tyler a lesson.'

'A lesson for what, Maz? That firework has just gone into the house. We have to wake him up in case there's a fire.'

'And then what?'

'What do you mean?' Daniel grabbed hold of both of Maz's arms, trying to shake some sense into her. 'Maz, we have to warn him.'

'No.' Maz looked up at the building. 'It's too late, and besides, they have fire alarms.'

Daniel turned back to the house, bile rising in his throat as he saw an orange glow spilling through a previously dark window. 'Maz, there's a fire. We have to do something.'

Now it was Maz's turn to grab hold of Daniel. 'Daniel, listen to me. I can't get into trouble.'

'None of us wants to get into trouble, but if we put a stop to things now, it won't be so bad. I'll call the fire brigade.'

'NO! Daniel, listen to me. The surprise I had for you, the thing I was going to tell you? I'm pregnant.'

'You're what?'

'Pregnant. With your child. Oh, and you should probably know I'm also Jack Tyler's daughter.'

'You're what?' Daniel's eyes widened, his mind cloudy just when he needed his thoughts to be clear. Was this another of Maz's pranks?

'Listen, Dan, Jack deserves everything he gets. Do you know what he said when I told him I'm pregnant? He told me to get rid of it. He told me to get rid of our baby. Just because I'm only sixteen doesn't mean...'

'You're sixteen?' Daniel clutched his stomach, feeling like he might throw up. 'You told me you were eighteen and about to go to university!'

'Don't pretend my age made any difference to you. It is what it is. You believed what you wanted to believe. Now, do you see why we need to get out of here? No one can link this fire to me or I'll have social services at my door before I've even been for the three-month scan. Come on.'

Dazed and confused, his mind scrambling to make sense of Maz's bombshell, Daniel let her drag him back towards the woods.

'What the hell's going on?' asked Steve, meeting them at the gate.

'Nothing, it's all OK. How's Sam?'

'In an awful state. I'm worried she's got alcohol poisoning. I need to get her home.'

'Where is she?'

'Lying under a bush over here.'

Steve led Daniel and Maz to Sam, who was curled up, shivering under a bush like a wild animal.

'Maybe I could carry her to the end of the drive and call an ambulance?'

'No!' said Daniel and Maz in unison. If Steve and Sam were unaware of the devastation unfolding at Saffron Manor, it was best kept that way.

'We'll lie Sam down in her kayak and attach it to the back of yours,' Daniel told Steve. 'You're the strongest and fastest, so it makes sense. Me and Maz can travel back in my kayak.'

'There's still the problem of getting Sam back down onto the beach.'

'We'll carry her between us, but whatever we do, we need to hurry.'

As Daniel helped Steve lift Sam, he was aware of the tang of smoke filtering through the trees. All he could think about was the immediate problem of getting Sam to safety. What had happened at Saffron Manor felt like a dream, not to mention Maz's revelation. Whatever happened next, Daniel knew his life would never be the same.

Chapter 65

The pale light of dawn seeped through the thin curtains, and Alice threw her pillow across the room in frustration. All night she'd been tossing and turning, the meeting with Celia and Jerry playing round and round in her mind. Part of her felt elation at discovering she was part of a family. She'd promised to visit them again in a few days and was looking forward to it, but the revelation about her dad hung heavy on her heart. Yes, he'd been to prison, but eighteen months wasn't that long in the grand scheme of things, and there were still twenty-three and a half years he could have been in touch.

That it was Luke she wanted to speak to about everything stung. Her skin still burned when she thought of his touch, and she'd never experienced such peace as when they lay intertwined, thinking she was now part of a team. Alice wished she could shut off the memories. How a few hours could have affected her so deeply made Alice feel weak and a fool for ever trusting Luke. She should have stuck with her initial instinct and steered well clear.

With a sigh, she climbed out of bed and yanked a pair of jogging bottoms and a jumper over her pyjamas. She needed to get out of the house, get into the fresh air, and try to clear her mind. Not wanting to wake May, Alice grabbed the first coat her fingers landed on and crept out of the house.

The village was deserted, cottages dark, curtains closed and lights off. A distant rumble of thunder left Alice questioning the sanity of being out at this time in unpredictable weather, but she pressed on, the sight of the sea doing as much to clear her mind as the damp air and fresh breeze. When she reached the beach, her eyes focused on the horizon, where a thin band of lighter grey signalled the arrival of morning.

A small wave crashed against the shore, sucking sand and pebbles beneath its foam as it retreated into a slate-grey mass. Alice walked to the water's edge and tilted her face towards the lightening sky. The air was damp, tiny droplets landing on her skin, shocking her out of her drowsiness. Her fingers tapped out a pattern on her thigh as *Reflets dans l'eau* by Debussy played in her mind.

Alice turned her gaze to the east and spotted a figure disguised by head to toe waterproof clothes walking along the shore. She wouldn't have recognised him but for the small Scotty dog scampering along at his heels.

For a moment she considered turning back, but she would have to face Jack Tyler sometime. With his eyes shielded by a large hood, he didn't spot her until Alice was within touching distance.

'Good morning, Jack,' she said.

Jack started and turned on his heel.

'Jack, please wait.'

'I've nothing to say to you.'

'Well, I have plenty to say to you,' said Alice, jogging to keep up with his surprisingly long strides. To make matters worse, the heavens opened, which was of no consequence to Jack in his waterproofs, but Alice, in her flimsy corduroy jacket, was quickly soaked to the skin. 'Don't you care that we're related?' asked Alice.

'You're no relation of mine.'

'But I am, aren't I? You're my grandfather. Your daughter Tilly is my mum.'

'I don't have a daughter called Tilly.'

'Fine then, Maz.'

'I don't have a daughter called Maz, either.'

'But you did, didn't you? Until you disowned her. How does it feel to be talking to me, Jack? You wanted her to get rid of me, didn't you?'

Jack stopped walking so suddenly Alice almost bumped into him. 'I did what I thought was right at the time.' He shook his head and carried on marching across the beach.

'And now?'

'Tilly made her choice all those years ago. She could have remained part of our family, but she wanted to strike out on her own. Always thought she knew best, did Tilly. And look where it got her, two kiddies by two different men and neither of them anywhere to be seen.'

'Did you even try to find her?' asked Alice, panting at the effort of jogging through the sand.

'Tilly didn't want to be found. She stopped being my daughter decades ago. We're no longer family, and you're nothing to me.'

The harshness of Jack's words stopped Alice in her tracks. He walked on, his stride determined, his eyes fixed straight ahead. She cupped her hands around her mouth and yelled into the rain. 'Whatever you think of me, reporting us to social services was a new low, even for you!'

Jack stopped, turned around and stared at her. 'I've made many mistakes in my life, young lady, but that isn't one of them. You're looking in the wrong place if you need someone to blame. It wasn't me. Now, please leave me alone.'

Alice couldn't understand how he could be so cold. It wasn't as if his life was filled with friends and family. Surely he was lonely? If even a lonely old man wanted nothing to do with her, Alice wondered what that said about her. She tried not to take Jack's dismissal personally, but as the distance between them grew, Alice lifted a hand and brushed water from her cheek. It was impossible to tell whether she was wiping away raindrops or tears.

Chapter 66

'Are you sure about this?' May handed Alice a cup of tea, and they both stared out of the open front door to where a man from the estate agents was hammering a sign into the ground.

'It's the first thing I've been certain of since we arrived in Saffron Bay.'

'But what if he comes back?'

'My dad?' May nodded and Alice sighed. 'He's had twenty-five years to find me, and I'm done with waiting. If we sell this place, we can move back to the city. You'll be able to spend proper time with your friends, you won't have a crazy bus journey at the start and end of each day, and once we've bought ourselves a flat, there'll be enough money left over to see us both through university.'

'You've really thought this through.'

'It's all I've been thinking about. Saffron Bay has never really been our home. It's a place that belongs in the past, a place where our parents screwed up their lives and ours with them. I just want to get out now. But don't worry, nothing will happen quickly. There won't be another move until after you've finished your exams.' Alice noticed May cast her eyes down to the floor. 'What is it?'

May shrugged, sipped her tea and leaned against the door frame. 'I don't know. Everything you're saying makes sense, but I suppose I've been getting used to the place.'

Alice's eyes widened. 'You want to stay?'

May shrugged again. 'The volunteering I've been doing at Margot's café has been really fun, and she's offered me a paid job once I've finished my exams. Also, I didn't tell you, but I went for a walk with Paige last week.'

Alice spat out her tea. 'You what?'

'I should have told you. I was wary at first, but it turned out she wanted to apologise. She's been having a really tough time of it, and I'm not sure the girls she hangs around with really get it.'

'But you do?'

'Dysfunctional families are kind of my specialty,' said May with a wry smile.

'Hang on, so you're telling me you and Paige are friends now?'

'It's early days, but yeah, we are, kind of.'

'Well, I didn't see that coming,' said Alice, watching as the *For Sale* board was nailed onto its wooden pole.

'Does Sylvie know about this?' asked May, pointing to the sign.

'Yes. I went to see her yesterday. She was more upset than I'd expected her to be, but when I explained my reasons, she said she understood.'

'She'll miss you, and your piano playing.'

'I'll miss her,' said Alice, surprising herself. She'd always considered Sylvie a neighbour, but now she realised she was a friend, and a good one at that.

'What about Luke?'

'We're not on speaking terms. I doubt he'll miss me.'

'You need to talk to him.'

'No, I don't.'

The handyman walked over to let them know he was finished, and after thanking him, Alice closed the front door. She and May walked into the kitchen, and May opened the fridge. 'There's nothing in here for lunch. Shall I head to the shop?'

'You've got revision to do. I'll go.' Alice picked up her purse and pulled on her coat. As she let herself out of the cottage, she noticed the salt in the air, the way the trees hugging the village were turning a vivid green as their spring leaves emerged and how the sea was a vibrant shade of turquoise. She would miss the views in Saffron Bay, if nothing else.

Sam was behind the till when she walked into the General Store. 'Alice, tell me it isn't true!'

'What isn't true?' asked Alice, picking up a basket.

'You're selling up.'

'Wow, word travels fast around here.'

'So it is true?'

'Yes.'

'But why?'

'For a list of reasons as long as my arm. It's the right thing to do, for me and for May.'

'You'll be missed,' said Sam. 'We've all got used to having the Lovedays back in town.'

Alice laughed. 'That's kind of you to say, but I think most people will be glad to see the back of us.'

'Actually, we were going to ask if you'd play the piano for the amateur dramatic society's next show. Most people who live here now moved here in the years since your dad left. The Loveday name means nothing to them, and they'd be keen to get to know you.'

'That's a very kind offer,' said Alice, 'and if we were staying long-term, I'd have loved to get involved, but moving is the best thing for me and May and I'm afraid I'm not going to change my mind.'

'Fair enough,' said Sam with a sigh.

A bell tinkled as the door to the General Store opened, and in walked Margot. Alice stiffened. Margot was the last person she wanted to see.

'Afternoon, Sam, Alice. I'm on an emergency milk dash, as we've had a run on lattes this afternoon.' Margot walked to the fridge and filled her basket with bottles of milk. She carried them to the counter, giving Alice a brief smile before settling her eyes on Sam. 'Is everything alright, Sam? You're looking a little glum.'

'Alice is selling up,' said Sam as she began scanning the contents of Margot's basket.

'What? But you can't!'

'I think you'll find I can,' said Alice, aware how cold she sounded but not caring.

Margot placed a hand on Alice's arm, but Alice shrugged her off. Sam frowned and narrowed her eyes. 'What am I missing here? Have you two had a falling out?'

'I'll leave Margot to explain that one,' said Alice, picking up her bag of shopping. 'Bye, Sam.'

Alice walked quickly through the village, but wasn't surprised when Margot caught her up.

'Alice, please, I need to talk to you.'

'I have nothing to say to you.'

Margot grabbed Alice's arm and forced her to stop. 'All I'm asking for is two minutes of your time.'

Alice folded her arms but didn't say no.

'Shall we go to the café and I'll make you a coffee?'

'We talk here or not at all,' said Alice, sitting on the bench Solly had been occupying when she first arrived in Saffron Bay.

Margot sat down beside her and let out a sigh. 'I'm sorry for keeping secrets from you, Alice. When you first arrived, it was such a shock realising how little you knew about your father.'

'But you didn't feel the need to rectify the situation.'

'I honestly believed that giving Dan the opportunity to explain himself was the right thing to do. Then, when I didn't hear from him, I panicked. I couldn't risk going behind his back. He cut me off once before, and as my only link to my son, Marty, I couldn't risk that happening again.'

'What about Marty's dad?'

'A one-night stand when I was young and foolish. Of course I tried to track him down, but I didn't even have a surname to go on. It was always just me and Marty until Dan came on the scene, of course.'

'You said Daniel cut off contact with you. When was that?'

'The first couple of years after he left. When he got back in touch, he was very apologetic, but never explained his actions.'

'He was in prison.'

'What?'

'His parents told me when I met them last week. I know people can send letters from prison, but maybe he was embarrassed.' Alice shook her head, bemused at having to defend him. She glanced at her watch, half of Margot's two minutes were gone.

Margot must have noticed, for when she spoke, her words came out in a rush. 'I should never have burdened Luke with what I knew. I thought he could look out for you, but I put him in a horrible position. None of this is his fault, Alice. I asked him not to say anything until I'd heard from Daniel. He was trying to do what he thought was right, and was angry at the thought of keeping things from you.'

Alice sighed. 'None of this changes the fact you both should have told me what you knew. And it doesn't change the fact that my dad doesn't want to see me.'

'But that's the thing, Alice. He does.'

'What?'

'I received his letter yesterday. He'd been away for a month, so only just got my letter. He's on his way down here as we speak. Alice, he's coming to find you.'

Chapter 67

'Knock knock.'

Alice looked up from the onions she was chopping to see Sylvie and Solly standing in the doorway. 'Oh, hi.'

'Sorry to barge in, but the door was wide open.'

'Urgh, I keep telling May to close it properly when she leaves, but she doesn't listen.'

'Is she meeting friends in the city?'

'No,' said Alice. She pulled a face and leaned against the worktop. 'She's gone for a walk with Paige Morris.'

'Paige?' said Sylvie. 'Are you sure that's wise?'

'No, I'm not.' Alice washed the knife and set it down, deciding the onions could wait. 'But May assures me Paige has turned over a new leaf and wants to be friends. It's not a friendship I want to encourage, but I can hardly start telling May who she can or can't hang out with.'

'Very true.'

'Would you like a cup of tea?'

Sylvie glanced at Solly, who nodded. 'That would be lovely, thank you, Alice. Why don't we make it? It looks as though you're in the middle of something.'

'It's fine,' said Alice. 'I was getting a head start on dinner, but there's no rush.'

'I see you've got the sign up,' said Solly as Alice pottered around the kitchen making tea. 'It seems a shame after all the work you've done on the cottage.'

Alice shrugged. 'It's for the best.'

Sylvie and Solly remained quiet. Alice glanced behind her and noticed Sylvie take Solly's hand, then give him an encouraging nod. He cleared his throat. 'Alice, I wanted to talk to you about the elephant in the room.'

Alice frowned and looked around. 'I don't see an elephant.' She smiled. 'Sorry, couldn't help myself.'

Solly gave a nervous chuckle. 'I've tried to give both you and Jack space to deal with everything yourselves,' he said. 'I've always tried to keep my nose out of other people's business, and that includes my brother, but I'm not sure that's always been the right approach. I'm your uncle, Alice, and as your uncle, I feel I need to step up where my brother can't.'

'Can't?' laughed Alice. 'Don't you mean won't? Jack's informed me I'm nothing to him and he wants nothing to do with me.'

'That's as may be,' said Solly, 'but I do. I was away when everything happened with Daniel and your mother, but I know enough to know it was you left paying for their mistakes. It isn't fair. I have little to offer, and my reasons for wanting to acknowledge our relationship are partly selfish. I never had a family of my own, and I'd like to be part of your life, yours and May's.'

'That's very kind of you to say, Solly. And I promise I'll stay in touch once we've left Saffron Bay. I feel no ill will toward you. You've never left me feeling anything but welcome here.'

'See,' said Sylvie.

'Why don't I talk to Jack? Try to get him to see sense?'

'About me?' Alice laughed again. 'I don't need anyone fighting my battles for me, Solly. I've managed on my own until now. Besides, Celia and Jerry are keen to spend some time getting to know me, as am I them.'

'Celia and Jerry?'

'My grandparents on my dad's side.'

'Oh, yes. I was away with the navy when the Lovedays lived in the village, so I've not met them.'

'You'd like them, I think. They're good people. More victims of my dad and Maz's mess.'

'Speaking of Daniel,' said Sylvie, 'have you heard anything from him? I must say, I was so shocked to find out Margot has been in touch with him all this time.'

'Not as shocked as I was,' said Alice, handing over two mugs of tea. 'Actually, I spoke to Margot yesterday, and she gave me some rather momentous news. It seems Daniel Loveday is on his way back to Saffron Bay.'

Both Solly and Sylvie's eyes widened. 'Goodness, how are you feeling about that?' asked Sylvie.

Alice sat down at the table. 'I honestly don't know. I've had butterflies in my stomach ever since Margot told me, but I don't know what they mean. One minute I feel terrified, the next angry, the next excited. The past twenty-four hours have been an emotional rollercoaster.'

'I bet,' said Sylvie. 'Do you know where and when you're going to meet him?'

'Yes, that's one thing I am sure of. I've asked Margot whether we can meet at the café. It feels like neutral ground.'

'Do you really want an audience?'

'Definitely not. She's said we can go there after closing time.'

'You're a very brave girl, Alice,' said Solly, reaching across the table and squeezing her hand.

'I don't feel it,' said Alice with a small laugh. 'But I'm ready to hear some answers, and Daniel Loveday is the one to give them to me.'

A hush descended as each contemplated the implications of Daniel Loveday's return to Saffron Bay. It was Sylvie who broke the silence.

'Has Luke spoken to you lately?' she asked.

'No. And there's no reason he should. We're not friends.' Alice sat heavily in a chair and picked up her mug of tea. She didn't want to think about Luke, especially after her conversation yesterday with Margot. Her feelings were too complicated, and with the imminent return of her father, she had bigger fish to fry.

'He's leaving Saffron Bay too.'

Alice looked up from her mug of tea. 'He's taken the job in London?'

'You knew about it?'

'I saw a letter when I was at his house once. How do you feel about him going?'

Sylvie's eyes remained fixed on Alice. 'I'd feel better if I thought it was what he really wanted.'

'What are you suggesting? That he's leaving because of me?'

'In part, yes.'

'I'm not responsible for any decisions Luke makes. And it's unfair to suggest I am. If you don't want him to go, tell him.'

'It's not that,' said Sylvie. 'I love having him so nearby, of course I do, but he's a grown man and I want him to live his own life. If moving to London were about starting again, I'd be all for it. But it's not. It's about running away.'

'In that case, it should be him you're talking to, not me.'

'But you're doing exactly the same thing,' said Solly. 'Can't you see that?'

'So what if I am?' said Alice, standing up and pushing back her chair. 'Aren't I allowed to do something for myself for once?'

'All we ask is that you take a little while longer to think things through,' said Sylvie.

Alice's shoulders sagged, and all the fight left her. 'My mind's made up and there'll be no changing it.'

'Come on,' said Solly, standing. 'I think we've taken up enough of Alice's time. We'll leave you in peace. Alice, I know your father returning is a huge thing for you to have to deal with, but please remember you're not alone. You have a family now. Lean on us if you need to.' He surprised Alice by pulling her into a hug, and she felt tears burn the back of her eyes.

'Thank you,' she muttered, as they walked out of the room.

Chapter 68

'How did it go?'

May paused in the doorway of Alice's room. 'It was interesting.'

'Interesting?'

May walked into the room, and Alice shuffled up to make room for her on the bed. 'She wasn't mean to you again, was she?'

'No, not at all. She was actually pretty tearful and grateful.'

'Grateful?'

'We spoke for a long time. She had a lot she needed to get off her chest. It turns out the other girls she's friends with all come from perfect families, and she's had no one to talk to about family stuff.'

'No family is perfect,' Alice pointed out.

'True, but none are quite as messed up as hers or mine.'

Alice put an arm around May. 'I'm so sorry.'

'You've got nothing to apologise for. You've practically raised me and done a brilliant job of it, too. I'm lucky compared to Paige. Yes, her mum is still around, but she doesn't have an Alice in her corner.'

Alice swallowed the lump in her throat. 'Did you go to Paige's house to hang out?'

'No.'

May looked suddenly shifty, and Alice narrowed her eyes. 'May, where have you been?'

'Hear me out before you blow your lid,' she said, turning to face Alice. 'We went up to Jack Tyler's house.'

'You what?' said Alice, jumping off the bed and glaring at May. 'In what world did you think that would be a good idea?'

'Both me and Paige wanted to apologise. I know you arranged my volunteering to make things up to him, but I'd never apologised in person, and it turns out that night wasn't the first time Paige had gone snooping around up there, so she wanted to apologise too.'

'What happened when you got there? He didn't pull out his baseball bat again, did he? If he did, I'm going straight to the police.'

'I told you to hear me out,' said May, sighing and shaking her head. 'He was pissed off at first, as you'd expect. In fact, he slammed the door on us.'

'Right. So you left without speaking to him?'

'No,' May's cheeks turned pink.

'May, what did you do?'

'We walked around the house and shouted our apologies through the window. Eventually he got fed up and let us in.'

'He let you into his house? You went into his house, after what happened last time?'

'He's not actually that scary,' said May. 'I think he's lonely. Me and Paige talked about it after we left. It's like he's been punishing himself by living in that one room all these years.'

'Punishing himself for what?'

'For driving Mum away, for driving the rest of his family away. I told him straight that what he did to Mum was terrible, but I also told him what she's been like to live with over the years. In my opinion, they're both as bad as each other.'

'She was a vulnerable young girl who was pregnant, and he chucked her out on the streets.'

'I know, but I don't think he meant to.'

'He told her to end the pregnancy.'

'And he feels awful about that too, especially now he's met you. He said he regretted saying it almost straight away, but felt he couldn't back down.'

'At least we know where Maz gets her stubbornness from.'

'I told him he should speak to Mum, if she ever comes home. They're more similar than he'd like to admit, and I think twenty-five years is enough time to hold a grudge. It's time they both moved on.'

'How did you get so wise and grown-up?'

'We've both had to grow up fast, haven't we?' said May.

'Too fast. So, how did you leave things with Jack?'

'Hmm, hard to say. I gave him quite a few home truths, so I wouldn't say we're friends, but he's got plenty to think about.'

'Right,' said Alice, inwardly groaning. For all May's optimism, it sounded to her like May and Paige had poked a hornet's nest. After their encounter on the beach, Alice was certain Jack had his mind made up about her, and now he'd think she couldn't fight her own battles and needed her fifteen-year-old sister as a guard dog. But Alice said none of this to May. Instead, she gave her sister a hug, congratulated her on building bridges with Paige, and wandered off to the bathroom to get ready for her next shift in the pub.

Alice had her fingers on the doorknob about to leave when someone knocked and she jumped out of her skin. When she opened the door, her heart sank.

'Hello, Alice.'

'Patricia.' The word came out as a sigh. 'I'm on my way to work. If you're here to complain about May, I know all about where she and Paige have been, and I can't say I approve either. But from the sounds of things, they were equally complicit in their little plan.'

'I'm not here about Paige.'

'Oh.'

'Can you spare a minute?'

Alice glanced at her watch. 'Literally a minute.'

'That's all I need,' said Patricia, following Alice into the kitchen.

Rather than offer Patricia a drink or a seat, Alice leaned against the kitchen counter, enjoying how uncomfortable Patricia looked hovering in the middle of the room.

'Have you spoken to Luke lately?'

Alice rolled her eyes. 'Why does everyone want to know that? No, I haven't and don't intend to speak to Luke. You're free to do whatever the heck you want with him.'

Patricia laughed. 'I don't want to get together with Luke,' she said. 'At least, not anymore.'

'Right.'

'I've never been one for sloppy seconds, and it's obvious to everyone in the village he's in love with you.'

'I highly doubt it.'

'If this is about him keeping secrets, you've got it all wrong. I know Luke better than most, and he'd never deliberately do anything to hurt anyone. If he didn't tell you about your dad, it would have been because he thought he was doing the right thing.'

'Why are you defending him?'

'Because he's a good man. Because I ruined his life once and this is my way of trying to make amends. You two are perfect for each other, and you're the only one who can't see it.'

'I don't get it,' said Alice, turning to fill a glass with water as a way of escaping Patricia's intense stare.

Patricia sighed, pulled out a chair and flopped down into it. 'Let's just say I've seen the error of my ways. It's not only Luke I mistreated; I totally misjudged you and your sister. I don't know what May's done, but it's like I've got my daughter back. She's happy, and I've not seen her happy in a very long time.'

'I'm glad we could be of service. Now, I really must go.'

But Patricia didn't move. Instead, she sat playing with her hands. 'There's something else I need to apologise for. I heard you had a visit from social services.'

'It was you who called them?'

Patricia nodded. 'I'm so sorry, Alice. I was jealous and bitter, and... there's no excuse for what I did.'

'It's OK.'

'What?'

'I said, it's OK.' Alice wasn't going to admit that Maisie Clark's assessment had gone better than she could have hoped. She wasn't going to admit that the foster carer's allowance she was now in receipt of had taken an enormous weight off her shoulders. She wasn't going to admit that the relief that it hadn't been Jack who called them was so great Alice could cry. But neither was she going to see Patricia suffer. 'It's water under the bridge, Patricia. I appreciate your coming here to apologise, but I really need to get to work.'

'Of course.' Patricia stood up. 'Well, I guess I'll see you around.'

'Bye.'

'Oh my God,' said May, appearing as soon as Patricia had closed the door behind her. 'Did that just happen?'

'It did,' said Alice. 'But as much as I'd like to talk it over with you, I've got to get to work. I'll see you later.'

As she walked past May, Alice found herself drawn into a bear hug. 'I love you so much,' said May. Alice kissed her sister's cheek, and found as she walked the short distance to work, she felt about three stone lighter.

Chapter 69

Luke walked into the pub and had to force himself not to walk straight out again. Nick didn't notice, striding straight to the bar and greeting Alice with an ease Luke envied. He thought he'd got her shifts nailed, only visiting the pub when he knew she'd be at home, but here she was, serving customers in place of Rita, who should have been on duty.

'No Rita today?'

Alice answered Luke with a tight smile. 'She's got a migraine, so I've been called in to help.'

'Right.'

'How are you?'

'Good. You?'

'Fine, thanks.'

'I'm sorry to interrupt this scintillating conversation,' said Nick, perching himself on a bar stool, 'but I'm dying of thirst here. One pint of Doom Bar, please, Alice, and whatever Luke is having.'

'Just a pint of lager, please,' said Luke, handing over a ten-pound note. Nick whistled and tapped his fingers against the bar as Alice poured their pints.

'*New York State of Mind.*'

'What?' said Luke as Alice handed over his pint. She ignored him and turned to Nick, one eyebrow raised.

'Got it in one,' he said, lifting his pint to her. 'Cheers.'

Alice smiled and turned her back on them to clean some glasses.

'Shall we sit outside?' asked Luke, longing to put some distance between him and Alice.

'Hang on,' said Nick, placing his pint down on the bar. 'You play the piano, don't you, Alice?'

'Yep,' she said, not turning around.

'*New York State of Mind*. You know it? As in, how to play it?'

'Yep.'

Nick let out a whistle, then leaned both elbows on the bar. 'Alice?'

With a sigh, Alice turned around. 'What?'

Nick pointed to the piano in the corner of the room.

'No. No way. I'm here to work, not play.'

'Just one song. Come on. You can see if someone walks in, and anyway, I'm sure Luke won't mind watching the bar. Please. It would be like all my Christmases had come at once. I've never met anyone who can do justice to that song.'

'What makes you think I can?' asked Alice, flinging a tea towel over her shoulder.

Nick shrugged. 'I've got a feeling about you. It's always the quiet ones you have to watch out for.'

Luke watched the interaction, thinking what an idiot his best friend was and how he didn't stand a chance of getting Alice to fall for his charms. 'Come on, mate. Leave Alice alone. She doesn't want to play the piano for you.'

Alice's eyebrows shot up. 'Really? Says who?' She placed her hands on her hips and stared at Luke.

'I thought you only played classical piano,' he muttered as she walked out from behind the bar and made her way to the piano.

'There's a lot about me you don't know, Luke,' said Alice, lifting the piano lid and spreading her fingers across the keys. She turned to Nick. 'Are you coming?'

'Yes, ma'am,' he said, saluting and standing beside her.

The bar went quiet and drinkers turned to look as the first notes sounded. A few bars in and customers were out of their seats, crowding around as Alice worked her magic, fingers running up and down the keyboard with a speed Luke had never witnessed. Nick's eyes were so wide Luke thought they might pop out of his head. He watched Alice, who was oblivious to everything and everyone in the room, with her eyes closed, her body swaying as her hands blurred.

A tiny nod of Alice's head was the only encouragement Nick needed to sing. It had been so long since he'd heard him, Luke had forgotten what a great voice his friend was lucky to possess. Together, Nick and Alice made quite the duo, intuitively working together as the music ebbed and flowed. Luke turned his head away, feeling a pang of jealousy rip through him.

When the song ended, the room burst into rapturous applause, with shouts of 'more' and 'encore' filling the air.

'You know *Georgia on My Mind*?' Nick asked Alice.

She replied with a smile, her hands tickling the keys. 'Is this too low for you?'

'No, it's the perfect key.'

'Great.' Alice closed her eyes again, and she was off.

Luke tried to tear his eyes away but couldn't. On a normal day, Alice could be spiky, self-conscious, with an outer shell that was at times impenetrable. But here, sitting at the piano, it was like watching a different woman. With a pang of sadness, Luke recognised her as the Alice he'd had in his bed. The Alice who relaxed enough around him to let her guard down. The woman he loved had shown him her true self, and he'd blown it. The woman he loved? Loved? Luke's hand trembled, the beer in his glass spilling over the sides. He walked through the door, escaping into the warm spring air.

He couldn't love Alice. It wasn't possible to love someone after a few short months. It was ridiculous, stupid, impossible. Luke sat down heavily on a bench and threw his head into his hands. He could try to talk himself out of it as much as he wanted, but there was no denying the truth. He loved Alice Loveday, a woman who hated him, a woman he had lied to, a woman who would probably celebrate when he finally moved to London and she never had to see him again. 'You fool,' said Luke, shaking his head. 'You total and utter fool.'

'Finally, something we agree on.'

Luke's head snapped up. He hadn't even noticed the music had stopped. Alice was standing right there in front of him, a smile tugging at the corner of her lips. 'I had no idea you were so good at the piano. I mean, Gran told me you were amazing, but I never thought...' Luke trailed off as Alice folded her arms across her chest. What had he done to put his foot in it this time?

'You can't think I'm that good if you came out here.'

Something in her tone gave him hope. Was she teasing? Luke stood up and took a step towards her. 'You want to know why I came out here?'

'I'm all ears.'

Luke ran a hand through his hair. It was time to be honest. After all, he couldn't make things any worse than they already were. 'I came outside because seeing you and Nick together made me jealous. I came out here because I couldn't bear to watch the woman I love a second longer and not be able to touch you, to shout my feelings from the rooftops. I'm an idiot, I know that, but from the second I met you, all I've wanted to do is protect you, help you. The last thing I wanted to do was hurt you.'

'You love me?' Alice was frowning like this wasn't good news.

'Yes, I think so.'

'You think so?' she arched an eyebrow then stepped towards him so their faces were inches apart. Her voice dropped to a whisper. 'Luke...'

'Alice?' called Nick, walking out into the beer garden. 'There's a queue at the... oh, sorry. Am I interrupting?'

Luke glared at his best friend. Wasn't it obvious? A flustered Alice announced she had to get back to work and ran back into the pub.

'Sorry, mate,' said Nick. 'I had no idea what was going on out here.'

'It's alright,' said Luke. 'I don't know what was going on out here either.'

'Women,' said Nick, sitting himself down on a bench. 'More trouble than they're worth.'

Luke sat down beside Nick. 'Do you really think that?'

'Course not,' said Nick, grinning. 'Especially not that one.' He pointed to Alice, who was serving the crowd of customers gathered around the bar. 'She's definitely worth it, and you'd better figure out what you're going to do to win her back, hadn't you?'

Chapter 70

Alice's hand hovered on the door handle. Ever since she had answered the phone to Margot earlier that morning, her resolve had been faltering. Could she do this? Did he deserve this from her? She turned, ready to walk away, but May took hold of her arm.

'You can do this, Alice. Just go in there and hear him out. This isn't for him. You're doing this for yourself.'

'Will you stay with me?'

'Are you sure you don't want to do this alone?'

'No, I want you by my side.' Alice took May's hand, gave her a watery smile, took a deep breath, and opened the door.

As promised, the café was closed to all other customers, but even if every table had been occupied, Alice would have known her father the second she laid eyes on him. His hair had lost the yellow tones and was now pure white. Deep crow's feet spread like fireworks from the corners of his eyes, and Alice felt a stab of anger that this was a man who often smiled. They locked eyes, and Daniel Loveday half stood, his chair scraping against the floor. Alice squared her shoulders and walked over to his table.

'Alice.' The name slipped like a sigh from his mouth.

'Yes, and this is my sister, May.'

Daniel, who so far had had his eyes fixed on Alice, shifted his gaze to May, his mouth falling open. 'It's a pleasure to meet you, May. Goodness, you're the spit of Maz.'

'So people keep telling me,' muttered May, conforming to the teenage stereotype and rolling her eyes.

'Please, take a seat.'

Margot appeared from the kitchen. She must have been lurking, waiting for them to arrive. 'What can I get you, ladies?' Her voice was too chirpy and sounded forced.

'I'll have a hot chocolate,' said May.

'Tea for me,' said Alice, too on edge to cope with one of Margot's strong coffees and not yet ready to meet the woman's eye or say please.

'Thank you for coming, Alice,' said Daniel, once Margot had left to make the drinks. 'It's good to finally meet you.'

Alice laughed and stared at her father. 'Meet me? You sound like you're greeting an acquaintance of Margot, not your daughter.'

Daniel looked down at the table. 'I'm sorry, but there's no manual for this kind of thing, is there?'

'I suppose not.'

'May?' called Margot from the kitchen. 'Could you come over here and give me a hand with the drinks?'

May looked at Alice, who nodded to show she would be alright by herself. 'Why did you come back?' asked Alice, once May had left the table.

'I wanted to see you. I wanted to talk.'

'Well, I'm sorry, Daniel, but you're twenty-five years too late for a cosy father-daughter chat.'

'She told me you were adopted.'

'What?'

'Maz. She told me she was putting you up for adoption. That's why I never came looking for you.'

'But the deeds to the cottage, you left them in my name. Why would you do that if you thought I was being adopted?'

'Maz promised she'd pass them on to the adoption agency.'

'I'm so confused,' said Alice.

'Would it help if I started at the beginning?'

Alice nodded. 'Start with the fire. I want to know what really happened.'

Daniel leaned forward in his seat. 'I'm so sorry for how I let you down, Alice. At the time, I thought I was doing the right thing.'

'You and Jack both.'

'Sorry?'

'Nothing. It wasn't you who started the fire, was it?'

Daniel frowned. 'How did you work that out?'

'I've lived with Maz for twenty-five years,' said Alice, unable to stop her lips forming in a half smile.

'Have you spoken to her about any of this?'

Alice shook her head. 'She's sent a few postcards, but I haven't been able to get hold of her since she went away.'

'Why does that not surprise me?'

‘Hey,’ said Alice, feeling an irrational need to defend her mum. ‘Maz has never been the best mum in the world, but at least she was there, sort of. Which is more than I can say for you.’

‘Fair enough,’ said Daniel, raising his palms in a motion of surrender. ‘As you seem to have worked out, it was your mother who started the fire. She claimed it was an accident, but I’ve had plenty of time to think about it, and now I believe she deliberately aimed those rockets at the house. Jack had given her an ultimatum she didn’t like, and it was her way of getting back at him. In her defence, she knew her mum and sisters were away, and probably thought Jack could put any fires out easily enough once she’d given him a bit of a scare.’

‘Why did you say you did it?’

‘She was pregnant with my child. I honestly believed she was eighteen, but regardless, I should never have slept with her in the first place. I behaved like an idiot that summer, and I suppose owning up to the fire was my way of trying to make up for that.’

‘But you went to prison!’

‘Only for eighteen months. It would have been worse for Maz. I didn’t want her to have to go through a trial while pregnant.’

‘You said you thought I was adopted?’

Daniel nodded. ‘The case took ages to reach court. I was still a free man when you were born. I went to visit you and Maz in hospital and got to hold you. It was the happiest day of my life, despite everything, but then Maz told me about the adoption.'

'You must have agreed to it.'

Daniel nodded and hung his head. When he looked up, his eyes were filled with tears. 'I didn't want you put up for adoption, but what choice did I have? My solicitor had told me I was likely to get a prison term, so I couldn't offer to have you.'

'You could have told your parents.'

'I'd put them through enough without the added stress of knowing I'd got a sixteen-year-old pregnant and their only grandchild was being put up for adoption.'

'They could have taken me in.'

'Maz didn't want that. She said the best thing for you was to have a fresh start. I said my goodbyes to you in the hospital, but I need you to know I've thought about you every day since.'

'You could have looked for me when I turned eighteen.'

'I wanted to, please believe me, but I didn't want to ruin your life. Maz promised she'd leave both our details with the adoption agency, so you could contact us if you wanted to. When I didn't hear anything, I assumed you were living happily with an adoptive family and wanted nothing to do with us. I can't tell you how angry I was when I learned Maz had kept you and never told me. After taking the blame for the fire, to take away my chance of being a dad felt so cruel.'

'When did you find out what she'd done?'

'When Margot wrote to me to say you'd turned up in Saffron Bay. To say it was a shock was an understatement.'

'It took you long enough to come down here. She must have written to you months ago.'

Daniel had the decency to blush. 'I was away when her letter arrived, and then when I read it I needed time to think. I know I should have come here the second I got her letter, but it messed me up good and proper. I couldn't believe what Maz had done to me. The last thing I wanted was to rush in all guns blazing and screw things up all over again.'

Before Alice could reply, Margot and May appeared, carrying a tray of drinks and another holding slices of cake.

'Thank you,' said Daniel, giving Margot a warm smile.

Alice felt a rush of jealousy. Margot knew her father better than she did. It wasn't meant to be that way. Numb and confused, Alice leaned back in her seat, unable to lift her eyes to meet Daniel's.

'How long have you been back in Saffron Bay?' May asked Daniel, taking a seat after getting an affirmative nod from Alice.

'I arrived in the area last night and got to the village this afternoon.'

'Where are you staying?'

'With my parents. They told me they met you,' he said to Alice, trying to catch her eyes. 'They liked you.'

'I liked them. They must have been pleased to see you.'

'Yes,' he said, 'it's been a while.'

'Where do you live?' said May.

'Scotland. I'm an estate manager in the Highlands. Not quite landscape gardening, but as close as I could get.'

The north of Scotland. Daniel Loveday had moved as far as he could get from Saffron Bay. Alice had so many questions for him. Did he have a wife? Did she have half-siblings? A wave of exhaustion washed over her, the enormity of the meeting taking its toll. Alice sat quietly, drinking her tea, eating her cake and listening as the others made small talk around her.

'I'm sorry,' she said, interrupting Margot's long explanation to Daniel about the community centre events. 'Do you mind if I head home and we catch up again over the next few days? There are practical matters we need to discuss about the cottage. You've probably heard I've put it up for sale.' The way Daniel's eyes widened told Alice that he didn't know, but had the good sense to keep whatever thoughts he had about her plans to himself. 'You've got my number,' said Alice. 'Let me know when's a good time, and perhaps you could come to the cottage?'

'I will do.' Daniel half stood up as though he might try to hug her, but Alice backed away.

'See you soon,' she said. Alice felt bad for leaving May behind, but there was somewhere she needed to be, and she wanted to go there alone. With one last glance at the café, Alice turned and headed toward Luke's house.

Chapter 71

'Oh, hi Alice. Are you OK?' Luke frowned at the woman on his doorstep. There was a wildness in her eyes, and her cheeks were flushed as if she had a fever.

'I don't know,' she said.

'Come in.' When she seemed unable to move, Luke put an arm around her shoulders. Alice looked up in surprise as though she'd forgotten he was there, but put up no resistance as he led her through to the sitting room. There was no hiding the packing boxes strewn all over the room, and he noticed Alice's eyes settle on them. 'What's the matter, Alice?' asked Luke, turning her to face him.

'I've just met my dad.' A single tear tipped from her eye, and Luke watched it trail down to her chin.

'Woah, that's big. Do you want to sit down?'

Alice nodded, kicked off her shoes, climbed onto the sofa and curled her legs beneath her.

'How was it?' asked Luke, sitting beside her.

'I don't know.'

'Let me make you some sweet tea,' he said, moving to the kitchen.

'I don't take sugar in my tea.'

'I think you need to today.'

'Alright.'

As Luke busied himself in the kitchen, he kept stealing glances at Alice. All the fight had left her, and she was a shell of the woman he knew and loved. It scared him, and as he stirred sugar around the mug, he wondered if she needed to see a doctor. He carried the mug of tea to her, and when she took it from him, he noticed the focus had returned to her eyes.

'Thank you,' she said. 'But don't blame me if I spit it out. I warned you I hate sugar in my tea.'

Luke flopped down on the sofa, breathing a silent sigh of relief. Alice didn't need a doctor; she needed a friend.

'Urgh,' said Alice, taking a sip and setting the mug down on the floor. 'Sorry to turn up in a state like this.'

'I'm glad you did. You've had a massive shock, by the looks of things. I'm glad you're not on your own.'

Alice picked up an ugly cushion and hugged it against her chest. 'May would have come with me when I left. She's been amazing through this whole thing, but it was you I wanted to see.' Her cheeks flushed a deep red.

Luke risked taking one of her hands in his, praying he hadn't misjudged the situation. 'I'm so sorry for keeping things from you,' he said. 'I never intended to hurt you.'

Alice gave him a weak smile. 'I know. I've realised that. And let's face it, you haven't been the only one. No one in Saffron Bay was forthcoming with what they knew when I first arrived.'

'Out of loyalty to Jack, I think,' said Luke, and Alice nodded. 'Besides, no one knew exactly what made your dad leave, not even Margot. Everything was guesswork and hearsay.'

'My dad didn't start that fire,' said Alice.

'Are you sure?'

Alice let go of Luke's hand and laughed. 'Yes, I believe him. It was my mum, though I'm not sure that makes things any better. I'm still the daughter of a pyromaniac, it's just a different parent to who I thought.'

'She did it to get back at Jack?'

Alice nodded. 'I don't think she actually meant to cause any damage. She was young, reckless and angry and not thinking properly.'

'Have you spoken to her about it?'

'No. She's sent a few postcards, and I have her email address to get in touch with her in an emergency. I've tried asking about what's been going on here via email, but all my messages have been ignored, so clearly she doesn't see giving me any answers as a priority.'

'She's probably ashamed.'

'That's very generous of you,' said Alice. 'In my opinion, she's nothing more than a coward. Do you know she told Daniel I was adopted? That's why he's had nothing to do with me all these years.'

Luke heard not only anger in Alice's voice but plenty of hurt, too. 'What an awful thing to do.'

'I know.' Alice jumped off the sofa and began pacing around the room. 'It's not even like she wanted to be a mum to me. She may as well have put me up for adoption, given the quality of her parenting. And to deprive me of my dad? I'm not sure I'll ever forgive her for that.'

'I may be way out of line,' said Luke, standing beside Alice, 'but do you think the timing of all this really was a coincidence?'

'What do you mean?'

'She would have known you'd get Seashell Cottage when you turned twenty-five, and would have known you'd rock up here and find all sorts of skeletons lurking in your family closest. I don't know the woman, but it seems very convenient she was out of the country when the proverbial hit the fan.'

Alice groaned, and instinctively, Luke wrapped his arms around her and pulled her close. The top of her head rested against his chest, and her hair smelled of flowers. 'My life is such a mess,' muttered Alice, her own arms wrapping around Luke's back.

'Everything will be alright in the end,' he told her.

'You don't know that.'

'No, but it sounded good.'

Alice laughed and pulled back until their noses were touching. 'It would be very easy to kiss you right now.'

Luke stayed silent, wanting nothing more than for her to do just that, but knowing the decision needed to come from her.

'But I'm not going to.'

Luke's heart sank.

Alice leaned further back. 'You're leaving. The cottage is up for sale. The dad I've not seen for twenty-five years has just turned up, and if that wasn't enough, May starts her GCSEs next week. Now would not be a good time to be getting into a relationship.'

'I don't have to take the job.' The words were out of Luke's mouth before he knew what he was saying.

'What? You'd turn down your dream job for me?'

Luke sat down on the sofa with a sigh. 'It's not my dream job. I'm only taking it because I don't know what else to do, because I feel stuck, because staying here feels like the safe option, even if it's stopping me from getting what I really want.'

'And what is it you want?' asked Alice, her voice little more than a whisper.

'I thought I wanted a family, two point four kids and all that, but it turns out I don't. What I want is you.'

When Alice didn't reply, Luke decided it was a case of in for a penny, in for a pound.

'I know you're selling up, but you may as well know how I feel about you before we go our separate ways. It's crazy to say, and I don't believe in love at first sight, but the first time I saw you, well, I think it's as close to love at first sight as I'm ever going to get.'

Alice's laugh wasn't the reaction Luke had been hoping for. 'Sorry,' she said, 'it's just that the first time you saw me, I was crying my eyes out in a graffiti-stained shell of a room. I was a snotty mess and probably the least attractive I've ever looked.'

'I thought you were the most beautiful girl I'd ever seen, despite the ugly crying.'

Alice laughed again, and this time it was a welcome sound.

'Most people would have run a mile at the state of the cottage, but not you. You pushed through everything that was thrown at you, and even with all the aggro you faced, May was always your priority. It was impressive. It impressed me. I've never met anyone like you, and if it's a choice between you and a job in London, I'd choose you every time. It helps that I hate London,' he added, trying to lighten the mood.

'Luke,' said Alice, running her hands through her hair. 'I don't know what to say. Selling the cottage seems like the logical thing to do, and although you say you don't want it, making you turn down that job doesn't feel right. You say you don't want kids right now, but what if you change your mind in a year's time? I've deferred my place at uni, which means if I go, it will be at least four years until I have a degree, more if I decide to do teacher training. You've waited long enough to get what you want. I don't want to be the person to make you wait even longer. Oh, and my head's all over the place, so I really don't think I'm girlfriend material at the moment.'

'I know, and I'm sorry to dump all this on you on top of everything else, but I wanted you to know how I really feel.'

'Thank you for telling me. You've certainly given me plenty to think about. How about we meet up later in the week once the dust has settled and talk things through?'

'Sounds good to me.'

Alice leaned over and kissed Luke on the cheek. 'You're a good man, Luke Richards,' she said, before standing and walking out the door.

Chapter 72

'Are you sure you want us here?' asked Luke for the hundredth time that morning.

Alice smiled at him and May. 'Of course I do. I wouldn't have invited you here otherwise.'

'Will Daniel mind?' asked May.

Alice shrugged. 'I don't see why he should. If he's planning on sticking around, we'll have plenty of time to spend alone, but this is all still so new to me and I wanted you both by my side.'

May smiled and Alice squeezed her hand. She'd been quiet since Daniel's return, and, after much probing from Alice, had admitted to fearing she'd be pushed out by the new father-daughter relationship. After being reassured nothing could be further from the truth, the old May was returning, if a little more cautious than usual.

'How are things with Paige?' asked Luke while they waited for their guest to arrive.

'Great.' May beamed and pulled out her phone. 'We went swimming in the bay yesterday and saw a pod of dolphins. It was so cool. Paige had a waterproof case for her phone and got some amazing pictures. See.'

Luke and May were still poring over the photos when the knock came on the door. Alice left them to it and walked out into the hall. She took a deep breath, checked her reflection in the small mirror beside the door, then opened it to Daniel. 'Hi,' she said, sounding as shy as she felt.

'Hello, Alice.' Daniel leaned forward into an awkward hug, trying to kiss her cheek but catching her nose instead. When he pulled away, his face was scarlet.

'Come in.'

Daniel whistled as he stepped inside the cottage. 'Goodness, this has changed a bit since my day.'

'You should have seen it before.'

'I did. Margot sent photos. I felt terrible handing over such a dump, but I wasn't even sure you'd accept the cottage, or if the adoption agency would pass on the details.'

'What would you have done if I hadn't?'

'Sold it probably. Speaking of which, I noticed the sign outside.'

'Oh yes, that. To be honest, I'm regretting putting the cottage on the market, but it seemed the right thing at the time. Now I'm wondering if I should delay for a while, maybe even a year. I've deferred my uni place, so I won't need extra funds immediately. May is keen to stay.'

'I can't pretend I'm not sad to see a For Sale board up outside, but the cottage is yours to do what you want with. But we should talk it over. There are eighteen years of missed maintenance payments, for starters, if it's money you're worried about.'

Alice frowned. 'I'm not interested in your money, Daniel.'

'That's good, because I don't have much of it,' he said with a laugh. 'But I have put a little aside for you just in case you got in touch one day. It would certainly help with living costs should you decide to go to university.'

It was too much to take in. Daniel hadn't even removed his coat. 'May is here, and my friend Luke,' she said. 'They're waiting in the kitchen. Shall we go through, or would you like a tour of the cottage first?'

'Let's go and say hello,' said Daniel.

As Daniel walked into the kitchen, Luke stood. 'I've heard a lot about you,' Luke said as Daniel shook his outstretched hand. 'And there's no mistaking whose father you are. You're like two peas in a pod.'

The awkwardness Alice felt mixed with a new feeling she eventually identified as pride. She had a dad. She looked like her dad. For the first time in her life, she was part of a family. The thought caused tears to burn the back of her eyes. But she still couldn't get used to seeing an older male version of herself. It was weird and would take a bit of getting used to.

'Hello again, May,' said Daniel.

To Alice's surprise, May stood up and gave him a warm hug. 'Hi, Dan. It must be weird for you to be back in the cottage.'

'It is a bit.'

'Please,' Alice said, 'have a seat. Do you want a cup of tea? Coffee?'

'I brought some beer with me,' said Luke.

'Now you're talking,' said Daniel, as he and Luke grinned at each other.

'Why don't we move through to the living room,' said May. 'I'm sure Dan would like to have a snoop around, and there's more space for us to sit.'

'Why don't you give Daniel the tour,' said Alice. 'And I'll make a pot of tea for me and May.'

'Sure,' said May, grinning at Daniel.

Alice found May's ease around Daniel uncomfortable. She wished she could feel as relaxed around him. Mind you, May had spent far longer in the café with him than Alice had. She'd come home full of excitement and information. May had had no qualms in asking the questions Alice was too overwhelmed to. Thanks to her sister's nosiness, Alice learned she was Daniel's only child. He'd had a few long-term relationships over the years, but none had lasted the distance. He was currently single, and had handed in his notice at the job in Scotland so he could get to know his daughter. Alice didn't know how to feel about that last part. It felt like a lot of added pressure had been placed on her shoulders. What if Daniel didn't like her and resented leaving his old life behind?

'Why are you hiding in here?' asked Luke.

'I thought you and May were giving Daniel the tour?'

'I've come to find a bottle opener, and to check on you.'

'I'm fine,' said Alice. 'I'm sorry we've not had time for a proper catch-up yet.'

'You've had other things on your mind,' said Luke, nodding his head towards the living room. 'How does it feel having him in your home?'

'Weird. And scary.'

'Scary? Why are you scared, Alice? Has he done anything to make you feel uncomfortable?'

'No.' Alice shook her head and stared out of the kitchen window. In a small voice she added, 'What if I'm not good enough? What if he doesn't like me?'

Luke walked over to her, took her hand and turned her to face him. 'That is the most ridiculous thing I have ever heard you say. You are more than good enough. That man in there is lucky to have you, and I'm pretty sure he already knows that. You're amazing, Alice.'

'But I'm not, am I? He'll have spent the past twenty-five years wondering what I'm doing, what I've achieved with my life. It must be so disappointing to turn up here and find I've achieved nothing at all.'

Luke laughed, and Alice scowled. 'I'm sorry,' he said, shaking his head. 'But I take back my earlier comment. That just there is the most ridiculous thing I've ever heard you say. You, Alice Loveday, have turned this crumbling wreck of a cottage into a home on a shoestring budget. You have raised your sister almost single-handedly for goodness knows how many years. You've worked your butt off to get yourself out of a bad situation not of your making. And we haven't even reached the bit about you being an extraordinary musician with the resourcefulness and determination to nurture your talent against all the odds. If Daniel Loveday isn't proud of the woman you've become, he doesn't deserve to be called your father.'

A cough made Alice and Luke spin around. Daniel was leaning against the doorframe, staring at them. 'I'm sorry, I didn't mean to eavesdrop. I came through to see if you needed any help.'

'I'll leave you to it,' said Luke, squeezing Alice's hand and walking out of the kitchen.

'I think I've got everything under control,' said Alice, flustered. She began piling mugs onto a tray and finding jobs that meant looking anywhere but at Daniel.

'Alice, please stop.'

Alice placed the milk bottle and jug back on the worktop and turned to face him. 'How much did you hear?'

'Enough to know you have very natural worries about things working out between us. But if there's one thing you don't need to worry about, it's whether you're good enough. You could have refused to see me, you could have screamed at me, you could have sent me packing. But you didn't. I may not know you well, but I've seen enough to know you're a remarkable young woman whom I'm honoured to call my daughter. If anyone should be feeling like they're not good enough, it's me. But that's why I'm here, Alice. This is a second chance for us, a chance for me to put things right. You have nothing to prove, and I have everything. But why don't we start with a cup of tea and a cold beer? After all, it's not like I'm going anywhere.'

The shape of Daniel blurred in front of her as tears filled Alice's eyes. Her dad was here, and he wanted to get to know her. She had no idea how the next few months would pan out, but this was a very good start. Alice picked up her tray, smiled at Daniel, and went to find the others.

Chapter 73

Alice wiped a hand across her brow and stared up at the house. She wished she hadn't insisted on the others waiting at the gates. Why had she thought it would be a good idea to come alone? The appearance of the house and grounds still shocked her. Alice could imagine how beautiful it would have been in its heyday, and the tragedy of that lost beauty made her feel a rush of shame. Jack had been right about her family's involvement in his loss, even if he'd got the wrong parent.

Just as she was about to knock on the front door, it swung open to reveal Jack Tyler standing with his hands on his hips.

'Alice, what are you doing here? Is this your sister's doing? Did she tell you about her visit?'

'I'm sorry May and Paige barged in here again.'

Jack threw his hands in the air. 'It was what I needed to hear. I've behaved despicably ever since you arrived in Saffron Bay. I suppose it was a tremendous shock, not that it's an excuse.'

'Is that an apology?'

Jack's eyes flashed, and Alice saw the old Jack flicker behind them. 'Yes,' he said, 'I suppose it is. May helped me see that none of what happened was your fault. I've spent twenty-five years regretting the way I pushed Tilly away, but I've been too proud to back down.'

'It's big of you to admit to your mistakes. Thank you for your apology. It means a lot.'

'I probably owe Tilly an apology too, don't I?'

'I'd say it's she who owes us. She's a grown woman. It's about time she took responsibility for her actions. If she ever comes back to the UK, that is.'

'Surely she wouldn't abandon you completely?'

Alice smiled. 'She'll probably put in an appearance once she knows the dust has settled. To be honest, though, it's easier without her here. Despite everything that's happened, I miss her, but I don't miss the chaos she trails in her wake.'

'That sounds like the Tilly I used to know.'

'Listen, Jack, I'd like to get to know you better. I'd like to meet my aunts and any cousins I have. My whole life I've thought it was just me, Mum and May. I never thought I'd have a big family I could be part of. But that's not why I'm here.'

'Oh?'

'You deserve to know the truth about what happened all those years ago. It was Maz who started the fire. My dad took the blame, and, as much as you'd like to continue punishing him, I think he's been punished enough. He went to prison for a crime he didn't commit, was hounded out of his home, and missed the chance of twenty-five years with his daughter. Maz, Tilly, told him I'd been put up for adoption.'

'Are you sure it was Tilly who started the fire?'

'Yes. But I also know it was you who had cut corners with fire safety, and you who had lied to your wife about having insurance.'

'How do you... Nevermind, I suppose it doesn't matter now. But regardless of whether I had insurance, I still would have lost everything in that fire.'

'You still would have lost your house, yes, and perhaps your wife and youngest daughters still would have moved away, but it's been your choice how often you see them. It's been your choice to live in one room like a hermit and hide away from the world. You've trapped yourself in an event from twenty-five years ago and refused to even consider a life beyond it.'

'What sort of life is there for me? Look at it.' Jack looked up at the house that still bore the scars from the fateful night.

'There's more to life than bricks and mortar, Jack. Despite your best efforts to push them away, there are still people who care about you, who want the best for you.'

'Like who?'

'Hold on a minute,' said Alice, typing out a hasty text message. 'You've taught me a lot, you know.'

'Me?'

'Yes. You've shown me what happens when you stand still and refuse help from others. I've spent my whole life trying to be sensible and not take any risks, but it's impossible to control everything. Terrible things can happen in life, but there's so much good out there too, so much excitement.'

'I'm glad I've been of some use to you,' said Jack, 'but I still don't understand why you're here?'

'I didn't come alone,' said Alice, looking behind her to the still empty driveway.

'What do you mean?' Jack's eyes widened as a movement over Alice's shoulder caught his eye. She turned to see a group of people walking towards them. 'You asked me who cares about you? Well, I brought some friends with me.'

'Friends?' Jack squinted to make out who was walking up his drive.

'We all need help sometimes. Let us help you get this place closer to what it once was. I'm a dab hand at fixing up properties these days,' said Alice, the hint of a smile on her lips.

'Hah, you think anything can be salvaged from this wreck, do you?'

'Maybe not the house, but certainly the grounds. Have you ever thought of building a new home in the grounds of the old?'

'I've never wanted to... I... I've... It took a lot of courage, you coming here.' Jack's voice softened, his eyes glassy as he looked down at Alice. 'I've done nothing but make your life difficult ever since you moved to the village.'

'And I understand why. To be honest, I was going to run away from it all.'

'Why didn't you?'

'Because my friends helped me see I'm part of this community, that I have friends. Just like you do.'

'I hope you don't mind us barging in like this,' said Sylvie, fanning her face with her hand as she came to a stop beside Alice.

'Yes,' said Solly, 'we fancied a spot of gardening.'

'I brought coffee and cake,' said Margot.

'And I'm crap at gardening, but I'm OK at cleaning,' said May.

'I've brought some refreshments for when we get fed up with coffee,' said Rita, lifting the lid of a picnic basket to reveal a selection of beers.

'And I'm here to apologise,' said Daniel, stepping out from behind the others.

'You came back?'

'I thought it was about time,' said Daniel, holding out his hand. Jack looked at it, around at his friends, then back at Daniel. When he took Daniel's hand, a cheer went up among the group.

'As you can see,' said Jack, 'the garden could do with a bit of a spruce-up.' He smiled at Daniel.

'We'd better get started then, hadn't we?'

Chapter 74

The pub was busy, not only with locals, but with tourists making the most of the long bank holiday weekend. For the start of May, it was unusually warm, and even this late into the afternoon the hazy sunshine still held plenty of heat.

'Ah, the VIPs,' said Rita as they made their way to the bar. 'Goodness me, you've not changed much, have you?' Rita stood back, looking Daniel up and down. Alice couldn't quite think of him as her father yet, but even so, Rita's obvious admiration left her a little uncomfortable. 'I bet you don't remember me, Daniel. I was a little kid the last time we met.'

'Of course I remember you, Rita,' said Daniel, sneaking a wink at Alice, who'd briefed him before they walked in.

Rita flushed with pleasure and took their drinks order.

'Is Luke here yet?' Alice asked.

'I think he's outside.'

'Do you mind if I go and say hello?' asked Alice.

'Not at all,' said Daniel.

'We'll meet you out there,' said May.

As Alice walked towards the door, it opened, and in walked Jack, followed by Sylvie and Solly, who were holding hands and both looking like shy teenagers. No one batted an eyelid.

'I thought we'd set a few tongues wagging at least,' Solly said to Alice as she walked over to greet them.

'I'm sorry, Solly, but I think your romance is the worst-kept secret in Saffron Bay.'

'And there was I thinking we'd cause a bit of drama,' said Sylvie, grinning.

Nick's wolf whistle from the far side of the pub was well timed, and Sylvie flushed with pleasure. 'The golden couple are making their grand entrance,' Nick called, and locals clapped, holiday makers joining in, despite not understanding the reason for the sudden applause.

'Ladies and gentlemen,' shouted Solly above the racket. 'Please let me introduce you to my fiancée.' He lifted Sylvie's hand high in the air, put an arm around her, then tipped her back in a ballroom move, kissing her lips to cheers from the assembled drinkers.

'Congratulations,' whispered Alice, squeezing Sylvie's hand as she slipped past them.

'Good luck,' said Sylvie, her eyes twinkling.

Alice spotted Luke and spent a moment watching him. He was sitting on a bench, his body still, his eyes trained on the horizon. 'You missed the grand entrance,' said Alice, sliding onto the bench beside him.

Luke turned to her and smiled. 'I hope someone caught it on camera.'

'You knew?'

'Solly came round yesterday to ask my permission. Of course I gave it.'

'You're happy for them?'

'Delighted. Solly will never replace my granddad, but I couldn't think of a better companion for Gran. He's a decent bloke.'

'I'm pleased you think so, given he's my great-uncle.'

'Oh yes, I keep forgetting about that. How was Jack when he arrived?'

'He slipped into a quiet corner pretty sharpish. I don't think he's ready to be in the spotlight just yet.'

'I don't blame him.'

'Why don't you come in and join the celebrations?'

Luke turned his gaze back to the sea. 'I don't really feel like it.'

'Why not? Is everything OK?'

He sighed and looked at his hands. 'I heard on the grapevine you got an offer on the cottage.'

'I did, yes, and a very generous one at that.'

'Hmm.'

Alice couldn't keep the grin off her face as she gave him a playful nudge. 'You know, you only heard half the story?'

'What do you mean?' Luke turned to her, confusion in his eyes.

'I got an amazing offer. That part is true. What you clearly haven't heard is that I turned it down.'

'Really? But why?'

Now it was Alice's turn to stare at the sea. 'Oh, you know, this and that.' She was teasing, but there was no doubt her decision had been made easier by Daniel's insistence he would help her with her university fees if she chose to go. Between that, shifts at the pub, and offering private music tuition on the evenings she was free, Alice knew she could manage with no need to sell up. But now wasn't the time for discussing boring financial matters.

'This and that?'

She shrugged. 'There are a few things, a few people, actually, I decided it was worth sticking around for.'

'People?'

'Daniel, obviously, Margot, Sylvie and Solly, Jack…' She turned to him. 'You.'

'Me?'

'I know you're off to London, but you'll be back to visit your gran. And we can catch up when you do.'

Luke's smile grew wide. 'You're not the only one who can turn things down.'

'You don't need to do that for me.'

'Too late, I already have. Anyway, it wasn't just for you. Yes, the job sounded amazing, but I've been building my business for a while now and have a loyal local client base. It would be a shame to give that up. You are the cherry on the cake, I suppose.'

'Well, my decision wasn't totally about you, either.'

'No?'

Luke raised an eyebrow, and Alice gave him a playful punch on the arm. 'May didn't want to leave either. She's now best mates with Paige, and I might be mistaken, but I'm pretty sure she's getting friendly with Rita's son Ted. Plus, my dad is planning to stick around, and I'd like to get to know him better.'

'But if we're going to be living in the same place, we might as well spend a bit of time together.'

'Good idea. There are tons of jobs around the house I could use your help with.'

Luke picked up on Alice's teasing tone and laughed. 'You know that wasn't what I had in mind...'

His lips met hers, and Alice wrapped her arms around his neck. 'There are still things we need to talk about,' she said, pulling away. 'Like the fact you want kids, and I'm nowhere near ready for that.'

Luke kissed her in reply. She couldn't say how long they stayed locked together, but they snapped apart quickly when someone coughed behind them.

'Alright if we join you, or is this a party for two?' asked May, plonking herself down on the opposite side of the picnic bench.

'We can stay inside if we're interrupting,' said Daniel, hovering a few paces away and looking like he would rather not have witnessed his daughter in a passionate embrace.

'The more the merrier,' said Luke.

'Pull up another bench,' called Solly as he and Sylvie walked towards them. Behind them came Nick and Jack, locked in conversation, then Patricia and Paige.

'Room for two more?' asked Sam as she and Steve emerged carrying a tray of drinks.

'Make that three more,' said Margot, holding the door open for them.

Luke leaned in close to Alice so that only she could hear him. 'You're right about me wanting kids one day, but I'm in no rush. What I want is you, and I'll give you as much space as you need for as long as you need it. You're worth waiting for, Alice Loveday. Besides, I don't think I could handle kids yet on top of this lot. We've got a big enough family as it is.'

Alice looked around at the motley crew gathered in the pub garden and smiled. She couldn't have conjured up a more random group of people if she'd tried, and yet they were the people who made up the heart of Saffron Bay. Just below the hum of conversation, they could hear the waves meeting the shore, and the screech of gulls circling above their heads looking for scraps.

Daniel didn't look completely at ease, Jack even less so, and Alice knew there was a way to go to build relationships with the men in her life. But she was willing to put in the work. With a start, she understood she was no longer alone, no longer solely responsible for those around her. She was part of a team and had people who would carry her if she needed it. There were still loose ends to tie up, not least her relationship with Maz, but Alice knew that would come in time. Besides, she'd never been looking for perfect, just a second chance to grow into the person she'd always wanted to be. And if Alice was certain of anything, it was that her second chance was stretching out before her, ready to be seized. Luke put his arm around her, and she leaned into him. Somehow he'd broken through her defences and stolen her heart. And unless she was very much mistaken, Saffron Bay had done just the same.

* * *

To stay up to date with the latest Saffron Bay series news and receive a FREE ebook, *The Island Girls*, join the LK Wilde Readers' Club at www.lkwilde.com

Acknowledgements

It was a cold weekday in early spring when the Saffron Bay characters took up residence in my mind and captured my heart. I had taken a few days off to stay in an Airbnb on the south coast of Cornwall, but rather than switching off, my brain began buzzing with story ideas, and the Saffron Bay series was born.

It's one thing to come up with an idea, and quite another to execute it. Creating the story you've just experienced took a lot of teamwork and behind-the-scenes support. My first thanks go to my ever-patient boys, Joe and Tom. They put up with me obsessively writing, bring me cups of tea, celebrate my highs and offer hugs when I'm at the end of my tether. They are the motivation behind everything I do, and I couldn't be prouder of them.

A big 'thank you' is due to Jo Egleton for her wise editing advice and endless encouragement. She is my first reader and biggest cheerleader, and her thoughtful suggestions always make me throw my head in my hands and mutter, "Why didn't I think of that?"

Thank you to my brilliant agent, Salma Begum. A year ago I never expected the words 'my' and 'agent' to appear in the same sentence! It's been a pleasure working with her over the past few months, and I can't wait to see what the future holds.

Thank you to Natalie Perman, who stepped in at the last minute to save the day and ensure the novel is proofread and polished. I really appreciate not only the hard work she put in, but the insightful feedback that once again, made me throw my head in my hands and mutter, "Why didn't I think of that?"

Without the encouragement of Audible, this book and series would have languished on my laptop for goodness-knows how long. They have brought the story to life, and I can't thank them enough.

Finally, thank *you* for picking up this first Saffron Bay book and joining Alice and Luke and the rest of the Saffron Bay residents as they uncovered secrets and found their happy endings. I hope you have enjoyed the story as much as I enjoyed writing it!

About the Author

Author and musician LK (Laura) Wilde was born in Norwich, but spent her teenage years living on a Northumbrian island. She left the island to study Music, and after a few years of wandering settled in Cornwall, where she raises her two crazy, delightful boys.

To keep in touch with Laura and receive a 'bonus bundle' of material including the novel *The Island Girls*, join her monthly Readers' Club newsletter at-

www.lkwilde.com

Or find her on social media- @lkwildeauthor

Finally, if you enjoyed this book, please consider leaving a review or rating on Amazon. Reviews are so important to indie authors as they're the best way to help more people discover the book!

Author's Note

If you would like to receive a FREE eBook, *The Island Girls*, sign up to the LK Wilde Readers' Club monthly newsletter at lkwilde.com.

Two women, one island. Is it big enough for both of them?

Islander Rose McGuire dreams of a future filled with romance. But when tragedy strikes, her world is turned upside down. Propelled into the arms of local scoundrel Alex Watson, her dreams soon become a nightmare...

Mainlander Anna Allinson lives a life of luxury but is trapped within a gilded cage. When a chance encounter with an island fisherman ignites a spark within her, Anna decides to leave behind all she knows and risk everything for love.

But island life proves far from idyllic as Anna struggles to adapt, and not everyone welcomes her arrival, least of all Rose.

As Rose and Anna navigate their tumultuous lives, events bring them together, forging an unlikely friendship and forming bonds that will pass down through generations...

Also By LK Wilde

People say you get one life, but I've lived three.

I was born Ellen Hardy in 1900, dragged up in Queen Caroline's Yard, Norwich. There was nothing royal about our yard, and Mum was no queen.

At six years old Mum sold me. I became Nellie Westrop, roaming the country in a showman's wagon, learning the art of the fair.

And I've been the infamous Queenie of Norwich, moving up in the world by any means, legal or not.

I've been heart broken, abandoned, bought and sold, but I've never, ever given up. After all, it's not where you start that's important, but where you end up.

Based on a true story, *Queenie of Norwich* is the compelling tale of one remarkable girl's journey to womanhood. Spanning the first half of the 20th century, Queenie's story is one of heartbreak and triumph, love and loss and the power of family. It is a story of redemption, and how, with grit and determination, anything is possible.

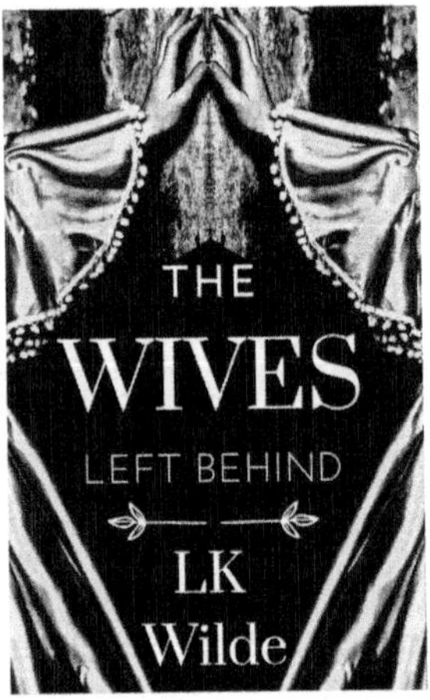

1840, Cornwall. The victim, the accused, and the wives left behind. Welcome to the trial of the century... Based on a true story.

When merchant Nevell Norway is murdered, suspicion soon falls on the Lightfoot brothers. The trial of the century begins, and two women's lives change forever.

Sarah Norway must fight for the future of her children. Battling against her inner demons, can Sarah unlock the strength she needs to move on without Nevell?

Maria Lightfoot's future looks bleak, but she's a fighter. Determined to rebuild her life, an unexpected friendship offers a glimmer of hope...

With their lives in turmoil, can Maria and Sarah overcome the fate of their husbands? Or will they forever remain the wives left behind?

Book 1 in the Cornish feel-good *The House of Many Lives* series

Kate is stuck in a rut, She works a dead end job, lives in a grotty bedsit and still pines for the man who broke her heart.

When Kate inherits a house in a small Cornish town, she jumps at the chance of a fresh start. A surprise letter from her grandmother persuades Kate to open her home and her heart to strangers.

But with friends harbouring secrets, demanding house guests, and her past catching up with her- can Kate really move on? And will her broken heart finally find a home?

Printed in Dunstable, United Kingdom

77878659R00245